Also by Larry Brown

R^{the}abbit Factory

Larry Brown

[signature: Larry Brown]

Free Press

NEW YORK • LONDON • TORONTO • SYDNEY • SINGAPORE

*f*P

FREE PRESS
A Division of Simon & Schuster, Inc.
1230 Avenue of the Americas
New York, NY 10020

FREE PRESS and colophon are
trademarks of Simon & Schuster, Inc.

For information about special discounts for bulk purchases,
please contact Simon & Schuster Special Sales:
1-800-456-6798 or business@simonandschuster.com

Designed by Paul Dippolito

Manufactured in the United States of America

10   9   8   7   6   5   4   3   2   1

Library of Congress Cataloging-in-Publication Data

Brown, Larry, 1951 July 9–
    The rabbit factory / Larry Brown.
        p.   cm.
    I. Title.
    PS3552.R6927R33 2003
    813'.54—dc21

                                        2002045591

ISBN 0-7432-4523-7

This one is for Coach Brown, Shane.

R^{the}abbit Factory

1

The kitten was wild and skinny, and its tail looked almost broken, kind of hung down crooked. It had been around the neighborhood for several days, darting here and there, dodging traffic sometimes, and Arthur had been trying to catch it, setting the Havahart cage in the yard and baiting it with anchovies, but even though the kitten seemed desperately hungry, it would not enter the trap. It only sat and looked at the bait, and at them. But there was no big rush. Arthur had plenty of money and plenty of time to mess with stuff like that whenever he wasn't sitting in front of the big-screen TV watching westerns. Sometimes he dozed off.

He brought his coffee to the love seat where Helen was watching through the big bay window. Outside was late afternoon, cold and wind, a cloudy sky, no sun. A few cars passed out on South Parkway. She hadn't switched to whiskey yet, was just having some red wine so far, holding her glass in both hands. Arthur sat carefully down with her. Snow was dusting down in the yard, tiny flakes whirling in the chilly breezes. He could see it swirling across the street. It was cozy there next to her and he thought maybe he could get it up today, if he got the chance.

"I think it smells us," she said.

Arthur sipped his coffee and with her looked at the kitten. He kept thinking maybe he could find something that would occupy some of her time. He thought maybe she'd like a cat, so he was trying for one.

"What do you mean 'smells us'? We're in here. It's out there. How can it smell us?"

"I don't mean in here, silly. I mean maybe it smells us on the trap. Our scent."

Scent, Arthur mused. He guessed it was possible. Just about anything was possible, looked like. Even getting to be seventy. He'd charged the trap to his American Express card and he'd seen drinks from the Peabody bar again on last month's statement. She seemed to be going over there a lot lately. He tried to get her to always take cabs since the trouble with the police. Sometimes she did.

"Don't you know anything about trapping?" she said.

"Hm? No," said Arthur. "But I'll bet you do." She knew a bit of information about a lot of things. She could converse on different subjects. She could converse fluently on penile dysfunction. She'd read a booklet about it, and he thought she might have seen a television program about it as well. She could watch the bloodiest show on TV, *The Operation,* and he didn't want to be in the same room with it. He wondered where else she went to drink besides the Peabody. She never told him anything.

"Well," she said. "I read a book by somebody. Trappers have to cover their scent or the animals will smell them and go away. They have to boil their traps in wood ashes and things like that to remove their scent. They have to wear gloves, and if they're trapping something really smart, like a wolf or a coyote, they can't even touch the ground."

Arthur glanced at her. It was plain to anybody that she was a lot younger than him. He knew other men looked at her. He knew for a fact without having any way of proving it besides hiding in the lobby ferns and spying on her that she talked to strange men at the Peabody.

"Come on. How can they trap if they don't touch the ground?"

"They have to put down something to kneel on."

"Like what?"

"I don't know. Some old sacks or something."

"Do they have to boil the sacks?"

"I don't know."

"You think we need to boil our trap?"

"I just think it smells us. Look at the way it keeps watching us."

Arthur watched the kitten watching them for a while.

"You don't even have a pot big enough to boil it in," he said. "That thing's two feet long. How about spraying some Lysol on it?"

Helen gave him her patient look and sipped her wine. He remembered a time when she'd clamp her lovely muscular thighs around his back like the jaws of a new bear trap. She'd be gasping, with her head thrown back and her mouth opening and closing and her fingers in his hair yanking, going, Oh my *God, baby*! That was a long time ago, true. Way back in Montana. Still.

"Be serious," she said.

"I *am* serious. I already bought some cat food, didn't I? I already spent fifty-two dollars and fifty cents for the trap, didn't I?"

They sat studying the kitten. It walked around the wire box, looked back at them, sniffed at the contraption. Finally it sat again in the dead grass and stared at the anchovies. Maybe its tail was just deformed.

"Looks like if it was hungry it would go on in there," Arthur said.

"It's got to be hungry. Look how skinny it is."

"How are you going to tame it down even if we catch it?"

"I'll cure it with kindness, I guess."

"What if it claws you? You ever been attacked by a cat?"

"No, but I know you have."

"They can be pretty vicious if they get mad."

"That's true."

"They can whip a grown dog if they make up their mind to."

"I've heard that."

"And if you get scratched, why then you've got that cat-scratch fever to worry about. Like in this Ted Nugent song I heard one time."

"Well, if I get scratched, I'll put some peroxide on it."

"Or alcohol," Arthur said, and sipped his coffee. They stayed there for a quiet period of time, just watching the kitten. Arthur looked at Helen, but Helen didn't look at him. He sat there a little longer. Her slip was sticking out just a bit past her knee. Arthur very smoothly moved his hand over to her knee. He didn't need any Viagra pill to schedule a hard-on for him. She just had to get him in the right mood.

"Now, now," she said, and flipped her skirt down and moved his hand. He returned his gaze to the kitten. It was all about blood, he thought. Pressure up, pressure down. He'd read somewhere that some guys had little rubber bivalves that had been surgically implanted and were hidden back behind their nuts. Pump it up, let it out, like an inner tube. He didn't even want to think about doing something like that to himself.

"I don't think it's going to let us catch it," he said. Damned if he hadn't gotten all upset again, thinking about how everything had turned out. "I think I'll go find a coffee shop and get some fresh ground." Helen didn't say anything. Maybe it was time for him to give it up. But it was hard to let go. So very hard to let go. Probably even when you got as old as old Mr. Stamp.

2

Later, near nightfall, he was in a coffee shop near Cooper and Young, sipping a cup, sitting on a stool. He was the only patron besides a drunk guy in a trench coat who was keeping quiet and minding his own business with a crossword puzzle, but he could see people passing on the sidewalk. The owner was reading *The Commercial Appeal*, shaking his bald noggin.

"Dickheads," he said, and turned the paper over.

Arthur wondered if maybe there was some place in Memphis where a person could rent a tranquilizer gun, load it with one of those darts like they used to knock out animals in Africa they wanted to study, or a big cat in a zoo when they wanted to work on its teeth, maybe just get a small, low-dosage dart, nothing too big, something for a kitten, hell, he reasoned, you wouldn't need anything big enough to knock down a rogue tusker.

He could imagine himself hiding behind a tree in their yard with a tranquilizer gun, waiting for a clean shot at the kitten. But he couldn't figure out how they'd tame it. He wondered if it would work to sedate it and hog-tie it and then force-pet it.

He looked across the street. His eyes were old but he could see people inside a barbershop. A barber was moving around somebody's head. It seemed late to be getting a haircut. The drunk guy in the trench coat put the crossword puzzle and a nubby pencil in his pocket and some money on the counter and weaved his way out.

But what if only somebody like a veterinarian could get his hands on those dart guns? Maybe they were federally regulated, like machine guns. It probably wasn't something you could just buy over the counter. There couldn't be too much demand from the general public for an item like that. He worried over it and was glad to have it to worry over. It kept him from thinking about his repeated recent failures at getting into Helen's exquisite bush. He couldn't remember the last time he'd gotten a boner, and wished he'd written it down. The stripper he'd visited hadn't done him any good. The doctor had mentioned vacuum pumps once. That sounded just a little bit dangerous. Plus, he didn't like anybody messing with his jewels.

He ordered a cup to go and looked across the street. A man in a trench coat stood on the sidewalk. It looked like the drunk guy again, but it was hard to tell from here. The owner set the coffee in front of Arthur and he pulled a dollar from his pocket for a tip and put it on the counter. He picked up the cup and his fresh ground, walked out, checked his watch, had to get on home quick, shit, *The Wild Bunch* was fixing to come on at seven.

3

The barbershop was not crowded. One sleepy old man in a white coat droned on a nappy couch, slumped sideways, his polishing kit beside him, brown stains on the tips of his interlaced fingers. The gray-haired barber moved on rubber soles gently around the man in the barber's chair, his keen scissors making almost soundless snips as locks of hair drifted onto the floor and the pin-striped sheet wrapped around his customer.

The man in the raised chair seemed at peace. The barber had just finished lathering his face with hot foam and the rich smell of it hung in an aromatic veil over customer as well as attendant. The tiles on the floor were green and white, a checkerboard of odd colors.

The man in the chair had his eyes closed. He had a deep tan—maybe from Miami?—and his finely manicured hands where they held each other in stillness were small for such a heavy man. An ancient plastic radio in the corner on a shelf was softly playing Elgar's "Sospiri."

All that could be seen of the man were his lathered face, his hands, the cuffs of his black pants, and his shiny shoes resting on the pedestal.

When the door opened, no head turned except the barber's. He stepped back out of the way when he saw what was happening and then crossed his hands over his chest, comb and scissors raised, eyes wide behind his thick glasses.

The muzzle of the gun came within six inches of its target. Perhaps the man in the chair had gone to sleep or at least drifted woozily in the barber's fragrant ablutions. The gun fired, bright blood sprinkling on the silent barber, a jarring explosion that momentarily silenced the music.

It fired again, an enormous sound in that closed space, the air filling with the sweet smell of glucose and the sharp odor of smokeless powder and the soaring of stringed instruments.

It fired again and then the barber stood with hot blood dripping from his glasses, his hands still crossed at his chest. The shoe shiner clutched his belly but did not open his eyes. The killer, who wore a trench coat and a mask kind of like the Lone Ranger's, turned and weaved out the door while taking off the mask, stepped between two parked cars, and was gone. Elapsed time inside the barbershop: nine or maybe nineteen seconds. The barber would tell the police later that it happened so quickly it was hard to say. The guy had been standing under the streetlamp out front drunk, earlier, though, he added. Looked like he was working a crossword puzzle.

4

Next afternoon a cab stopped on the brick parking lot in front of the south entrance to the Peabody hotel, downtown. Frankie Falconey stepped out and looked at his shoes. Claude the doorman was smiling at him and holding the cab door open with a white-gloved hand. Frankie paid the cabbie and the doorman closed the door and the cab pulled away. There was still some snow lying here and there. He had a whopper of a hangover.

"What's up, Claude," he said, and kept looking at his shoes. The shit wouldn't ever come off after it dried. And damn his head felt bad.

"Everything's cool, Mr. Falconey. The birds are out again."

Frankie looked up.

"What birds? I don't see no fucking birds. You mean these flying rats the city won't shoot? All they're good for's crapping on your car. Or in your hair."

The doorman just smiled. Taxis and private cars were letting people off and taking riders in. There were women sporting fur coats. A few well-dressed dudes in black hats going in had acoustic guitars in cases. Horns were blowing on Second and the pigeons flapped and rose in whirling flocks, blue, green, gray, dull colors with pink beaks, over the parking lot and above the old hotel. Frankie could remember when the place had been just about shut down, back in the early seventies when he was just a kid, the dark hallways, the moldy carpet. But they'd fixed it up really nice now.

There was one spot, just a speck of dried blood, right there on the toe of his right shoe, just about over the toe next to the little one. Frankie raised his foot and wiped the toe against the back of his pants leg, rubbed it hard against his calf. He checked it again and saw that it was not gone. He turned toward the door anyway, shooting his cuffs and patting his hair briefly with his hands.

"She in?" he said.

"She's in," Claude said, and held the door open. Frankie pressed a folded five into his hand. He liked to keep everybody greased, made him feel like Bobby DeNiro in *Goodfellas*. He went on up the hall past some shops.

He went up the steps past the two big bronze dogs and into the lobby with its polished floors and its brightly lit chandelier and its square marble columns where music was playing from a black baby grand that was tinkling itself in a corner. A monstrous bouquet of colorful flowers sat in front of the elevators atop the circular fountain where the mallards took their twice-daily baths. As usual the lobby was full of people with cameras waiting on the ducks or having drinks or chatting in richly upholstered chairs pulled up beside the round tables. Lots of voices were talking. He walked over to the bar and found an empty tall chair and waved at Ken, who was busy making three Bloody Marys. Frankie looked around to see if anybody famous was sitting in the lobby today. He'd seen Billy Joel in there one afternoon having a drink, but hadn't asked him for an autograph. You couldn't ever tell who might pop in. Clapton maybe if he was doing another show at the Pyramid. B.B. might walk in with Lucille in her case. There were people in tourist T-shirts, some laughing Japanese people in horn-rimmed glasses and big coats, a few guys in suits drinking draft beers, some college-age kids maybe up from Ole Miss for a night on the town. Ken rang up a tab and placed the bill in front of a customer with a pen and then came over and put a small duck-embossed napkin in front of Frankie on the bar's black slab.

"How's it going, Ken? You win any money on the football?"

Ken was already pouring a shot of Himmel. He set it on the napkin.

"Ah, the Titans . . . if they'd get their shit together. . . . I don't know what they're thinking."

Frankie lifted the shot glass and sipped half of it. It instantly made him feel better, calmed his nerves and furnished a comfortable afterglow. He looked at the glass he was holding. His fingers were still shaking the tiniest bit. He sipped again and set it down empty. Ken refilled it.

He knew he'd done exactly what he was supposed to do, even if he had been drunk. He'd had to get drunk to be able to do what he did. But he didn't leave any evidence behind. He hadn't left any fingerprints on anything. The gun was on the bottom of the Mississippi River, the mask in a trash can just outside the fairgrounds, the trench coat at the Salvation Army. So why did Mr. Hamburger want to talk to him this soon? Who knew? Maybe there was another job lined up for him already. Maybe even a fat bonus for a job well done.

"You see Anjalee come in?"

Ken nodded and picked up a wet glass to dry. He wiped it hard with a dinner napkin and the glass squeaked. He cocked his head toward the lobby and spoke to the glass.

"I caught a glimpse of her going across the lobby. You ready for me to send it up?"

"Right, let me get this one down."

Frankie picked up the second shot and drained it, then stood up, digging in his pocket for some money. He put a ten on the bar and waved as he left. Ken smiled.

"Thanks, Mr. Falconey. See you later?"

"Maybe so. Take care, Ken."

The bartender looked after his retreating back. He waited a few moments and then picked up the money and turned toward the register.

"Yeah, right, asshole," he muttered.

5

In a very nice room 420, a country girl named Anjalee was lying on the bed and on a crocheted afghan her grandmother had made for her a long time ago. She was reading in the paper about a New York–style barbershop slaying near Cooper and Young when he stepped in with the key. She had on leopard panties and pink booties. She was sipping on Mountain Dew spiked with Absolut Citron and smoking a Camel filtered. She put the cigarette in an ashtray but didn't stub it out, and stretched out on her flat stomach and pulled her panties down to her knees and then raised her nicely rounded behind into the air and waved it around some. She knew what he'd do: step into the bathroom, take a leak, flush, wash his hands, dry them, step out, open the door for the room service guy, bring the whiskey over, fix a drink, drink the drink (or maybe two), take a condom (he was plainly terrified of catching some STD from her) from his pocket. The whole routine sucked. It wasn't romantic anymore. He'd told her he wanted romance, even if he was paying her, and for a while they'd had it, and now they never had it. He wasn't being considerate of her feelings anymore. Now he just showed up and mounted her. For a long time, she'd been pretty impressed by the Peabody, and had hoped it would lead to things like nice dinners at places like Automatic Slim's, but it never had, and now she simply heard the phone ring some days and picked it up and it was him on it, saying two words: Friday, two, or Tuesday, four, or Sunday, one. And she went.

And waited.

Like this.

To fuck him safely.

For more money.

He was quiet now, coming out of the bathroom, zipping his pants.

On cue the bell rang and he went to the door. He didn't open it wide enough to let the guy in, just took the bottle and passed some money out and shut the door, locked it, put the chain on, and sat down in a chair near the wall.

She stayed on her stomach, looking at him with her ass in the air. He opened the bourbon and poured some of it into a crystal glass, dumped in a handful of ice cubes from a waiting chrome bucket. She watched his eyes when he started drinking and wasn't looking at her. He was staring at something past her, way out past the windows, that look in his eyes he got sometimes that made her wonder what he could be thinking. She didn't know where he got his money. He always had plenty of it. She thought he was probably a small-time hood, based on her observations of some of his thuggy friends and from overhearing a few of their stoned conversations about robberies and beatings and trips to the Shelby County Jail. But he didn't like questions. She thought she'd ask one anyway.

"Excuse me," she said. "You gonna come over here and get you some of this or what?"

He just kept sipping his drink. She guessed he was in another one of his shitty moods. He had gotten up, turned on the television, and slumped back down into the chair, and now he was watching something on ESPN. He'd watch any kind of sports. Precision swimming. Professional duck-dog retrieving trials. Those people chopping wood real fast even. Actually that stuff was pretty fun to watch. She thought she'd like to try that logrolling in water.

"Well, horse*shit*," she said, pulled her panties back up, and got off the bed to fix herself another drink and get dressed. "If you'd rather watch the damn TV than get in bed with me, I'll just go down to the bar and watch the ducks."

"I've got a lot on my mind."

"Oh yeah? Like what? Must not be me."

He raised his head.

"Hey. Don't bitch at me, okay? If I want somebody to bitch at me, I'll get married. One of your purposes is to not bitch at me."

She stepped into her skirt and pulled it up and fastened it around her waist. One of her purposes. Yeah, well, one of the purposes of fucking was to maybe get to come once in a while, too, but she didn't much, did she? It was all about him all the time, wasn't it? His needs, what he wanted. She poured some more Absolut into her glass and walked over and got a few ice cubes from his bucket. She looked down and saw a red spot on his shoe.

"What's that on your shoe?"

"A pigeon shit on me."

"Looks like blood to me."

"Well it ain't. Okay?"

He fixed her with a look she didn't like. She turned away from it.

"Wow," she said. She sat back down on the bed and got her cigarette from the ashtray and finished smoking it while she drank about half of what was in her glass. He wouldn't even look at her. She guessed he was tired of her.

After a while she got up and put her bra on. She slipped her feet out of the booties and into her shoes and pulled her sweater over her head. Let him sit here and watch the stupid television while she got paid for it. She got her brush from her purse and went into the tiled bathroom and brushed her hair. Her makeup was still okay. She grimaced at the mirror. No lipstick on her teeth. Maybe she needed to try a new tack with him.

Back in the room, she picked up her drink and sipped it, swirling it slowly around in her hand, studying his inert form.

"We goin' out to eat?" she said. "You said we could."

"I don't know yet."

"I could stand some Italian. I love that lasagna over at Papa Tutu's. God. It's heaven."

"I don't know yet."

"They got the best bread sticks I ever had."

"I ain't made up my mind yet."

"When you gonna?"

"I don't know yet."

She stomped her foot.

"What the *fuck*, Frankie? Do you want me to leave?"

"No," he said to the TV, and took another sip.

"Then why in the hell don't you *talk* to me sometime?"

" 'Cause I'm watching Kyle Petty in a car race, okay?"

And he was. They had a vibrating camera in Mr. Petty's car. The walls and fences and grandstands were zooming by at some incredible rate of speed. Frankie didn't look at her anymore. Fuck him. She didn't have to stay around his mopey ass. She could go have a drink and watch the ducks come down and get in the fountain, splash around, quack.

"Okay. Fine. Whatever. You sit right here and be Mr. Unsociable Asshole. I'll be in the bar if you want me."

She drained her drink and slammed it down and headed for the door.

"Why don't you tell Ken to send me up a shrimp cocktail?" he said.

6

Anjalee had to take a bus over to the old folks' home a few days later because she had a flat and was running late. She was still on probation from when the couch cops had nabbed her at Fifi's Cabaret, and this was her community service. All the judges had gotten so big on that. They'd let you pick up trash or if you had a little education teach English to some of those from Asian shores or Pakistani mountains who yearned to know it better in order to buy convenience stores they gave names like Quik-Pak or Sak.

Her grandmother had died in one of these places down in Water Valley and she remembered how much her grandmother had suffered and so she didn't mind it so much because everybody who kept living got old and needed help, and one day she would, too. She was a little tired so she was sitting down in the lounge taking a break. They made her wear a white uniform and creaky shoes and a white hat, and she had no medical training whatsoever. Most of the days she worked were spent rolling old folks over or rolling them over the other way or feeding them or emptying their bedpans or listening to them complain about their feet or their backs or their digestive processes or their old tickers that didn't tick so good anymore or their miserable arthritis or the cold spots inside their bodies or just innumerable things that in their combining sometimes made her afraid of getting old. On the other hand, she'd seen a few of the old folks having sex, withered and wrinkled bodies singing joyously in the throes of hot lust, liver-spotted hands gripping each other, and whenever that happened she stood guard outside the door. If anybody came along, she said the patient was using the bedpan and the other old folks' home workers just went on down the hall because they didn't need any more work, saved them from wiping another ass. Who wanted to wipe an extra ass?

She put her feet up in a chair. She drank her diet Coke and smoked her cigarette clandestinely, what with it being prohibited in there and all, it being a place that was kind of like a hospital but not exactly, but some of the die-hard smoker old folks had smokes smuggled in by relatives and raised their windows and lit up and exhaled out them just like Anjalee was doing right now.

A few of the old folks had died, too. It seemed to her that sometimes they'd just take a notion to up and croak overnight because one day they'd be laughing at Opie and Andy and eating their applesauce and the next day stretched out cold as a mackerel. Mr. Pasternak, Miss Doobis, Mr. Munchie, Mrs. Haddow-Green, each now dead with a new stranger in their bed. Sometimes she wished she was back in Toccopola fixing hair.

She heard Miss Barbee's swishing footsteps and chunked her Camel out the window and fanned the air with her hand and then with her white hat and stuck it back on her head. Miss Barbee came in and sniffed the air like a bird dog and Anjalee told her a patient had burned some tissue just now, not over two minutes ago, and Miss Barbee, who was a beautiful Swiss chocolate brown and large with gigantic tits and feet and ass and a melon head, too, put her hands on her hips, said, "Oh yeah, I bet," and then, "Well, come on here, we got to go wipe Mister Boudreaux's ass, old fool done shit all over the place again."

Anjalee got up and followed Miss Barbee down the hall, squeaking along in her shoes, trying to keep up. They turned in at the end of the hall and there sprawled on a bed like a skinned squirrel was Mr. T. J. Boudreaux, formerly of New Iberia, shit smeared on him from head to toe. Anjalee had always felt tender toward him because he mumbled what sounded like sweet Cajun nothings to her while she was feeding him his lukewarm gruel.

"*Got* damn!" Miss Barbee said. "We gone need a fire hose to clean his ass up this time!" She closed the door.

She went over to the side of the bed and put her hands on her hips.

Mr. T.J. was trying to say something, but nothing intelligible came out of his mouth. Anjalee thought he was probably trying to apologize for the mess. She knew Mr. T.J. couldn't help it. He peed in the bed all the time.

She'd started over to the closet for some clean sheets when she heard a *WHOP!* Her head turned toward the bed and she saw Mr. Boudreaux's top half hanging out off the other side and Miss Barbee drawn back to let him have it again.

"You nasty mess!" she yelled. "I'm sick a wipin' yo ass!" She reached over and slapped him the other way, *WHAP!*, and all Anjalee did was look for what to hit her with and that turned out to be a nice heavy steel pitcher on a table. Miss Barbee didn't see it coming because she was so busy. Anjalee swung it with both hands by the handle and KAPOW! knocked Miss Barbee's crisp white hat clean off her head. Miss Barbee as she was falling and farting turned and made a feeble grab for Anjalee's arm, but Anjalee had been to a few four-rounders at Sam's Town in Tunica with Frankie, back before things started turning sour, and she feinted quick and waited until Miss Barbee was almost on the floor and then *BEEONG!* popped her again right over her left eye with it and watched her go down like a steer in the killing pen, so hard her ugly-ass head bounced on the floor. Mr. T.J. was still talking Cajun gibberish in the bed and he was crying a little, too, but Anjalee knelt down next to Miss Barbee with her white-stockinged knee on the floor and looked at her. The skin was split deeply above her eye with some fatty bloody flesh showing and she was bleeding from the ears and nose and as Anjalee knelt there watching, a stain began to spread out from her panty-hosed crotch where her uniform dress had risen up on her fatpuckered thighs. The pitcher had two dents in it.

"Well fuck a mule," Anjalee said. She got up and then backed away.

She went to work on the old oysterman rapidly, washing him, putting his dirty pajamas in a plastic bag, shifting him back and forth while she replaced the sheets and put clean pajamas on him. Then she closed the door behind her when she went out and down the hall and got her sweater from the coatroom and left, trying not to walk too rapidly, out the side entrance, a voice raising a question behind her, down the steps and over the wet sidewalks and once she hit the street, running, until her mind caught up with her and told her to slow down and not attract attention on the way to the bus stop, get home and change the flat, move the car, try to be a little bit cool.

7

Arthur got all upset over TV news at lunch about a hit man conducting his business right across the street from the coffee shop he'd been in. To calm down he got in the Jag and drove over to the Mall of Memphis, and then after getting across the parking lot without being run over, he browsed along a pet shop's sidewalk windows, checking out the items there, collars and dog dishes, parakeets and cockatoos in wire cages, hamsters on their rolling treadmills busily trying to get the hell out of Dodge. A few listless puppies in sawdust soaked with puppy pee. Sad and puzzled little things with their heads cocked to one side, and the sight of them probably capable of breaking Helen's heart. She slept like a frog in cold mud beside him after drinking until late most nights, then dozed and flopped around and groaned late in the mornings while he got up quietly and dressed and drank coffee and made his breakfast and watched the big TV while he waited for her to come down with her hangover and start mixing her cure. But he knew she slipped out sometimes, too. For Rocky Road, my ass. He'd written Dear Abby about all his problems and that evidently hadn't done any good. Dear Abby hadn't even run it in her column. Dear Abby wasn't even writing her own column anymore according to a little note at the bottom of her column. Maybe she'd gotten too old, too. He gave out an enormous inward sigh. What was he to do if he didn't go back to the doctor?

Helen still had needs. And so did he, at least sometimes anyway. Not a whole lot. Just once in a while. But he could hardly stand to admit defeat and accept that he'd gotten too old to cut the mustard by himself. Maybe he did need a pump. A dick pump. Good God. More money. The DUIs had already cost him a bundle.

He didn't see a tranquilizer gun in the window, guessed he'd have to go in and ask. He hoped they weren't smart-asses. A bell over the door rang when he went in, accompanied by the peace-inducing music of aquariums bubbling, the irritating squawks of tropical birds. A stocky young man was behind the counter, wheat hair, shirt too big, tie too loose, propped back on a stool reading a tattered paperback, spacecraft on its cover, by a guy named Effinger. Arthur read the title: *The Wolves of Memory*. The young man didn't look up. The shop reeked of Pine Sol trying to cover up dog shit.

Arthur cleared his throat. That usually worked, but the young man still didn't look up. He seemed intent upon his book.

"Excuse me," Arthur said. "Would you happen to have any tranquilizer guns?"

"Nawsir," said the young man, who turned a page.

"I have a wild animal I want to catch," Arthur said, feeling slightly foolish over saying "wild animal."

"If it's a possum, you can call the dogcatcher folks."

"It's a cat, actually. A rather small one. A kitten, really."

"Cats are weird," said the young man, still not looking up, and Arthur didn't know why this cat problem had to come about now alongside these other problems with Helen's drinking and his dick. It seemed to him that one problem at a time ought to be enough. What Helen needed was some help. But she didn't want to hear that.

"I really need some help," he said, trying not to sound like he was pleading. "It's my wife I'm trying to catch it for."

The young man put Effinger down. He reached under the counter for a pack of Marlboros and a lighter, propped his feet on the counter, lit up.

"That's a bad habit for a young person to take up," Arthur said.

"I been smokin' since I was six. Why don't you get a trap?"

"I've already got a Havahart trap. He won't go in it, she, whatever it is. I think it smells me. That's what my wife said anyway. She read it in a book."

"Is it in your yard?"

"Well, sometimes."

"Is it scared of you?"

"I haven't done anything to it."

"Cats can be like that."

"Yes they can," Arthur said. "They can be pretty vicious, too." He leaned up against the counter and fiddled with a small stack of chartreuse Post-its, turned and looked at some red swordtails and neon tetras, then examined a thumbnail casually. "I was attacked by one when I was a child. It stalked me when I was sitting in a car and I had to roll all the windows up to keep it from getting me. I told my parents all that beforehand." He looked up at the young man. "And they just laughed. They weren't laughing after that cat attacked me, I can tell you that. They were painting my little legs with a bottle of iodine."

"Aw yeah? Your daddy kill the cat?"

"No he didn't," Arthur said. He hoped his disappointed tone was plain. He still didn't know why his daddy hadn't killed the cat. It looked like his uncle would have volunteered to kill his own cat himself, but he didn't. He looked at a python in a cage. It had eaten some animal and there was a lump in the middle of it. He wondered what it was: gerbil, rat? It seemed his daddy had been dead almost forever now. He still thought about him often, though, and about the times he'd taken him fishing for fat bluegills at Tunica Cutoff. They used to catch piles of them. They'd pee on you when you took the hook out. He remembered how good they were to eat, fried in black iron skillets and grease in the kitchens of houses built on stilts. Old rotted boats dark and silent under shade trees. Life had been a lot simpler then. Fewer choices.

"How'd it get you?"

"Had my back turned. Making a peanut butter and jelly sandwich."

"I can come over and probably catch it but it's gonna cost you."

"How much?"

"Fifty bucks."

"*Fifty bucks?*"

"Fifty bucks."

"That seems high. How do you propose to do it?"

"Little help from a little friend."

"Can you come over in a couple of days?"

"Okay. Twenty up front, thirty when I hand him over."

Arthur stood there, reaching for his billfold, feeling half angry and somewhat helpless, wondering where this could possibly lead. All this trouble and for what? One little lost animal saved from the world and hundreds of thousands of others being bred at the moment. Was it worth fifty dollars of his money? Wouldn't it probably just tear up the drapes and the rugs and piss on the furniture? Would it change anything between him and Helen? Probably not. She was just like she'd always been. Horny.

"You'd better call first," Arthur said. "My wife likes to sleep late in the mornings."

8

Frankie was working a crossword puzzle and waiting at the corner of Danny Thomas and Beale for a guy to come walking by on the sidewalk and make a sign to him. People were going by him and standing around him and horns were honking and the exhaust fumes from pickups and vans and cars and buses and carriage horses were rising up into the cold air. A guy down the street selling flowers wasn't having much luck.

There were quite a few people out and he figured a lot of them were Christmas shopping. A man walked by on the sidewalk, looking directly at him, then made a fist and lifted his thumb, and a black stretch Caddy eased to the curb next to Frankie while the back door opened. He got in and pulled the door shut. The car began moving and the dome light came on. The inside was upholstered in soft leather and the driver was hidden behind a pane of black glass. A tall and stern-looking man wearing glasses and a very good suit was sitting across from him with a slim aluminum briefcase on his lap, and it was obvious that he was not in a good mood. Beside him on the seat was a tiny long-haired dog, black and white, with a polka-dot ribbon around its neck. The little animal showed him its teeth. Frankie chuckled.

"What's up with the guard dog, Mr. Hamburger?"

"Never mind the dog. What's up with you?"

Frankie smiled and leaned back.

"Well, I don't know. Lenny said you wanted to see me."

Mr. Hamburger never took his eyes off him and watched him in a way that made Frankie think of a rattlesnake he'd seen Anjalee watching on a Discovery Channel documentary just before it hit a mouse at blinding speed. But anybody who'd gotten his dick mutilated by a gasoline-powered posthole digger would probably stay in a bad mood.

Mr. Hamburger raised the lid on the briefcase. The little dog peeked in as his master lifted an eight-by-ten photo from it. He presented it.

"Does this man look familiar to you?"

Frankie took the picture and studied it. An ordinary photo of a man with deeply tanned skin, short black hair neatly combed, with just a little gray showing. He handed the picture back. No hard question there. But why the question?

"What is this, Mr. Hamburger? We both know who that is. You gave me that picture at the Como steak house." He glanced sideways. The glass in the car windows was very tinted.

"Who is it?"

What the fuck? He wasn't sure now what to say. He didn't want to say the wrong thing. Something was definitely wrong but he decided to try to make light of it.

"What's this, some kinda joke? Okay, ha ha, it's real funny. Where we going anyway?"

Mr. Hamburger just kept watching him, holding the photo. The car kept moving smoothly, past the big buildings that stood in their own shade, as if somebody had wired all the lights on green just for them. Frankie looked out the window, then faced Mr. Hamburger again. He was starting to get just a little bit scared.

"Had a haircut lately, Frankie?" Mr. Hamburger said.

"Nah, I ain't had no . . ." He stopped. "What *is* this?" he said.

"Mr. Leonardo Gaspucci got a haircut the other night. A quick one, they said. You know anything about Mr. Gaspucci's haircut, Frankie?"

He knew he was in some deep shit now, but not why. He hoped to get enlightened but he doubted he would. There was probably no way to jump out. The doors were probably locked. And just then they all locked. *Click.* He swallowed hard.

"Look, Mr. Hamburger. I don't know what you're talking about, okay? I did what you told me to. Did I do something wrong?"

Mr. Hamburger put the photo back inside the briefcase and closed the lid. The little dog that had been peeking inside the briefcase turned its attention back on Frankie and began showing its teeth again. Mr. Hamburger petted it, stroking the long strands of black hair and white hair sensuously, slowly, careful as a lover. Frankie wondered if they were heading to the loop for I-40, and if so, where they were going. Either Arkansas or Mississippi. Why in the hell would they be going to Arkansas or Mississippi? Unless they were going to the steak house at Como again for a juicy T-bone. He couldn't imagine why they'd be going to Arkansas.

"Would you like to know who Mr. Gaspucci is, Frankie? Would you be interested in hearing that?"

He turned his reptile eyes upon Frankie again and waited, but there were no questions showing on his face. There was only one thing to say.

"Sure, Mr. Hamburger."

"Mr. Gaspucci was getting a nice haircut the other night, Frankie. The works. Shave, talc, nose and ear trim, the whole deal. Then somebody came in and messed up his haircut for him. I mean messed it up big time."

"Who's Mr. Gaspucci?" Frankie said softly.

"You wouldn't last long in Chicago, Frankie. Mr. Gaspucci is *not* the man in the photo. That man's still walking around selling people posthole diggers. I saw him, Frankie. And I paid you a lot of money to make sure I wouldn't."

Frankie laughed, snorted momentarily, then chuckled. His grin got wider and he chortled, feeling a lot better now, realizing now that Mr. Hamburger was just playing around with him and that it would be over in a few more minutes, and he would let him out somewhere, and he could find a bar, and get a drink that would calm his trembling hands. Lenny never had told him that Mr. Hamburger pulled practical jokes. Maybe this was the way they did it in Chicago. Scare the shit out of somebody and then have some belly laughs about it. He'd have to tell Lenny about this over drinks. Maybe even this afternoon. Wouldn't that be fun? Oh how they'd howl. Call for another drink. Eat some goldfish from a bowl. He could call up Anjalee and tell her to get ready and take her somewhere nice. Maybe Huey's, close to the Peabody. They had a very good burger and you could get a drink. Shit, maybe even try that Automatic Slim guy's place.

"That's a good one, Mr. Hamburger, that's a real good funny one, reminds me of my uncle, used to tell me stuff all the time and I'd believe it, and I mean dead serious like you, too, he had this great delivery—"

"Shut the fuck up, Frankie. Mr. Gaspucci was involved in the vacuum cleaner business. He was a regional sales director for the

Hoover company and he had a kid in school at Yale, pre-law. Want to know why he was getting a haircut?"

Frankie couldn't say anything. He just had to listen. The little dog kept snarling silently, showing his nice clean white teeth.

"He was getting a haircut so he could go to Hoover's annual motivational conference in Phoenix. He was going to meet his father there and they were going to play golf. Golf, Frankie. Mr. Gaspucci and his father got together six times a year and played golf. They played at Palm Springs, at Hilton Head, at Doe Island, at Old Waverly down in Columbus. It was their thing. It was what they did together. You know why? Because Mr. Gaspucci senior had busted his balls to get Leonardo into college and get him graduated with a business degree and you know what he did to get the money, Frankie? He sold Hoover vacuum cleaners. He sold them door to door, Frankie, and he even worked weekends and eventually, once he had his degree in business, Leonardo joined the Hoover company himself and rose through the ranks to become a regional sales director. They had a great relationship and they never had quarrels and they loved each other as much as men can, and you know what you did to Mr. Gaspucci, Frankie, you want to know why you're in here with me and the man in the picture is out there and why we're riding through town like this, you want to know what you did to Leo Gaspucci?"

The car was speeding up onto the ramp to cross the Mississippi at the Hernando de Soto bridge. To Arkansas. Frankie was almost weeping into his lap because he knew he wasn't going for a big fat Como cut off a cow now. He said: "What?"

"You fucked up his haircut. You were supposed to whack this asshole who just happened to *vaguely* resemble him. Who wasn't supposed to arrive for twenty-seven more minutes. Yet you were seen waiting outside, drunk like a dumb-ass. And if the cops grab you, it's only a matter of time until they'll have me. Because you'll squeal."

"But he came on in! Please! Mr. Hamburger, *wait* a minute . . . I just thought he was . . . kinda early!"

They were on the bridge now and going faster and Frankie could see the gray arched and riveted steel beams above them and the rails of the bridge flashing by. Far below lay the father of waters, slow and muddy, wide and ancient, home of monster catfish, alligator gar, Mark Twain, and mid-South TV's favorite fisherman, Bill Dance. Mr. Hamburger didn't seem to notice, only reached inside his coat. The little dog growled gently, low in his throat, but not to the hand that stroked him.

"Sorry, Frankie. We're not responsible for what you thought."

9

The bar at Gigi's Angels on Winchester was dim, the clientele all men, drinking heavily in heavy smoke. The floor was full of empty chairs. Two tired-looking dyed blondes, a little lumpy and stretch marked from childbirth and naked but for silver panties, were moving slowly on the stage, under faint blue lights, to Chris Rea. Lighted candles along the back mirror and among the bottles flickered whenever the door opened. The sailor had spoken nervously to the bartender about the possibility of a woman and when she came out from behind a door the sailor saw her look at him. She winked and he nodded and took a big drink of his beer. In a moment she was near his elbow, luxuriant in tight black, a low-cut sweater that showed her breasts generously, her hair loose and shiny like some kind of animal's mane.

"What's your name, sailor?"

"Wayne Stubbock," he told her. "Are you really . . . ?"

"Really what, Wayne?" she said as she signaled to the bartender. "Be cool, okay? I got caught on a couch by some cops one time. In another place I used to work." She smiled again and pulled a pack of Camel filtereds from her pocket. The bartender set a clear drink with ice, a slice of lime floating, at her hand. "Thanks, Moe," she said. He saw a nice bracelet on her wrist, twisted silver. He had a small headache again. But he didn't have them every day. They were probably nothing.

"I mean . . . God. Are they all like you in Memphis?"

She reached for a book of paper matches on the bar and opened it and tore one loose, tossing her hair back before she lit it, then scraping it hard across the little rough patch and pressing on it with her finger so that when it flared and she lifted it flaring and smoking to her mouth he could see himself twinned in her eyes for one brief flash of recognition. Her lips pulled on the Camel, sucked back the smoke, and a small hole opened in her mouth and blew out the match. She winked. And in that moment he was in love.

"I'm a country girl. You just got lucky 'cause I quit my other job."

She looked away from him for a moment and reached for her glass, lowered her eyes and sipped from it, then before she took another drink and set it down cast her gaze around again as if sizing up the night.

"How long you in town for?" she said, and eased her hand over onto his knee and then lifted her eyes to his and looked into them with an unwavering stare. She had big eyelashes. It was almost scary being next to her. He had never seen one like this up close.

"Just one night," he said. "Tonight."

"Well, hey, I guess you better make some hay while the sun shines, huh?" She lowered her voice. "What you want, baby?"

She moved her hand higher on his leg and up the inside of his thigh. There was heat in her hand and she was still smiling at him and sipping at her drink and holding it hanging beneath her fingers, swirling the ice around in the glass with an unstudied grace. The thought of being naked with her made his heart start beating hard against his breastbone, just like it did whenever he got ready to fight.

"I want to marry you," he said, before he could stop himself.

She didn't laugh. Her eyes got solemn and she stopped swirling the drink. She raised her chin.

"Where you headed?"

"Indian Ocean."

He thought of all the iron and steel moored at the shipyard in Pascagoula, and of all the welds in the hull and the weapons racked in the armories and the food frozen in the freezers and the planes with their folded wings and the sleeping pilots and the sleeping marines and sailors and even of the sleeping Sea Sparrow missiles in their beds. He didn't know what would happen to him if he jumped ship and stayed, but already those kinds of thoughts had begun to form.

"You want a blow job?" she whispered. "I'll give you one for fifty that'll make you remember me on your deathbed."

He had to think. Something was wrong because here was this thing happening. She wasn't supposed to be here. She was supposed to be back on his daddy's farm with him, and he'd build the house on the back pasture his father had set aside for him, next to the lake he'd fished in as a boy, under the wide shade of old post oaks. He'd teach the children to fish for walleye and they'd ride the tractors with his father. Summer lawn-mowing while she hung out clothes and cooking burgers on a charcoal grill. Buying all the toys at Christmas. They'd have love in the afternoons.

"I want to marry you," he said. "I ain't never . . . what's your name?"

She took a drag on her cigarette before she answered, and let the smoke come out with her words.

"Anjalee," she said, and seemed a little sad. "But I don't need to marry you, sailor. You better take a blow job while you can get it."

She drained her drink and motioned for another one. The bartender looked at Wayne, and she nodded. When the drink came, she picked it up and got him by the arm. He didn't know what was going on but he followed her, around the end of the bar into some darkness and through a black door that she locked behind them, just the two of them in the dark and then climbing up stairs where scant light showed above, and onto a landing that headed a hall of doors. She took him into the third room on the left. One candle was burning beside a condom packet on a table next to a small bed where a nice black leather coat was lying. She closed the door behind them and dropped quickly to her knees and, setting down her drink, opened up the front of his trousers. When he came in the rubber a few minutes later, panting like a hot puppy with his trousers down around his shoes and his fingers wrapped in her hair and barely standing he was moaning and groaning and crying and dying because he knew she would leave him and find another.

10

The pet shop young man came as promised, right up the sidewalk after he got out of a beat-up old Buick Century. Helen saw him stop in front of the house and with her drink got out of the recliner.

"Who in the hell's *that?*" she said.

Arthur sidled up beside her, smelling the coffee in his hand. Once in a while, he had a gin and tonic with her to be sociable. But she could drink all by herself just fine.

"It's somebody I hired to catch the cat."

"Oh yeah? How much'd you have to pay him?"

"Twenty bucks," said Arthur, sipping from his steaming cup. "Thirty more after he turns it over."

She kept watching the young man. He was walking up and down the sidewalk. He carried something that was alive in a tow sack.

"I don't think it's even out there anymore," Helen said. "And what's that he's got in that sack?"

"I saw it this morning, walking around. It's probably hiding. I don't know what he's got in the sack."

"How do you know he can catch it?"

"He said he could. He seems like a nice young man."

Helen stepped to the dining room table and removed a chair that she placed by the window. She sat in it and looked out for a bit. He sipped his coffee. He knew that three months was a long time to go without for somebody who liked it as much as she did. He guessed she was tired of trying. But so was he. Whenever he looked at it now, the head of it seemed to be turning purple. Was it dead, had part of him died? Sometimes it felt cold, rubbery. Like there wasn't any blood circulating through it. Like your arm when you sleep on it at night sometimes.

"I feel sorry for that boy out in the cold," she said.

"He's getting paid for it."

"I wish I knew what he had in that sack."

"I guess we'll find out," Arthur said. He stood close to Helen and eased his hand onto her shoulder. She reached over her drinking arm and patted his hand just for a second, and then Arthur took his hand away. He knew how wet she could become. She was evidently coated on the inside with the slickest and most lubricious oil imaginable. He figured she still harbored vast reserves of it, deep, hidden within her body like a petroleum deposit buried beneath a mountain. He hoped nobody at the Peabody was drilling for it.

The young man stopped in the yard and set the sack down. The sack moved and jerked about. Arthur didn't know if he liked the look of that. He'd thought maybe he would have something on a long pole with a snare or a loop on the end of it, but it was plain now that he hadn't come equipped with anything like that.

"What's he got in there?" Helen said. "A monkey?"

"Beats me. He didn't say what he was going to use. He just told me he could catch it."

"What's his name?"

"I don't know. I didn't ask him."

"Well, for heaven's sake."

"What?"

"You hired somebody and you don't even know what his name is? Where did you find him?"

"Over at the pet shop at the Mall of Memphis. You know, Studebaker's?"

"God." She sipped her drink. "That's such a stupid name for a pet shop."

"Well . . . I guess if that's your name . . ."

"What were you doing at the pet shop?"

"I was looking for a tranquilizer gun for the kitten. You know, one that shoots darts? You know, like those you see on TV? You've seen them, like the ones they use over in Africa and places? I saw them shoot one into an elephant that was running amuck one time. Well, actually they shot five or six into it. They had to keep reloading their gun. I think they were using extra-large darts. I didn't figure I'd need any that big."

Helen looked out the window again, frowning. She seemed pretty disgusted with him.

"I can't imagine what you could have been thinking," she said, and flounced the edge of her dress over her pretty knees as she sometimes did when she got agitated with him. Out in the yard, the young man took a long look around, then pulled a leash out of his pocket and opened the mouth of the sack. What started coming out was a scarred old pit bull, brindle colored, tiger striped, nub eared, a runt.

"Oh shit!" Helen said, and lurched up, sloshing some of her drink on the carpet. Out in the yard, the young man had snapped the leash onto the pit bull's collar and was kneeling and petting him. Arthur could see the wide tongue of the dog licking his hand. The dog moved with difficulty, as if his legs were bad. The young man stood up and led him forward and the old dog limped along beside him.

"What's he doing out there, Arthur? If he lets that dog hurt that kitten . . ."

"I don't know what he's doing just yet. Why don't we wait a minute and see?"

"I don't know if I want to see or not. Don't you know they train those dogs to fight by letting them kill kittens?"

"I didn't know that," Arthur said.

"Why, hell. They've outlawed them in England because they've killed so many children. Don't you know that?"

"It's news to me," Arthur said. She was getting kind of mad. She got kind of mad easier when she was drinking. She got kind of mad sometimes when he couldn't get it up, too. She'd yelled at him once. Then left.

"Don't you ever read the papers?"

"Just the funnies mostly. I like 'Snuffy Smith.' And 'Dear Abby.' "

There was a flurry of motion at the corner of the house and the dog dove at something. The young man was yelling, pulling at the leash, his breath coming out in a white fog, and when Arthur glanced at Helen she had raised a hand to her horrified mouth. She set her drink down and turned away.

"I can't watch this," she said. "Not in front of my own house." She had her fingers over her eyes.

"Look," Arthur said, pointing.

"How could you do such a butthole thing?"

"It's not what you think. Look."

"No. I'm not."

"You'd better. He's caught your cat for you."

Helen sniffled and turned slowly. She took her hands down from her face. The young man was leading the pit bull toward their front door, and the dog had the kitten in his mouth similar to the way a pointer retrieves a downed quail. The kitten was writhing in the dog's mouth and frantically scratching its muzzle with all four feet, but the old dog just ignored it and kept limping forward. Arthur could see that the kitten was yowling, because its mouth was wide open and he could see its teeth. Once they got closer, he could also see that the kitten was going to the bathroom all over the place. Then the young man stopped next to the steps out front and said something to the dog and the dog stopped and sat. Its muzzle was bloody from where the kitten had scratched it, was still scratching it. Its face was a mask of old cuts, and healed stitches of leathery-looking skin, but its eyes were bright and in them Arthur could see what he thought was a kind of love. It made him feel so good he smiled. The young man lifted his hand and waved at Helen and Arthur and smiled. They waved back. It was starting to snow again.

11

In an old building on Front Street, just above the river, a guy named Domino D'Alamo read a work order and then took some fresh meat out of the walk-in cooler that was next to the lion-meat freezer. He was wearing gloves and he had a coat on over his apron. The radio in the back was turned up loud since he was hard of hearing. A pimply prison guard had fired a twelve-gauge shotgun right next to his ear one day just for the fun of it, one beautiful April day down in Mississippi, when spotted orange butterflies were out on the roadside daisies while they cut the tall grass with sling blades, and the free folks just drove on by all day long.

He was cutting meat at night in this little shop now, by himself, which suited the shit out of him, since he didn't like people very much. The lion-meat freezer had a big sign Mr. Hamburger had written out with a thick black Magic Marker: "Lion Meat Only." Nobody else ever messed with the lion meat because nobody else wanted the stinking job. The weed Domino kept hidden in there was high grade, worth $100 on the street for a quarter ounce, or $6,400 for a pound, which was his usual load. He kept it in a box stamped PRIME RIB that he marked for his own identification with a single slash of a red Magic Marker.

He unwrapped the fresh meat from the cooler. Sometimes the lion meat was old beef. Sometimes it was old mutton or pork. He was sure the lions didn't care what it was. He figured they'd eat anything, goat, horse, mule, burro, whatever. This stuff wasn't lion meat and it hadn't been in there yesterday but it was so fresh it still had some blood oozing out of it. He guessed maybe Mr. Hamburger had brought it in sometime.

This meat was in some strange chunks and didn't really resemble any meat he'd ever seen, but he knew there were plenty of other kinds of meat in the world. What he wished he could get his hands on again was some whitetail. Now there was some good stuff. It was about the best stuff he'd ever put in his mouth. But it was hard to get your hands on whitetail if you didn't hunt. And Domino didn't hunt. The only whitetail he'd ever had was roadkill that had been brought to the prison kitchen sometimes. And since he'd worked in the prison kitchen his last two years, he'd always gotten some of it. Along with the warden, who was crazy about it, too.

He'd been lucky to land this job straight out of Parchman. You could pick a lot of cotton in eighteen years. Domino was one of those people for whom prison rehabilitation worked in that he'd learned a marketable skill and had made connections that were helping him in the outside world.

The weed came in once a month from a connection Domino had now in Oregon, on a UPS truck with one of those friendly guys in a brown uniform carrying a five-gallon bucket of drywall plaster. Mr. Hamburger had okayed the deliveries to his place when Domino told him that he had a Sheetrock operation on the weekends (a lie) and had to sleep in the daytime (not a lie), which was when United Parcel Service made their deliveries, so somebody else who worked the day shift always signed the chart for him, since it was evidently just drywall plaster. Domino dug the wet plaster out from around the package of weed late at night, waterproofed it and wrapped it in old meat that was about to turn bad, stuck it in a marked box, and froze it in the lion-meat freezer into one solid chunk that would take a chain saw to cut apart. It worked out real good for everybody. The lions got fed. Nobody got hurt. Domino knew he might get hurt if Mr. Hamburger ever found out what he was doing. He'd heard things about the mob and Chicago. Everybody had. But Domino didn't ask any questions. He just went about his work.

He cut through some big pieces of the fresh meat with a sharp knife and a bone saw, still wondering what it was. Maybe it was elk. Maybe one of Mr. Hamburger's rich buddies had gone on a hunting trip out West and bagged an elk and hadn't been able to eat all of it. He looked closer. He was sure it wasn't whitetail. If he'd thought it was whitetail, he'd have kept some of it for himself.

Actually, the lion guy got a pretty good deal. He only paid fifty cents a pound for the meat even if it was porterhouse steaks, even if it was filet mignon. But going down there wasn't like going to a zoo where the lions were walking around pretty healthy and intact. Some of these lions couldn't walk around too good because they had only three legs. Some had half a tail, or one ear, or not many teeth because they were so old, and the lion shit smelled really bad. He knew the guy tried to keep the cages clean, and was just trying to help the lions, who had been mistreated and neglected by previous owners, but Domino could take one look into their big yellow eyes and see that they would eat him, too, if they could get to him, even if some of them did have only three legs. While he was down there, he dropped off the weed at an empty house in the country down close to Water Valley. He made a phone call beforehand and the money was always sitting on the front porch in a plain brown paper bag. He left the box, picked up the bag. It went about as smooth as a baby's ass. And he'd already made the phone call for this trip.

He started taking the boxes out and stacking them on a two-wheeler, and carrying them outside, and started sticking them in the sealed cooler of a reefer truck that he used for deliveries. He put the prefrozen, marked weed box in first. He had to make several trips because there was so much lion meat today, as well as a package wrapped in garbage bags and already frozen, heavily taped. The work order stated that he was to dump it somewhere but not give it to the lions. It was probably guts. He put his arms around it when he picked it up.

He was actually looking forward to going back out in the country and making his casual rounds. He was already thinking about a Pizza Den sandwich for supper.

He went up to the empty second-floor office and smoked part of a cigar outside on the rusty fire escape, high above the river, since Mr. Hamburger didn't like smoking inside. It was snowing again, flakes drifting down on the brown, moving water, falling far out there over in Arkansas, like a picture. He watched a tugboat come by, heading upstream with three barges, way out there. He could see a deckhand walking around. No telling where the guy was going. Lucky fucker. Going up the river like that, you'd probably see some whitetails drinking water. That would be like a picture, too.

He went back down and ground the fresh meat up and shaped it into some mounded two-pound packages and pulled some shrink-wrap over the white foam pans. He always wrote "Hamburger Dog" on them, but today either some asshole had stolen his Magic Marker or he couldn't find it, so he just left them blank. It was no big deal. Mr. Hamburger knew what it was. He'd written the work order. After that he went back out and stuck them in the back of the reefer truck and cranked it up. They wouldn't freeze hard before he got to Como. It wasn't the first time he'd fixed up a bunch of dog food for his boss. He was supposed to deliver the dog food out to Mr. Hamburger's house on his lion-trip way out of town, as usual. He never had seen the dog on his trips out there because he'd never gone into the house. But he figured the dog had to be a big bastard, as much meat as Mr. Hamburger had sent out there. Maybe he was a Rottweiler. Or a mastiff. All he knew was that he was glad he didn't have to pay for his dog-food bill.

He'd wondered often why Mr. Hamburger was always in such a bad mood. He'd almost bite your head off if you said good afternoon, so naturally nobody ever did.

12

Miss Muffett bumped softly on her plastic leg down the long hall, toward the cavernous kitchen she had to use. The big house in the little town of Como, thirty minutes south of Memphis just off I-55, was loud with its silence. It was a nice old town with large oaks and stately homes and mostly quiet streets. No mullet-headed punks running up and down with monster bass speakers going. You could sit out on the porch in summer. Most of the time, her boss was never there. Not these days. Not since his tragic accident six months ago. Now he tried to stay busy. He always thought he had to tend to his business in Chicago even though he was supposed to be retired. But Chicago had been good to him. So good that he'd been able to expand his meatpacking business to Memphis a few years ago. For the last few nights he'd been working in his shop out back. She'd seen the limo pull in there a few nights ago. But she never went out there except to get some meat out of one of his coolers. She didn't want to bother him. She guessed he tried to work out his anger with work. He was the one who'd insisted she help him dig the postholes so that he could fence in the backyard for the little dog. She'd told him three times she was scared of machinery. She didn't blame him for being angry with her. But it wasn't exactly the kind of thing they could talk about either. The doctors had already said there was nothing they could do for him. Just like with her leg and her daddy's boat motor out on Sardis Lake so many years ago. Her daddy didn't mean to cut her leg off with the prop. And it almost killed him when he did. He went to his grave still apologizing to her for it, and crying over it. But some things you couldn't do anything for. You just had to get used to having one real leg and one made out of plastic. You had to get used to doing some kind of job that wasn't too hard but that still brought in some money, like housecleaning, which she'd done for years all over Como and Sardis and Senatobia, or even house-sitting and dog-sitting for rich people like Mr. Hamburger. It wasn't so bad. Miss Muffett knew that things could always be worse.

The floors were shining from her diligent mopping with Mr. Clean. She looked behind a tall potted plant. Two small and perfect dog turds lay there, one crossed over the other in an X, almost identical, almost hidden. He had his own little personal dog door built right into the wall there in the kitchen, so why did he keep messing in the house? Because it was cold outside sometimes and he didn't want to go out to use the bathroom, that's why. He was very crafty about where he left his surprises. She believed he did it on purpose and it never failed to piss her off.

"You little shit," she said.

She wondered where he was. Sometimes he hid in closets and was small enough to crawl up under the couch in the great room and sleep there undetected for hours. He moved through the house like a ghost, silent. Sometimes he showed her his teeth. And she'd never done one thing to him, hardly, had only tried to discipline him a few times, train him. He just didn't like her, never had from the first when he was a puppy and she was keeping him and caught him crapping on the fine white-oak floors and warped him a good one with a rolled-up *Glamour*, which in all honesty was probably a bit heavier than a rolled-up newspaper. That was her right as the housekeeper. The dog shouldn't have held that against her, she thought, but he evidently did. She'd tried to pet him and make friends with him plenty of times since then, but he wouldn't let her. It seemed to her that he was holding a grudge. Rather than come whining or begging to her for water whenever his pan was dry, he would make an incredible leap from the rim of the second-floor guest bedroom's bathroom tub to the seat of the commode, like a cat, and would get on the back side of the seat and put his forepaws down inside on the sloping front of the commode and lower his head, drinking on a downhill grade. She'd seen him do it. He'd drink for a long time, until he got his fill, his long-haired back sticking up through the hole in the toilet seat like some weird wig. She'd watched him once, when she'd heard the faint click of his toenails coming, hiding in the broom closet out in the hall and peeking past the corner of the cracked door.

Getting back out was harder for him. He had to pick up one paw at a time and get them up on the seat of the commode, and he slipped that day and got his back feet wet. But she figured he had it down to a routine by now. So he wasn't dumb, not at all. And since he wasn't dumb, he had enough sense to know by now that he was grown and he wasn't supposed to go to the bathroom inside the house. But did that stop him? Hell no. He was so cunning and strategic with his deposits that sometimes she didn't find them for weeks, and by then they had turned chalky white and were hard, like peanuts. She'd cuss him while she bent down awkwardly and picked them up with toilet paper. He was hiding again somewhere, right now. Probably avoiding her. Didn't want to be friends. Didn't want to let bygones be bygones. Probably up under the couch again. He was kind of a spooky little dog. Once she'd wakened to a terrific thunderstorm, one so severe the power had gone off, on a night when Mr. Hamburger had gone on another trip to Chicago, and in a flash of blue lightning she'd seen the little dog lying on her chest, whining. She'd risen screaming since it had happened in tandem with a nightmare about him, one where he was eating her feet, actually some of her toes on a three-cheese pizza, and she'd thrown him to the floor so hard it had injured one of his legs, and he'd limped for four days, and she had worried, and on the fifth day he had stopped limping and Mr. Hamburger had come home and caught him up in the hall and hugged him and kissed him, acted a fool over him like he always did.

She bumped over the floor and looked behind a couch. He wasn't there. She looked for the little dog for about twenty minutes, opening doors quietly, taking careful steps, peering around corners one eye at a time. But he was nowhere to be found. She even went looking upstairs. Then she felt something watching her in Mr. Hamburger's study and turned around slowly. He was lying on a shelf about two feet above a desk full of shipping bills and ledgers. He looked like nothing more than an old dust rag, so still he was. She couldn't imagine how he'd gotten up there.

She raised her hand to try and pet him but he raised his lips and showed her his teeth. Okay. Well. She turned and bumped out and closed the door and shut him in there so he wouldn't go outside and dig in the yard and get all messy while she was gone. Her boss wasn't coming back for about another week and she thought she might slip out for a while tonight. But she wouldn't be gone for long. He'd be okay by himself for a while. She'd be back later.

13

Anjalee parked her junky Camry just around the corner from her apartment building and left it and walked up the street and peeked around the corner before she stepped out. More snow was coming down and the few people on the sidewalks were bundled up and hurrying against it. There were two police cars parked in front of her building. The lights weren't flashing. They were just sitting there. Oh *fuck*. She'd have to go back to Gigi's Angels and keep staying there until Frankie called for her. The couch cops might not know she was working there yet. And the regular cops would put her *under* the penitentiary if they nabbed her for Miss Barbee. She didn't know if Miss Barbee was dead or alive. She'd looked in the paper a few times but she hadn't seen anything about it. But if she didn't go back to the old folks' home for community service, she violated her probation. She'd get raped with a billy club in jail. Maybe have to muff-dive somebody's old stinky box.

She got back in her car and turned it around in a parking lot overgrown with dead weeds. In ten minutes she was back at the strip joint. She put her car behind the building. A few customers were sitting on stools in the dead midafternoon. A rock tune was blaring. One girl was dancing but not very enthusiastically. She didn't see the neatly dressed old guy who wore a gray raincoat and who had come in there for the last few afternoons. He was not a regular and nobody knew who he was. He just sat there on the corner stool and drank gin and tonics. She'd talked to him once.

Since nobody was behind the bar, Anjalee went around to the

end and raised the part that was mounted on hinges and let herself back there and got a cold mug from the little icebox and drew herself a Sam Adams and poured a shot of mezcal and picked up a salt shaker and grabbed a wedge of lime from a tray full of them and set everything across the bar and then ducked back under the thing instead of raising it again and took her stool out front.

Maybe Frankie would call soon. Maybe even today. She didn't want to tell him she'd been turning tricks again. But she hadn't heard from him in a few days and she couldn't do without money, smokes, drinks, food. And where was she going to go now? Where could she go where they wouldn't find her? They might even come looking here. The detectives might be out on the street with her mug shot, since she had one, showing it to people and asking them if they knew her. And somebody they might ask might know her. They might say, Yeah, I know her, that's Anjalee, boy she's hot, turns tricks over at Gigi's Angels sometimes, there's a room upstairs.

Which reminded her that she needed to go up there and get her good leather coat before somebody stole it.

She licked the web of her hand and poured some salt on it and grabbed the mezcal and slammed it and bit the lime hard and licked the salt off her hand and then picked up the beer and drank some of it. Another tune started up and the stripper moved into it sluggishly. Anjalee wondered if she ought to just go on home.

"Hot Juanita!" somebody yelled, and threw a dollar at the girl.

"Wore-out Juanita's more like it," the girl said over the music.

Moe came back in and saw Anjalee and smiled and winked. He had a bad temper sometimes, but she had him pretty well wrapped around her finger. Some other people came in, two men in suits, two men in car coats with shopping bags, towing a blind guy, and they got him up on a stool and ordered him a margarita on the rocks. The blind guy was wearing a fox stole. The two men in suits called for shots of whiskey and lit cigarettes. They were standing pretty close to where the nice old guy in the raincoat had sat those few times, and she thought about that afternoon she'd met him. Back before all this stupid bullshit happened.

"Good afternoon," he'd said.

She had to figure out what she was going to do. Maybe she could stay at Frankie's place for a few days, wherever that was. All he'd ever told her was that he lived in midtown.

He pulled back the stool next to hers and said: "Mind if I sit down?"

"Free country."

The two guys in suits down the bar watched her and talked and nodded and watched her some more. One winked.

"Yes it is," he said immediately. "It certainly is a free country and I for one am glad of it. Things would be pretty sad if it wasn't a free country." He took a drink of his gin and tonic and set his glass down on the napkin and said: "It's also good to be alive. There's a whole lot of people who can't say that."

She drank some more of her beer. She probably needed another shot. She looked at the guys. They were grinning like a pair of mules eating saw briars. She'd heard her daddy say that once. Jesus, she still missed him.

"Had a lot of snow lately, haven't we?" the old guy said, although he wasn't looking at her.

One of the guys held his drink up and nodded to her. She smiled at him and wondered how much money he had on him.

"I wish it would snow the whole city over and stop everything from moving," she said, and looked at him. He was studying a dusty deer head mounted above the bar, in the back. UT Volunteers and Tennessee Titans and Memphis Tigers caps hung on the horns.

"You a sports fan?" he said.

"Naw. Not really. I been to a few fights at Tunica."

Maybe if she took them on together she'd make more.

"Me either." He shook his head. "I don't even get excited over the World Series. Everybody else does. I guess there must be something wrong with me."

"My boyfriend's nuts about baseball," she said. "Football. Hockey. Basketball. Car racing. Horse racing. Drag racing. Dog racing."

"I like westerns," he said. "Old stuff mostly. John Wayne. Alan Ladd. Randolph Scott."

Moe came down the bar to get a beer from the cooler back there. He opened it and turned around.

"I thought you went home already," he said to her.

"I decided to come back."

"You gonna be around tonight?" Meaning did she want him to put out the word that she was available for rolls in the upstairs hay.

"Maybe so. I don't know yet."

"Well let me know when you do. Couple guys down here askin' can they buy you a drink."

She ducked her head a couple of times and after watching her for a few seconds he moved away. She didn't know what she was going to do.

The old guy left her alone, raised his face, and watched the stripper dance for a bit. After a while he called for another drink. When the bartender started making it, he turned to her.

"Would you like something else, miss? Looks like you're getting depleted there."

She looked up at him. He had on a pale blue paisley tie and his shoes were shined and he kind of resembled Richard Harris only shorter and plumper. She'd seen A Man Called Horse *at the drive-in outside Pontotoc once, when she was very small and pale, while somebody was on top of her mother in the back seat, grunting. She had concentrated on the movie even when the sounds behind her got too loud to ignore, when the grunts began to climb toward breathless short screams. She had sat there with no popcorn and watched Richard Harris being hung on horsehair ropes by the meat of his chest to the beat of rawhide drums and stayed as quiet as a hiding rabbit since her daddy was dead and all appeared to be lost.*

"Okay. Sure. Mezcal and a Sam Adams. Thanks."

Some more people were coming in now and before long it would start to get dark. Voices rose in laughter and talk. The two guys who had been watching her finished their drinks and left. Maybe she needed to think about cutting some action before long. Maybe if she made a long night of it she wouldn't even need to worry about Frankie's money. But no matter how much she made, she wouldn't be able to go back to her apartment and get her drawings and stuff.

She hated that. She'd drawn one from memory of her grandmother sitting on a paddleboat in Charleston Harbor, going out to look at Fort Sumter. Maybe she did need to go home. But that would be hard to do without some money. Her mother didn't have any. And there'd probably be some grubby asshole with a pot gut hanging around. There always was.

After the fresh drinks came, the old guy turned to her again.

"I'm not trying to be nosy or anything," he said. "I'm just wondering if you work here. I've seen you behind the bar."

She picked up her beer and sipped it. He seemed like a nice old guy. He looked pretty harmless. Like somebody's uncle. Like Mr. Pasternak.

"Well," she said. "I guess you could say that."

"Are you a dancer?"

It was odd to her that he said "dancer" instead of stripper. It was like he was showing her a little respect. She decided she liked him.

"Sometimes."

"Are you going to dance today?"

"I don't know," she said. "I usually do my dancing late at night."

He looked at one of his thumbnails and seemed uncomfortable.

"I was just wondering," he said. "Do you have a costume with you?"

"A costume?"

"Or whatever you dance in."

"I've got something I can go put on if that's what you mean."

Now he seemed shy. His face turned just a little red and he cleared his throat. That was something you didn't see much in here.

"I was just wondering," he said.

"Yeah?"

"How much would it cost me for you to go put your costume on and dance a little?"

"You mean just for you?"

"Yes," he said, and looked into her eyes. There was something in his that was soft and vulnerable, as if it pained him to say what he was saying.

"I don't know. How much would you like to give me?"

"How about fifty dollars?" he said.

She was already sliding off her stool.

"Hell, mister, for fifty dollars you can go upstairs."

"What's upstairs?" he said.

"Come on and I'll show you," she said, and reached for his hand.

But when she got him up there, and took off everything except her panties, and did a little sexy dancing for him, he couldn't get it up, not that she saw it, because he didn't take any of his clothes off, only admitted that he was having a problem with his wife, and she felt bad for him, because she thought maybe he was going to start crying, and she thought it was pretty sad, but he gave her the fifty dollars anyway, and she was ashamed of herself for taking it, but she did, since she needed it.

The door opened, and a group of guys came in, some Memphis firefighters she knew from Fifi's Cabaret when she used to work the couches, and she saw them looking at her. They were regulars in here now and good tippers and loved to drink the hell out of some cold beer when they got off duty.

"I'm in for the night, Moe," she said, and he said okay. What she needed was a sugar daddy. Somebody who could take care of her the way she wanted to get taken care of. Stay on South Beach in Miami during the winter maybe. Or fly to some island. First class. All expenses paid.

14

Since he was just a dog, the little dog didn't know the names of things like squirrels, or man, or trees, or meat, or a ride to Overton Park, or a walk, or hunching, or meat markets, or spreeing gyps, but he could see all those things that were on the outside each time he went on a ride to Overton Park, so he dreamed on his shelf of chasing those things with fuzzy tails until they went up those things he sometimes raised his hind leg and peed on, and he dreamed of the scent of a something he'd smelled that made him want to hunch, on a walk one time with the man he liked, and he dreamed of all the things he got to eat whenever he went to that place with the man he liked where there was only meat, more meat than any little dog could eat.

He woke, looked around, and leaped lightly down onto the desk. He stretched, yawned, gathered himself, aimed for the drafting table five feet away, and launched. His paws slid on the slick, slanted finish of the table when he landed, and he skidded a little bit, and he scratched and scrambled around some, but he was able to catch himself by backpedaling rapidly and using his toenails. It was only a short hop from the rolling chair to the ottoman next to the easy chair and a minor bounce to the floor from there. He went back over to the desk he'd just left and raised up on his hind legs to hook the handle of the second drawer with his teeth and pull it open. He looked at the things inside there for a long time and finally chose one. There was lots to choose from in the drawer the man he liked kept filled for him. Beef jerky. Dog-food-aisle treats of the most delicious kind. Imitation bacon and Pup-Peroni. But his water pan under the desk was dry as an old cow bone.

He carried his goodie over to the rug and went back to the desk to push the drawer closed with his head. Then he gnawed the cellophane off the Slim Jim he'd selected and began to munch it, wagging his tail a bit, not understanding the implications of his salty snack and the closed door, since he was just a dog.

15

The pit bull released the kitten on command into a steel wire-cage the young man had brought over in his car. They shut the door before it could jump out and then Arthur dozed off. Helen put the cage in the pantry to let the kitten calm down some and then put some nuggets of cat food in through the bars. The young man's name turned out to be Eric and she talked to him in the warm kitchen while Arthur napped on the couch. She poured Eric shots of Chivas over ice and kept sipping her drink. Later, she pushed the pantry curtains aside and checked. The food was all gone. The kitten was curled in a corner, sleeping. Those were good signs. She went back to the kitchen and fixed another drink. She had a pretty good buzz going and it was making her horny. It always did. He hadn't done anything in three months. And Ken. Why did she keep getting drunk at the Peabody and then fucking *him*? She didn't even *like* him. And then the next day when she'd sobered up she always promised herself she'd never do it again. Hell no. Never again. Then she got drunk a couple of weeks later over there and did it again. It was what they called one of those vicious circles. And now because of those two DUIs she had to worry about the cops all the time. But it didn't seem fair not to be able to drive the Jag over to the Peabody on a pretty fall afternoon, and get out on the cobblestones, and give the keys to a valet, and let him park it while she went on in to the bar. What was the point of even having a Jag if you couldn't drive it where you wanted to?

Arthur snuffled and woke up. His nap had taken about twenty minutes. He looked around for a few moments as if he didn't know where he was. He was so eager to please her. Hoping she'd let him try again. But what for? Why didn't he just stop spinning his wheels and go to the doctor and get a prescription for the shit and start taking it? Twenty minutes? Twenty minutes was a long time. A lot could get done in twenty minutes. Entire cities could die in flames in twenty minutes or you could have a baby. You could fuck your brains out for twenty minutes if you had somebody capable of fucking your brains out. Like that young man right over there. She looked at Eric. Then she looked back at Arthur. He knew damn well she was horny. But after all this time of trying, after taking her clothes and underwear off again and again and trying everything she knew to get him going, she was tired of messing with him. He refused to try the pills, even after the doctor told him they might help him. He'd said it wasn't natural. She'd said: Well, is a kidney transplant? And they had no children. And never would. Not now. Nope. Couldn't even adopt, apparently. It was too late for that. He was too old. She suspected that he had always been too old.

It was true that if it hadn't been for him, she might still be slinging drinks in Missoula. Or even Bozeman. But she missed Montana, too. Especially in the summertime. When you grew up in a place that beautiful, it was hard to forget it. She missed the vast brown hills that rolled away in the distance, and the mountains and clear streams and the eagles and the lakes blue as glaciers. Even after all this time, she still missed driving out Rock Creek Road on moonlit nights and drinking beer and fucking boys on the swinging bridge. What she didn't miss was seeing her daddy's little trailer in East Missoula with his one skinny tree in the yard. But if she went back, she'd have to go see him. And he was only two years older than Arthur.

She thought about fingers on the inside velvet of your thighs. A sweet mouth kissing this and that. She stopped herself. She didn't know how much longer she could take it. He refused to seek any help. He didn't seem to realize that she had needs. And he was almost seventy years old.

She stooped to the floor with her glass and petted the pit bull on the muzzle. He was lying beneath the kitchen table eating a few pieces of bologna that Arthur had gotten him from the icebox. She'd wiped the blood from his muzzle and scratched his back with her hairbrush. He licked her hand energetically as she petted him. Just an old chewed-up sweetie.

Arthur's decline had come gradually. For a long time, they'd both made excuses for him. Finally the night had come when they had to admit to each other that Arthur had a problem. But it didn't mean she had to just live in frustration, did it?

Wasn't it easier to just read a book? Have a few drinks? Let him go on to sleep and then slip out? Wasn't that better on everybody involved? If he didn't know it, how could it hurt him?

"Arthur, why don't you pour Eric another shot?"

"I don't want to get him drunk. He's got to drive back."

"Mind if I smoke?" Eric said. "And no offense, Mister Arthur, but I can handle my booze. You can ask anybody at home."

"Go right ahead," Helen said, before Arthur could interrupt. "Arthur, get him an ashtray, too, please."

Arthur scratched his head. "I don't think we've got any."

"Well, maybe we should buy some," she said.

"I can use just anything," Eric said, already pulling out his pack. "A jar lid'll do. Shoot, I can use an empty Coke can."

"We don't keep much Coke around here." Arthur was rummaging around in a drawer and she could hardly take her eyes off Eric.

"So," she said. "How long you been in Memphis, Eric?"

"Couple of months," he said.

"And were you in the pet shop business in Mississippi?"

Arthur was banging around in the cabinets, muttering, moving pots.

"How about a bowl?" he said, his head behind a cabinet door.

"Bowl's fine," Eric said. He already had a pretty long ash hanging off his cigarette. Arthur got the bowl under his smoke just before it tipped off. "Thanks, well, no, ma'am it wasn't really the pet shop business. We raised dogs, bulldogs, pit bulls, weenie dogs, poodles, peek-a-poos and some beagle hounds me and Deddy and Mister Nub run rabbits with in this rabbit factory we made outa chicken wire. We had a dog trailer and we'd go over to First Monday at Ripley and set up and stay all weekend. It was pretty big time."

"It certainly sounds like it," Helen said. Did he say *"rabbit factory"*?

"My granddaddy had a beagle one time so scared of rabbits he had to let her ride up on the Bush Hog."

"My goodness." She was going to ask about the rabbit factory but got interrupted when Arthur tilted the bottle over Eric's glass again and Eric nodded and thanked him. He puffed contentedly on his cigarette.

Helen sipped her drink and tried to think about what she was going to do. He didn't want to do anything but just sit around the house and check his stocks on-line and watch those old westerns, and she was so tired of that she was about to scream. Checkers had gone the same route.

The snow was still falling outside the window. She knew there were people somewhere sleeping out in it. In Missoula they begged for money just off the interstate. And in three or four days, depending on how hard she wanted to drive, and the weather, she could be back out there. It had been nagging at the back of her mind. Just leave him. Go back home. Get a divorce. Try to find somebody else who could make her happy. In another ten years, he'd be eighty. And she'd be fifty. And there weren't going to be any children by anybody if she waited much longer. She knew that now. She still didn't want to accept it, but she knew it. She had to think about her own happiness. There hadn't been any for her here in a long time.

"Cool," Eric said. "This is great. Kind of cozy, like."

Helen smiled at him. On a small screen, like a faint movie in her head, she could see herself kissing him. Up against the counter. On the couch. On the back seat of her Jag. Several different places.

16

It was just dark down in Mississippi, out in the hills of woods on the black and lonesome winding roads with dirty snow melted along the sides, scattered lumps of snow all over the place. Domino cruised in the freezing night air with the window cracked in the cab of the reefer truck to let his cigar smoke out. The truck didn't have a radio in it and it was just as well. He had to play everything so loud that it was starting to drive him deaf in the other ear, too. He guessed he'd have to get a hearing aid one of these days. He'd dropped off the dog hamburger at Mr. Hamburger's place in Como and put it into a cooler that was inside the big shed in his back-yard, and had driven on down the interstate and gotten off at Batesville and turned east on Highway 6. He was going to get a room at the Ole Miss Motel in Oxford like he always did and spend the night, get a good night's sleep, drink a little bourbon in the hotel room, try to find some nature shows on TV, take the meat on down to the lion guy the next day, and last, drop the weed box off at the empty house and pick up his money. He didn't want to be around those big cats at night. A few of them had gotten out a few times and had to be shot by the sheriff's deputies. One of them had killed somebody's pet dog in a yard and had been eating it when it got shot. It had been in the paper. He wanted to be down there in the daytime so that if one of them got out again he could see it coming in time to climb a tree.

He knew where there was a beer joint down on 315 in Panola County, so he turned off 6 onto it and cruised down that way. It wasn't late. Not much past seven. He'd get a sixer and some pigskins and cruise around on some country roads for a while, dump those frozen guts somewhere, and still have plenty of time to get to town and hit a liquor store and grab a sandwich at Pizza Den, maybe a whole roast beef and gravy, and then check in. The lion meat would be okay overnight in the cooler on the reefer truck, since it was down to about five degrees in there right now. That shit was hard as a brickbat. After a couple of hours in there it was.

It was a few miles down the road to the beer joint. It was farming country. Fences and cows. People had pickups. He met quite a few.

He saw the store up ahead, the lights over the pumps. He pulled in and shut off the truck and went inside and got a cold six-pack of Schlitz tallboys and a bag of hot, barbecued skins and a few cigars, paid the guy, got back in the truck, popped a top, and went on up the road with a beer between his legs.

After a few more miles and a few more curves, he crossed a river under a bridge with steel arches over it. He could see the river in the dark, long and straight, lined with naked winter willows. Up ahead there was a curvy cut-through road that would eventually lead him back to Oxford and he put his blinker on, slowed down, and turned off. He breathed out a contented sigh. He liked being in the country and had gotten used to it down at Parchman. He for one appreciated the fact that once you got out of Memphis you could see trees and land and farms and shit like that. Sometimes even whitetails. He turned his head for just a moment to admire a wooden fence somebody was building around a pasture and then immediately smacked a pretty nice buck. *BAPLOW!* Somebody would've liked it mounted on their mantel. It had leaped from roadside green cedars squarely into the middle of the road at the moment he'd turned his head. The whitetail rebounded from the grill and went skidding and turning across the road, white belly hair flying, a sad ballet. He felt the lick in the steering wheel beneath his hands and his beer came out from between his legs and landed on the floorboard and spilled all over the seat, all over his legs, too. Next thing he knew he was sitting on the side of the road. The whitetail was kicking in the road, illuminated by the headlights. It was a strange one-horned whitetail. And he couldn't believe his luck. Domino was simply overjoyed. A whole entire whitetail, and it was all his! All he had to do was get it back to Memphis. Boy oh boy. Whitetail country-fried steaks with milk gravy, whitetail tenderloin in a red-wine sauce, juicy whitetail roasts cooked slowly in a Crock-Pot with onion gravy and carrots and potatoes. If he just had a woman to share it with. To cook for. How cool would that be? Well. Maybe later. Save some money. Work hard. Stay out of trouble.

Domino put it in neutral and pulled the hand brake and got out slowly, shaking just a bit. Beer dripped out over the rocker panels. It was all over his legs. He picked up the can and pitched it across the road. His cigar had gone out and he felt a bit addled. It had happened so quickly that he hadn't had time to do anything but hit the whitetail. He went around to the front of the truck. The hood and grill were dented in but he didn't pay much attention to it because Mr. Hamburger had insurance. He was more interested in looking at the whitetail, which was still kicking. Just think how fresh.

"Get you some whitetail," he said to the whitetail.

Now he was in a dilemma. How was he going to keep it overnight until he could make his deliveries and clean all the boxes out of the back, and then stick the whitetail back there? He could stick it up on top of the back end of the reefer truck and maybe tie it down if he could find some rope, but he couldn't just leave it out there in the Ole Miss Motel parking lot overnight. Somebody would come along and steal the whole damn thing while he was asleep, probably. He doubted if the Pakistani people who ran the Ole Miss Motel would let him keep the whitetail overnight in his room. And hell, it might ruin overnight if it wasn't refrigerated or kept outside in this cold weather. He didn't know what in the shit to do. He walked closer to the whitetail. It looked like it was trying to move. He wished it would go on and die. Maybe he should throw those frozen guts out of the back right here. Make some room.

Domino didn't walk too close. He'd read stories in outdoor magazines in barbershops while he was waiting for an open chair about hunters who had shot whitetails and approached them, thinking they were dead, and then suddenly the whitetail jumped up and gored the hunter, sometimes fatally. He didn't want to get gored, even if it had only one horn. And he wondered what had happened to the other horn. Maybe some hunter had shot the other one off. Or maybe it had broken it off in a fight with another whitetail.

He thought he'd better get his knife. Just in case it got up and tried to gore him. Or maybe he should just go on and stab it to death. There was a long-bladed boning knife in a sheath on the floorboard on the other side and he reached and got it and stuck it inside his shirt. Then he took another look at the whitetail.

It looked like it was dying. It was still kicking some, but not very hard. He'd just wait. It might not take long. Then, on the other hand, it might take all night. And he didn't have all night.

He relit his cigar with his still-shaking fingers and decided to wait a while. He walked around in the road for a few minutes, looking up, smoking, and it was kind of partly cloudy. It looked like more snow. He could have whitetail steak and eggs for breakfast once he got it cleaned and cut up. He could butterfly the tenderloin and sauté it in butter.

And just then he heard something with a loud muffler coming. He looked over his shoulder. The glow of lights was reaching up the hill behind him. He was very conscious of the weed being in the truck. But there was really nothing to worry about.

Nothing to worry about except maybe going back to prison if something he couldn't foresee were to happen out here. For a whole pound of weed.

The vehicle came on. He watched a dump truck come over the hill, slow down next to his truck, and then stop. "Go on, dumb-ass," he said. It was very cold. He thumped a few ashes in the road.

He heard the grinding of gears. The truck moved slowly, swerved wide around the whitetail, and went on down the road, changing gears, gaining speed, the muffler rattling. He listened to the sound of it growing smaller in the distance and he listened until the sound of it was gone. He was freezing his ass off in his thin coat.

He could dump the guts plus some of the lion meat. Throw it away right here. Hamburger would never know the difference. Hamburger didn't know how much he had. He was back in Chicago. It would take a little work, but he could take out enough boxes to make room for the whitetail, and toss them off the side of the road, and leave the box in that had the weed, and stick the whitetail back there. He walked around to the back end and opened the latch on the cooler. Cold air rolled out. He grabbed the first box he saw and pulled it out, got a good grip on it, and stepped off the road with it. The box was heavy, about eighty pounds, but Domino had pumped a lot of iron in prison. The ground was kind of slick with snow in spots, and he had to go slowly and step carefully. He carried it about fifty feet from the road and dropped it. He took his cigar out of his mouth and looked around. This was going to take a while. And he hoped nobody came along. He sure hoped a cop didn't come along. A cop would want to ask questions, would want to see his license, might want to poke around in the back, and what about the whitetail? He couldn't take it away from him, could he? Maybe he could. And how much lip could he give a cop, considering the weed in the truck? The thing to do was get the shit emptied out fast, load the whitetail in there, get the hell away from here and on up to town. He was about halfway out of the woods when he heard another vehicle coming, fast, from the other way.

This one was a car, really hauling ass, and it barely slowed down, just enough to swerve wide around the whitetail and go on. *Jesus,* Domino thought, *It's cold as a well digger's ass out here.* It roared on past and went out of sight down the dark road. It kept on going until it, too, was out of hearing.

After things got quiet, he went back to the truck. He got hold of the frozen bag of guts. And felt inside it then what felt like a human hand. It felt exactly like a human hand because it had four outspread fingers and a thumb. Then he felt around on what felt like a foot. He could feel some toes. A big toe for sure. And then a . . . head? And just as it hit him what he'd been cutting up in Memphis earlier in the evening, and what he'd delivered out to Mr. Hamburger's house for his big dog to eat, the noise of another bad muffler and the beam of a searchlight on a cop car swung over him and froze him in place as it rattled and shook onto the road from where it had been hiding and lying in wait for him or somebody like him, less than a hundred feet back, a dark place under a few ancient loblolly pine trees. Huge mothers. Tremendous. Each one weighed more than the car. Easy.

17

County constable Elwood "Perk" Perkins had heard the truck hit the deer, the squeal of tire, the whump of body, while he was changing CDs. He'd been sitting down the hill there in the dark all by himself with his sandwiches in his auctioned-off-by–Blue Mountain, Mississippi Police Department Ford Crown Vic—you could still see BMPD faintly on each front door beneath the white paint he'd sprayed from a shake-up can he'd gotten at Sneed's Ace Hardware—should've put two on it—and the shit didn't match anyway, had a few runs in it—listening to the radio traffic on his police radio he'd bought himself and to Patsy Cline and Jim Reeves and Ray Price on his Walkman, because he had discovered that if he took his own sandwiches and parked off the road and totally immersed himself in chewing and the songs of people like Hank Williams and Merle Travis, in his mind he could go to another place. He could actually go out of his mind. There was this music playing and they were singing about plowing the last mule on the last row of cotton on a ridge in south Tennessee. It didn't get any better than that. Unless it was Miller time. Then it got better than that.

The car had two hundred and sixty-something thousand miles on it. And smoked. Rings probably shot in the ass, he figured. He was going to get a better one next year that would do more than sixty without coughing and cutting out and farting unburned fumes all over the place, in case he had to make hot pursuit after somebody. He needed to get that muffler fixed. And find out why the whole car kept shaking sometimes.

Perk was hoping to get to the Grand Ole Opry and the Bluebird Cafe in Nashville and Dollywood in Knoxville both, on vacation next summer. It was said that Dolly came to her place six times a year. Maybe he'd be lucky enough to be there when she was there. If she could just hear *one* of his songs. At one time he'd wanted to take his deputy sheriff ex-girlfriend Penelope up there. But just when he thought she was almost ready to give him some, she'd caught him cheating with his old flame Earleen Lundt in the back seat of his cruiser parked down on Papa Johnny Road, and she had broken it off. Now whenever he met her on her patrols she gave him the big Fuck you with her finger, which hurt, especially if he was hauling his daddy to town for groceries. But he figured she wouldn't go without a man for long. She'd find somebody. Probably some intellectual since she'd been pretty intellectual herself. Liked to look at photographs and shit like that.

He turned on the blue lights as he eased closer to the guy with the bag, who had turned around now and was looking at him. Some dork trying to dump something, looked like. Or maybe he had unsafe brakes since he'd hit a deer. He wondered what Earleen was doing tonight. Maybe on her break giving blow jobs out behind the Sonic in Water Valley. Maybe he'd cruise by there later for a foot-long chili-cheese dog. With onions.

He pulled his car over and he got out with his hat on. Really a cap.

"Evenin', mister," he said. The car was rattling loudly behind him. Shaking, too, so that the headlights wobbled.

"Huh?" the guy said.

Perk nodded toward the deer that was still moving some.

He guessed he'd have to shoot it. He'd had to shoot lots of wounded deer that drivers had hit. He'd gotten pretty good at it, could usually get them with a head shot from about ten feet. He practiced on Saturdays in his daddy's pasture, but he knew he'd never be as good a shot as Penelope, who could shoot the pants off him and his brother Rico and most of the other cops he knew. He decided he'd better raise his voice over the muffler noise.

"Raise hell with a fender, don't they?" Perk almost shouted.

"What?" the guy said. To Perk he looked nervous. Strange-looking man, too, wearing a long bloody apron under his flimsy coat. He hadn't shaved in about a week and he had a dark-blue knitted tobog-gan on his head and a cigar in his mouth and he had very thick rubber boots on his feet, the kind you'd wear if you were going after polar bears maybe. And holding some kind of a garbage-bag package as if he were about to carry it into the woods. A door was open at the back of the truck and there were some boxes back there. The truck was sitting there idling. The truck had a Tennessee tag. Shelby County. Memphis. The deer was still kicking, but not very energetically now. Perk looked closer. The deer had only one horn. All this looked a little peculiar to him as he walked closer, so he said loudly:

"How 'bout comin' on down here and let me get a look at you, sir."

"Huh?" the guy said.

"Come on over here, sir, you're almost blockin' the road!"

The guy threw the bag down and the cigar down and ran into the woods like a crazy person with asylum employees after him.

"Wait a minute, come back here, hold on . . . ," Perk said, but by then the guy was nearly gone. What was he running for? He walked after him a little way, and for a while he could see the white tail of the apron flopping, but then the guy must have stopped somewhere and hid. It was quiet off the road once he stopped crunching around in the scattered frozen snow. He could hear his cruiser rattling. He could see it shaking. He'd left his flashlight in the cruiser. If he went back for it, the guy might run completely away. But what was he guilty of?

He stood for a short time just listening. Then he picked his way carefully back, crunching over fallen limbs, and got his flashlight from the seat. The deer had begun a low groaning and grunting that sounded almost like some kind of tribal chant. He started to shoot it. *Poor bastard gonna die anyway,* he thought. *Shit. Save a bullet. Might need that bullet.*

He eased back into the woods. It was awfully cold. It was worse than that. It was bitter. It felt like the North Pole. God, he'd hate to have to live at the North Pole.

"Okay now," he said, pretty loud. "You might as well come on out. I'm gonna get your tag number, see. I can find out where you live."

Tall trees with their naked winter branches stood around him saying nothing. His breath whistled out in small and gentle white explosions. His feet were getting cold, clad in only thin nylon socks and plain black leather boots. And shit, Christmas was right around the corner. He didn't have his shopping done yet. And by now everything had been picked over at Wal-Mart probably. The car kept rattling and shaking behind him. It was actually kind of embarrassing when you pulled people over.

He couldn't understand why the guy was hiding. People did dumb-shit stuff, though. Rico had told him that drunks would roll down their windows at a roadblock and blow their beer breath all over you and swear up and down that they'd had only one or two. Six-packs, they meant. Didn't the guy know he was going to freeze to death out here?

"Hey, mister!" he yelled. "Whoever you are! You better come on out! It's gonna get cold as a witch's tit!"

Just then some more snow started falling, landing soundlessly on his shoulders. Maybe they'd have a white Christmas this year. He waited for a few more minutes. He turned his face up and watched the flakes drifting down. Maybe he could go out to the mall tomorrow and try to get a few things. He knew his daddy wanted a fish cooker and some Jeff Foxworthy deer-hunting videos. He thought he'd get Rico a deluxe three-burner Coleman stove to take camping out. He liked camping out. Or used to. When he was married to Lorena he did, and the two of them went all the time. John W. Kyle State Park. Down to Enid. Up to Tishomingo. It was a damn shame they'd split up. Perk had always really liked her. And Rico seemed like he was losing control more and more all the time. Perk was afraid he was going to wind up killing somebody if he didn't get some help.

"Okay, bud," he called. "I'm callin' a tow truck for your truck. I don't know what you're hidin' for, but we'll find out."

There was nothing, no sound.

"Last chance," he called. "I heard it was goin' down to zero tonight." That was just some bullshit to try to get him to come out of the woods, because it was only supposed to go to eight. "I wouldn't want to be out here."

The snow was falling faster. Suddenly it doubled in intensity. His coat was getting covered. It was covering his boots and flakes were hanging on his arms, so soft, so melty. He started singing a song under his breath, one he'd been working on in his head for the last few nights:

> *When my eyes saw the light*
> *From your window last night*
> *I was standing alone in the street.*
> *I could tell it was you*
> *In that red dress so new*
> *Kicking off shoes I'd put on your feet.*

"Okay, well," he said to himself. He worked his way back with snowflakes drifting across the flashlight's brilliant beam. The guy had dropped a box, already partly covered with snow, in the woods. He stopped and looked down at it. No telling what the other thing was.

> *I held on to your wine,*
> *Hadn't been gone no time,*
> *Long enough for you to meet*
> *Some slick-looking Clyde*
> *Who was starting to ride*
> *My sweet thing clean under the sheets.*

He kneeled next to the box and touched it. He picked up the lid. It was full of frozen meat. It looked like there were some old steaks and some old roasts and some old ribs but there were no wrappings on any of the meat and it was all frozen together into one solid chunk that looked strange. How would you cook it all at the same time like that? Was he throwing this stuff away? What for? And why was he picking this place to do it if he was from Memphis? Did they not have garbage cans in Memphis? What was the bloody apron for if he wasn't some kind of butcher? Okay, well, maybe the guy was clearing out the truck to make room for the deer. But hey, that was illegal, taking from the side of the road a deer you'd hit. You were supposed to call the game wardens and let them dispose of it properly.

The deer had stopped moving. He'd have to call the DOT, tell the road guys there was a nice buck up here they'd want to pick up in the morning. Well, nice if he hadn't broken that horn off. And if the dork in the apron wanted to run around in the woods the rest of the night, that was his business. He'd make a note of the tag and a description of the truck and then call a wrecker to get it off the road. He thought about seeing what was in the bag.

He warmed up instead, sitting back inside his cruiser with the heater blasting on high and his fingers thawing out and sipping the last cup of lukewarm coffee from his thermos. He got his pad and pencil out and wrote the chorus for his new song, which he'd decided to call "Some Other Fool."

> Don't call me up for lunch
> And damn sure not brunch,
> Don't talk in my ear about rules.
> Just remember the day
> You were french-kissing Ray,
> Don't play me for some other fool.

The deer was dead by then. He got back out of his cruiser with his coat unzipped and walked over to it and got it by the remaining horn and dragged it over to the shoulder of the road, slipping around in the roadside snow, getting his boots mushier and wetter, beside an almost solid wall of little bushy cedar trees that were in partial darkness since his cruiser was right behind the truck. And as it sometimes happened with his new songs when they were in the heat of being born, the words just wouldn't stop coming:

I tried my best,
Couldn't get enough rest,
She's got an itch that needs scratching all night,
Had to sleep in the day
While she gave it away
And in the mornings
Did the milkman's wife.

There was a sharp blow just below his left shoulder blade and he looked down to find the bloody point of what appeared to be a long-bladed knife poking through the front of his shirt. He just had time to turn a bit and see the strange-looking man with the bloody apron stepping back into the cedar bushes, his teeth chattering, saying something he couldn't quite make out because he was falling dead toward the side of the road.

18

The ship had been under way for a while and Wayne was lying in his rack in the steel cubicle he shared with three other guys, an open *Playboy* across his chest. He couldn't concentrate on reading because he had another headache. He reached up and turned his little lamp off and listened to what was around him instead. Henderson was in his rack writing a letter home. LeBonte was working on his accounting school correspondence course, and Young was asleep, snoring lightly. He wondered what Anjalee was doing back in Memphis.

"You goin' to sleep?" Henderson said. He'd raised his head and was scratching his chin.

"Nah. Just laying here. Who you writing?"

"My mama. I ain't wrote her in a couple of weeks."

"How's she doing since that operation?"

"She's a lot better. I had a letter from my sister last week. We been so busy I ain't had time to write."

Wayne lay there and didn't say anything for a while. Henderson wrote some more and then put down his tablet and pen.

"Well if you ain't goin' to sleep, you want to go get some coffee?"

He knew he wasn't going to be able to sleep for thinking about what she'd done to him. He wished it could have lasted longer. It was the largest thing that had ever happened to him. Including knocking out Stevenson in Philadelphia two months ago. The headaches had started after that fight.

"I might as well, I guess."

"We get on down there, might still be some of that chocolate pie left."

"You gonna turn into a chocolate pie."

It only took a few minutes to get down to the galley, and it wasn't full at that time of night. Some scattered groups of sailors were sitting around talking. Two crew-cut marine guards in camo and green T-shirts were eating hamburgers and playing chess. There was just a skeleton crew behind the steam tables and they'd cook eggs to order if you wanted them, but Wayne didn't want any eggs. He looked at some sandwiches and passed on them, too. He had to watch his snacks and try to stay at his proper weight, and not get over two hundred and one pounds, the limit for amateur heavyweights. Right now he was holding fairly steady at one ninety-seven.

"That tuna salad's really fresh," a cook called out.

Henderson took one, and a bag of barbecued potato chips, and a piece of pie. This headache wasn't just terrible. Some were.

"I thought you just wanted some coffee," Wayne said, reaching for two cups. He filled them from the decaf urn and poured milk and sugar in both, then got a spoon and stirred.

"You ever seen Henderson come in here and not pig out?" said the cook.

"Growin' boy got to have his snacks," Henderson said.

They settled at a corner table where some rock and roll was playing at a low volume. Henderson had gotten after them one time to get some Jackie Wilson and Otis Redding and they had.

Wayne sat there and sipped his coffee and watched Henderson eat. He wanted to tell him about this girl he'd met, just didn't know how to. This girl. This whore in Memphis who gave him a blow job for fifty bucks. Henderson would think he was apeshit. A couple of pilots in nylon coveralls came in and grabbed some candy bars and went back out. The marines had pushed their trays aside and were studying their board. Henderson started talking about Ali and Ray Robinson. Wayne saw a cook dozing in a chair. He could feel the ship moving beneath him, carrying him on out, away from her, plowing through the waves. There were faint creaks here and there. He could hear the clatter of the dishes back in the scullery. Somebody dropped one and it broke and somebody else said, Well no fucking shit, sweetie.

Where did she live? Where was she from? How old was she? What was her last name?

There were too many things he didn't know. He didn't know where to start. He didn't know anything at all about her except her name and what she did. And that she was a country girl. How was it going to sound to Henderson? Nutty like a fruitcake. Like he'd lost his frigging mind.

He didn't tell him.

19

It had gotten completely dark and Eric had passed out. Arthur had to put him to bed on the couch and throw a comforter over him. He turned the light out in there and came back into the dimly lit kitchen. Helen had opened another bottle and her makeup had smeared because she was crying. She had the radio going to some station that was playing Bessie Smith. Arthur came up behind her and put his hands on her shoulders. He was really hoping he could get it up. She turned and kissed him full on the mouth and he eagerly returned it. She started breathing harder and he put his hand on one of her breasts and rubbed it. She opened her mouth and moved it up along his jaw and put her hand on him. He squeezed her breast harder.

They kissed more. She rubbed him some but he was as flaccid as a dead flounder.

"You feeling anything?" she said.

"Maybe so . . . I think maybe . . . it feels . . . it feels like . . . almost . . ."

"You think we can do something?"

"I hope so. I sure would like to."

"I would, too. I'm about to go crazy."

"I know you are."

They wound up in the bedroom, and the same thing happened, and this time she did cry. He went downstairs and had a cup of butterscotch pudding in the dark, watching somebody on the Discovery Channel digging up a woolly mammoth with the sound low so as not to wake Eric or the pit bull sleeping beside him, whose name, they'd found out, was Jada Pinkett.

20

The little dog had tried scratching for a long time already at the thick wooden door, and even though he had succeeded in marring it to the point where it would need to be taken down and refinished, he hadn't made any serious progress toward getting through it and walking down the hall to the toilet for a drink. He'd hopped up on the seat beside the bay window a few times and looked out. Part of the wet roof was near the window. If he could have gotten out there, he would have been able to walk down the shingles to the rain gutters to find leaves piled up at the corners that pooled a little melted snow.

He went back to the dry water pan and licked the inside of it. Then he lay down on the rug next to the desk and ran his pink tongue out.

He was still for a long time, his eyes closed almost to slits. He lay with his back legs splayed out and his head between his front paws. He turned his head at something, maybe a ghost, then sat up and with his hind foot scratched at the ribbon around his neck.

For a long time, he lay looking at the door. Once something passed, out in the hall, and his ears perked up, then lowered again. He got back down on his belly and watched the door, his chin on the floor. He had sad eyes.

But that didn't last long. He got up and walked around the room again. The windows dripped with melting snow outside. He jumped back up on the window seat and watched it come down on the other side of the glass. He licked at it.

Finally he went back to the door and sat down in front of it and barked. Then he got up on his feet and started barking and growling at the same time, lunging at the door. From outside the room there came the faint voice of somebody yelling for him to shut the hell up. Maybe he took that for encouragement. He barked for quite a while, maybe as long as three or four minutes. But there was no other voice to either encourage or impede him. After a while he just slowed down and stopped on his own.

He went back to the water pan. Then he jumped back up on the window seat and stood on his hind legs and gnawed at one of the pieces of wood that trimmed the glass panes. There was the small sound of his tiny teeth knocking against the glass. He chewed steadily, and slivers of wood began to fall away from the window. Specks of paint began to gather on the window-seat cushion.

Maybe he got tired because sometimes he stopped and rested.

Once when he stopped, he barked a single bark that sounded almost like a question. Then he went back to gnawing again.

Splinters were coming out now. He kept at it. Finally he seized a piece of wood in his teeth and tore it off at the joint. Now there was a small gap in the glass. Cool wind eased through it in a trickle and touched his nose. There were sounds and smells from the outside world leaking in.

He bumped a glass pane with his head. It didn't move. Out past the window a car pulled away from the house, going down the driveway, out onto the street. The little dog watched it go and wagged his tail happily a few times.

He looked left, he looked right. He looked at the water pan beneath the desk and then started gnawing on another piece of wood. Tiny pieces of paint started flaking off again. Some more splinters fell. Somebody watching might even have said that he seemed to know what he was doing, such a busy little beaver he was.

21

Miss Muffett decided she'd just drive around some, find a bar somewhere out in the country, maybe over close to Holly Springs, go in, have a few drinks and talk to a few men, see what happened.

She hadn't checked on the little dog, but if he could bark he was okay. She knew she'd have to let him out of there eventually, let him go to the bathroom out in the yard. The thing about it was that he wouldn't mess in Mr. Hamburger's study, of all places. That was the only place in the whole house where he wouldn't mess. She got her pistol and locked the house and got in the car and pulled out of the driveway and headed up the street, toward the interstate. He never called anyway. He wouldn't even know she was gone.

She wanted to talk to some men and see if maybe somebody would want to have a little fun with her tonight. If she did find somebody, she could tell whoever it was that she had a very nice house up at Como they could use, and that her boss was gone to Chicago again, and that he kept a well-stocked bar in the great room, and that it would be perfectly all right for them to have drinks in there before they did it and that they could even do it in there if he wanted to. It didn't matter, wasn't any big deal. The house and her vagina would be open to him, whoever he was. She had plenty of cash in her purse for drinks to lubricate likely candidates.

She drove over the railroad tracks out to the overpass and it wasn't snowing anymore. She didn't pay any attention to the mobile home that was sitting about sixty feet in the air on some steel girders at Moore's Mobile Homes but turned left on the other side of the bridge, got onto the ramp, and merged with the traffic flowing north on I-55. It took her about fifteen minutes to get to Senatobia, where the junior college was. She turned off at the ramp, slowing down since it was marked 30 MPH on a yellow sign.

At the end of the ramp, she stopped and looked both ways. A pickup was coming from the east, and she had to wait for it. When it passed, she saw that there were a couple of young men with beards in it. They had on red hats and orange vests. There were guns in a rack behind the seat. Deer hunters. She wondered where they hung out to drink beer. She started to follow them but didn't, just turned right on Highway 4 and eased her foot down on the gas pedal. She went past a few houses with redbrick siding and then over some hills of pastureland. Soggy cows were standing around waiting for somebody to feed them. There were some wet fields that had long been picked clean of cotton, and a big green tractor with a Bush Hog and a flat was sitting at the end of one of them. Then there were some woods and some patches of kudzu that had turned brown after the first frost. She turned her headlights on.

There were some serious woods on up the road a ways. It was kind of like going through a tunnel in part of it, because the trees were thick on each side and the limbs hung low, and they were ragged and torn, she suspected from the tall trucks that barreled through this road all the time, taking a shortcut between Highway 7 and I-55.

She didn't meet a whole lot of traffic. There were a few houses scattered here and there, mostly pretty run-down affairs with cars parked in muddy yards, dim yellow lights showing through the windows where plastic was tacked. Then some more woods. She passed one store. It was closed, windows knocked out, rusted shopping carts out front.

And then she saw it. It was set back in a grove of dark pines but there was a light over the front door. She slowed, put on her blinker, and turned in. About ten pickups and one van were sitting in the parking lot. It looked like every one of the pickups had a gun or two in a rack behind the seat. There were probably some dead deer lying in the backs of some of them. The sign over the door said PINES LOUNGE. There was advertised on another sign a catfish special with all the trimmings on Friday nights for $8.95, all you could eat, looked like a deal if their hush puppies were any good.

But since it was Wednesday, they weren't eating any catfish when she stepped inside the dim room. Instead there was a popcorn smell like a movie theater lobby, with Johnny Horton doing "When It's Springtime in Alaska" on the jukebox. It had great speakers, sounded like a taped-live Johnny Horton concert. There was a long bar with bottles of beer and drinks scattered up and down it, and stools scattered around as well. There was a place in the song where the girls singing backup did this thing with their voices lilting high that made a chill run up Miss Muffett's spine. Some unshaven guy in a wheelchair and a hospital gown and black nylon socks sat near a table, his shaking fingers holding a cigarette jittering smoke while his other shaking fingers lifted a full shot glass to his lips. There were a bunch of men in muddy brown overalls and camouflage coveralls and red-checkered wool jackets and Carhartt jackets, and some of them had camouflage caps on their heads. Some of them hadn't shaved in years. They were playing pinball machines and eating popcorn and barbecued pigskins and drinking beer and whiskey and smoking cigarettes and talking and yelling and laughing. A few of them quieted down and looked at her. Some wiseass in the back said something about strange. It looked like on first glance she was the only woman in there. Second glance, too. But she wasn't worried. She thought she might have hit paydirt. It had taken her only about thirty-two minutes to get over here and that was pretty incredible. She had left the quiet confines of the big house where she spent so much time alone and now she was with some living breathing people, and not a dog that wouldn't hang around her, or a boss who wouldn't talk to her very much because of an accident he'd had that was not all her fault even if she *had* accidentally hit the throttle and caused the turning auger to wrap around the front of his pants, and she was going to have a drink or two, and she was going to talk to some of these men, and she was *going* to have a good time. She sat down on a stool.

They had Christmas lights hung up all over, which made the place seem cheery and homey and warm. She looked at some of the men. One of them was a tall handsome man with thick brown hair, in a long leather coat, and he was tethering a white hound on one of those dog reels by having the cord wrapped around one leg of his stool. He was smoking a thin cigarette and wearing dark green glasses and Miss Muffett saw suddenly that he had only one hand. He had to put his cigarette in the ashtray to take a sip of his drink. She wondered what had happened to him. Probably not a boat propeller.

There were quite a few stuffed deer heads hanging on the walls as well as some stuffed bass, some stuffed crappie, the head of an alligator, the head of a black something that looked kind of like a dog but wasn't. It was a horrible-looking thing with long white snarly teeth. She opened her purse, wondering how she could break the ice with the nub guy. Except for the thing snarling down from the wall, it was a completely comfortable atmosphere and she wondered why she hadn't done something like this before. The pinball machines were ringing and there was a layer of smoke up above the lights of the bar. She didn't know for sure what she wanted to drink. She didn't drink much. She wondered what the man with the nub was drinking. She looked but couldn't tell.

A gray-haired but youthful-looking bartender with hefty biceps in a tight T-shirt saw her and picked up a coaster and walked over to her and put it down in front of her.

"Hey," he said. "How you?"

Miss Muffett was startled by the blue in his eyes. It took her a moment to reply. His eyes looked like chips from a turquoise stone.

"Fine," she said. "Just fine, thank you."

"Good. What can I get for you this evenin'?"

He was mopping with a clean rag at the bar top, picking up a shaker or a bottle of ketchup, wiping at spilled salt. He looked up at her, his eyes a polite question. People with empty bottles and glasses were waiting for him to wait on them.

"I don't know what I want," she said. "How about a beer?"

"Sure. What kind?"

She didn't know one beer from another. She never had paid any attention to beer. It was just beer. It said so right on the label, just like cooking oil.

"Hey, Scotty, bourbon and Coke down here?" some guy said.

"I'll take another Miller when you get a chance," another one said.

"Okay," he said. "What kind of beer you want, lady?"

"Just any kind."

"Just any kind?"

She nodded.

He didn't act like he thought that was weird but merely got a mug from the back side of the bar and pulled down on a chrome lever and started filling it. Maybe she should have asked for a bourbon and Coke. She could always try that if she didn't like the beer. Or what about a martini? They were supposed to knock you on your ass, weren't they? She figured it might be easier to get picked up if she was sloppy drunk, so she wanted whatever would do the job. She eyed the one-handed man clandestinely. He was *so* handsome. The bartender was turning back to her. He brought the beer and set it down on the coaster.

"Dollar-fifty," he said, and stood lingering impatiently. She paid him and tipped him a dollar and he thanked her and turned away. Then he started waiting on the other people.

Miss Muffett turned dreamily on her stool and listened to the music and started looking around. There were a bunch of guys in the back at a table, shooting pool. One of them had a ponytail that hung out the back of his cap where the little adjustable headband was. One fat guy in starched Duck Head overalls was Pavarotti with a larger beard.

She looked at the beer. She guessed she'd have to drink some of it. It was as dark as Coca-Cola and it had a thick and foamy brown head. She picked it up and took a sip from it. It was hard to keep from making a face because it tasted so incredibly bitter to her. Yuck City! When she looked up, the bartender was watching her. She smiled at him and took another drink. The second one made her gag. The bartender saw her and walked back over with a worried look on his face.

"You don't like it, huh."

"Hey, man. How about a Fighting Cock on the rocks over here?"

"Well . . . actually . . . no," she said. "I think maybe I should just get a bourbon, maybe a bourbon and Coke . . ."

"A bourbon?"

"Yes."

"Mind if I ask you a polite question?" He was smiling now.

"Why no."

"You know any more about bourbon than you do about beer?"

It seemed that several people were listening to this conversation. They seemed to be waiting for what she was going to say next.

"Not really," she said. "I don't drink much."

"You don't?"

"No."

He leaned in. "Is that beer bitter to you?"

"Well, yes, it is. A little. Actually, quite a lot. To me, anyway."

"Some people have to develop a taste for beer."

Somebody hollered: "Hey, Scotty, Schlitz and a Blatz and a Schmidt's and a Schaeffer and a Rollin' Rock?"

"Well, how do you ever develop a taste for it if it tastes so awful the first time you try it?" she said. "I mean, why would you want to keep trying it? That's like getting beat up and enjoying it."

The bartender laughed and put both hands on the bar.

"You want me to make you a drink that tastes real good?"

"That would be wonderful," Miss Muffett said.

He cocked his head for her to tell him the truth.

"You aim to get drunk?"

"That's what I came in here for," Miss Muffett said.

"Fix her a lemon drop, Scotty," one guy said.

"Naw, man, make her a sloe gin fizz," another one said.

"I don't know much about drinking," she said to those around her in a general way. And then she saw the handsome one-handed dog man with the thick hair leaning against a wall and talking on the telephone, but the dog was still tied to the stool. She was able to watch him since he had his back turned to her. He looked somewhat mysterious in his long leather coat.

The people standing around her started leaning in toward her and giving her their names. There was Ricky and Ben and Joel and Matt and Michael and Mark and Traver and Keith and Horatio Potter who lived just down the road and trapped part-time. She asked Horatio what the snarling thing up on the wall was and he said it was a coy-dog he'd killed, a cross between a coyote and a dog, nasty sumbitch, wasn't it?

Scotty brought a drink in a narrow glass with different colors: pink, yellow, white. It had two straws but no parasol. Perhaps a pink poo-poo?

"Here go. Lock them lips around this," he said. "Scotty's tsunami, on the house."

"Why thank you," Miss Muffett said, and slid her mouth over one of the straws and sucked. Mmm, mmm, she inwardly went. She'd never had one this good, like some special new candy.

"Wow, Scotty," she said. "I could drink about ten of these babies."

"Yeah, but you'd be on your ass," Scotty said. "Shit's dynamite."

"I feel like a little dynamite tonight," she said, and bent to slurp at her straw. He watched her for a moment. Then he grinned.

"Well hell," he told her. "Rip it up, girl. If you want to party, you come to the right place."

"Don't get too far away," she said. And she turned her eyes back toward the man with the nub. Who was looking at her.

22

It was quiet at Gigi's Angels. There were only a few drunks nodding at the bar. All the girls were temporarily off the stage since business had been bad and Moe couldn't afford to pay them around the clock. Anjalee's business had been zero. All the firefighters had gone home. It turned out they were spending all their money on Christmas presents. Was she even going to get her mother anything?

She let herself back behind the bar and got a cup of coffee and tilted some bourbon into it, then went back around and got her cigarettes from her purse and lit one. A horn blew outside and one of the drunks stirred and got off his stool, stumbling some, and went toward the door. The horn blew again and the guy paused to get his coat off a rack near the cigarette machine. He went on out and the door slammed after him. Anjalee sipped her coffee. Frankie hadn't called, and she couldn't call him. He'd always been funny about his phone number, never would give it to her, told her it wasn't that kind of relationship. It was beginning to look like it wasn't any kind of relationship at all. He'd probably found somebody else. She'd been halfway expecting that for a while, so it wouldn't be any surprise. If that was true, she wouldn't be getting any more money from him. She thought about that sailor wanting to marry her. He was a nice guy. She should have said yes.

She missed her apartment so badly she didn't know what to do, but there was no way she could go back there. Even if she hadn't killed Miss Barbee, she had certainly fucked her up enough to get sent to jail. All her clothes, her shoes. A couple of sweaters she might need in this weather. All her art supplies. She wondered what would become of her things. She guessed when her rent got overdue the landlord would come up and unlock her apartment and haul her stuff out and give it to somebody, maybe the Salvation Army. Then, on second thought, she figured the cheap prick would sell it all and keep the money. He never would come up and fix her leaky sink that was still leaking. Or light her pilot light. Had to call Memphis Light Gas & Water to come over and do that. Cheap prick.

After a while she got up and skipped the coffee and just got more bourbon. She smoked another cigarette and munched a few peanuts left in a bowl. She was hungry. Already she was getting nervous about walking around in daylight. It wasn't going to be any way to live. But without any money, she couldn't even go home.

One of the remaining drunks raised his head and said something unintelligible, then dropped his face down on the bar.

And then through the door came Lenny. He saw her immediately and she turned toward him. She liked him because he didn't give her the creeps like some of Frankie's asshole buddies. He wasn't one of those guys who wouldn't look you in the eye or was always playing around with his dick inside his pants. She'd had a few drinks with him in a bar he and Frankie had been in one night. He'd been nice to her and told her that her dress was pretty. Back when Frankie was giving her enough money to buy some good clothes. Like when she'd gotten that black leather coat that was still upstairs. She needed to go up and get it.

"Well hello, beautiful," he said, once he'd stopped beside her.

"Hi, Lenny."

"You want to date me tonight?" he said, didn't sound like he was kidding.

She looked him up and down. It didn't sound like a bad idea.

"I don't know. Have you seen Frankie?"

He coughed briefly into his fist before he answered.

"I think Frankie's probably out of town, honey."

That seemed odd. Frankie hadn't said a word about going out of town. He reached out and touched her arm, then leaned on the bar.

"I was going to buy you a drink, but you've got one," he said. He looked around. "What do you have to do to get some service around here?"

"I guess Moe's in the back."

"Can you call him?"

"Call him?"

"Yeah."

She looked at him. He had on a good suit that fit him well. And his shoes were actually some nice cowboy boots. They looked like Tony Lamas. They had a cool green-lizard toe. That damn Frankie. What did he mean going out of town and not telling her?

"I can pour you something," she said. "What you want?"

"I want a vodka martini, very dry."

She shook her head. He was easy on her eyes.

"I don't know how to make one of those."

"Maybe you should learn."

Well, maybe she should. Maybe he had plenty of money, like Frankie. If he was in the same business as Frankie, he probably did. She smiled at him.

"Or we could always go somewhere they know how to make one," he said.

"I know a good place," she told him.

23

The little dog got stranded on the roof, looking down to trees in the yard, cars with their lights passing on the street in the mushy squishing snow, a moon sky smoked gray by fast-moving clouds. The stopped-up rain gutters held plenty of water and melting snow and he stood there slanted downhill drinking from one for a long time.

He went back to the window to try and get back in where it was warm, but it was too high above him now, the roof too steep to let him make a decent jump. He'd been lucky not to roll his little butt right off the gutters when he'd first jumped through the hole left by the loose pane he'd pushed out with his head.

The roof was wide and long and had peaks in it. The little dog could get around on it pretty good and he spent some time checking most of it out, only thing, there wasn't much of a place to lie down where it wasn't slanted, and maybe for that reason he wasn't able to get any sleep. What he did was drape his belly over the ridgeline, half in front, half in back, and try to sleep that way, but it must not have been very comfortable for him, might have even hurt his little pooched-out belly, because he kept getting up. It was cold, and the wind was blowing, and he never did go to sleep, even though he seemed to try more than once to achieve that natural dog state.

Most of the night passed with him watching it. Lights below that shone on the yard went off. The traffic slowed and almost stopped. A siren sounded far off and died. The small town quieted, as if the dark had brought some angel of peace with folded wings into the streets to smoke cigarettes and hang out at deserted corners for the duration of a single freezing night. There was only the hum of semis in the fog out on the interstate to cut through the silence, and he, a solitary little dog, didn't know what they were.

Near daylight, shaking with cold, he whined beneath the window. There was nothing out there for him to eat. The man he liked wasn't around anywhere that he could see. He couldn't smell him either. So he went down to the very edge of the roof, ran back and forth a few times, taxiing, looking down and whining, and then he jumped, his ears lifted out from the sides of his head like the fragile wings of birds, into the darkness that swallowed him.

24

When Miss Muffett woke up, she didn't know where she was. It wasn't completely dark, but on the other hand, she couldn't see anything very clearly. Somebody was next to her, but she didn't know who it was. Then she figured out that she was in the back seat of a car. Was it her car? She couldn't tell. It was getting to be daylight. This was very different from waking up alone in her own bed, as she did a lot of mornings in her mostly lonesome life. She'd wanted love for so long that it was just an old achy pain now. Somewhere along the line she'd settled for simple fucking.

She reached out her hand to feel what was around her. She felt what felt like somebody's hairy leg. The leg had a laced-up boot on it. Her neck was hurting.

"Who is it?" she said.

"Huh?" a sleepy voice said.

"I said 'Who is it?' " she said.

"Aw, you know who it is," the voice said, and then after a moment of silence some light snoring started up, air flowing over soft tissues, an open mouth. Her leg was off and she found it on the floorboard. Her underwear was off and she found it on the floorboard. It turned out that she was lying half on top of this person and she had to move around on the seat to get herself situated enough to get her underwear on and once she did, she pulled her leg up from the floor and strapped it on and pulled down her dress.

She looked down at her chest. Her bra was all twisted around and her dress was open on top. She looked at her boobs. They had suck marks on them, of all things, vague blue-and-red bruises around her nipples.

It looked like she might have had a great time but she wished she could remember more of it. One of the things she could remember was talking and laughing in the bar with those nice people who had kept buying her those really good drinks. Somebody had gone out for sandwiches at one point and brought them back in and she remembered pigging out on a salami-bologna-cheese hoagie with sliced tomatoes and peppers and oil, so maybe she'd been passed out at some point. She remembered dancing with the tall dog man with the brown hair beside the rainbow of lights coming out of the jukebox. She remembered the way his nub had felt against the small of her back. His name, she remembered, was Faisel, and he was a logger. He'd blown his hand off, when he was sixteen, trying to demonstrate the recoiling barrel on a Remington Sportsman 48 twelve-gauge shotgun. The dog, Amos, belonged to his ex-wife, Camelopardalis, whom he had described as a failed and bitter poetess, but he still had to take care of it sometimes when she was on her Mary Kay route. She'd already won a pink Cadillac. Faisel had said it was the ugliest fucking thing he'd ever seen. He'd also said his friends called him Nub.

Now that she was waking up a bit, she could remember a few more things. She remembered driving around in the country in her car with Faisel at the wheel, Amos in the back. They'd tried to drop him off at Camelopardalis's place in Michigan City, since she was supposed to be back, but there was a note on the door saying that she'd gone out for ribs at Horn Lake with some of her friends and that she'd be back in a few hours, and asked Faisel, in the note, to keep Amos overnight for her, which hadn't made him happy. He'd been for leaving Amos tied to the doorknob with the leash, but Miss Muffett had talked him out of it, saying that somebody would probably come along and steal him since he was a hound and it was hunting season. She also remembered during the course of the evening confessing her own little dog problems to Faisel, but she couldn't remember what he'd said, and that was in another bar, someplace he took her to, a roadhouse, she couldn't remember where it was, only that some people were on a stage in leotards and vests and big pants and blond dreadlocks playing tuba music like none she'd ever heard, stuff that was oomping and bumping and rumbling. She didn't know where the dog was now. Didn't really give a shit, either. Seemed like they might have dropped him off somewhere.

Her head was hurting. Felt like it was about to pop. Then: Oh crap. The little dog was still home by himself. He might have been forced to poop in Mr. Hamburger's study.

She tried to sit up. It was hard to. It was her car, all right, but when she looked around, she didn't recognize the place where the car was sitting. There was some mud spattered up on the windows, and the windshield was streaked with muddy arcs. Out beyond the windshield, she could just make out the bleary forms of some run-down steel buildings with weak lights and some junked heavy equipment, dozers, cranes, yellow backhoes with flat tires.

"I've got to go," she said, and began trying to extricate herself. It was indeed Faisel's sleeping face she looked down on. She kicked him suddenly.

"Get up!" she said, and started crawling between the front seats. She could see the keys hanging from the ignition.

"And get your clothes on," she said. His pants were halfway up his legs, but he had his underwear on. She wondered how they'd managed it. *If* they'd managed it.

Once she got in the driver's seat, she reached out and grabbed his leg and shook it.

"Hey! Faisel! You've got to wake up! We've got to go!"

He moaned and stirred and yawned and rubbed his chin with his nub. She cranked the car.

"What time is it?" he said.

"Time for me to get my ass back to Como."

"Can you hold it just a minute while I get my clothes on?"

"What happened to my windshield?" she said.

He sat up in the back seat and started arranging his pants. He had to scoot up and then down, tugging at them with his hand and his nub. He'd slept on his balled-up coat for a pillow and his hair was messed up pretty bad. She pushed the wiper button and the wipers came on, but no stream of water actually sprayed out, just a few impotent spurts.

"Oh crap," she said. "Have you got a handkerchief?"

"A what?"

"Handkerchief. Look at this. What'd you drive us through?"

"Me?" Faisel said, trying to get into his coat. "Shit fire, you's the one drivin'. You said you's takin' me on the scenic tour. Don't you remember?"

"No," Miss Muffett said. And she didn't. Not shit.

He handed her a huge red bandanna and she got out and rubbed at the windshield with it but it didn't do a whole lot of good. Finally she had to concentrate on just wiping a hole in the middle so she could see well enough to drive. She tossed him the muddy bandanna when she got back in and then she put her seat belt on. She turned her headlights on.

"You want to get in the front?"

"I might as well," he said. He opened the back door and got out and closed it and walked around in front of the hood, and Miss Muffett studied him as he went across. She wished she could remember if it had been any fun or not.

Once he was seated, she told him to put his seat belt on and he did. She pulled the car down in D and started looking for a place to turn it around. Faisel lit a cigarette and cracked the window and she eased off into the unknown.

"Where are we?" she said.

"On the scenic tour."

She drove slowly, looking around. It dawned on her gradually that they were in an enormous junkyard with gravel roads in between the wrecks. Rusted hulks of machinery lined the drive she was on, some of them towering up thirty feet or more. Cars were stacked on top of each other. In the middle of it was an enormous drive-in movie screen all gray and tall. Faisel pointed to it.

"They shot a movie up here last year and built that thing and just left it. It's a movie prop. It ain't real."

"It looks real."

"I know it does. This is where we parked so we could . . . you know."

"Well, where is it?"

"Holly Springs."

And it turned out it was. It took her about two hours to get back because she had to take him to the bar and his truck, and then she had to get gas, and something to eat, and some BCs and some orange juice, and there was a bunch of white dog hair all over the back seat, and she had to stop at a coin car wash and suck all that out with a hose, crawling around on the back seat on her plastic leg. She didn't like for her car to get all messed up.

25

Arthur slept late. He got up with his hair mussed and had to comb it. Eric was still snoring it off under the comforter. Jada Pinkett was asleep. The kitten was arched in the corner, its hair standing up, and it spat and slashed twice at him when he got close to the cage. He wondered how they were going to let it take a shit without some dirt in there.

He'd spent the rest of the night in a chair in the living room with a rug thrown over him. It was the only thing he'd been able to find.

He went in there and put the rug back down on the floor and straightened it out with his foot. He could hear what sounded like a fire-truck siren going somewhere, maybe down Southern. They had a station up there. It faded away.

Upstairs he peeked through the bedroom door and saw Helen sleeping. Hungover again probably. It looked like she'd get tired of it.

Back in the kitchen, he started coffee and went out front to get the paper. He didn't bang the door when he closed it.

The paper wasn't on the doorstep. The asshole paper kid had thrown it out on the walk leading up to the step again, and it was lying right on top of some snow. The walk was kind of icy. And he had his house shoes on. Now he'd have to go back in and get his galoshes, or just forget about the paper. He hated to go to all that trouble. But he really wanted to read the paper. It would be something to occupy his mind and not let it dwell on what had happened again last night. It was starting to get embarrassing.

He stood there in the cold wind in front of the door and looked at the houses on each side of him and at the traffic passing down South Parkway and under the big leafless trees. He asked himself what he would do if the shoe was on the other foot. What if she had something go wrong with her, say she developed a fungus up inside her, or her vagina started making too much bad bacteria, or all the mucus in her body dried up, and it caused her to not be able to have sex, what would he do then? Assuming that he was functioning okay in the penis department, of course. There was just some piece of him that temporarily wasn't working exactly quite right and they had to find out what that was, and if that meant going to the doctor and talking to him again, then maybe that's what he needed to do. He couldn't keep on like this. He had to remember that she was younger than him. Her sex drive was still strong.

So that settled that. He'd go back in and get his galoshes and get his paper and by then the coffee would be almost ready.

He turned around to go back in and the door was locked. He banged on it.

"Hey."

He banged on it some more.

"Hey, Eric! Get up and let me in! Hey, Eric!"

It was a good thing none of the neighbors was out. This was about the third time he'd done this in a month. He always lost his keys.

"Hey, Eric!"

The door suddenly opened and Eric stood there over him, holding the doorknob, weaving.

"Locked myself out," Arthur said, and stepped back in. "I was just getting my galoshes so I could go out for my paper."

Eric's hair was tousled and his eyes were red and he was scratching at his belly and yawning, but he waved a hand at Arthur and shook his head with his eyes half closed, still yawning, still sleepy.

"S'okay, Mister Arthur. I already got my boots on."

He went out the door rubbing at the side of his face, stumbling, his arm in one sleeve of his coat. Arthur watched him and saw a few birds scatter as he moved toward them. Helen was always throwing out seeds for them, or old bread or crackers, and they hung around in the yard sometimes. Eric picked up the paper and dusted the snow from it and came back and clomped his boots at the step, knocking the snow off.

"I better take these off," he said, handing Arthur the paper.

"Well, that's not necessary, really, I . . . ," Arthur said.

He already had them off and walked sock footed back across the room and found his cigarettes and lighter on the couch where he'd slept.

Arthur closed the door and thanked Eric for getting the paper and Eric said he was welcome. Arthur could see the red light shining on the coffeepot, which meant it was ready. Jada Pinkett was sprawled like a dog who was dead.

"You a coffee man, Eric?"

"Shoot yeah. You got some ready?"

"It's ready. How do you take it?"

And then, after a few exchanges of light chitchat, Eric began to tell him the history of Jada Pinkett, who had fought seven times in the pit, and who, though runtlike, had six times been victorious. At the end of the seventh fight, in back of a big chicken house in Paris, Mississippi, with thirty-four drunk people watching, and after suffering severe blood loss from a pumping vein on his left hind leg, he had been slowly choked down into the dry brown dirt in the second roll by a much larger and badly disturbed brindle bull named Tarzan Duran, from Athens, Georgia, and Eric thought maybe Jada Pinkett had suffered a near-death experience that changed his personality and made him stop wanting to fight and hating cats and start loving to catch little tender things like kittens and baby rabbits and play with them instead. Dog fighting had gotten a bad name, Eric told him, because of those people who wanted to put a stop to hunting once and for all and claimed fishing was cruel, too, to the fish.

They got up more than once to get more coffee and Arthur found some doughnuts that weren't too stale in one of the cabinets and opened the box and put them on the table between them. Eric ate two and Arthur ate one. When Jada Pinkett woke up, Eric took him for a short walk and when they got back, Arthur opened a can of beef stew and let him eat it on an old newspaper. Eric, watching him eat, said his daddy had named him as a pup while holding him on his lap after seeing Jada Pinkett on MTV. Why? he said. Who knew? His daddy just liked the name, he guessed. Eric leaned closer and told Arthur that his daddy had won thousands of dollars on the dog, and he said it again, *thousands* of dollars, and Arthur asked him who from, and Eric said rich Delta ex-planters who had leased their land to the riverboat casinos, and were making ridiculous amounts of money each month not raising cotton, like three hundred thousand dollars a month, some of them, and had money to throw away, to build cool hunting cabins out in the wild river bottoms, with massive solar panels and concrete driveways that were miles long, and state-of-the-art satellite systems that pulled in over sixteen hundred channels, to install piña colada machines in the cabins where you just pushed a glass up against the machine and it spit one out. Boy, Arthur thought. He should have kept all that Tunica land his daddy had left him. But shit. How much money did a man need? He didn't need any more. What would he do with more? Buy a big boat? Why did they need a big house with servants? He'd had that growing up and he didn't want it. The main thing was just to be happy. But that itself was hard enough to do. If she was happy, would she drink so much? That old nagging worry of twenty years kept nagging through: *She only married you for your money, Dilbert-head.*

Arthur heard a toilet flush upstairs. And he thought he heard the soft sound of the bedroom door closing, but couldn't be absolutely sure because it happened at a moment when Eric was still talking. He couldn't let on to Eric that he had a bunch of things troubling him. So he leaned back.

"Sounds like a whole way of life," he murmured.

"It gets tough sometimes," Eric said. "Y'all gotny eggs?"

Arthur found sharp cheddar cheese and half a Virginia ham in the icebox and he chopped hunks of both on a laminated block while Eric broke six eggs into a bowl and beat them with a whisk. Beside the stove Arthur found Teflon-coated pans. She'd probably sleep late. Then come down feeling bad. Then fix a Bloody Mary. Start all over again.

He looked up to see Helen standing at the foot of the stairs in her silky robe, the hem of her gown showing just below the rabbit trim, her feet in fur-lined slippers. She'd brushed her hair. Did she have lipstick on?

"Well, hey, she's up," he said. Jada Pinkett was browsing beside his knee for more juicy snacks. He bent over and picked up the wet messy newspaper with gobs of carrots and dog tracks in the beef-stew gravy left on it and stashed it in the trash can. "Good morning," he said, but he didn't know what he would have said if Eric hadn't been standing there, pouring the egg batter into the two skillets he'd preheated and coated with oil.

She seemed calm. She even smiled.

"Good morning," she said, and walked on over, gave Arthur a light kiss on the ear. Eric turned at the stove.

"You sleep good, Miss Helen?"

"God," she said. "I've got to have some aspirin."

"Overdo it a little bit?" said Eric, with a tiny smile.

"You can say that again," she said, and started looking in the cabinet where she kept all her pills. "I may have to fix myself a Bloody Mary."

"Make it two if you don't mind," he said.

Arthur wasn't surprised. He went over to the stove and gauged the progress of the omelets. The slowly crisping edges had slid away from the sloping walls of the pan and in the center of the quaking yellow mass there was cheese melting and cooking together with thick bits of ham, a genie wisp of fragrant steam rising that reminded Arthur of things his mother used to make for him at their big house in the Delta, out there in the old pecan grove. He could still smell in his head the pies she used to make, maybe blackberry the most since it was always their job to pick the berries, together, and he could remember the purple stains on his fingers, and the summertime heat, and the clean dirty jokes she told wearing her long dress and bonnet and laughing, and he could remember the view from the kitchen window, all those cotton wagons, filling up the whole back field in the summertime, twenty or thirty of them, grass growing up around them, all the tires his daddy had to get his men to fix in the fall. Took that many wagons to get it all in. But he never had wanted to farm, like his daddy. All that heat and dust. All that mud. If you didn't get rain, you were screwed for that year. And he'd done all right with his daddy's money, first in oil, then in the stock market. All you had to do was just leave it in there and you'd be okay. Better than okay. He had a lot more now than what his daddy had left him. Eric had the pans by the handles, sliding them back and forth a bit, making sure they weren't sticking. Helen had gone into the liquor cabinet and was reaching for a bottle. Arthur didn't say anything. He watched her get one of those six-packs of tomato juice from the pantry and listened to her coo to the kitty for a bit and the hissing was louder than the cooing. When she came back to the sink, she got a glass of water and opened a plastic bottle and took two pills, leaning her head back to get them down with the water.

"Crap," she said. "I don't know how we're going to tame that kitten down." She went to the icebox and got a lime and some Worcestershire sauce and some hot sauce and some pickled okra, and then she got some glasses and ice and started mixing and slicing. He made some more coffee and got three plates down. He'd halve his with Helen. But she saw him do it and said: "If you're getting a plate for me you can put one back." So he did. Then he got to thinking about those adoption people. Those adoption people had always thought he was too old. They never would come right out and say it, but he knew that was what they'd thought, in all their tidy little offices: *Too old. Almost a geeze-ball. Didn't get married until he was almost fifty? And what the fuck does she know about raising a kid? Stamp them "Rejected."*

He should have tried to get one in Russia. Russia had plenty of them. But she hadn't said anything about trying to get a baby in a long time now. She just carried the grieving of it around inside her like a stomachache. He still felt guilty over his lazy sperm. They were probably all dead by now.

"They're ready," Eric said, and pretty soon he had them on the plates. Arthur found the silverware and got napkins while Helen sat on the high stool and sipped her drink. Eric had already downed half of his by the time he put their breakfast on the table. Helen bummed a cigarette off him and found the bowl he'd used the night before and actually lit up and then coughed a delicate cough. Arthur didn't say anything. He just sat there and ate and watched her. She was beginning to seem like somebody he didn't exactly know. Like something had changed about her during a night's sleep. Her hair looked longer somehow. She looked younger. And he didn't believe he had ever seen her look more beautiful. It was all he could do to keep eating. He kept thinking about her crying, how the sobbing had sounded, how he'd been almost able to feel the anguish that was in her heart.

By the time breakfast was over, Eric had gone ahead and gotten a beer from the icebox and Helen had mixed herself another drink.

"You guys are starting a little early, aren't you?" Arthur said. He'd kept quiet for a long time. He just couldn't stand it anymore.

"Hair of the dog that bit me on the ass," Eric said.

"Works for me," Helen said.

"But don't you think you should eat something?" Arthur asked her.

She just waved a casual hand. "I'll boil some eggs. Something."

"Well," he said, looking at both of them, hoping that maybe Eric would decide to get going now if he gave him the gentle hint that they were ready to get on with their normal day of being with each other without him around. "I need to get my galoshes on and shovel some of that snow off the walk. Start my day."

"Good," Helen said. "That sure needs doing. It gets so slick sometimes I'm afraid I'm going to fall. Eric, honey, I hate to keep bumming."

"No problem, I got two packs. You need any help, Mister Arthur?"

"Well, not really," he said. "It's kind of a one-person thing, one person, one shovel, won't take me long probably, I'll just go get my galoshes," he said, a little miffed, and went up the hall to get them from the closet. Didn't Eric need to get on to work at the pet shop? And wasn't Helen ever going to put some clothes on?

His galoshes had always been too big for him. He knew you were supposed to wear shoes with them, but it always turned out that he never had his shoes with him whenever he got ready to put the galoshes on. He had to be careful walking around in them or they'd slip off his feet. In snow he kept his arms out like he was ice-skating.

He could hear them laughing in the kitchen, and Helen got up to get something from the icebox. Was she getting something else to drink? He watched *Jerry Springer* every day for the fights those people almost got into and he didn't want an impromptu booze party in the kitchen to mess that up. But surely that wouldn't happen. Eric would have to leave and go to work sometime. Probably way before lunch.

He had to go back to the broom closet to get the shovel and he carried it back through the hall. He went out the front door and checked to make sure it was unlocked.

He glanced toward the kitchen just before he shut the door but he couldn't see what was going on. He could hear them laughing.

He shoveled at the front step for a while, halfheartedly. He saw his neighbor, old Mr. Stamp, out shoveling his step, too. They waved at each other. He'd be as old as Mr. Stamp eventually if he kept living. Was Mr. Stamp able to get it up? He'd bet money he wasn't. He wondered what they were doing in there, what they were saying. They were probably having a good time. Maybe they were dancing to the radio like she did sometimes. That was okay, if they wanted to dance to the radio. He was afraid she felt like her life hadn't been fulfilled. And now it was too late. He was almost seventy and it was hard to believe. He didn't know how all that time could have possibly passed so fast since he could remember so well the days when he was a child and in many ways it didn't seem that long ago. But he guessed it was like that for everybody. When his mother was born, they didn't have computers. Or televisions. Going to the dentist was probably hell on earth.

The day had turned so sunny that snow was melting in the street in front of the houses, and on the sidewalks. The sunlight looked pretty good to Arthur after the gray days of winter. It would be almost spring in a few more months. All the birds would be back by then, the sparrows, jays, robins. Helen would be buying bags of bird feed to scatter out front. If the cat stayed around, it might turn into a problem if it got out of the house. But she didn't even have it tamed yet. And might never.

26

The cruiser was rattling loudly. Domino got a good grip on the knife and yanked it. Only a little trickle of dark blood came out, staining the snow, not a whole lot. He wiped the knife off on the cop's pants and put the knife inside the sheath and stuck it back inside his shirt. He already had the gun, a loaded stainless-steel .380, with black plastic grips and a couple of clips. But he wasn't planning on having to use it on anybody. It just depended on what happened. He was taking it just in case. He didn't know what else he could have done. Not just run.

He'd seen him open that box and look in. He might have walked back up and looked in the bag. He might have wanted to see if there was anything in there besides meat. But there was no need in thinking about what might have happened. This is what had happened. All he could do now was try to get away. He was going to move the cruiser. It would be risky. But so was this. He'd already moved the bag into the woods. Who the hell was that?

He got the cop by the feet and started pulling him like a stick of pulpwood off the road and into the woods before somebody else could come along. It was just bad timing. It was just being in the wrong place at the wrong time. He was almost too stiff with cold to move, but his feet were warm in the boots he always used in the freezers.

It was tough pulling. The cop was heavier than he looked, for one thing, because he was short and wide, and had thick legs and arms, and Domino guessed his weight at about two-ten, more than him. Built like a football player. It was also slippery. But the exertion was helping to drive some of the cold away. The only thing was that his fingers were stiff and hurting with cold even in the gloves.

He had to pause for a rest. He knew he was out of shape. His breath was whirling around him in clouds of white fog. He knew his pulse had to be going nuts. He was scared shitless. This was a lot different from what he'd done to Doreen. That had been one thing. This was something else.

But he couldn't let himself think about it too much. If he thought about it too much, he wouldn't be able to do what he had to do if he was going to get out of this. He picked up the feet and pulled again. The snow had slacked off but there was still some coming down.

He finally got the cop a few hundred feet off the road. Everything was dark against the scattered snow. He pulled him behind a brush pile next to the bag. If it kept snowing, he thought it would cover them up. He stood there looking. He had to try and think of all the possibilities. The car kept rattling.

Of course they'd come searching with their police cars once somebody missed the cop. They might find some blood, depending on how much snow fell between now and then. They could test the blood and probably find out something from it, like how long it had been there maybe, what type it was. They might even get out in the woods and kick around and discover the bodies. But they could never connect him with it if he got away now. There was always some calculated risk in moving dope. It got done all the time, but some people got caught doing it, too. None of this would have happened if he hadn't hit the whitetail. And he'd only been in trouble with the police that one time. He knew what had happened to him. Domino had been found wrapped, crying, in a blanket in a trash can at a gas station in Tupelo by two gas station attendants, and one of them had given him to his sister, Doreen, who'd had some weird ideas. She'd had some weird ideas about Christmas, like no toys for snot-nosed kids like him, and even the early and absolute denial of the mythical sky rider, the sleighmaster Santy Claus, and weird ideas about some other things, too, chief among them that sex with preteens was okay, and she had never allowed him to attend school, partly because she thought school was evil, partly because she was afraid the authorities would find out that she had him and what she'd been doing with him. He'd sewed her drunk ass up in a quilt one night while she was passed out on Corbett Canyon and burned her all up in a Christmas Eve house fire in 1986, when he was fifteen, because she'd slapped and punched a lot between drunken bouts of sex once he got old enough to do that, but had kept him in a very cold basement sometimes when he was too little to do anything about it. And he finally just got scared she was going to kill him and did it first. The judge didn't believe his story, and gave him life. But he'd earned his probation. It didn't matter now. It was done. All he could do was try to get away. Then he could go to Oregon and live out there in the woods right next to the ocean. Raise the shit himself. They got a lot of rain out there, so things probably grew well. Maybe he could get a hang glider and jump off some of those cliffs.

He walked back through the woods for the last time, hurrying now. The door was open on the cop's shaking cruiser, and Domino got in. A Walkman was on the seat with a bunch of CDs. He picked up a few of the CDs and read the titles. He'd learned to read from *Reading Rainbow* when Doreen was at work. He'd picked up Townes Van Zandt's *Rear View Mirror*, Hank Williams's *Rare Demos First to Last*, and The Gourds's *Stadium Blitzer*.

There was a brown paper bag on the seat of the cruiser and he picked it up and looked inside it. Some kind of sandwiches. He shut the door, but it hung, and he had to shut it again. Piece of shit. The cruiser was still rattling loudly and when he pulled it down in gear it started shaking a lot worse and the muffler started going *bang bang bang bang bang bang bang.*

27

When Miss Muffett got back to Como, it was nearly nine o'clock. She knew she had to get up there quick and let the little dog out of the room, and then watch him all the way out the door to make sure he didn't stop and pee somewhere in the house. But he probably already had. He wouldn't have been able to hold it all this time. But whatever mess he'd made, she'd fix it to where her boss wouldn't see it. He was very particular about his study. He didn't like to return and find that it had been messed up in his absence. He might frown over that. She was actually a little afraid of Mr. Hamburger's temper. It had always been bad, and now it was even worse. But again, that was certainly understandable. She just wished the whole thing had never happened.

She herself was about to die to pee. She stopped in one of the downstairs bathrooms and yanked her panties down and her dress up and slammed her pale cloven butt down on the toilet, breathed a sigh of relief while she peed and peed. Ooh it felt good.

Pulling her plastic leg up the stairs one step at a time, she started feeling guilty about leaving the little dog alone in the study. She suddenly realized that she hadn't checked to see how much water had been in the pan. What if it was dry? But a dog couldn't die of thirst overnight, could it? She suddenly had a horrible vision of the little dog stretched out dead on the floor of the study.

But he wasn't on the floor when she opened the door. At first she didn't see the missing windowpane. Then she did. The little shit had gone out the window, for sure, to fall to his death. And all this time she'd thought he was so damn smart. Chewed his way out, looked like, from the splinters.

Well, it wasn't her fault, she told herself, and she went to the downstairs closet to put her coat back on. Mr. Hamburger couldn't blame her for it. But he probably would. Just like with the posthole-digger deal. She was actually kind of surprised that he hadn't fired her. She guessed he needed her.

She looked around in the yard for the longest time for the small dead and broken body, in the melting snow, bracing herself for the shock of seeing him. The little dog wasn't there.

She looked all over the yard and behind the bushes and around the big shed two or three times with her nose sniffling and wiping at it with the side of her thumb and there was not a little dog to be found. Maybe he dragged himself off and died somewhere else. She stood there looking at the ground, wondering what to do next. And couldn't think of a damn thing.

28

Deep inside the ship, cruising through the black water of the Atlantic Ocean, Wayne couldn't get to sleep for a long time because of thinking about Anjalee, but he finally did, and then sometime during the night a tremendous shock went through the vessel and woke him up and there was an awful immense groaning noise that came from somewhere down below. A bell was ringing. He could hear an alarm going off, *BaBaWOP, BaBaWOP, BaBaWOP.* Then some other bells started going off. Something else was screeching like a smoke detector.

Henderson turned on his light and rolled over.

"What the shit, bro?" Wayne said.

"We done hit somethin'."

"Hit something? What the hell could we hit out here in the middle of the ocean?"

"I don't know," Henderson said. He sat up suddenly. He'd been sleeping in his clothes. He rubbed excitedly with his fingers at some sleep in the corner of one eye. "They ain't no tellin' what all's swimmin' around out here, Wayne. Might be one a them gigantic squids."

Something very wrong had happened. A collision of some kind. And everybody knew that collisions were not allowed in the United States Navy. Wayne sat up and started putting his clothes on. Henderson grabbed his flip-flops and stuck them on his feet. They hurried out to the passageway together.

29

Eric sat there in the kitchen while Mister Arthur shoveled the walk out-side and got comfortably tight again, on the cold and spicy Bloody Marys she'd fixed for him and then on some beer from the icebox, and then on screwdrivers that Miss Helen made while giggling and jiggling her perky boobs around. She'd gotten a tad towheaded and had put Dean Martin on her compact Bose CD player and Eric had decided that back in the day, Dude could damn sure wail. The front of her robe had come open and her gown was slit up the side and sometimes he caught a glimpse of her long and shapely thigh, the curve of her slick, muscled calf. She'd taken her house shoes off and including her feet she was as nice a woman as Eric had seen. The nice was coming off her like heat off his granddaddy's stovepipe.

He didn't know what the hell to do about her. She didn't have a bra on and it was hard not to stare. He liked Mister Arthur, and didn't want to have the kind of thoughts he was having about her, but they just kept coming, and he'd already imagined himself doing some things with her. It was hard not to. And all the time she was looking at him with a slight smile on her face that was hard to read. Was it an invitation?

If it was, invitation to what?

What about Mister Arthur?

How long would he shovel the walk?

Was he misreading the whole situation?

Was she drunk as shit?

Was she as drunk as she got last night?

Did she do this very often?

Did she drink too much?

If so, why?

Would she want to drink with him, maybe, some more sometime?

Would that lead to something?

How would he feel if it did?

How old was Mister Arthur?

How old was she?

Were they having some kind of problem besides the cat?

He smoked another couple of cigarettes with her. Finally he raised his wrist and looked at his watch. He didn't really want to go. Just felt like he had to, Mister Arthur out there shoveling the walk by himself in the snow and all. He was intruding on their time together probably.

"Boy, look at the time," he said. "I guess I ought to think about gettin' outa here. I got to sober up and get to work sometime."

Miss Helen had her legs crossed. She reached a hand out to him, and squeezed his briefly.

"I don't *want* you to go," she said. "You're fun." She looked down for a second before sipping from her glass. "Arthur's not fun sometimes, if you must know the truth."

He didn't know what to say to that. He didn't know what kind of perfume she was wearing but whatever kind it was would give you a hard-on. Jada Pinkett was sprawled on the floor, sleeping again. Snoring. Almost worse than his daddy. He wondered if he could call in sick. Naw, shit, not today, Jada Pinkett needed some dog food.

"Well, I got to get to work sometime," he said. "I ain't even sure what time. I always have to work till ten."

She raised her eyes.

"Why don't you call and see? The phone's right there."

"You don't care?"

"No, go right ahead. Maybe you don't have to go just yet."

She got up and moved clumsily over to the window when he stood up to go to the phone, her drink in her hand. She stood there looking out while he poked the numbers. It rang a few times and then Antwerp answered it. He hated to have to talk to Antwerp simply because Antwerp always managed to make him feel dumb and hickified and he just never had punched his stupid ass out yet, the job and all, big discount on the Purina.

"Uh, Antwerp, hey. This is Eric."

"I know who it is!" Antwerp shot back. "It's the guy who didn't clean the iguanas' cages and left 'em for me. Let me tell you, man, it's caked pretty hard. You're gonna have to shape up and start pulling your weight around here."

Eric said: "Look, asshole. All I need from you is what time I need to be in today."

"Sounds to me like you'd better sober up," Antwerp whined.

Eric could hear some parrots in the background and the sound of serious electric guitars booming through some bass-heavy speakers. Antwerp always turned his music up extremely loud if there were no customers in the store, which might have explained why so few came in when he was there, which was probably why he did it.

"Can you just look on the schedule for me?" Eric said.

"Hold on."

The phone was laid down on the other end and there was a bumping noise in his ear. He listened to the music. It wasn't heavy metal. It sounded like Slobberbone. He thought it was "I Can Tell Your Love Is Waning" and he started humming it standing there. He sipped on his screwdriver. Miss Helen turned from the window. Her robe was fully open now and her gown was made of some thin material and he could see her nipples pushing against the fabric and the shape and size of her breasts. There was nothing left to the imagination. There was just a piece of cloth between them. He heard the phone being picked back up.

"You're supposed to relieve me at two and keep it open until ten. Plus you're supposed to sweep up and feed all the birds. And the gerbils. I've already fed the puppies and the lizards."

Then Miss Helen moved closer to him. She said almost soundlessly: "I don't *want* you to go."

"Okay," Eric mumbled into the phone, and heard Antwerp start with a question, but he put the phone back on the hook. She was standing right in front of him and he could see into her eyes and there was something scary deep in there and he could smell that maddening perfume. He was wondering if maybe she wanted him to kiss her. But what if he tried to kiss her and she didn't really want him to? What if he didn't kiss her and she wanted him to?

Eric in the midst of his fear/lust/confusion heard Mister Arthur scuffing the snow off his galoshes out front, and drew back from her, and there was sudden sadness on her face. Then it turned to anger, he supposed toward Mister Arthur. She pulled her robe around herself and grabbed her drink and hurried out and went back up the stairs. He was breathing hard, and standing there in the kitchen alone he wondered if Mister Arthur would be able to smell her perfume on him when he came in because it smelled to him like he was standing in a dizzying cloud of it, where she had been, like an animal that had left its track.

30

Domino, cruising in the dark, listened to "White Freight Liner Blues" while he was wearing the earphones and thought it was pretty kickass, and he ate one of the dead cop's fresh-fried bologna on whites with mayonnaise. It felt strange to be eating a dead man's supper, but he was hungry and upset and trying to calm down. This was all Hamburger's fault. Domino had moved the cruiser and hidden it about a half mile down the road and then jogged back to the reefer truck and loaded the whitetail. He was trying to reassure himself that everything was going to be all right. That nothing had changed. There was no reason to change his plans. He *couldn't* change his plans. He had to drop off the weed and get the money whether he dropped off the lion meat or not. He was going to go on with his routine, drive on up to Oxford, hit C&M Package across from the hospital, get a pint of bourbon, hit Pizza Den on University Avenue for maybe a whole muffaletta instead of a roast beef with gravy and a big bag of chips and go right on down the street to the Ole Miss Motel and check in. The whitetail was in the back and would stay good and cold in there overnight. He knew he needed to gut it sometime. Pretty soon. He had the knife. He could always do that after he dropped the weed off. Tomorrow. Tomorrow would be a better day. Tonight he could talk to the Pakistani man when he checked in and then lie in the slightly seedy Ole Miss Motel and eat his sandwich and drink his bourbon and watch some nature shows on the television with the volume turned up and try not to think about what he had done. It had taken him a long time to stop think-ing about what he had done to Doreen, not that he ever actually had stopped, but it had taken him a long time to get to the place where he didn't just think about it constantly while he was chopping cot-ton or picking it down at Parchman. He knew this thing was going to be the same way. But at least tonight he'd be in the motel, and he'd have the bourbon, and he could drink it until he was drunk, and then he could sleep. Tomorrow would be a better day. And each day after that it would get dimmer in his mind. Or at least he hoped it would. He didn't want to let himself think about whether the guy had a family or not. He hadn't been wearing a wedding ring. But that didn't mean he didn't have a family. He must have had some-body. Out there in the world somewhere there was probably some-body who would miss him. Maybe even cry over him. He'd wished a million times that he'd had somebody who would have cried over him, instead of leaving him in a fucking garbage can in Tupelo. And who was that in the *bag*? Why was somebody *in* a bag?

He finished the sandwich and balled up the zip-lock thing it had been in and threw it out the window. When he rolled the window up, the red temperature light was on in the dash.

Oh shit.

He took the earphones off his ears and his foot off the gas and slowed down. The red light didn't go off. It stayed on. He didn't understand it. He'd driven this same truck down this same road plenty of times, all up and down I-55, out to Como a million times delivering steaks, all over Memphis delivering meat, and it had never once gotten hot on him. It wasn't even that old. It couldn't be over two or three years old. The reefer box and the refrigeration unit were used, but the truck chassis and engine were pretty new. So why was it hot?

He was going to have to shut it off. That was all there was to it. If he didn't stop and shut it off, it would ruin the engine. Lock it up. If it ruined the engine, he wouldn't be able to drive it anywhere. He'd be stuck.

How far had he come? Five miles? Ten? He'd started eating the sandwich as soon as he'd left. And how long had that taken? Five minutes? How far could you travel in five minutes? Not far enough. Not nearly far enough away from what he'd left behind him.

Shit. Was he around any houses? He didn't see any right at the moment. He was going very slow now. There were just some fields where it looked like cotton had been picked. There was what looked like a junked school bus on the side of the road. There was a broken-down house with brown wilted kudzu all over it that the frost had killed. There was a cotton gin down here somewhere but he didn't think he was close to it yet. He thought there might be some houses around it. Somebody might have a phone. But who was he going to call?

Whatever he did he couldn't keep going. He was going to have to shut the truck off. Pretty soon. Before it cracked a head or something. If he cracked the head, he'd have to call a wrecker. And the wrecker would have to tow it to a shop. And the truck wouldn't be running. And all that stuff in the back would start to thaw out after ten or twelve hours. And if it thawed out and stayed thawed out long enough, it would start stinking. And that pound of weed was back there. And it would be a big stinking melted mess of meat. And the whitetail was back there. And all that might look kind of funny to somebody in town. It might look funny to some shop mechanic. Who might call the game warden. Who might poke around in there and decide it was too much for him and call the city police.

He stopped. He didn't have any choice. The light was burning bright: HOT. And now steam was coming up from the hood.

Son of a bitch. He was right on the highway. He started up again, looking for someplace to at least get it off the road. There was a green sign up there. Maybe there was a side road there. He knew it was getting hotter and hotter. It hit him then. They were going to find out he'd killed that cop, was what was going to happen. Either that or catch him with the weed. Then they were going to send him back to the penitentiary. He was going to be back in prison. Maybe even on death row this time.

No he wasn't. He was going to get out of this shit someway. He wasn't going back to that place. He sped up a little. The green sign got closer. The green sign said PAPA JOHNNY ROAD. He didn't have any choice. He swung onto the dirt road, went around a curve behind some trees, and pulled to the edge of it, off on the left, and killed the motor. Then the lights.

The motor was making a horrible noise. Even with his bad ear, he could hear it just fine. It was rattling and he could dimly hear steam hissing and now it was just boiling out all over the hood.

Now he was really scared. The motor was knocking like hell and something sounded like it was frying. He opened the door. The interior light came on and he reached down for the black rubber-coated flashlight, one of those six-cell things that would sit flat on the floor without rolling around. He reached under the steering wheel on the left and pulled the hood latch.

He got out and went around to the front. He turned the flashlight on. That's when he saw the broken piece of whitetail horn that was sticking into the radiator. If his hearing hadn't been so bad and Perk's car hadn't been so loud, he probably would have heard the radiator hissing a lot sooner. But. The pimply prison guard had taken care of that for him a long time before. Kind of like a preordained thing or a snowball effect when you considered all the elements over the years.

31

It was cold where Perk and what was left of Frankie lay in the dark and the snowy woods. No cars passed on the road and it was late now. Snow drifted down from the black limbs above in silent dropping and piled up and became deeper and began to cover up Perk's face, which was on its side and surprised with one open blue staring eye, and settled in his hair, even melted a little on the neck of his cooling body, but not much longer. The temperature was steadily falling and falling, dropping toward zero, rare cold for this country of snakes and cows and flathead catfish.

Except for the wind, it was very quiet.

In the silent dark, the trunks of the trees stood somehow unclear against the growing white carpet, which itself had no light and showed itself only because it was white. Something moved out there at a distance, out beyond the dead trees slanted among their living brothers, out behind an old rusted fence. The first coy-dog drifted out of the woods and lifted its nose high. A mongrel mix born in a culvert. Like a shark it would eat anything. Its muzzle threaded the air and moved until it found the fresh scent of blood and locked on it and then it began to walk forward. Behind it others slinked, quiet shapes threading their way among the silent trunks and fallen logs, the dark vines, over the dead grass beneath everything that lay waiting for the promise of spring.

32

The road was cold and deserted, winter locked in. Domino had been walking and walking and nobody at all had come along. He'd stayed next to the truck for a long time, thinking that somebody might come along, that maybe somebody who lived down Papa Johnny Road would turn in going home and stop to see if he needed any help, and the only thing he'd known to try if that happened was to maybe ask if he could get a ride up to their house with them and see if they had a phone book and try to find a shop somewhere that had twenty-four-hour towing service and repair service and maybe get the truck towed into town and try to get the radiator fixed tonight. Other than that he didn't know what to do. He didn't feel like he could just leave the truck with the weed in it. He didn't want to take a chance on taking out all the boxes just to get to the one that had the weed in it with the truck still so close to where he'd killed the cop and left the bag. He was nervous about his out-of-state tag because he knew how cops were about out-of-state tags. He was torn between staying with the truck and getting away from it.

But nobody had ever come along. So he'd started walking. He'd walked and walked and walked and now his feet were hurting and his hips were hurting and the boots he had weren't the best ones for walking. They were made more for keeping your toes warm. They were doing okay with that.

He should have gone straight. That's what he should have done. That's exactly what they'd told him to do when they'd let him out. The warden had actually been a pretty nice guy, and had developed somewhat of a fondness for Domino, and he'd had a short talk with him on the day he'd been released.

"Go straight, kid," he'd said, even though Domino wasn't a kid, the warden sitting kicked back in his chair with his ostrich-skin cowboy boots up on his desk. And Domino had assured him that he would. Now look where he was.

He had the gun hidden inside his pants and the knife was still inside his shirt. He'd thrown the Walkman and the CDs into a bunch of privet bushes. The road curved a lot and he'd already gone by the gin. It was deserted, no pickups parked out there, no lights that would indicate somebody working late inside.

He thought he'd been walking for at least an hour. Maybe over an hour. He'd taken one of the Schlitz tallboys with him, but it had been gone a long time. He wished now that he'd stuck another one in his pocket.

The more he walked, the more he thought it might be a bad idea to try to find a towing service or a repair service. What if he succeeded in getting it towed to town, but then couldn't find a place that did overnight repairs? The stuff would thaw out if the truck sat there long enough without getting cranked up. He'd still have the same problem. What he needed was another vehicle. It didn't even have to be a refrigerated one. If he could just get his hands on a vehicle, he could drive it back to the truck, turn the headlights on the reefer box, and pull out enough boxes to find the one that had the weed in it. Then what he could do was just drive the weed box on over to the empty house tomorrow and drop it off. Since he'd already made the phone call, they were expecting it, and the money would be there. The lion meat would all be ruined, but Mr. Hamburger would just have to understand that accidents sometimes happened. And what the hell was Hamburger going to say crossways to him now anyway? The whitetail would ruin, too, sure, but fuck that now. At least he wouldn't get caught with the weed, close to a dead cop. And somebody dismembered in a garbage bag.

But where was he going to get a vehicle? Even if somebody came along, what was he going to do, hijack somebody? If he did hijack somebody, what was he going to do with the person after he got through with the vehicle? Kill him? Kill her? What if there were children? Where exactly was he going to stop?

But he didn't have time to think about that for long, because by the time his good ear picked up the sound of something coming up behind him, he was already beginning to see the road getting lit up in front of him.

What if it was another cop? He had a dead cop's gun on him and a bloody knife inside his shirt. He was down here all alone. If it was a cop, he might not have any choice but to shoot him. And then where would he be? Not in a different boat.

But it wasn't a cop car that slowed behind him and pulled alongside him. It was a blue Dodge minivan with one headlight out, and Domino raised his hand and waved as it stopped. He couldn't see inside it. He couldn't tell who was driving it. He didn't know if it was a man or a woman, or an older person or a teenager. He wasn't going to know who it was until he opened the door, and he wasn't going to know what to do until he opened the door, whether to come on out with the gun or not.

But he had to do something. His hand reached out for the door handle. His fingers closed around it. He pushed the button. He pulled the gun out of his pants and raised it. When he opened the door, the guy already had his hands raised. He was wearing a coat and a sweater and glasses and what looked like a homemade muffler. He had wide eyes. He also had long pale fingers and wild curly hair.

"Shit! Don't shoot!" he said. He looked like he might be an intellectual from all the books piled up on the dash and the seat.

33

Merlot didn't like guns and thought there were way too many of them in America, so by the time he saw this one, pointed at him, and being stoned, it was too late to do anything but put his hands up and say: "Shit! Don't shoot!"

The man holding the gun looked awful. He looked like a butcher with that bloody apron. Merlot was trying not to shake and let the guy see it. But he was pretty outraged, too. He didn't want to put up with this bullshit. He put up with enough bullshit at the university. And he got paid for that. Twice a month. With health insurance. And a credit union.

"Don't try anything funny," the guy said. He knocked some books off the seat and down on the floorboard, and Merlot saw immedi-ately with even more outrage that he was one of those people with no regard for *your* stuff.

He couldn't help saying: "Hey, man, I paid a lot of money for those books."

The guy got in and closed the door. He was stepping all over the books. The guy pointed the gun at Merlot. Little black hole. Right in his face. Some death lay in there, waiting to come out.

"Move this thing on down the road," he said.

"Where to?" Merlot said, since the little black hole was scary.

"You gonna have to speak up," the guy said. "Just go," the guy said, and poked him with the gun, on his arm, hard, so hard it hurt.

"Hey, man, that *hurts!*" Merlot said, pretty loud. He had a roach in his pocket. He was just riding around. Taking a break from grad-ing papers. Bored out of his mind. Worried as always about Candy. What did he stop for? Just because the guy looked like he needed a ride. And where the hell were the cops when you needed them?

"Hurt you worse you don't move your ass."

Merlot did like he said. He tried to watch the road and tried to cut his eyes sideways to get a look at the guy, but the guy said: "Don't watch me, watch the road."

Merlot wondered what kind of gun it was. How did he know it was a real gun? Merlot didn't know anything about guns other than the fact that he was afraid of them, but somehow it didn't look like a real gun. It didn't look like any gun he'd seen in TV shows or movies. What if the guy was just pulling his leg? What if it was a water pistol? Or a starting pistol? He raised his voice again.

"Mind telling me what kind of gun that is?"

The guy looked at the gun, then back up at Merlot.

"Asshole, it'll shoot your ass is all I know. You got a light?"

"A *light?*"

"Push in your cigarette lighter there for me. You know you got a headlight out?"

"Yeah, yeah, I know it." He'd been meaning to get the damn

thing fixed but he'd been so busy getting ready for Christmas break that he just hadn't had time. And Candy getting worse every day. Now this shit.

Merlot was going about twenty and pushed the lighter in. They didn't speak while it was getting ready to pop out. The radio was turned low, but Merlot could hear the voice of a man speaking about pills for your nerves in these uncertain times. What if he slammed on the brakes and jumped him?

The lighter popped out and Merlot reached for it, but the guy beat him to it. Merlot looked at him. He had a big fat smelly cigar in his mouth and he was holding the red, glowing lighter up to it. Some smoke started coiling from the end. Merlot could really smell it. It smelled horrible. It reminded him of moldy couches he'd sat on as a child and deserted theater lobbies and some other things he'd just as soon not have to think about right now.

"And speed up," the guy said.

Merlot sped up. To about thirty. Stoned, that was plenty fast enough. He was holding the wheel with both hands when he went around the curves.

"Is this a carjacking?" Merlot said loudly. "Is this what this is?"

"Put whatever label on it you need to," the guy said. "And you're gonna have to turn the heat up a little. Cold as a polar bear's butthole."

"What do you expect? It's winter. It's deer season. People are out in the woods in flannel coats and shit."

Merlot reached and pushed the lever over one more notch, which put it on medium. The guy rolled the window down just a little after first pushing the lock and unlock buttons and making all the doors click several times, until Merlot said: "The one in front," and wanted to add, "Dipshit," but didn't, and the guy found the right button.

Merlot wondered if he should turn the radio up. He wondered if the police were looking for this guy. He had to be a desperate guy if he was going around carjacking innocent people like him. If he was desperate, then why was he desperate? He must have done something pretty bad. He might be an escaped convict who'd broken out of jail somewhere. There might be a big search going on for him right now. And here was something else to think about while he wasn't doing anything but driving this asshole around:

What if they were looking for the guy and had roadblocks set up and he had to blast through one at gunpoint in the minivan? Why hell, there'd be a hail of bullets, wouldn't there? What if it was like *Bonnie and Clyde?* They'd get cut to bloody ribbons like Warren Beatty and Faye Dunaway, wouldn't they?

"How much gas you got?" the guy said.

"Almost a full tank," Merlot said. "I just gassed it up yesterday." He waited a moment. "It dropped a dime, so I went ahead."

He waited again, but the guy didn't say anything. Maybe he didn't hear him. He was busy smoking his cigar. Merlot could watch him from the corners of his eyes. He could keep his eyes mostly on the road but kind of lose focus and let them slide to the right just a bit and he did that some more until the guy said: "Keep your eyes on the road."

The guy seemed to be really enjoying his cigar. He was wreathed in smoke, leaning back in the seat, watching the farms and woods and fences and fields pass, sometimes a few dim, yellow lights. Merlot's daddy had smoked the stinkingest cigars he'd ever smelled in his whole life. And this guy's was almost as bad.

But if he *was* an escaped convict, what had he done to get put in in the first place? That was the thing Merlot wanted to know since he liked to question everything objectively. Was he a simple thief or was he a serial killer? Had he done some computer crime or had he molested some schoolchildren? Had he ever killed anybody before? In other words, would he use that gun he was holding if it was real? Was he capable of it? Did he have the guts it took to pull the trigger? And was it even loaded? How did he know it was? It was also possible that the guy might have another hidden weapon on him. Like a knife. Maybe even two. Mightn't a butcher?

A cop car passed them casually and went over a hill. But in a val-

ley three minutes later they met it coming right back with its lights
on dim, and when it came alongside them, Merlot could see the star
on the side and as soon as Merlot could see it in his side mirror he
could see that it had hit its brakes and was angling to the opposite
side of the road. It looked like it was going to turn around. Oh yeah.
It was definitely turning around. He was going to get stopped for that
headlight being out. The cop had seen it in his rearview mirror when
he passed. He was surprised it hadn't happened before when he was
riding around. Now some new shit was going to hit the fan. Now
they'd see how bad Mr. Gun-Toting Antisocial Bully Butcher here
would be against forces of good who were also armed with guns.

So, should he say anything? Huh? Should he say anything?

What if saying something was worse? What if there were bullets
flying? What if the guy killed the cop? What if the cop accidentally
killed him, Merlot? Hell, bullets got to flying, innocent people got
shot.

So should he say something? He decided he should.

"That cop's turning around," he said.

"Mother . . . *fucker*," the guy said in a calm but incredibly pissed-
off way, and Merlot could see the cop car backing quickly from the
other side of the road, and the blue lights came on before it even got
fully turned around. The guy found the ashtray and put the cigar out.

"He's pulling me over," Merlot said. "I'll have to pull over."

"No. Don't pull over."

"What? What do you mean?"

"I mean don't pull over. Keep going."

"But what if he pulls up alongside me?"

"Keep going."

"What if he tries to shoot my tires out?"

"Keep going."

By now the cop car was right on his tail and there was no mistaking it, the cop wanted him to pull over. It was an effort of will to
keep his foot off the brake, but he was very conscious of the gun
pointed at him.

The guy said: "If you pull over, I'll shoot you."

That made Merlot pretty indignant.

"So you've got it all figured out, have you? What if he tries to ram us or something?"

"Anybody ever tell you you got a big mouth?"

"Not since my old man died."

The siren came on in the cop car behind them. Then in a straight stretch of road the cop car pulled up beside him and kept pace. A voice came over a loudspeaker: "Pull over now, sir! Pull over right now!"

"What am I gonna do?" Merlot said.

"Keep going."

"It's a cop! I'm supposed to stop!"

"Keep going."

Just then the interior light came on in the cop car, and Merlot could see that it wasn't a man driving the cop car. It was a woman, a black woman with a medium 'Fro, in a blue uniform, and she had the mike up to her mouth. He could see even from there that she was very well endowed, about like Dolly Parton was endowed.

"Pull it over!" the voice said. It was a nice voice but really loud. She was running right beside him and Merlot could have almost looked right into her eyes if he had taken them off the road for a few seconds, but he couldn't. He tried to give her a helpless look, but he knew she wasn't getting it. The blue lights were flashing everywhere. They lit up a frozen rabbit. They lit up a dead and frosty-tailed mule that somebody had evidently just *left* on the side of the road for the road guys to pick up.

"Speed up," the guy said.

"Speed up? She's right beside us."

"She?"

"It's a female cop. I can see her."

"Oh yeah?" the guy said. "Lemme see."

He leaned over and Merlot caught a whiff of his breath and knew it had been quite a while since this guy had bothered to floss. Whoa.

He bet he didn't have a steady girlfriend. Neither did Merlot. Candy being the way she was, it was hard to have a regular girlfriend. Or even one he could bring over, invite to stay for dinner, attempt to hump on the couch afterward.

"Roll your window down," the guy said.

"This is the last time I'm telling you," the voice over the loud-speaker said, pretty loudly.

Merlot pushed the button for the window, uneasy doing it, wondering why the guy wanted it down as it started coming down. But before he could think for very long about it, the guy leaned over and stuck the gun out and pulled the trigger and a window on the passenger's side of the cruiser shattered and the cruiser swayed, squealed its tires, slid sideways, and stopped.

Merlot could see it in his side mirror, receding, sitting there, blue lights going, siren still screaming, the interior light still on, and a glimpse of the woman cop, but there was just that glimpse, and then the guy told him to roll the window back up.

Merlot did what he was told, but he was sick, sick sick sick. Oh he was sick! *What'd you roll the window down for? Dumb-ass!*

34

"Oh shit!" Lenny screamed. He was lying on his back on the bed. "Oh God! Oh my God!"

Anjalee raised her head and smiled a wicked smile at him, put one finger to her lips, and swung her hair back from her face briefly before lowering it again. He put another pillow behind his head.

Later they lay back on satin sheets in the plush Peabody suite that was a hell of a lot nicer than any room Frankie had ever put her in, eating nachos with melted cheese poured over them and shrimp cocktails and crackers and for her a tossed salad with pepperoni and chopped-up bits of provolone. He'd ordered up a bottle of Dom and two glasses. He didn't watch any sports and she seemed pleased with that. It turned out they both liked Larry King, but he didn't have anybody on worth a shit that night. CNN had taped live coverage of some crooks in the stock market getting arrested in New York and people yelling at them. It turned out that Anjalee was a long-time *Zorro* fan just because of Guy Williams, so they watched him and Don Diego and Sergeant Garcia and then they watched a Lucy show on *Nick at Nite,* the one where she was working on the candy factory assembly line and had to cram a bunch of it in her mouth when it got to going way too fast for her to keep up with it.

They got food all over the nice bed. They did it again, slowly, carefully, even lovingly. They kissed tenderly. He wondered how much she was going to charge him. He wondered if it would be more or less than what she had charged Frankie, the dumb son of a bitch. He was a hamburger by now. Or a dogburger.

Later they took showers and got dressed and went out. He had a driver for his car, a man in a chauffeur's uniform who didn't say a word, only drove them through Memphis and down I-55 to the exit at Senatobia where he turned off and headed for the casinos at Tunica, the bright lights of the little Vegas in the Mississippi Delta. Where even the legendary Merle had played. And he decided something on the way down. He decided he wasn't going to say shit about what was probably left of Frankie.

35

"Well I don't give a fuck what you think!" Helen yelled through the locked door. Then she threw some lipstick and gloss at it, lotions, creams, emollients.

36

They had stopped engines and it was hard to believe until the NBC and ABC news crews' helicopters started arriving and landing on the flight deck, along with some Coast Guard people, and then pretty soon they were on the news itself. Wayne saw it with Henderson in the TV room, which was almost deserted, since a lot of the crew who were off duty were up on deck trying to see what was going on, and Admiral Zumo was on his way out to have a personal peek they said.

Something must have gone wrong. Somebody must have said something they shouldn't have said or maybe when they said it somebody else misunderstood what they'd just said and maybe that was how an *NBC News* cameraman wound up leaning out over the edge of the flight deck unseen behind a crowd of enlisted men who just happened to be standing there with a couple of third-class petty officers holding on to his belt while he was taking unauthorized video film of the whale that had been struck by the propeller but not killed. Wallowing out there in the rolling waves, blood staining the water around it, and Wayne standing there watching it knew that America would see the blood and the whale suffering and that a great outcry would come. Hell yes. They were mammals, not fish. They bore their young alive. They didn't bother anybody. People had soft spots in their hearts for them and would spend two days in the hot sun trying to get them back into deep water whenever they found them run aground in a pod at Cape Cod.

There were all kinds of rumors floating around the ship. Some said the prop was broken, and that they were stranded. Some said the whale had a baby, and that the baby was out there crying and swimming around its dying mother, although nothing like that had appeared on the TV screen just yet, but being in the military, they knew how the government could suppress information, at almost any time, and for almost any reason, say, something that might be sensitive, like secretly invading another country, and if there was indeed a baby whale swimming around and crying because its dying mother had been struck by an aircraft carrier from the U.S. Navy, they'd damn well want to suppress it from the general public until they could decide what to do. Shit. There was no telling how long it took to decide what to do about them dead little green men they found crashed in Roswell back in '47, is what Henderson said.

It was rumored that Peter Jennings was on the ship. It was rumored that Prince was on the ship. It was rumored that the captain had been on the line with the President, that the President was waiting for developments while playing a little golf and catching Billy Joe Shaver at the Continental Club in Austin, that something had gone wrong and some film had been released that shouldn't have been. The President didn't appear to be pissed yet.

Most everybody was confined belowdecks. They could go to the galley and eat, they could work or sleep or study, but they could not go up.

Things got pretty boring pretty quickly. Wayne and Henderson played cards, watched a movie, ate some sandwiches, played some dominoes, heard some more rumors, took a nap.

Then when they were back in the TV room to catch Steve Earle and Robert Cray on *Sessions at West 54th*, the captain gave them the straight scoop over the intercom, at 2230. Yes, it was true that the ship had hit a blue whale normally not seen in these waters, a whale that may have been sick and running a fever and whose sonar might have been subsequently impaired. Yes, the ship's propeller had severely injured it, quite possibly critically. Yes, there was a whale calf involved, about a twenty-two-footer. The ship was stopped for an investigation, which was SOP for any collision, and since they were only three days out they would probably be going back to some port, but right now they were about to be involved with some civilians in a rescue effort for the calf. That was all. The intercom went off but then there was a long whining fuzzy buzz with enough feedback to where they thought maybe Neil Young was onboard with his electric guitar and wahwah pedal, about to come over the loudspeakers with "Mother Earth."

"Sheeeit, Wayne," Henderson said, turning back to the television and reaching into a big bag for some more Fritos. "We ain't never gonna get to the Sea of Arabia messin' with this whale shit."

37

Merlot went nuts from fear when the guy tried to light his cigar again. Sick! The guy took his eyes off him for just a few seconds to fumble around at the bottom of the dash for the lighter, and in that small window of opportunity, thinking about what the butcher guy might have done to the innocent lady cop, and what he might do to him later, he jammed both feet on the brakes, grabbed the gun, and elbowed the guy in the teeth as hard as he could. Sick! And since grabbing the gun scared the living shit out of him, and was like something he had never done before in his whole life, and since he was seized by adrenaline and given extra-normal strength from those two weird little organs coming off the top of his kidneys, he held the gun with one hand while it fired one round through the windshield post *BOOM!* and another one through the windshield, which spiderwebbed *BLAM!*, and another one right through his new Pioneer CD player with Bass Booster *BAM!* and caught the guy by the thick hair on the back of his head that was sticking out from under the knitted cap with the other hand, and slammed his face and the cigar into the windshield. It went *KaPLOW!*, and some books fell off the dash, and the guy kind of rolled his eyes, then crossed his eyes, but Merlot was still plenty revved up on the adrenaline rush, so he slammed his face again, not even noticing that the van had stopped by then, or that the cigar was getting smashed all over the place, or that books were getting scattered everywhere, and just kept on slamming his head kind of hysterically and heaving since he was still so scared.

The door jerked open. There was a blinding light in his eyes.

"Don't move!"

Merlot didn't move. The voice sounded familiar.

"Hands in the air!"

It sounded like the lady cop. But the light was so bright he couldn't see. Son of a bitch! It was like the landing-gear light on one of those 767s! Coming straight in for you! The problem was that his left hand was still holding the gun and his right hand was holding the guy by the back of the head and he didn't want to drop the gun and maybe risk it going off or drop the guy and maybe have him come back to life. Or her.

"I can't put my hands up," he said.

"Why not?" the voice said. He knew it was the lady cop now but he couldn't see her. He felt like he was getting permanent eyeball damage.

"This guy tried to carjack me," he said. "Are you all right?"

The light in his eyes was turned off. He had to blink a few times. He saw her then. It wasn't a 'Fro after all. She had rounded black hair that was sheened and formed around her face and the sides of her head like a bowling ball. She had large wet doe eyes and full smoochy-looking lips and a broad but graceful nose. She was about ten pounds overweight and she was about the sexiest thing he had ever seen. And she was locked and loaded on him over the muzzle of a big revolver, both her hands steady on the grip. Then he noticed that the very tip of the muzzle, the part where the front sight was mounted, was wavering the tiniest bit. Death lay waiting in that little black hole, too.

"I can't turn loose," Merlot said.

She lowered the gun and stepped closer. She grabbed her flashlight again from her pocket and shone the beam on the guy.

"He carjacked me," Merlot said again. "He pulled this gun on me when I pulled over."

She didn't say anything. Merlot kept looking at her and holding the gun with one hand and the guy's hair with the other. He thought he was out.

"I think he's out," Merlot said. "I slammed his face a few times. You sure you're all right?"

"Give me the gun," she said. "Is the safety off?"

"I don't know," Merlot said. "Has it got a safety? I don't know anything about guns except I'm scared of them."

She stood there for a moment and seemed to be trying to make up her mind. Then she put the flashlight and the gun away.

"I'm not the bad guy here, ma'am. I'm just making a citizen's arrest."

"Who are you?"

"My name's Merlot Jones," Merlot said. "I teach out at Ole Miss."

"All right. Give me the gun. Be careful with it."

"Yes, ma'am." Merlot turned loose of the guy's hair and the guy's head slumped over on him. His nose was bleeding and some of the skin was busted over one of his eyes and he had bits of smashed tobacco all over his mouth and chin and the blood was getting on his clothes.

He pulled the guy's limp fingers out of the gun and it didn't go off. Thank God. He was trying to be really careful with it. He was pretty scared just holding it and his hands were shaking now from thinking about what he'd just done.

"My hands are shaking," he said. "Can't help it."

"I can see that," she said. "Be careful. Here."

He handed it to her with it pointing away from her and she took it. She expertly jacked it open and ejected the live shell, where it spun in a bright brass arc and clattered to the road and rolled and then stopped. She pulled something from the handle and stuck it in her pocket, and put the gun in her other pocket. She seemed to know a lot about guns.

"I'm coming around to the other side," she said. "Don't move."

"I'm not going anywhere."

He watched her go in front of the windshield and thought she could easily be a model for one of those large-ladies' lingerie catalogs like Erma or whatever her name was, the kind he liked to look at. He liked some meat on a woman's bones. A big woman was extra warmth in the winter.

The other door opened. She didn't look at him. She took hold of the guy who was bleeding, and pulled him up, and looked into his face.

"You grabbed the gun and did this, too?"

"Yes, ma'am."

"You know you got a headlight out?"

Merlot nodded, looking into her eyes, which seemed to be getting bigger the more he looked, knowing he'd yearned for something all his life, and knowing now that it was her face. He suddenly had a crazy thought. He wondered if maybe she'd like to go home with him sometime and meet Candy.

38

There was a huge sycamore in Mr. Hamburger's fenced-in backyard and in it was a nest that had been painstakingly built from leaves over a period of two months by an old white-nosed fox squirrel that lived in the neighborhood and scampered across power lines and traveled from yard to yard and raised some cute babies once in a while. The nest was about three feet out and two feet down from the edge of the roof, and Miss Muffett had seen the mama squirrel on the roof a number of times, but it had never gotten into the attic to tear up newspapers or race around up there on the insulation or gnaw the insulation off the electrical wires the way squirrels some-times did as far as she knew, so she was cool with it, long as it didn't bother her, she wasn't going to bother it. But there was a little more to it than just that.

Miss Muffett actually liked the squirrel and even enjoyed feeding the squirrel and she would often put out nuts for it, sometimes Jiffy peanut butter on jar lids. It seemed to like crunchy best.

She walked out the back door in a real bad mood to feed the squirrel some pre-Christmas brazil nuts that were on sale and looked down and saw a small piece of rectangular glass lying in the yard and heard familiar yapping and looked up high in the tree and higher until she gasped and fainted dead away, toppled gently over into the deeply mulched flower beds, good thing no sharp bricks were poking up in a border like some folks have. Might have messed her *up*.

39

Arthur dozed off in the waiting room and had to be roused by a nurse, who took him back to an examining room. There was a long wait, but he finally got seen.

"Looks like a blood-flow problem to me," the doctor said in his office after the examination, leaning back in his rich leather chair, pouring a double shot of Stolichnaya over big square ice blocks in a crystal glass on his desk. He went ahead and lit up a Doral Light, too. The walls were paneled with good dark wood and there were pictures of his smiling grandchildren on them. One was riding a spotted pony while the doctor held the halter.

"What are you saying?" Arthur said.

"Jesus," the doctor said. "All I'm saying is all last week I was getting up at two A.M. to take a whiz after a couple of pops."

Arthur waited politely. He wondered what Helen was doing now.

"Because I'm old, too, you know?" the doctor said. He sipped his drink. An intercom on his desk said something garbled. He turned a knob and it quieted. He raised his tired old eyes over the glass and looked morosely across the desk.

"How much do you expect at your age without some help? You're not some young bull full of piss and vinegar, you know. You ever heard the term 'slowing down'? Or 'getting old'?"

"I still have desire," Arthur said. "So does Helen."

The doctor took such a large drink that he almost choked. He made a few *KAFF, KAFF* sounds, then cleared his throat, sucked in a lungful of smoke, blew it out.

"Whew. Don't we all," he said. "Don't we all. A hard penis is nothing but one that's full of blood, Arthur. And we have a blood-flow problem here. That's about as simply as I can explain it, being a doctor. Now, you don't want to go on Viagra because you say it makes you feel unmanly. You don't want to schedule your sex because you're uncomfortable with that. I can go with that, even if I don't accept it as valid. But my God. Patients, without the benefit of attending eight years of medical school, always know so much about themselves and their conditions that it continues to astound me daily."

"But . . . ?"

The doctor held up the cigarette hand, which trailed smoke.

"Will you let me finish? Please?"

Arthur sat quietly. Like a lamb before the slaughter.

"Now. I can fix you up with a good pump."

"A good pump."

"Yes."

"A good dick pump, you mean," Arthur said bitterly.

The doctor sighed. He set his glass down and picked up the phone and punched a number and waited for it to ring while he took quick furtive puffs off his smoke. He spoke into it. He lowered his head. He asked a question. He muttered some things into it that sounded like model numbers. He said Fine, fine, then Thank you, and hung up. Then he stood up.

"It's your lucky day, Arthur, we've got some in stock. You can pick it up and pay the girl out front. I take all major credit cards."

"How do I know that's what I want?" Arthur said.

"It's either this or Viagra or reconsider some type of surgery."

"No!" Arthur said.

"No need to get all hot about it," the doctor said.

"I'm not hot," Arthur said. "I'm just . . ." He stopped. "I don't know what I am anymore."

"You're a normal human male, Arthur. Who's getting up there a little in years. Who has a wife who's a good bit younger than him. You have to have some help. Why do you think they make these things? Because it's a common problem. That's your key word right there, 'common.' "

Arthur was afraid he was in for a lecture now. Once the doctor got on a roll, he could just keep on going. You didn't want him to get started on arteriosclerosis or the black plague.

"Okay. So it's common. But knowing that doesn't make me feel any better."

"Don't be bitter, Arthur. Now, I've got some company brochures here if you'd like to take one with you. Of course there'll be one in the packet explaining how to use the pump. It's pretty self-explanatory actually. You just stick it in and . . ."

Arthur thought about it for a few seconds.

"How much is this thing going to cost me anyway? I just paid fifty bucks to a kid to get a cat caught." He didn't mention the fifty bucks to the beautiful young stripper.

"To do a what what?" the doctor said.

"It's a long story. I'm just trying to do something to make Helen happy."

The doctor smirked then and took another drink and puffed on his cigarette some more.

"Arthur, you take this thing home and you'll make Helen happy, believe me. It's three or four hundred, plus tax."

The doctor waited. He seemed about to make a shooing gesture.

"I've got other patients today, Arthur. Do you want the brochure or not?"

"I guess so," Arthur said, and got out of his chair. The doctor reached into a pile of pamphlets that were scattered on the corner of his desk and handed one to him. There was a picture on the front of a white-haired couple riding horses on a beach. The picture was in color. Shallow waves were rolling in behind them. They looked slightly happy. The man seemed stoic and looked virile for his age. The woman looked like she might not be the most amazing fuck on the whole beach. They were wearing sweaters and jeans and they were barefoot, riding the horses, which were wearing saddles. To Arthur there was an unspoken yet grim message in the picture of some older people in trouble who were hiding it from the world but gamely trying to do something about it. He realized that they were like him. But not like Helen. She didn't fit into that picture. It seemed so awfully scary to him that he put the pamphlet in his pocket quickly.

"Let me know how it goes," the doctor said. He turned up his glass and winked at him, and Arthur booked for a fat man's ass on out of there.

40

Domino was in a holding cell in jail, where the female deputy sheriff had dropped him off and filled out forms while the intellectual-looking guy he'd tried to carjack sipped coffee in the lounge as he told the other police officers what had happened. Domino had heard and seen some of it. They made the guy he'd tried to carjack tell it several times and he told it exactly the same way each time and then they left him alone and told him to get himself some more coffee and that they had some fresh chocolate doughnuts, too, and that they were sorry about the bullet holes in his minivan, but that he'd have to leave it with them, and then after their investigation was complete, they'd get it towed to the shop for him and let him know when it was ready, and then after a while the guy he'd tried to carjack said he figured his insurance company would probably furnish him with another car since what happened was probably covered, and then he and the female deputy sheriff left together. All this happened after the crime scene investigation itself, out on the road at the scene of the interrupted carjacking, while Domino waited in the back of a warm patrol car handcuffed and bloody and sick with worry and hurting like shit with knots all over his head. They were holding Domino until they could figure out what all he'd done. They definitely had him for assault with a deadly weapon on a police officer and attempted carjacking, but so far Domino hadn't said anything. He was just keeping his mouth shut, just waiting for that one phone call he knew he was allowed. His head was scabbed up and swollen and they really hadn't given him the proper medical attention as of yet. He knew they'd have to sometime. Maybe he could escape then. Maybe he could just run. There wouldn't be a thing to lose by trying. If they found the cop. If they found the truck. If the meat thawed out. Yeah, he needed to make a call.

The only thing was, he didn't know who to call. He didn't know any lawyers. He didn't have any friends. He guessed he'd just wait and see what happened. It didn't look like there was anything else to do. It didn't look like he'd be able to escape from here. The thing he happened to be in at the moment looked like it would be pretty escape-proof unless you had some high-speed hacksaws or maybe an acetylene torch or Harry Houdini in there with you to give you some pointers.

They'd be out looking around in the country down there. They'd find that junky fucking cruiser. Maybe they already had.

There was a big cop in a suit out there, one who had come in later extremely pissed off and who'd been trying to get him to talk. Even now he was just sitting there sipping a Pepsi, watching him through the holding-cell bars. He looked like a mean motor scooter, too. And he was just staring at him.

Domino leaned back against the painted block wall. There was a bunk but it wasn't big enough to lie down on. He wasn't going to say anything. That was how people got in trouble. They talked. They signed things. They applied for credit instead of paying cash. He knew how the world worked. Or he was pretty sure he did. But who in the hell was that in the garbage bag?

The plainclothes cop got up. He walked slowly down the hall, toward the holding cell. Domino could hear his feet on the tiles. He stopped in front of the cell and stood there. Great big son of a bitch.

"Still don't want to talk?" He sipped some more of his Pepsi and belched.

Domino didn't say anything.

"You will," the cop said calmly. "You'll sing like a yeller canary gettin' his guts mashed out his asshole when I get done with you."

He took the last drink from his Pepsi, turned, walked back up the hall, dropped his can into the trash, and picked up a ring of keys from a desk.

He was kind of far away, but Domino could hear him fine. And he noticed then that he hadn't seen any other cops for a while. He hadn't noticed any of them leaving, but it seemed it was just the two of them there now. He wasn't sure at all how that had happened.

"You know why, you piece a shit?"

Domino didn't make a sound. Quiet as a mouse. Or a cat.

" 'Cause my name's Rico Perkins. And my little brother's name's Elwood. We cain't raise him on his radio, but he's got a gun *exactly* like the one we took off you. He's a constable. But I'll bet you already know that. 'Cause I think you done met him."

And he started walking closer. Domino didn't say anything. But he could see the family resemblance right away. This guy was taller, though.

41

Anjalee's hair was spread on a pillow and she lay on her belly with one nice leg bent and the other one straight, her eyes closed, her breathing regular and steady, her breasts flattened beneath her, half the sheet barely covering the simple naked beauty of her lovely ass.

Outside the room there were dim sounds in the hall, women talking, knocking on doors sometimes, vacuums running. Doors were opening and closing. The hall elevator sometimes *ching*ed.

Cars and buses and vans and trucks passed below in the streets, the noise of their horns and exhaust muffled by distance.

She turned onto her side and pulled some more of the satin sheet over her and held her thumb and forefinger an inch apart and in her sleep said very clearly: "That damn baloney was *that* thick."

42

Some neighbor must have heard the dog yapping up in the tree and called 911 while Miss Muffett was fainted out, because here came the Como Volunteer Fire Department from their station right across the street from the steak house. Sirens howling, lights flashing, red trucks with gold letters and hoses and ladders in the driveway, guys in turnouts drinking coffee in foam cups, guys wandering around the yard in black boots with yellow toes helping Miss Muffett up and talking on those portable radios. A few of them had made the emergency run to the house six months earlier to extricate bloody Mr. Hamburger from the bloody posthole-digger incident in the backyard that day. But there was a different tactical problem for them now. The little dog was about fifty feet up. Or maybe sixty. It was a big tree. He was up there checking out the birds, like an ornithologist.

CVFD didn't own a one-hundred-foot aerial platform like Memphis or Oxford, but there was a fire-equipment dealer in Southaven named Shed Roberts who just happened to have one in his parking lot that was in the process of getting gold letters put on it before it got delivered to the Memphis Fire Department. Some of the Como firefighters sometimes played poker and drank whiskey with Shed or had steaks at the Como steak house with him on his company tab, and one of them had seen the ladder sitting there coming back from a strip club in Memphis the night before, and one of the firefighters told Miss Muffett that Shed was more than glad to drive it down once they called him just because he loved playing with the things, and would have had one in his yard to scrape his house and paint it and clean the leaves out of his rain gutters or even put Santa and some fake reindeer on the roof if he could have afforded it, since a good one ran about $645,000 plus tax and delivery from the factory up in Pennsylvania.

They maneuvered the bucket platform with two truckies riding in it through the branches of the sycamore, which was leafless since it was winter, which made it easier for them to get it close. One truckie clipped a safety line to his waist and opened a narrow gate in the bucket, and while his partner held on to the waistband of his smoked-up turnout pants, stepped out into the air, reached for the little dog, and got him.

A small clutch of neighbors had gathered, a few old folks, some kids in coats, also a television crew from WTVA-9 in Tupelo that had been cruising down I-55 and had followed the ladder in since Shed had been running the red lights and blowing the air horn just for the fun of it, and a weak cheer went up as the ladder started retracting down to its bed on the engine, which was parked in the driveway, really humming and roaring, making all kinds of racket.

The Tupelo TV folks wanted an interview, probably hoping they could get it on the news as a human-interest story that night, but

Miss Muffett didn't want her plastic leg to be on TV and she didn't want anybody to tell Mr. Hamburger that they'd seen his dog on TV because he'd jumped into a tree because she hadn't left him any water in his pan. She took the little dog and went inside and shut the door. Then she peeked out the curtain to see if they were still waiting. Hell yeah. Like a bunch of vultures.

43

Helen was sitting at the dressing table in her bedroom, putting on some makeup, fixing her hair, sipping on a drink. Arthur had given up trying to talk to her through the locked door but had yelled through it that he was going to call the doctor right now and see if he could fit him in today but she didn't really care anymore. She was trying to apply her lipstick. If he hadn't had all that money, she never would have married him. It was a mistake and she could see that now. The horrible thing was that it had taken so long. She'd given him twenty years and she wasn't going to get those twenty years back. But what the hell had she been thinking twenty years ago? Nothing. Not about the future, that was for sure. Only about how easy life would be. No more waiting tables. No more taking care of a bunch of drunks in the Union bar every night. No more worrying about how you pay the light bill this month.

She was going out for a while and when she came in she'd just tell him the truth, which was that she'd made a mistake, and yeah, had married him because he was rich, but that there wasn't any need in compounding it by letting it go on any longer. She'd tell him she wanted a divorce, and that she wanted the Jag, and some money, and he could keep this house. A house was nothing. A house was just wood and wallpaper and you filled it up with deer heads and doilies. You could have one of them anywhere. Any mountain, any meadow. In Montana you could.

She'd go back home and start over. She'd invest her part of the money once she got it and live off it the same way he'd been doing all these years. She'd find a house in Montana or build one, one made from logs, with a sloped red roof and lots of glass and that would sit in the back of a field of yellow grass in the fall at the foot of a gray cliff that was two hundred feet high. Maybe find a man who could give her a baby. She wasn't too old. Forty wasn't too old. She'd seen in *People* magazine where Beverly D'Angelo had married Al Pacino and had given him twins and she was over forty. And her mother had a cousin in Idaho who raised potatoes with her husband and had a baby when she was forty-three. She'd read somewhere that some woman in India had delivered a healthy baby at the age of sixty-seven. So it wasn't impossible. She was going to tell him. It wasn't like she hadn't almost done it twenty times already. But last night had been the final straw. If he wasn't going to even try to get any help, if he couldn't even make love to her, if she didn't even have that, and had to find it with other men, and especially an asshole like Ken, then there wasn't any need in staying any longer.

Eric was supposed to get off at ten. But she thought she might pay him a visit before then. She checked her lipstick in the mirror and picked up the last of her drink and finished it. She'd slow down on her drinking for right now. She was going to the Peabody eventually, but she wasn't going to get drunk and fuck Ken again for sure. That was over. No doubt about it. Bet on it. She wasn't going to let the police get her again, either, because she was going to be careful. She didn't want to have to look at those dead babies on that table again. Who would?

44

Rico took Domino to the Oxford hospital in a car with a wire mesh barrier between the front and back seats. His hands were cuffed behind him and he got let out in the back parking lot where cars and pickups were sitting with frost and snow on them and where steam was coming from a pipe that ran up the side of the building. Stars stood high above. Some nurses were getting off duty and talking as they went to their vehicles. It was very cold.

Rico didn't say anything, just got him by the arm and took him in through the emergency-room entrance. The lights were bright inside. Domino stopped when Rico stopped and stood in the middle of the waiting room. A man with a bloody head was moaning in a padded chair while a woman held a bloody towel up to the side of his face. A black child with pigtails lay crying in another woman's lap, and Domino could see that her arm was broken, oddly bent. Deep and mournful sobs were coming out of her thick and moving lips, and gobbets of yellow snot from her nose. Some other people sat in what appeared to be trances and stared at a television playing the David Letterman show.

"You stand right here," Rico told him, and Domino did. Some Christmas wreaths were hung up on the walls. There was a coffeepot on a table and some foam cups were sitting next to it.

Rico went over to a low glass partition and a lady who was behind a desk. She lifted her face as he began talking. Domino didn't listen. All he wanted was one chance.

A security guard came through a door. An old guy. He had a uniform on, but he didn't have a gun, didn't even have a nightstick, and he looked a little sick himself. Maybe on the verge of admission. He walked through the waiting room and Domino turned his head and saw him go outside and pull a pack of cigarettes from his pocket and light one and stand there smoking, walking around, flicking his ashes, his breath blowing out in the cold air.

Rico came back.

"Go on and sit down," he said. "We gonna have to wait."

Domino looked around. There was a chair a few feet away. He eased down into it but he wasn't able to lean back very comfortably because of the handcuffs. Having his hands behind his back like that gave him bad memories of Doreen. He looked at the TV. Dave was talking to Alec Baldwin and they were laughing. Domino liked it when they threw watermelons off the top of a building. He wished they'd do that. Instead they broke for a commercial.

Domino sat there for a long time. Rico leaned against the wall but didn't take his eyes off him. The guy with the bloody head got called back. The child with the broken arm got called back. The security guard kept going in and out, smoking cigarettes, letting cold air in.

The guy he'd tried to carjack had busted his head pretty good, felt like. It kept throbbing. And the son of a bitch had fought back against a gun. He hadn't expected that. The orderly who finally came to get him was pushing a wheelchair and Rico came off the wall.

"He don't need no wheelchair, man," he said. "He can walk fine."

The orderly hesitated. He seemed to be looking for a place to put the chair.

"All right," he said, and bent over and folded the wheelchair together and slid it up against the wall.

"Get up," Rico said, and Domino stood up. The orderly went to a door and stood holding it open while Domino walked through it. Rico followed close behind.

The door closed after them and they were in a wide hall where gurneys stood and where a man at the far end was mopping. Somebody was screaming loudly in a room back there somewhere. They followed the orderly up the hall and turned in with him to a small scary examining room that smelled of rubbing alcohol and had one padded metal chair and a padded table with a piece of paper stretched over it. There were shelves and a cabinet at the back. Through an open door, Domino could see the back side of the emergency-room office and the woman Rico had been talking to. She was talking on the phone now and looking at some papers in front of her and trying like everybody else to ignore the screaming.

"Okay," the orderly said. "Get up here and sit down and let me get a look at you."

Domino did like he was told. It was a little difficult to get up on the table with his hands cuffed behind his back, but he managed it. Rico leaned against the open door to the hall. Domino could see a small gun hanging on his waist. The person in the room back there kept screaming.

The orderly took Domino's head in his hands and tilted his face back to the overhead light. He probed with his fingers here and there.

"That's a nasty cut he's got right here on his temple," he said. "I expect the doctor'll want to stitch that."

Rico didn't say anything. Domino kept quiet, too. And he wished whoever it was back there screaming would either shut the fuck up or die. He'd heard people scream like that while they were getting raped at Parchman. Or stabbed with screwdrivers. It made it hard to sleep for wondering if you might be next.

"I've got to go get a few things," the orderly said, and went through another open door behind him.

Domino just sat there. There was something buzzing somewhere.

"Me and you gonna take a little ride after they get through with you," Rico said. "We gonna ride out in the country and see what we can see."

Domino just kept quiet. He didn't like the look on this cop's face. He looked like he might kill you just for the fun of it.

The lady from the desk up front hung up the telephone and as soon as she did it rang again. She answered it and talked for a few seconds and then swiveled around in her chair.

"Officer Perkins?" she said. "There's a call for you."

Rico walked halfway across the room but he kept his eyes on Domino.

"I can't come in there right now, ma'am, I've got nobody to watch my prisoner."

"Well, let me see if I can stretch the cord that far," she said, and came on in the room with it. It just barely reached. Rico had to turn his back to her after he took it so that he could keep watching Domino.

Rico talked for a few moments, and Domino saw a sudden rage come over the cop's face.

"All right," he said, finally, and handed the phone back over his shoulder without looking at the lady. "Thank you, ma'am."

"You're welcome," she said, and looked frightened, and disappeared behind Rico.

Rico's face had turned a little white and he walked slowly over to Domino. He was clenching and unclenching his fists.

"They found my brother's car," he said in a low voice. "You better hope to God he's okay."

Just then the orderly came back in with a plastic tray of bandages and some medical tools. Domino didn't see any scissors in there.

"Okay," the orderly said. He looked at Rico and waited for him to move out of the way.

"You mind, Officer?" he said.

Rico moved out of the way but not very far. He was staring a hole in Domino. And Domino didn't even want to know what he was thinking.

The orderly had been working on him for only a few minutes when the doctor came in. He was a small black man with a short-clipped beard and he was wearing a blue uniform and some puffy paper covers over his tennis shoes. He did not look or sound like he was from around there. He looked and sounded like he was from someplace like Sudan or maybe Nigeria.

"I will take it from here," he said to the orderly. "How about checking on the lady in four?"

"Yes, sir," the orderly said, and left.

The doctor rooted around in the tray and pulled a few things out, then set them back in. He muttered something and left. Domino kept sitting on the table and trying not to look at Rico. The screaming went on and on.

"You better not have done nothin' wrong to my brother," Rico said.

"Fuck you and your asshole brother both," Domino told him, since he didn't like threats, especially with his hands cuffed or tied behind his back.

Rico had started over to him when the doctor walked back in with a pair of scissors. He stopped.

"What is this? This is a hospital."

"I know what the fuck it is," Rico said.

"Okay, swell," the doctor said. He came on over to Domino and set the scissors in the tray and looked at his head. Domino could feel his fingers touching him. They felt warm and reassuring.

"He has a pretty nasty cut here," the doctor said, to nobody in particular. Rico didn't answer. He was back leaning on the wall with his arms crossed.

"Can you lie down?" the doctor said to Domino.

"Not too good," he said. "Not with these handcuffs on."

The doctor turned to Rico.

"Can you take these handcuffs off this man while I stitch him?"

Rico thought it over for a few seconds. He frowned and shook his head.

"I'd rather not, Doctor," he said. "Can't you just do it with him sittin' there?"

"Well, yes I *could*," the doctor said, in a really smart-ass Sudanese or maybe Nigerian tone. "I could stick this needle in his eye if he jerks his head around, too."

Domino could see it happening before it happened. He saw the chair there by the wall. He saw how many steps he needed. The person in the back kept on screaming. It looked like it was getting on everybody's nerves.

"I really hate to, Doctor," Rico said over the screaming. "This man's dangerous."

"Do you want him treated?"

"Well, yes, I'm required by law to get him treated."

"Well. I can't do what I need to with him sitting up. I need to look at this eye. And he needs to be flat on his back for that."

Rico just stood there. The screaming went on and on, only high and weak now, like some strange new song. Maybe the drugs were kicking in.

"What, Officer, are you afraid he will run off?"

"I don't know what he may do. Or what all he has done yet. That's what I'm tryin' to find out. But I need him patched up tonight."

The little doctor let out a deep sigh. He turned his eyes for a moment toward the screaming in the back. Then he looked at Rico and spoke in a surprisingly gentle voice, full of logic and reason.

"Officer, we have got a lot of hurt people in here tonight. And we have got some more coming in just a few minutes from an auto accident on Highway 7. If I don't do this now, I may not get to do it for another two hours. Or maybe four. Do you want to wait that long?"

"I can't," Rico said. "I've got to go somewhere."

"Well, how about cooperating with me then?"

Rico moved very slowly. Reluctantly. He reached slowly for the handcuff keys that were in a pouch on his belt. He came over. He walked behind Domino and Domino could feel him holding on to the cuffs, could hear the tiny click of the key as it opened one cuff, then the other. When Rico walked back in front of him, he was holding the cuffs in one hand. He looked down for just a moment to put the cuffs in the leather holder on his waist and Domino grabbed the scissors from the plastic tray and stabbed the little doctor in the throat at the same time he came off the table and went for the chair. Rico almost stopped him. He was plenty big enough. He was strong enough. And he was almost fast enough. But not quite. The chair caught him across the face and blood flew and Domino tugged the gun loose from Rico's belt as he fell and then he was running hard for the door.

45

Eric got to work on time and left Jada Pinkett sleeping on the back seat of his car, and thought about slapping Antwerp upside his head if he said anything, but Antwerp didn't say anything after he took a look at Eric's face. He just punched out and left, took his jambox with him. Eric had asked a few times for Antwerp to leave it so that he could listen to Robert Earl Keen and the Robert Earl Keen band while he was working, but Antwerp never would because he was a stingy son of a bitch, Eric supposed.

He swept up and fed the birds and the gerbils. He looked to see how many rabbits they had now besides the one breeding pair. Four half-grown ones in a cage, two white, one brown, one black-and-white spotted. Eric had already put the buck back in with the doe so that there'd be another fresh batch coming along in about two weeks or less. Rabbits didn't sell very well unless they were furry babies and cute and made kids want them and throw screaming temper tantrums, wanting them to the point where they'd get down on their hands and knees and beat their heads on a concrete floor, and it was hard in the pet-shop business to keep yourself supplied with young bunnies unless you could breed them right there on the premises, but the problem with that was that some tended to get not bought and unless you disposed of them some way, then they themselves grew to breeding age rapidly and started making rabbits by the cageful, and it could turn into a pretty expensive, buying-rabbit-feed-by-the-Purina-fifty-pound-bag-and-carrying-lots-of-buckets-of-rabbit-shit-out-somewhere operation pretty soon, as Eric's boss, Mr.

Studebaker, had found out, not knowing much about the pet shop business at first, just always wanting a pet store kind of like the random kid who never got a Gibson Les Paul or a Telecaster for Christmas but instead some crummy microscope. But Eric didn't mind. Eric gladly took care of the extra rabbits for him about once every three weeks. There was a dirty parking lot out back where the Dumpsters and the empty skids and the bundled-up and flattened cardboard boxes sat and he kept a hammer handle by the back door, and once he was outside with the rabbit hanging upside down in his hand, by both back legs, all it took was a simple really hard *WHAM!* between the ears, and then it was a dead rabbit, nothing but meat to dress. He was so practiced that he could do it back there in just a few minutes with a keen Old Timer he'd used on probably a hundred squirrels and maybe two hundred rabbits down in Mississippi. Heads feet and guts in the Dumpster. Hope no kids come along and look in. Each pet shop bunny yielded a carcass of about two pounds of clean white meat that you could cut up and dip in an egg-and-milk batter and then roll in some seasoned flour and drop into a black iron skillet with some hot oil and let it crisp up golden brown. Let it simmer a while on low with the lid over it after it was done, it was just as good as fried chicken. Maybe better. His daddy had showed him how to make some gravy in the skillet with a little flour and salt and pepper, and you could open one of those five-biscuit cans of biscuits and stick them in the oven, and when they were done, it was as good a meal as any man could want. He didn't have a place to cook them just yet, so he was saving them in plastic bags in the freezer section of an old refrigerator in the back. And it was getting pretty full.

He gave a parakeet some water. He threw into the garbage a white, stiffened rat. He checked on Jada Pinkett, who was still snoozing and slobbering on the back seat. He'd finished Effinger's book and he'd read all the Philip K. Dick that he had and he had a ragged hardback *Martin Eden* by Jack London that he'd found cheap at Xanadu bookstore, on Winchester. And he thought maybe reading would take his mind off Miss Helen, but he didn't know if it really would or not. He couldn't get it out of his mind. The way she'd looked. The way she'd smelled. And then somebody came in. He had a monkey inside his battered leather flight jacket.

Eric stood up and said, uncertainly: "Hey. What's up."

He was a small older man, a bit larger than a jockey, dark skin, somewhat hunched. An elfin Eskimo.

"I have a primate I wish to sell," he murmured, his eyes roaming mildly from side to side in their sockets. "It's a Malaysian Gibboon. His name is Bobby."

The monkey was no bigger than a squirrel. It was gnawing its fingernails like a nervous woman and rolling its eyes fearfully.

"Looks like a squirrel monkey to me," Eric said. "But we don't buy nothin' from the public. We got dealers we deal with."

The little man wore gloves without tips at the fingers, and he stroked the monkey's head while he looked around the shop, taking the time to turn to the individual faces of those animals and birds that weren't asleep.

"The loneliness of the cage," he mused. "Your cage, mine. What does it matter whose? Somebody cages us all, don't they?"

"Excuse me?" Eric said. The guy looked wacko but the monkey just looked sick. Its eyes were dull and mucus was coming from its nostrils. The guy had a Kleenex in his hand, had obviously been wiping its nose.

It probably had some disease. That thing didn't need to be in here. Old fellow looked bad, though. He hated to run him out. But he had to think about his job, too, since Mr. Studebaker also cut him a deal on ear-mite drops and heartworm pills for Jada Pinkett.

"Look, mister," he said. "I ain't tryin' to be ugly or nothin' but that thing looks sick to me and I know my boss wouldn't want a sick animal in here with all his healthy ones. I think you need to take it to the vet or somethin'."

Eric watched as some tears broke from the corners of the little man's eyes. Something seemed to have cracked inside him.

"There's nothing wrong with Bobby," he said. "Bobby's gonna be okay. Aren't you, boy?"

He looked down at the animal and rubbed the top of its head and it vomited a thin dribble of foamy yellow puke down its front and over his jacket and hand. And then he just lost it and cried and cried, stood there, shaking but almost soundless, bent over slightly and holding the nasty shivering thing close to him.

"Mister. Come on. *Please?* You need to get that thing on out of here."

He hated to have to say that. But there wasn't anything he could do for him. Maybe he'd had him a long time. Maybe he was like his kid to him. You never knew. Some people bought sweaters for their dogs or wore them around in bags on their chests like papooses. He'd seen that once in Nashville. But you could see a lot of stuff in Nashville. Like some real pretty whores on the sidewalks, walking around in hot pants. You could just buy them. If you had the money.

"I thought maybe you could save him for me," the elf wept. "I can't afford the proper veterinary care."

Eric didn't know what to say after he saw all that. After a while the elf gave up and turned and shuffled out with his monkey. Eric stepped to the door and for a long time watched him go up the sidewalk surrounding the mall. He could see him stopping to talk to people, and people turning away from him. Some had Christmas gifts already. Others were holding hands. A lot of them seemed to be happy. Up the sidewalk the little man was still stopping people. But not very many of them stopped for long. They all had their own Christmas deals going probably.

46

The rescue effort failed. A bunch of Seals in cold-water scuba gear and loaded with shark repellent went out from a side compartment in black rubber boats with twin Johnson engines and they tried to help the mother whale, but she was too grievously injured to be saved by human hands.

Wayne and Henderson stood on the deck at about 1500, looking down, a sunny afternoon but cold, watching them surround in boats the whale mother below in the mostly deserted Atlantic. Even from high up there, Wayne could see the three terrible cuts across her side, and the bulge of her gray intestines spilling out into the water with some blood. A Greenpeace boat out of Norfolk had pulled next to them and the water between the enormous ship and the environmentalists' vessel was stained red. Everybody was looking for sharks.

"That's a low-down dirty shame," Henderson said. "That thing swimmin' around free as a bird. Nursin' that baby like a cow."

"They ain't gonna catch that calf, neither," Wayne said. No shit. The Greenpeace guys had brought rope nets with floats and had made an effort with small motorboats to herd the calf into one of them, but the calf had turned over one of the motorboats and almost drowned three of the six volunteers who were on it by hitting them, in its fear and panic, with its tail a couple of times, which should have been no big surprise since it weighed a couple of thousand pounds. One of the Greenpeacers had a concussion and a few subdural hematomas and a broken nose and three broken fingers and had to be airlifted out by one of the Coast Guard choppers sitting on the deck. They had given up after that, and now they were all just kind of sitting around watching it, and watching the mother die. The calf was shy now and hung back.

All the newspeople had left on orders from the Pentagon because the Pentagon was pissed. So many people wanted to get up on the flight deck that the captain came over the intercom and said he didn't think it was much of a thing to watch, kind of like a flood, but those who wanted to could go up in shifts if they were off duty.

"Shit," Henderson said, looking at Wayne. "Cap'n all worried about his job now he done had a collision. All he usually worried about is gettin' him a cold Schlitz after supper and kickin' back to watch *Bonanza.*"

"How you know he drinks Schlitz?" Wayne said.

"Poo-Head. Works in the officers' mess. Takes him one up."

They looked down. The wind was blowing in Wayne's face and the bottoms of his bell-bottoms were wet. The whale lay on her side, trying to maintain her position so that she could still blow her exhaled air out of the water. She rose and fell slightly with the motion of the ocean. The Seals and the Greenpeace guys had surrounded her with their little flotilla of boats and nets. Some of them were touching her. Still others at her head were saying things to her. She was almost too weak to move now and the Seals were not scared of anything anyway. Nobody knew when they were going back. That decision hadn't been made just yet. That decision was up to somebody bigger than the captain. All Wayne knew was that they were going back. And he felt bad for the whales. He decided he would stay on the deck as long as he could.

He and Henderson stayed out there until dark. Wayne worked for a while in the armory and let a couple of marines check out their M-14s so they could clean them for an inspection. He read a woodworking magazine and cut his fingernails. He thought about Anjalee and wondered what she was doing right now. She might even be sitting in that same bar.

After a few more hours, his relief came in and he went for a roast beef sandwich with hot mustard but didn't see Henderson in the galley. He talked to some boys he knew who were flight deckhands and they'd been watching the whale event unfold, too. One of them said it looked to him like the whale would die pretty soon and another one said he thought it might take days.

After he finished eating, he still wasn't sleepy, so he went back up to see if he could get back on deck and he could. The lights were up on the bridge as if for flight operations. He walked to the edge of the sailors, who all had their pea coats on now with the chill night air, and he was surprised to look down and see that the Seals and some of the Greenpeace guys were still in the water dumping shark repellant and using lamps they had rigged on their boats as well as some spotlights from the carrier. It was still about the same story. Lurking nearby was the calf. Wayne could see it, a vague shape under the water waiting around at the edge of the men and boats that were gathered around its mother.

It kept spouting, and now it had started a weird crying that Wayne could hear even high up on the deck. A thin keening, and dark all around, except for the pools of light down there in and on the water, and the swells rocking the whalesavers' boat, and even when Wayne stood there another hour, she wasn't dead. He was almost frozen by then. The group on deck got smaller and smaller. Finally he had to go, too.

Wayne set his alarm and thought about Anjalee for a long time. He built houses in Ohio for the two of them in his mind. He heard Henderson come in just before he fell asleep.

The clock went off at 0600 and Wayne hit it with his hand and then lay there. It was dark except for a tiny light over LeBonte's bed, and he wasn't in the bed. He lay on his back, warm under his wool blanket. He couldn't hear anything but Henderson doing a slight droning number.

He dressed quietly and put on his pea coat and went back up on the deck. It was very cold. Only a few sailors were out there. Dawn was just breaking and the ship was making a long slow turn under a weak orange light against the horizon, smeared gray clouds over it. The rocking swells were wide and there was nothing on the horizon but more of them. He looked down. The mother whale was gone, along with the calf. All the navy divers were out of the water. The Greenpeace boat was only a memory now.

"She drowned," a guy next to Wayne said.

He thought about that. To be born in water and die in it.

"What about the calf?"

"I don't know, man. I guess it figured we wasn't cool after we killed its mama."

The sailor had his hands in his jacket pockets and he motioned toward the water with his elbow.

"One of the Seals, he said he thought it was asking us for help."

"I heard it," Wayne said, and he suddenly wanted hot sausage and three over easy and knew he could have them. Toast and jelly. Hash browns. And he was going back to Memphis somehow. When he found her this time, he wasn't going to let her go.

He kept standing there. He hated to think about it out there in the wide open, a baby, swimming along all by itself, looking for a new pod where it could hang. How would it find others of its own kind? Was it calling to them, even now? He knew they sang to each other, from Iceland to Jamaica. Were the songs bouncing off under-water cliffs that went deep into the water? How did anybody know how far those songs could go?

He just hoped it would live, after all the shit it had gone through. He hoped for that as hard as he'd ever hoped for anything in his life. Not counting kissing Anjalee naked in a bed.

47

Arthur found the instructions pretty easy to follow. The whole thing had cost him $335.00 plus tax and his model was the Pet-Co Surge II, which the pamphlet described as "an ergonomically designed single-piece unit that allows users single finger or thumb pump activation." There were some cheaper models he could have gotten into as well and for sixty more bucks he could have opted for the top of the line, the Rapid II, which was powered by a "super strong" nine-volt battery motor, and, according to the pamphlet, was "Perfect for men with diminished hand strength." Somebody about a hundred years old, he guessed, with palsied, shaking fingers, still trying to get it up. Maybe old Mr. Stamp next door had one of those.

He pulled the commode lid down and sat on top of it while he read the instructions and some testimonials from satisfied customers. There were satisfied customers in Cherokee, Alabama, Marion, Arkansas, Dayton, Ohio, and Las Cruces, New Mexico, and he noticed after unpacking everything there in the bathroom that his model had come with an educational videotape and a discreet carrying case. You could take it on vacation. You could pay for one with Medicare. It said so right there in the booklet. He hadn't known that some of the government's money was going for stuff like this. U.S. taxpayers shelling out their hard-earned for a hard-on seemed unreasonable, but no more so than paying people not to raise two thousand acres of soybeans or financing studies of studies. He looked again at the couple on the horses. He pictured the guy in the picture doing what he was about to do. The whole thing seemed pretty broke-dick even to somebody as broke-dick as him.

He raised his face and looked at nothing on the wall where the paper was decorated with roses wreathed in vines, red and white and yellow. He was trying to remember what it had felt like the first time they'd done it in Montana. He couldn't. Maybe it was just time for him to give it up. It wasn't like it was something he hungered for all the time anyway, now, especially after everything that had happened. He'd felt a lot of humiliation over it, still felt a great deal. But if he wanted to do it with Helen again, what else could he do? It was either Viagra or this. Or an operation.

No.

Maybe he needed a drink first. He didn't know where Helen was. Her Jag was gone, but sometimes she did some shopping or went to restaurants. He knew she went to the Peabody bar sometimes, too, but he was afraid he'd get mugged on Beale Street.

He held the thing in his hands and looked at it. He saw the rings that were included. He understood that after he got his motor running, he had to put on a ring that would trap the blood until he got through with it. He wondered what would happen if he dozed off while it was still on. Would there be any permanent damage?

Maybe he needed to watch the tape. But how much sense was that going to make, to watch some guy like the one on the horse put himself into a plastic tube and suck all the air out of it? He just didn't see how it could work. But he was going to try it since he'd paid $335.00 plus tax.

He put it all back in the box except for the tape and hid the rest of it behind the door beneath the vanity. Then he went downstairs.

It was quiet. He looked in the pantry. The kitten was sleeping and Helen had opened the cage door because there was a bowl of cat food in there with it, a full pan of water. Maybe it was going to calm down. Maybe they'd be able to eventually keep it around the house like a regular pet. He hoped so even if he had been attacked and slashed and traumatized by one in his childhood. Maybe Helen would take an interest in it.

He went to the window and looked out to see if it was still snowing. Everybody else did. Everybody else seemed to have a pet or two. Already he missed Jada Pinkett. And Eric even more. Helen seemed to like him a lot, too.

48

"Lord have mercy," Penelope said. "I dig it when you do that, baby."

"Do what?" Merlot said, indoor pale and naked as a jaybird beneath her, and then chuckled, his head on the pillow. He took another long lazy lick at her leathery brown nipple and said: "Ooh. You want to look at this, School Nurse?"

She raised up. They were over at her neat little house just north of Water Valley, in the country. He wasn't ready to take her to his house yet since he was afraid Candy might have shit on the sheets again and wanted to get over there first and make sure Mrs. Poteet had cleaned it up just in case Candy had.

"Is it something wrong, Mister Professor?"

The weed she had was some potent stuff. Had taken it off some stoned Czech dude at the bus station one day. Penelope said keeping it didn't seem like stealing since it didn't really belong to anybody anymore unless you wanted to count the entire state, which was actually a whole lot of people who didn't even know anything about it and never would and wouldn't miss it, and although individually some of them wouldn't do it, collectively and regulated by the lawmakers and the people like her paid twice monthly to enforce the rules, the "state" would eventually just pour some kerosene over it one afternoon and set it afire for the fun of it. Merlot said God made pot the same day He made potatoes, according to how you read your Bible.

She had Alejandro Escovedo's *Gravity* playing on the big Kenwood speakers she'd paid for with money she'd won playing the slots at Hollywood, in Tunica. There were lots of violins and cellos. The shades were down. They'd done it in the living room on the couch first, then on the kitchen table, and then in the bathtub. It was pretty restful to finally be in the bed. He was about to get sore and red and run dry both, but naturally he didn't want to stop.

"Uh, School Nurse, yes, I think it's a small . . ." He searched for the proper word. "I think you'd have to call it a protuberance. It's like a small potato. Somewhat elongated."

She giggled with delight, stoned like him, maybe worse.

"Well, do you think, maybe . . . Mister Professor . . . it needs a good massaging?"

"Eh, I think maybe you could palpate it and see." He giggled some, too.

"Ooh, lover," she said, all serious, her eyes going serious, ducking to kiss him again. "Ain't nobody ever made me come the way you do."

And then she started kissing on his neck again and held him down and grinned at him and pressed her lips close and started blowing against his skin so that her lips vibrated and made noises like somebody passing gas uncontrollably while he flapped his arms and shouted happily for her to *quit it*!

49

Anjalee woke and stretched and yawned. It was quiet, with only the hissing of the heat coming through the ceiling vents. She didn't know what time it was. They'd stayed at the casino until three. He'd won big at blackjack. Very big. About forty-five hundred.

She was alone in the bed. She found her cigarettes and lighter on the bedside table and turned the lamp on. A few glasses that sat in rings of water held the remnants of drinks. Ashtrays with stubbed-out cigarette butts wearing her lipstick. She lit a fresh one and pulled the pillow up behind her and then got the other one and propped it back there, too. She stretched and yawned a long slow yawn with the cigarette in her fist.

She looked for a clock and finally saw on a small brown box some luminous red letters that read 11:47. Almost lunchtime, and she was hungry. She wondered if he'd paid the hotel bill before he left. If he hadn't, she'd have to sneak out.

There was a thick red robe with the hotel monogram on it hanging in one of the closets and she put it on and tied it around her and went into the bathroom and brushed her teeth. She was rinsing out her mouth and spitting into the sink when she heard the doorbell ring. She stopped and shut off the water. What if it was the cops?

But how would they know she was here? It was probably only housecleaning. It was probably time to check out.

She went back into the suite and the doorbell rang again.

"Yes?" she called.

"Room service, ma'am," came a muffled answer.

There was a peek hole in the door and she peeked. No cop. A nerdy-looking guy in a gray tunic was out there. He had on white gloves. She opened the door and he flashed her a polite smile. He had a table on wheels with him and it was covered in a large burgundy cloth.

"I didn't order anything," she said.

"Late breakfast, ma'am. Where would you like it?"

She looked. Her clothes were scattered. But there was a table fairly clean.

"Over there, please. Come on in."

He wheeled it in and she could hear dishes rattling gently. Once he stopped it, he removed the cloth to reveal covered dishes with metal lids, all kinds of condiments, syrup, napkins, coffee, a cup and saucer, juice, a dish of kiwi fruit covered with clear stuff, silverware.

"What's all this?" she said.

"Late breakfast, ma'am. Comes with the suite. Enjoy."

He didn't wait for a tip or anything, just went on out the door and pulled it shut. When she heard the lock click, she took the lid off one of the dishes. There was a large mound of hash browns with buttered toast. Another dish held sausage patties and bacon and fluffy-looking scrambled eggs. Another was full of pancakes. The last lid hid an envelope sitting on top of a note. She picked up the envelope and looked inside. It was full of used fifty-dollar bills. It didn't take her long to count it and there was eight hundred dollars in it.

The note:

Had to go, baby, but I'll hook back up. Go buy you some clothes.
Stay here long as you like, it's on me. I'll call. You rock. Lenny

She could go shopping this afternoon. Stay here? Hell, why not?

There was food and a good TV and a very nice bathroom and bed and a place to hide until she could decide what she wanted to do. She got a chair, pulled it up to the table, unrolled her silverware, and grabbed a fork. The cops probably wouldn't look for her in a place this nice.

Then she stopped. She looked at the money again. Hell. She could go home now. But it wouldn't hurt to buy a few clothes since she couldn't get anything out of her apartment. If she hung around Memphis much longer, the cops were going to pick her up.

She laid down her fork, picked up a piece of bacon, and bit into it. She was going to have to make a move. Pretty soon. But there was Lenny to think about. What was he going to say if she skipped town with eight hundred of his dollars?

Hell. If she never came back to Memphis, what would it matter? There had been nothing but trouble for her up here lately. And there were other places where she could work. There was Atlanta. There was Nashville. Chattanooga even. She could go anywhere in the whole country if she wanted to.

But she had to eat. She picked her fork back up and took the lid off the eggs. She smelled them, kind of hoping they'd smell like her grandmother's, and they did, a little bit, maybe, good enough to eat anyway.

50

Miss Muffett mopped the kitchen floor and vacuumed the carpet in the great room and sucked the dirt off the drapes, too. The people outside had gone by the time she got through. She thought maybe she'd make the firemen a carrot cake and take it over to the fire station before Christmas.

She went upstairs to the room she stayed in and took her leg off and dropped it on the floor and lay down on the bed and put one arm over her eyes. She hadn't gotten a phone number from Nub and didn't know how to get in touch with him. She guessed she could call directory information. Everything was still so cloudy in her mind that it seemed now more like a dream. She hated she couldn't remember the lovemaking. It was kind of like it almost didn't happen. It wasn't a satisfying feeling. Next time she picked up a man, she wouldn't drink so much.

She figured the little dog was hiding from her somewhere. That was okay, if he wanted to hide. Right now she needed a nap more than anything since she was so tired.

It was silent in the room, in the big empty house. She dimly heard something kick on and run for a while and then go off. There was a clock ticking. It ticked her softly to sleep. Outside the window the snow fell in soft ragged flakes over the woods and fields and rivers and roads of north Mississippi, under a sky low and gray. Black ducks shot overhead, past the big house, wheeling south, wings driving fast to the coming dark.

51

Penelope got notified by phone that she was being placed on administrative leave with full pay until the investigation was over, which was routine whenever shots were fired. She seemed upset when she got off the phone, but he didn't pry.

After she told Merlot what was happening, she sat on the bed naked and cross-legged eating a banana to get her strength back as well as for the potassium. Merlot was rolling a super-thin joint, which he then licked and sucked on the ends until it was nearly perfect. He had eight others already made, lined up on her bedside table, drying. He glanced up at her. When was the right time to tell her about Candy and how it was with them? Would it be best to wait? Maybe so. There really wasn't any kind of deception going on. Was there?

Penelope stripped the skin off the banana and shoved the rest of it in her mouth. Her cheeks bulged while she chewed. God, he loved her lips. They tasted like grapes. She dropped the peel on the floor.

"I need to get back home and check on things," Merlot said. "I've got to teach class tomorrow and give out grades. Then I'm done."

"Ummhummumm," she said.

"I'll probably get another car from my insurance company. There's a party before long and I'd like you to meet some of the people at the school, maybe some of my students who aren't going home for Christmas. They're pretty cool kids, some of them."

"You like kids, Merlot?"

"I love kids. I wish I was still one myself."

She laughed, but then got all shy and said: "Yeah, but I mean do you want some one day?"

He stopped rolling. She had finished chewing her banana. Her lips were shiny with banana grease.

"Yeah," he said. "With you I do. About ten of them. Or maybe twelve."

She crawled across the bed to him and kissed his naked leg.

"So," he said. "You got some time off, huh?"

"Yep. Sure do."

"And right here at Christmas. What you gonna do with it?"

She rolled over onto her back. She folded her hands across her massive flattened titties.

"I don't know. What do you want to do with it?"

"Are you asking me?"

"I'm asking you, baby. You are my baby, aren't you?"

"I guess I am now," he said.

"You better be."

"Well . . ." He laid the joint aside with the others and folded down the top of the baggie and put it beside them. He got his pillow and propped it up against the headboard and slid closer to her. "What would you think about a little trip?"

"A trip?"

"Yeah. Just a little one. Say, for a few days. I'm through after one more class. And giving out grades."

"How long does that take you?"

"Couple of hours."

"Ooh I love trips," she said. "We went to New Orleans on the bus one time when I was ten and I just about died from excitement."

She rolled over onto her side and his heart gave a leap when her titties rubbed up against him. He picked up one of the joints that was dried and found the lighter on the table beside it and fired it up. It was the best shit he'd smoked in a long time. He took a couple of tokes and flicked the ash in the ashtray and handed it to her.

"Where would you want to go if we went somewhere?" he said.

"I don't know. Where would you want to go?"

"You want me to tell you?"

"Tell me, baby." She sucked on the joint.

"Okay. I'd like to drive down the Natchez Trace and go to Natchez and stay in Texado. I've always wanted to do that."

"What's that?"

"Texado? It's the oldest house in Mississippi. It was built in 1790 when this whole state was still a Spanish territory."

"Oh shit, baby," she said. "That Natchez Trace is pretty nice, isn't it?"

"Fifty miles an hour," Merlot said, and took the joint back to suck on it. "No stinking trucks allowed. They don't even let UPS on it. Nothing but streams and woods and deer and wild turkeys."

"And this old place is nice?"

"Oh yeah. I saw some pictures of it in a *Southern Living* Mama had one time. We could call ahead of time and see if we can get in.

We probably can since it's close to Christmas. They got a casino down there, too."

"I know it. I love to play those slot machines. I hit that hot streak at Tunica that time. Can we play the slot machines?"

"We can do anything you want to. We're free birds."

What he didn't say was that he hadn't made up his mind yet what to do about Candy. He knew Mrs. Poteet would stay with her for a while longer. He thought maybe if they took off for a few days and did some riding and talking he could break it to her gently.

"When you gonna take me to your place?" she said.

"I don't know. It's probably dirty."

"I don't care."

"Probably a bunch of dirty dishes in the sink."

"I'll wash 'em for you."

"My carpet hasn't been cleaned in a while. Garbage is probably full."

She propped herself up on her elbow.

"Is there some specific reason you don't want me over at yo house, white boy?"

He sucked on the joint and then passed it back to her. She held up a hand.

"I'm good."

"Oh. Okay." He took two more hits off it and then put it out. "It's just a mess," he said. "All my papers and shit are probably all over the place."

"You got as many books in it as you got in your van?"

"More," he said.

"Well, you let me know whenever you get ready to go," she said. "Now c'mere and gimme some sugar."

And he didn't have to worry about it anymore right then, which was real good.

52

It had been a long day and it was a big surprise to Eric when Miss Helen walked in around nine. He could see right away that she'd been drinking. Her lipstick was a bit smeared, but she had a smile on her face. Some kids were looking at green-and-white parakeets. A married couple was looking at a puppy. Miss Helen walked over to the young rabbits' cages and he saw her stick her fingers in through the bars to touch one of them. The little rabbit sniffed at her fingers. He didn't guess he'd tell her what would be happening with some of those guys in a few more weeks, out back by the Dumpsters.

She wandered around the shop, acted like she was thinking about buying a pet. He tried to watch her without letting the people in the shop know he was watching her. But he watched her. He watched the movements of her legs in the tight jeans she was wearing and he watched her face and her breasts inside the leather coat she was wearing. The kids bought two parakeets so that maybe they could have baby parakeets and he sexed the birds quickly to be sure they were male and female and sold them a cage and gave them some feed and told them how to take care of them and they paid and left.

The guy of the couple came up to the counter and wanted to know if the bichon frise he was thinking about buying came with any kind of warranty and when Eric told him it didn't, he left, too, and then his wife followed him out all pissed off and bitching at him.

When the door slammed, Helen looked straight at him.

"Let's go have a drink when you get off," she said.

"I can't close till ten," he said. It was true. But what about Mister Arthur?

"You know where the Peabody is?" she said.

He had to think about it for a few seconds. He thought about Jada Pinkett eating the beef stew in Miss Helen's kitchen, about Mister Arthur opening the can for him, putting the newspaper down, petting him while he ate, talking to him. Mister Arthur had been really nice to him. So had she. It had felt good being in their house. It had made him feel not so bad about being away from home this close to Christmas.

"I never have been in there," he said. "But I know where it's at. What about Mister Arthur? Will he care?"

"Arthur doesn't have to know anything about it. He doesn't know everything I do anyway."

He didn't know what to say. She looked good. Better than good. But she was older. There was that. A grown woman. Not no girl. That was all he knew, girls, and not many of them. Actually only one that way, Rae Loni Kaye Nafco, a kind of large girl his age with a very pretty face who lived down close to Potlockney. She'd bought a puppy one time, a black poodle, while his daddy was gone off drinking and fishing with some of his buddies, and Eric had said some things she'd laughed at, and she kept talking to him, and stroking the puppy, and acting like she didn't want to leave, and then he'd opened a couple of beers, and then they had taken a seat on a bale of hay, and then she had kissed him, and one thing had led to another pretty quickly, especially after she told him she was on the pill, and they had done it in the barn. Then a few very satisfying times at her trailer with fresh puppy shit on the kitchen floor. And all that had happened right before he left home. He missed her now. He missed home even more.

"What does it matter about Arthur?" she said. "You barely know him."

She walked a little closer to him. She was wearing a zippered sweater under her coat and the zipper was down some now, almost halfway, and the cleavage of her breasts was showing. He could smell that perfume again and he felt almost weak.

"There's no reason to be scared of me, Eric," she said.

"Aw, I ain't scared," he said, which wasn't true, since he was plenty scared, thoroughly scared, scared shitless.

"I'm going on over," she said. "I'll be at the bar. Just park on the street somewhere and walk on over. When you get there, we'll get a table."

She didn't even wait for an answer from him. She zipped the sweater back up, stuck her hands in her pockets, then turned around and walked out. Watching her go, he couldn't help but notice that she had a fine ass.

53

Arthur was sitting on the toilet with the lid down, naked except for his socks, in the privacy of his own bathroom. He didn't have much hair on him anymore, hadn't in a long time. And a lot of his skin was pretty wrinkled. He was uneasy that Helen wasn't home yet. He'd wakened during the night, a month back, and she hadn't been in the bed, and when he'd gone downstairs, she wasn't down there in the living room either. But she'd come back in about a half hour later with a half gallon of melting Edy's Rocky Road ice cream, opening the front door like she was trying to be quiet, getting flustered on see-ing him sitting in the living room with the lamp on and a magazine, in his housecoat and pajamas and slippers, saying that she had run over to Kroger. Had developed a sudden craving for some Rocky Road. But he'd smelled liquor on her breath when she walked by him, and figured she'd been to a bar. Probably the Peabody. And when he'd tried to question her about why she'd been drinking and driving again after all the trouble she'd already been in with the police, she'd just slammed the ice cream into the freezer and gone into the bathroom and slammed the door. But stuff like that was nothing new for her. Temper tantrums. Now she'd been gone for hours and he had no idea where. He wanted her to come on back because he was afraid of who she might be with and what she might be doing. Was something going on that he didn't know about? Did she have somebody else? Was there another man somewhere she was seeing? Had he waited around too long to get some help? What were those stains on the back seat of the Jag and who put them there? What if she was driving around drunk again and got another DUI? The judge had already told her right there in the courtroom downtown, in front of everybody, that he'd put her in the state penitentiary for a while if she did it again, and that if she didn't believe him, for her to just show up in his court on a DUI charge again.

He was also afraid of the pump-up thing but he went ahead and did what the instructions said and amazingly, it worked. It got big and it got hard and he slipped the rubber ring around the base of it and walked around the bathroom proudly with it sticking up at a pretty good angle for an old guy, he figured, even admired it in the mirror. Turned sideways and checked it that way, got the profile. He was surprised and almost embarrassingly pleased by how well the thing worked. And then he just let out a big sigh and started taking the band off. All pumped up with no place to go.

54

Anjalee moved her Camry down the street from the Peabody and took a cab over to Gigi's Angels. She thought that would be safer. She asked the cabdriver to wait and went inside and there were only three people sitting at the bar. Nobody was dancing and there wasn't even any music playing. The whole place looked like it was about ready to shut down. That made her feel like she was making the right move. Get off a sinking ship before it went down. And she *had* to get her good leather coat from upstairs.

"Hey, Moe!" she said. He stuck his head out from the back almost instantly. He was chewing something rapidly and he walked to the beer cooler.

"Well," he said, swallowing, looking her up and down. "I didn't know if you'd be back or not."

"Just for a minute. Has Frankie called? Left a message or anything?"

"Nope. Lots of people were asking were you coming back after you left. Some more of those fire boys came back later. Jesus, can they drink some beer. You coming back tonight?"

"I don't know," she said. "I may have gotten a better offer."

He looked at her with a puzzled face and pulled a beer from the cooler.

"I've got a few things upstairs," she said. "Some clothes and my good coat. Can I go get 'em?"

"Yeah, sure. Or leave 'em here with me, either one. What's going on?"

"It's nothing, it's just . . ." She didn't want to ask him if police had been around because he'd know she was in some kind of shit, and she'd just as soon he not know that about her right now in case she needed him later. So she put on her sweet face.

"I'll come back in sometime and have a drink and we'll talk about it. Okay? It's just a lot of stuff going on right now."

"Okay," he said, and then he opened the beer and went on back through the door.

She went upstairs to the room where her things were hanging. She got her good leather coat. There were a few short dresses and a pair of shoes and a jean jacket and she got it all over one arm and hand and went back down. She went out to the waiting cab and it was gone. Her left arm was grabbed along with her right, and in just a moment there was one on either side of her, big ones in plainclothes and her stuff in a pile at her feet. People looking. Some of them just standing still, staring. The cops were actually pretty polite but they wouldn't let her take her other clothes since she was going to jail. One of them went to the door and yelled for somebody to come outside and get her stuff. Moe came out and got the stuff but he didn't say anything, just watched her with an awful look on his face, like he wished he could do something. They cuffed her and put her in the back seat and it didn't have any door handles on the inside. One of the cops drove and the other cop smoked cigarettes and cussed the traffic and she was terrified because they had her ass good this time. And plus they wouldn't talk to her.

55

Helen began getting hit on by men as soon as she walked into the lobby. A couple hit on her on her way to the bar and wanted to buy her a drink but she just gave them a smile and a head shake and kept on going.

She liked the Peabody bar. It was usually filled with well-dressed working people in the late afternoons and she knew that some of them had come there straight from their jobs at banks or law firms or real estate offices downtown and within walking distance. She liked the idea of that. But she'd never brought Arthur to this place. He wouldn't fit in, or he'd say something goofy and embarrass her. He might turn to a total stranger and start trying to talk to him about Randolph Scott. Or even Tim Holt. He was like a damn ency-clopedia on those old westerns. Remembered movies he'd seen when he was a teenager in Tunica. She didn't give a shit who Woody Strode was.

She stopped in front of the bar and smiled as she waited for some people who were leaving to get their coats and keys. And how did he get it in his head that she was so crazy about animals? She liked them okay, sure, the way you like raisin bran once in a while, but she didn't need that wild-ass cat. It probably had rabies or something. Parasites maybe. She didn't know where he got some of the ideas he came up with. Like looking for tranquilizer guns in a pet shop. And look now what that had led to. Eric, out of the blue. The world had gotten a lot more interesting. Then she had a sudden, exhilarating thought: What if she took him with her? To Montana? Wouldn't that be getting a brand-new start?

The people got their stuff together and finally started getting out of the way. She pulled out a stool and took a seat. Eric seemed very innocent and she was excited by that. Ken smiled and waved while talking busily to another customer. Asshole. She found the Virginia Slim Lights she'd bought, in her purse, and lit one and looked at the row of bottles behind the bar. She didn't know what she'd do if Eric didn't come on over. But he'd come. She knew he would. She'd seen how he looked at her. There was no mistaking a look like that. They'd have to get a room here or go to his place. He never had said where he lived. She didn't want to do it in the Jag in the parking lot anymore like she'd been doing with Ken. It was too risky. There were always cops walking around downtown or riding their bicycles.

She slid an ashtray closer. Ken kept screwing around but that was temporarily okay because she hadn't made up her mind what she wanted yet. She'd already had three draft beers and two shots of Rumpel Minze in another bar, but all that had been over the course of a good while. She could switch to whiskey, and she still wouldn't be drunk when he came in a little after ten. If he came in. She was afraid he was scared of her. *My God, honey,* she said to herself. *Don't be scared of me. I just want to take a few minutes of your time to show you a few things your mother never did.*

"Hello," a smooth, husky voice said close to her. She turned her head to see a man in his early forties, curly coal-black hair, dressed in trim tan slacks and a charcoal coat over a white shirt.

"Hi," she said, after a moment. After that moment Ken came over.

"Helen," he said. "Sorry to make you wait. Everybody wants to talk football. Only game in town." He winked.

"Don't they, though," she said. Winking at her like he owned her. "What can I get you?"

"I wanted to see if I could maybe buy you a drink," the guy butted in and said.

Ken looked at him. Helen looked at him. He was a fairly decent-looking dude but he had a pocket-pen protector. She didn't want him to be around when Eric got here. Some guys would buy you a drink and never leave. Some guys thought buying you a drink entitled them to some privileges, like sitting in a bar beside you all night boring you almost to tears over their old girlfriends and how much money they made and what kind of car they had and how they went to Cancun three times a year and blah blah blah and rah rah rah. He could buy her a drink. But she wasn't going to let him tongue-kiss her or anything. She didn't think. But who knew? Who would have thought she'd wind up fucking this loser behind the bar who had holes in his socks and his underwear, too? And all he had to listen to was Barry Manilow. Every time she went over there, it was the same thing. Fucking Barry Manilow. Over and over. Endlessly.

"I don't believe I know you," she said.

"That's true," he said, and he stepped forward with his hand out. Ken stood there watching, looked around at the other customers, and waited. "My name's Tyrone Bradbury."

"Oh," she said, and smiled. "Well. Are you any relation to Ray?"

He laughed and shook his head. She liked the way he put his hands in his pockets.

"No, but I get asked that sometimes." He was clearly nervous. But he looked up. "I just saw you and wanted to introduce myself. I didn't see a wedding ring on your finger."

Which was true. It was in her pocket and she'd put on a silver-filigree-mounted topaz to cover the white ring of skin.

"I didn't mean to bother you," he said. "May I ask your name?"

"Oh, I'm sorry," she said, and put out her hand. "I'm Helen."

He took it and he had a warm and firm clasp.

"It's nice to meet you, Helen. So, can I buy you a drink?"

"Well. I may be meeting somebody after a while," she said. "Around ten or a little after."

She looked at Ken after she said that. She thought his eyes were going to cross.

"That's okay," he said. "You don't have to talk to me all night just because I buy you a drink."

"Oh. Well, okay." She turned back to Tyrone. "Pull up a chair." He did. Ken was waiting, and watching her. She leaned forward with her breasts up on top of the bar. He was sure watching then. "Ken, Ken. What do I want tonight? You've got all that stuff back there and I don't know what I want."

Tyrone had gone back to his table for his drink and brought it over with a wet napkin because he'd sloshed some of it, looked like a scotch and water. She remembered that Eric liked scotch. She was aware of Tyrone sitting down next to her but she was looking at the bottles. They were rowed up back there and in a small pyramid at the bottom under blue neon glass. She could have one drink or two and get this guy to get a room and get it taken care of easy probably. Or she could wait for Eric and maybe get nothing. He was having a thing about Arthur. She could tell that already.

"What do you want, Helen?" Tyrone said.

"I don't know. I don't . . . freaking . . . know."

"It's about quit snowing," Tyrone offered. Nobody responded. He sipped at his drink and some ran off on his hand and he looked for another napkin and then reached way over for one and then almost toppled his chair and spilled about half his drink and righted the chair and muttered something. Some drunk in the back laughed pretty loud but Tyrone acted like he was deaf. Ken got some napkins and started mopping the bar with them.

"I want a Crown and Coke," she said, and Ken wadded the wet napkins and said: "Crown it is," and, "I'll get you another one, sir."

She swiveled around slightly toward Tyrone and he smiled.

"Thanks," he said to Ken. He'd spilled some on his coat, too.

"I don't think I've seen you in here before," she said, as he dabbed with a handkerchief and muttered.

"No," he said, looking up. "I'm just here on business."

"What business are you in, Tyrone?"

He scooted his seat closer, a smile on his face. Ken was making her drink back there and looking over his shoulder at her. Cars were passing on the street outside. She felt warm inside knowing that she was waiting here for Eric to come see her. She felt a way she hadn't felt in a long time. It was something to look forward to, and she couldn't think of many things she *could* look forward to. Going home sometime tonight sure wasn't one of them. She was going to be nice to Tyrone. But she was going to hold out for Eric.

56

The trouble with the land down behind the hospital and in the general area south of town, for an escaping criminal, was that it was all getting developed to the point where there weren't many patches of bushes left in which to hide, and even roads that used to be made of dirt were now paved, some with curbs and streetlights. Contractors from out of town were working their way through the streets and building all the time, paving old cotton fields and pastures, running out the rabbits. Coons could live anywhere, still did, even in the oaks on the courthouse square, and jogging Ole Miss coeds knew there were deer raising their babies in the woods beside Fire Station no. 2.

Probably the reason that Domino got away was that it probably took a while for Rico to call somebody, being hurt like he was, or maybe somebody from the hospital called for him because of his being hurt, and then it probably took some other police a few minutes to get down there, go inside the emergency room, see Rico bloody, get the lowdown on what was going on, maybe call for some backup, a matter of a few more minutes, and then actually get somebody on the ground down behind the hospital to start looking for Domino. And by that time he had already sprinted out the door and past the old sick-looking security guard who was sucking on another cigarette and across the parking lot and down the hill below the parking lot and across the lower parking lot and had jumped the ditch between there and Graceland old folks' home and run behind that parking lot and around the end of a tall plank fence and down another hill to a big green-roofed building where Dr. Buddy Spencer had his family medical practice and behind that building and between the young trees that had been planted and mulched and across the far south end of South Eighteenth, took a chance and got on the street long enough to cross the bridge over Burney Branch, then jumped off the street and ran into the woods and sage grass that lined the steep sides of Highway 7.

But he had better sense than to hide. A rabbit ran sometimes because he had to. One short-barreled revolver with no more bullets than the ones in it was no match for all the firepower they could train on him.

He did stop on one knee and lower his head to catch his breath. He was behind some bushes that had turned brown from frost and there were some thick patches of stuff above him that he would have to climb through in order to cross the highway. And the traffic. The traffic was going to be the worst because the cops were coming and some of them would probably be in the traffic.

His breath came out white in the cold air, and he had no plan. His only plan was to get across the highway and then try to get some distance from the road if it meant crossing a pasture or woods or fences. He had to lose them here. It was the only chance to get away.

He wasn't ready, but he made himself ready. He had his hand wrapped outside the trigger guard and he started forward at a fast clip, wading through the sage grass with his arms high. He bulled through a patch of briars and said nothing when they tore at his cheeks. He squinched his eyes almost shut and felt them tearing at his clothes and almost holding him back so that he had to lunge against them and flatten them down with his feet and turn and twist away from them like a drunk trying to dance and even then they kept trying to hold him. But he tore free and ran toward the foot of the bank. It was steep, and slick with mud from the melted snow. He had to put the gun in his pocket, and pull himself up from tree to tree, grasping at saplings and slipping and sliding in the mud. His breath was coming hard and he looked over his shoulder as a police car with blue lights flashing turned in from Highway 7 and screamed down the curve in front of the Pakistani fried chicken/gas station and he watched the car go across the bridge he'd crossed not three minutes before, and climb the hill toward the hospital.

Another one took squalling the curve at the intersection of South Eighteenth and Belk Boulevard with its blue lights flashing and its siren screaming. It lost traction on the rear wheels and swung wide, and the rear tire peeled up smoke as it straightened and climbed the hill and went out of sight. He didn't look anymore.

He could see the top of the road, above him. He had to get down on his hands and knees and claw at the ground sometimes, but he kept pushing with his legs and holding on to the trees and in less than a minute his eyes were level with the road. He crawled up onto the shoulder and kneeled there. Cars were coming, but he couldn't see any blue lights. They were coming at about sixty miles an hour. From the north two were coming side by side, with another one behind them maybe a few hundred feet back. He got up on one knee and waited for the two, and looked down the highway to the south, and he could see headlights coming that way, too. He couldn't stop on the median. He'd have to go for it.

The two cars got closer. One put on its brights and almost swerved. The other slowed and fell back.

"Come on," he said. "I ain't got all night."

The first car passed him and the other one had slowed to less than thirty, which caused the car behind it to start out to pass.

Domino went.

The front car's brakes slammed on and he heard a tire squeal and ran right in front of it, thought for a weak moment in his heart it was going to get him, even fancied that he felt the fender brush the back of his pants, but the car only blared its horn and went on up the road. He jumped down into the ditch and ran up the other side and the road was full of cars and trucks coming. There were bright lights on high poles all along the highway. He headed toward the traffic, trotting south down the shoulder, looking over his shoulder to see if blue lights were coming. They were. Fast. And he wasn't going back to Parchman.

He ran into the traffic and two cars slid wide toward the ditch on either side and another spun with its horn blaring *BWAAAAAAAAA!* and slammed into a pickup that was trying to avoid one of the cars in front and these last two were center-punched almost immediately from behind by a gravel truck that showered them with some of its load when the rear end lifted up and its headlights shattered into bits of flying glass. Tires were screeching all over the place.

He saw a car pinwheel twice end over end above a cloud of dust and a pile of torn metal where lights were aimed crazily and horns were blowing and steam was rising from buckled hoods and twisted frames and in that cloud of dust was somebody up above it, flying with no wings to the side of the road. He ran through the smoke and the shattered plastic, broken bits of red lenses crunching beneath his boots.

He heard a woman say, quite clearly, even calmly: "Mother, oh my."

Then he was through it and climbing another bank of grass. He clawed his way up it and ran over a low mound of ground and kneeled behind a young tree to look back for a second to see the shit he had done. God almighty. He'd done fucked some people up. Killed some of them maybe. There wasn't any way to turn back now.

The blue lights were pulling in and stopping and more were coming from up the bypass. At this elevation he could see them coming, screaming, and he knew that some of them were probably state troopers. Pissed off, with pump shotguns just itching to shoot somebody like him. He got up and jogged away into the darkness of the golf course, where the short grass made for easy running. He would cross that highway again somewhere south of here. Later.

57

Wayne's new orders came in on a noisy orange-and-white Coast Guard chopper that landed on the flight deck about 1620. Guys in coveralls and orange helmets passed out the mail and some cakes and cookies from home. The captain called Wayne into his tiny stateroom where he was working at his tiny desk. Wayne stood at attention before him, wondering what the hell he'd done.

"Stubbock?"

"Yes, sir."

"At ease, sailor, look. SEC-NAV wants you over at Camp LeJeune ASAP for a match with this jarhead Johnson from Third MAW. I know it's a rush job, but Admiral Hoozey called this in. Happens to be a big fan of yours. And I got a lot of shit to do. I may be getting shit-canned right out of this man's navy for running over a sick whale. That's some pretty ironic shit, ain't it?"

"Sir? The admiral? Is a fan of mine?" Wayne said.

The captain nodded.

"The admiral saw you in Philadelphia and won fifteen hundred on you off the army brass. When you knocked out Stevenson two months ago. I picked up three hundred myself. Buys a lot of cold Schlitz, Stubbock."

The captain had his pen in his hand and it was poised over the papers. How could he tell him he needed to go back to Memphis, not North Carolina? How could he tell him about Anjalee? He tried to stall.

"Sir, uh. That's not long to train for a fight."

The captain visibly recoiled and then recovered.

"Let me tell you something, sailor. Sometimes the United States Navy has to fight with no warning at all. Look at Pearl Harbor, sneaky bastards. You can stay on this tin can if you want to. I'm just waiting for retirement anyway. I'm short. I'm so short I can sit on a dime and swing my legs."

Wayne didn't know what to say. What about his headaches?

"I'm so short I can walk under a *door.*"

"Sir. Uh. I need to get back to Memphis sometime. Would it be possible for me to get some leave after the fight?"

The captain looked puzzled. "You just got some shore leave. Why you want to go back to Memphis? You're from Ohio, aren't you?"

He didn't know what to say. He said it.

"I left something there, sir."

"Well . . ."

The captain looked back up.

"What'd you leave? A girl?"

"Yes, sir," Wayne said reluctantly. And then he stood straight and strengthened his voice. "Yessir. A girl."

"All right, well . . . in that case . . . hmmm . . ." The captain hummed a few lines of "I Left My Heart in San Francisco" while tapping his fingers and then picked up another piece of paper and scribbled something on it and stamped it and handed it to Wayne.

"Look here. I got a woman in Tampa with tits that'll make you weep when you have to leave port. You go whip this marine for the power and the glory of the United States Navy and I'll give you a ten-day furlough. Guaranteed. There's a colonel at LeJeune I'd like to win some of my money back off of anyway. We were in San Diego together. Asshole used to cheat me at pinochle."

"Are you serious, sir? Ten days?"

"I'm serious as a heart attack, son."

"Yessir."

"Go pack your stuff, then. That chopper's burning fuel waiting for you and it's getting dark."

He had to say good-bye to Henderson quickly. Everything he owned ended up in one olive-drab duffel bag. They stood in the passageway together, and Wayne tried to talk fast, but he just didn't have time to explain it all.

"Well shit," Henderson said, shuffling his feet. "You just takin' off, just like that? I thought me and you's gonna watch a bunch of movies this weekend."

"I know," Wayne said, and then he stopped. "I meant to tell you something. I met a girl in Memphis. And I . . . we . . . I'm going back down there. But I've got to fight this marine. I got to beat this marine."

"I want to *see* it," Henderson said. "I want to be there to *pull* for you, man, you the man with all the *shit*, man, you the *man*, man!"

"You can't . . . I've got to go to North Carolina . . ."

"I'll ask for a transfer."

"How long will that take?"

"I don't know."

Then the captain stepped in between them, suddenly, from out of nowhere.

"What the hell's going on? You burning taxpayers' money on that deck, Stubbock. You better get it in gear."

The captain for some reason had his helmet on. He hardly ever had his helmet on.

"Yessir."

The captain turned away.

"Sir?"

The captain stopped. The straps of his helmet were swinging. He turned around.

"Can Henderson come, too?"

The captain got hot quick. He hardly ever got hot quick. Maybe the captain was losing his marbles over the whale shit. Maybe he'd been away from those big boys in Tampa too long. Maybe the permanent vacation he was about to get would calm him down some. And a big fat monthly paycheck for the rest of his life. With PX privileges.

"I don't give a shit! Go pack, Henderson, I'll send your paperwork later." He turned away. "Hit a whale. Jesus. Even Nimitz never hit a frigging whale." And then he wandered on off down the hallway, muttering to himself loudly about how the President didn't know what a dork Admiral Zumo was.

Later: The chopper was sitting thrumming and jetting thin black smoke with its blades slowly winding up and it began with a small piercing whine that slowly grew into a noise that was steady and deadly and that soon blasted out every other sound, going *WOCKA-WOCKAWOCKAWOCKA WOCKAWOCKAWOCKAWOCKAWOCKA!* The blades lifted and Wayne and Henderson, bent over with their duffel bags, scurried across the deck with their clothes rippling and climbed aboard and then it lifted off with its wheels rolling slightly and went about fifty feet aloft in front of the bridge and then turned above the deck and lifted higher and tilted and turned back toward the southwest, and its blades whipped into the night, and the chopper itself went out of sight except for its little red light that blinked steadily on its way to the great pine forests of North Carolina, where lived in those deep-green woods platoons and companies of running American warriors who sang an old song about kicking ass from the halls of Montezuma to the shores of Tripoli.

58

The cops had her in a room with a mirror in it. The ones who had nabbed her had given her to some other guys as soon as they'd gotten her to the jail. Anjalee knew from watching a million TV shows that it was really a two-way glass, and that another cop or maybe two or three more cops were sitting behind it, watching her talk to the plainclothes guy and listening to everything she said. They'd been talking to her at a desk with a bright overhead light. The room was none too clean. Broken tiles and smashed peanut shells. Some very flat cigarette butts.

They'd already done the good cop/bad cop thing with her cigarettes. One cop had played good and would let her have a cigarette and one had played bad and wouldn't. Right now the one playing good was back in the room with her, so she was smoking. She didn't like him as much as the one playing bad. The one playing good had bad breath and dandruff and long nose and ear hair poking out all over the place, actually needed to have that seen about pretty soon with some type of barbering person.

The one playing bad was kind of small but muscular and had a nice clean head of hair and pretty cool clothes with good shoes, she always noticed shoes. He was outside somewhere. Maybe looking at her through the two-way glass. She wished he'd come back in because she was hoping she could fuck her way out of this.

"So," Good Cop said, shelling some wet goobers from a paper bag. "Why'd you work over Miss Barbee over at the uh . . . ?" He paused to chew and consult a card on his desk. "Pleasant Years Nursing Home?"

"I had my reasons," she said. Pleasant years my ass.

He leaned forward. It was hard to keep from staring at the tufts of hair protruding from his ears. But she didn't really want to look at his nose, either. She settled for staring at the middle of his forehead.

"They better be good ones. You could be going up the river on this one. I see on your rap sheet where you couldn't make it as a hooker in our fair city."

He dawdled with a rubber band for a little bit. He'd brought back the ashtray that Bad Cop had taken away and she thumped some ashes in it and took a long slow drag, let it trail out her nose.

"Some of your boys are worse than some of the ones they're after."

He raised his eyebrows. They even had dandruff in them. He had about the worse case she'd ever seen. An epidemic on his head.

"She slapped this old man," she said.

The cop didn't say anything for a moment. He just gazed at the wall.

"Are you sure?" he said without looking at her.

"She slapped him twice."

Now he did look at her.

"Why'd she slap him?"

She waited a moment before she answered, thinking about her grandmother. She remembered how her grandmother had smelled.

"He messed in the bed."

The door opened and the one playing bad cop stood there.

"Are you willing to testify to that?" he said.

She straightened in her chair.

"What do you mean? Why?"

"A few old people died over there who weren't very sick according to some relatives who called it in. We think maybe she's got something to do with it. We're getting ready to do an investigation."

The names and faces, the watery eyes behind the glasses hit her with a new shock: Mr. Pasternak, Miss Doobis, Mr. Munchie, Mrs. Haddow-Green. Sweet old farts every one. She leaned back and crossed her legs.

"Hey, close the door, Ronnie, huh?" the one playing good said.

The one playing bad came on in after he shut the door and sat down at the scuffed table. He was wearing an empty brown shoulder holster over his burgundy sweater.

"I like your sweater," Anjalee said.

"So does my girlfriend who made it. You want me to tell her, Acey, or you want to?"

"Why don't you tell her, Ronnie." Acey said, and then scratched with all his fingers at his scalp briefly but furiously.

"You know there's people who can help you with that," Anjalee said.

"Who? I've tried everything!" he shouted. "I'm about to go absolutely! Fucking! Wacko!"

"What the shit, Ace." Ronnie said. ".Having a bad-hair day?"

"Sorry, Ronnie. Look. I gotta go wash my hair with this medicated crap my wife got me. You give her the lowdown about her probation and all that bullshit. I'll be back later."

And he got up abruptly and rushed out of the room. The door slammed. She didn't feel anybody watching her now but Ronnie. His eyes were brown and sad, like a sick beagle's.

"Look," he said. "Miss Barbee's healed up enough to be transferred from the Med to here and we're holding her until we can find out if we can charge her with anything. But your ass is in a crack, 'cause you violated your probation by not going back to work at the old folks' home."

He leaned over a little bit. He was half smiling.

"You know what it means. Handcuffs. Wearing an orange jumpsuit. They can strip-search you and look up your ass any old time they want to. And take it from me, the women in the Shelby County Jail are not the gentle refined kind who'll offer you a bite off their Hershey bars. You know we can send you off. Or just keep you here."

He'd said it now and she was scared shitless all over again. What'd she ever come up to this fucking place for? She remembered all those women-in-prison movies at the Pontotoc drive-in with her mother moaning and groaning along with some guy in the back seat.

"Yeah. I know."

"Where the hell you from, anyway, Mississippi or some fucking where?"

"Yeah. Toccopola," she said in a small voice.

"Another hick comes to town."

"So did Elvis."

"Oh crap." He laughed a short one. Then he picked up some papers on the desk and looked at them and then dropped them. "This is your arrest report. You got nabbed by the couch cops giving blow jobs at Fifi's Cabaret? Jesus. That rat palace should have got shut down a long time before it did. I heard Fifi got deported back to Kyrgyzstan."

"Yeah. But they didn't actually catch me giving anybody one."

He folded his arms across his chest.

"It's against the law to *try* to rob a bank, kid. Or to offer up your sweet monkey for money. In this state anyway. When'd you start selling your ass?"

She looked up at the wall and away from him. She swung her leg.

"A long time ago. But I worked in that club for a while."

"How long did that go on?"

She turned her face back to him. Still swinging her leg.

"Not long. I met this guy. I've been with him for a while. I mean, I stayed with him for a while. I've got somebody else now."

That seemed to amuse him.

"Why don't you try for a regular relationship with somebody that doesn't involve them paying you for sex?"

She shook her hair out of her eyes and looked back over at him.

" 'Cause I guess I kinda like the way it feels."

His eyes changed and so did his body posture and his voice got lower.

"How much do you charge?"

"It depends on what I need. Right now I need to get the fuck out of here."

He leaned back and studied her. He lowered his gaze and looked long at her breasts. Like he was thinking them over. He gave them that little smile again.

"You know what?" he said slowly. "I'll bet we can work something out where you can be released on your own recognizance in case we need you to help us out later. I mean, with the approval of your probation officer, of course. You'll have to check back in with him but I can probably straighten it all out."

Anjalee looked around. She stopped swinging her leg.

"Where's he at?"

"He's probably around somewhere. We'll go find him. But it might take a while."

"That's okay. I wasn't doing anything anyway."

"Well, come on, then. My car's outside."

59

The little dog must have had a wet dream. That's what it looked like. He whined and jerked in his sleep in the laundry room, behind the washing machine, for a pretty long time and his legs looked like they were running except that they were stretched out on the floor, pedaling like somebody on an exercise machine. Then his little red rubber rod came out and he leaked some stuff right on the floor. Then he went back to sleep. Or never woke up. No telling what Miss Muffett would have said if she'd seen that. She might have shit a brick.

60

Merlot called Farm Bureau in Oxford and told them about his minivan getting shot up, but they weren't surprised, oh no. They knew all about it because it had been in the paper that afternoon along with the stuff about the massive car wreck out on the bypass in which, amazingly, nobody had been killed. His agent, who was an avid coon hunter and owned a number of champion treeing Walkers that were standing at stud for three hundred dollars a pop and was forever trying to get Merlot to go out for a night in the woods with him, in a low and confidential voice also informed him that the unidentified man who had attempted to carjack him had escaped from the hospital where he'd been taken to get doctored for the wounds Merlot had inflicted on him, and had superficially stabbed a Dr. Kubuku, from Nairobi, and had superficially wounded a police officer whose name the paper hadn't released. There was also a search going on for a missing constable down in Yalobusha County, some guy named Perkins. That was in the paper, too. Merlot was pretty flabbergasted that the guy had escaped. His agent, D. C. Henry, told him it was no problem, that they had a *shonuff* nice late-model Four-Runner Limited repo they could let him have until the cops turned loose of his minivan and it got fixed. It had low mileage. Penelope drove him into Oxford after they did it again and over to the office on the west end of town so he could sign some papers and they almost never got away from there for having to tell the story to people over and over and introduce Penelope over and over. The only problem was that the Four-Runner was sitting in a lot over at the agency in Batesville, which was run by a guy named Smiley, but that turned out to be not a problem at all since Penelope happily drove him over on some of her administrative-leave time and they picked it up. It was a pretty cool ride. They got the keys and walked around it admiring it and then got inside it and cranked it up. It was a pearl color with gold trim on the outside and nice tan seats that got warm when you flicked a switch and it had a very good sound system with a six-disc CD changer in it. They didn't know that the deadbeat it had been repoed from had left it with almost a full tank of gas because he was inside Larson's Big Star on University Avenue buying a suitcase of Bud Light and some pigskins and a few Slim Jims when the repo boys grabbed it off the parking lot with a special wrecker made just for grabbing repos off parking lots in thirty seconds or less. Merlot went back inside and signed some papers to take care of all that and then kissed Penelope good-bye in the parking lot. She was seated but leaning out the open door of her red Blazer, pale smoke jetting from the tailpipe. Merlot stood inside the door and squeezed one of her cyclopean breasts surreptitiously and softly while he gave her a long kiss that he figured looked like Dick Burton giving it to Liz Taylor back in their heydays. After a while he pulled back and looked into her eyes. They were moist, but she didn't blink. She didn't blink much.

"You gonna call me tonight?" she said.

"Absolutely. I've just got to teach this last class and then get my grades together."

"When we gonna go over to your house? I want to see your place."

"I don't know . . . like I said, it's dirty and needs to be cleaned up . . . maybe in a day or two . . ."

"You don't want me over at your house," she said, all pouty suddenly, and she somehow managed to look abused. "What, I ain't good enough to bring home?"

"I just want to clean it up first," he said.

She drew back. She looked at her nails. They were white and glossy and short.

"Well, okay. You better call me."

"I will."

"Maybe we could go out to eat."

"Maybe we could."

"Don't you be flirtin' with none of them little old skank gals in your class, you hear me?"

"I won't."

" 'Cause ain't none of them little gals got any stuff near as good as what I got for you."

"I know that's right."

"Well. Long as you know."

"I do. Believe me, baby, I do."

"Why? You done screwed some of that little bony ass with that big old thang? I bet they done some yellin'."

"Hell no."

She turned her chin up sideways a little.

"Baby. Come on. They didn't do no yellin'?"

"I mean no I didn't . . ."

She laughed at his reddening face with her pretty teeth white as ivory, her rich voice deep, her cheek in a strong brown curve. She chucked him under the chin with her fist, softly. She kept looking at him from up under her eyelashes. Girls knew how to do stuff to you. Boy did they. This one was melting him like Silly Putty on a hot day.

"I'm just playin' with you, baby."

"I know it. I like you to play with me. You can play with me all you want to."

"I plan to. Tonight."

He stepped back and she shut the door and pulled off. He watched her circle through the parking lot and go down the hill and stop at the highway, then heard her toot the horn before she headed back.

Merlot got in and drove fast, back to Oxford and the campus. It was early in the afternoon and a lot of students had already left for the Christmas break, so there wasn't any problem finding a parking slot near Bishop Hall. He stopped by his office and got all his notes. He hurried upstairs and picked up his grade sheets in the English department office and then almost never got out of there for people wanting to talk about his carjacking, even some people who worked in offices down the hall, and he had to tell it three or four times but he finally said he had to get to class and they understood and finally let him go but told him they wanted to get together for a drink or two sometime in the near future and hear the whole story and he said okay and walked down the hall to the classroom but nobody was there. That was good because he didn't have his class together.

So much had gone on in the last couple days. He'd been smoking all that dope and they'd made a bunch of love, about nine times. All he was going to do anyway was give a summary of the semester, and he could do that off the top of his head. He sat there going over the notes he'd made over the semester but none of the students started drifting in. Then two did. By the time he'd been sitting there for ten minutes, he realized that was probably all he could expect, so he launched into a discussion about the things they'd read, kind of an overview, and he could tell that they were just as ready to get out of there as he was, and had already had about all they could stand for one semester, just like him, so he cut it short and let them go real early. They asked if he was okay because they'd seen the paper and he said he was and wished them a merry Christmas and they left.

After class he hustled over to the grill, through the dead brown leaves that were blowing across the campus in the chilly wind, and picked up a cup of coffee and a club sandwich and then went back to his overheated office and spread all his papers out on his desk and ate his sandwich and drank the coffee until it got cold, and worked up his grades. He signed all the papers and filled in all the little boxes and then took them back up to the English department office, which had closed by then, but he had everything in a manila envelope with his name on it and he just crammed it in under the door.

After that he drove around for a while. He didn't know what to do. He wasn't ready to tell her about Candy yet. Maybe they ought to just take on off, just go ahead and go. Maybe he could tell her in Natchez.

He circled the square in Oxford. The city electric department had hung wreaths on all the light poles and all the stores had Christmas decorations out. There was Christmas music playing on loudspeakers mounted in front of city hall. People were out shopping. Some were carrying bright gift-wrapped packages. A shitload of people were in the bookstore. Neilson's had people going in and out. He thought about going by City Grocery and having a drink, because he knew that some of his colleagues from the English department would probably be in there, celebrating the end of another semester, but he knew if he got in there he'd probably catch a buzz and stay too long, and he wanted more than anything first to check on Candy. So he went by his house.

Mrs. Poteet met him at the door. A natural redhead, her now-raven hair was piled high and she was wearing a tight red dress with sequins and a daring slit up the side. She gave him a fierce hug with her bony freckled arms.

"Hey, Marla. How is she?" he said.

"She's asleep," she said, patting him on the back. "I'm so glad you're all right. It was in the paper."

"That's what I heard."

Merlot walked down the hall and into the room. Candy was lying on her bed and she was asleep. Her ribs were rising and falling slightly with her breath. She hadn't shit in the bed. He thought about the first time she'd slipped into the bed with him, and how he hadn't told his mother about it, until the morning she'd walked in and caught them together. But she never had said anything. He guessed she'd always known that they'd one day wind up sleeping together. But they didn't now. She'd gotten too old for that.

He didn't wake her to tell her good-bye. She looked peaceful. What if she died while he was gone? He went into his bedroom and packed some clothes and underwear and socks, another pair of boots, got his toothbrush and toothpaste and his shaving gear from the bathroom, then went to the kitchen for some cash from under the cookie jar.

"I guess I'm going off for a few days," he said to Mrs. Poteet. She was sitting on the kitchen counter having a glass of red wine. She had the stereo going and was listening to C. J. Chenier doing "Bad Feet." "You got enough wine to last you?"

"We're good," she said. "A bunch of people called over here today wanting to talk to you. They all saw that thing in the paper. Was it horrible?"

"It was horrible enough," Merlot said. "Hell, I might as well have a glass with you, Marla. I'm not in that big a hurry."

"Please do," Mrs. Poteet said, and got him a glass from the cabinet without getting down. She poured him a full one and then lit a thin cigarillo. She had crossed one leg over the other in the tight dress. In her prime she'd been a stripper named Louisiana Red. Now she was about eighty years old, but still evidently pretty hot. She had more than one boyfriend now that she was a widow, and once, after attending a poetry seminar in St. Petersburg, Merlot'd found three empty condom packets in the bathroom garbage can. And had chuckled looking at them.

He leaned against the counter, close to her, and sipped his wine.

"I met somebody," he said.

Mrs. Poteet's eyes watered and filled almost up with tears but didn't brim over until she lowered her face and shook her head, slinging a few of them on Merlot's leg.

"Oh! I am *so* glad," she said.

"I'll bring her over sometime. She's got to meet Candy."

"Well, maybe you shouldn't wait too long."

"How's she been lately?"

Mrs. Poteet lifted her glass and sipped, then lowered it and held it with one hand. She rubbed the ash from her cigarillo on the edge of the ashtray.

"Every day's about the same. I don't think even she wants to live much longer. You could always call Dr. Dees. He's got that painless steel."

"Yeah, that's true," Merlot said. It was an old discussion.

The clock ticked. The television was playing low up front. A car went down the street outside. He hoped it wouldn't snow anymore.

"What's her name?" Mrs. Poteet said.

"Penelope. She's a cop."

"That's such a lovely name. Are you falling in love with her, Merlot?"

He took a big drink of his wine.

"Shit. I think maybe I already have."

He set his glass down and went to the phone on the wall.

"I'll be gone a few days probably. I'll call you and give you my number once I get somewhere. I think we're going to Texado in Natchez if we can get in. I'm gonna call them. Probably stop somewhere tonight. But you've got my cell phone, too."

"Yes I do. Well then. I might have a couple people over tonight if that's okay. I've got a few friends who are just dying to watch *Dancing Outlaw* and I told them you had *Vernon, Florida*, too, so we might just get into an orgy of video watching tonight." She gave him a look. "And maybe some other things, too."

"You go for it, girl. Buy some more wine if you need it. If you need any money, it's right there under the cookie jar."

"I know where it's at. I don't need anything," Mrs. Poteet said, lifting her glass.

"You want to get stoned? You want a couple of joints?"

A smiled leaped on her face and she leaned forward eagerly.

"Why, Merlot, have you got some?"

He reached into his shirt pocket and pulled out two and put them in her hand. She stared at them and he grinned when she dropped her jaw.

"This stuff does the trick."

"Coo-ool," she said. "I know just who to call."

He called information and got the number for Texado and a nice lady answered and they exchanged a few pleasantries and he found out that they could get in tomorrow night, preferably before six P.M. if they wanted dinner. He said that was cool and thanked the lady and told her 'bye and called Penelope and told her to start getting ready. On the way out, he squatted down and got a few CDs from the rack in the living room and told Mrs. Poteet 'bye and drove on down to Penelope's house, stopping on the way for some rubbers at a Texaco station just off 315 that sold hot gizzards and cold minnows. She wasn't ready and he had to sit on her bed and wait for her to pack her clothes and her gun, and he didn't understand why she was taking it, but he didn't say anything, and when she finally got ready, they took off from her house in the Four-Runner happily still burning the deadbeat's gas. He sped driving over to Tupelo and they got on the Trace there. Merlot said it would make for a longer, more scenic ride if they got on it there instead of down close to Columbus. He drove while she sightsaw but it was starting to get dark. They saw a few groups of deer but he guessed the turkeys had already roosted. There were some pretty creeks beside the road, where the water ran over rocks and trickled through trees. It was nice to be able to drive at a leisurely pace and not have all those monster trucks breathing down your neck. Why did they sometimes creep up close behind you and start blowing their horns and scaring the shit out of you on downhill grades in the steep, curvy mountains of the Pisgah National Forest in North Carolina? He still didn't know if she would understand about Candy. He'd made a very short call on her phone while she was in the shower and Mrs. Poteet said that Candy was awake now and fine but missing him.

"You know," she said, leaning on his shoulder for a while. "I just love going where I've never been."

She loved food the same way he did. She wouldn't make a peep while you were trying to watch a movie but would bring peanuts and pretzels and chips and dip and wine and frigid beer noiselessly. She knew all about baseball and played on the police league fast-pitch softball team in the summers, and pitched. Merlot was already thinking up names for the kids. They'd name one KuShondra, another Raymond, maybe a Herman.

They spent the first night in a perfect house off the beaten path, a place they found by just getting off the Trace close to Starkville and cruising over to Columbus and driving around in the city until they saw a friendly-looking police officer taking a smoke break on a bench and stopped and asked him about a place to stay. His name was Calvin and he said there was a great bed-and-breakfast called White Arches just up the street and told them what street and exactly how to get there and told them to just knock since it was so early and the old lady who ran it would come to the door. And he was exactly right. There was a huge old brown house with a wide brick walk and white trim around the windows and a deep front porch where wicker rocking chairs were set up and the porch ceiling was high and lined with bead board and the front doors were tall and very thick with leaded glass panels and brass latch plates and knobs and there were giant magnolias in the yard and even a small lighted goldfish pond with curved stone benches where you could sit and read a book if you wanted to, the old lady said, except that it had gotten too dark to read by then. There were some woods up behind the house, owls in the woods, she said gaily, told them they might hear them hoot hoot hooting!

The old white-haired lady was tiny and bent over slightly with a small hump in the middle of her back but she welcomed them in, babbling like she was on Ecstasy, and said she had a room or three ready and that if they would like to drink some wine and nibble on some Brie and shrimp and give her an hour or so, she could have the maid fix up some dinner for them. The room was upstairs and Merlot and Penelope carried their stuff up into the bedroom, which was full of antiques, and it had a high four-poster bed with a canopy and a dark-green velvet drape. There was a pair of French doors that opened onto a short balcony. The ornate wallpaper was slightly torn in a few places, but a delicate bedside table held a bottle of red wine, a bowl of fruit, two glasses, and a corkscrew. The maid, in a crisp uniform and a starched cap, knocked and then entered with a tray holding a warmed wedge of the cheese and a knife and an array of crackers on napkins and a small bowl of peeled pink shrimp along-side a bowl of cocktail sauce and another one of lemon wedges and a bottle of green Tabasco. She set it down on the coffee table and went back out butt first with a little bow.

Merlot dropped the luggage and sat on the bed and pulled out one of the joints and fired it up. The bed had five or six thick pillows piled against the headboard and he leaned against them. Penelope closed the door. Then she locked it. She was looking around, touching a leather couch, taking off her blouse, smiling, shaking her head over a footstool made from an elephant's foot. The ceiling was high and carved with wood intricacies by some long-dead carpenter and the windows were draped with sheer white material over the blinds.

"Pretty nice, huh?" Merlot said, and passed her the joint. She snuggled down beside him and took a few tugs on it.

"Wow," she said. "Did you see that straight-up piano downstairs? That thing's got to be two hundred years old."

She took one more toke and then handed the joint back to Merlot. He took a few more hits and then moved some little tied-up lace bags of colored rice from a brass tortoise shell and mashed it out. He handed her a glass and got the corkscrew and opened the wine and poured them half a glass apiece. They sipped and lay back on the bed. Merlot smiled at her.

"And did you hear the old lady cackling with happiness? Hell yes she takes American Express! I thought she was gonna carry our luggage up."

Penelope giggled in her deep and lovely voice.

"She's a sweet old thing, ain't she? Reminds me of my mamaw. I bet this house has been in her family since the Civil War. I bet we'll sleep good in here."

"Yeah, if we get to sleep any," he told her, and bent her back on the bed, since her snow-white bra was showing about a foot of deep brown cleavage. There was a tiny silver star pinned high on the left cup that he knew she wore just for fun. But her gun was in her bag. Loaded probably. It had made him a little nervous to have it in the Four-Runner the whole way down here and it was still making him nervous to have it in here in the bedroom with them but he didn't say anything. Not then.

Later: Dinner that night was candlelit in the deserted dining room, muted but certainly not sad, fine dark wood on the walls where hung pictures of stiff old white people long turned to dust beneath engraved slabs of stone, fine linen on the table, crystal glasses, a whole browned duckling with an orange glaze, truffles in sauce, more good wine, and the creamiest mashed potatoes Merlot had ever tasted. The maid came in from time to time to bring more homemade rolls or butter. After they'd finished, the old lady came out with her book from her room where she'd been reading, and asked them if they'd like to share a brandy and a coffee with her, to which they said they'd be delighted. She said she'd be back in a few minutes.

Penelope was radiant in a clingy dark-blue knit dress with a neckline that would stop a man in his tracks, her hair pinned up in a tight, shiny bun, and Merlot couldn't get enough of just looking at her. Even though he was pretty full, he was already smiling at the thought of being naked with her on that big soft bed with the canopy, holding her good brown body in his hands, and then going to sleep beside her, safe and warm in Columbus.

"You turn me on," he said, and she squeezed his hand across the table. He could already imagine the food they were going to cook together. She knew all those Creole recipes for jambalaya and all that good New Orleans food. He could show her how to make bread. He could show her how to make biscuit pudding like his mother's. They could call his mother up, maybe drive down to Gulf Shores and see her sometime.

She picked up her wine and sipped at it. She'd been a little quieter the last few minutes and he wondered if something was bothering her. But he held off asking her. It might not be any of his business. And he hadn't known her that long. She kept sitting there and sipping lightly on her wine.

"What's wrong?" he finally said.

She smiled too quickly.

"Nothing."

"Don't bullshit, baby."

Then she looked away and rested her chin on her hand for a moment.

"I shouldn't be here, Merlot."

He leaned back in his chair and picked at a scrap of truffle with his fork. It seemed almost cruel to train pigs to hunt them but not give them any when they found a nice juicy patch. They probably fed them the rotten ones.

"Why not?"

She took her hand down and put both of them in her lap.

"I ought to be back there helping them look for Perk."

"The cop who's missing?"

She was slow to raise her eyes and look at him. Finally she did.

"Yeah. I knew him pretty well. Or at least I used to."

It wasn't so much what she said. It was the way she was looking. So. Okay. There it was. She'd been lovers with this missing constable maybe. But did he expect her to be a chaste virgin? Hell no. She was thirty-three. Would it have been unusual for a female police officer to be at some point in her life sexually involved with a male police officer? Shit no. Not unless it would be unusual for a female dill-pickle slicer to be involved with a male dill-pickle slicer. And the same thing could be said for dogcatchers and librarians, or those who climbed tall poles with spikes on their boots and tools swinging from their belts. Maybe they'd shot their guns together on the weekends.

"Well," he said. "I'm not here to ask you a bunch of personal stuff about your private life before I met you 'cause I just met you."

She toyed with her napkin. She seemed suddenly at a loss for the proper words.

"I know you did. And you're a sweet man."

"Don't beat yourself up. You're off duty."

She nodded and looked down at the floor.

"That's right."

"You're actually suspended from active duty for two whole weeks. With pay."

"That's true."

"So they probably wouldn't let you help look for him even if you were still back there. Would they?"

"I don't guess they would," she said. "They're pretty strict about stuff like that."

She looked up at him, and her eyes were almost wet. Her nostrils flared.

"I just thought maybe I should tell you about him. I don't want any secrets between us about . . . stuff like that."

Merlot held her eyes with his. The question kept running through his mind, face-to-face with her like this. Was now the time to level with her about Candy? She was damn sure leveling with him about this damn constable.

"Baby. I'm not asking any questions."

"I think I'm going to call sometime and see if they've found out anything."

He tapped his fork gently on the edge of his plate and then laid it down. He wasn't sure what to say about all that. He lifted his wineglass and sipped from it briefly.

"Do you think he's dead?"

She didn't answer at first. Merlot set his glass down and ran his hand over the tablecloth. It was littered with a few bread crumbs that he swept together with the edge of his hand and then put them on his plate. He dusted off his hands. He looked up at her.

"I don't know. Rico would have made the guy tell him where Perk was if the guy hadn't escaped from the hospital. If the guy knew. If he's got anything to do with it. And he probably does. He carjacked you pretty close to a place where Perk parks sometimes."

"Where Perk parks? Who's Rico?"

"Elwood's brother. Perk's brother. He's a detective. We left before he got to the jail, but I know he was on his way over there. And he would have made him tell."

"How would he be able to do that?"

She sighed and took a sip of her wine.

"He would have probably held a knife to his balls. He did that to a guy who robbed a bank with some friends in Coffeeville and Rico wanted to know where the rest of them were. He found out, too. That's how he got promoted to detective."

"Holy shit," Merlot said slowly. "You were dating his *brother*?"

About that time the old lady returned with a tray and brandy glasses and a bottle of Christian Brothers. So they had to stop talking about all that, and start sipping brandy and listening to the old lady, who was originally from Starkville, where the legendary Johnny Cash himself had once been nabbed for picking flowers, back when she was about fifty, although there was no plaque that she knew of in the town to commemorate the historic event. At least not yet.

61

Bad cop Ronnie took Anjalee over to the mostly deserted Mid-South Fairgrounds, kind of close to Fairview Junior High and Christian Brothers College, pulled up behind a clump of naked trees, and humped her rapidly on the cold vinyl back seat of a cold city police car with the motor running, raising his head once in a while and looking around and then humping some more. She thought, What if some schoolkids come along, taking a shortcut? But she didn't have to worry about that for long. It took him only about three or four minutes. His whole face turned red and a big vein leaped out in his neck. He did these snorting noises, too. She didn't get a lot of fun out of it but after that he drove her back over to Gigi's Angels and let her go, told her to keep her nose clean. She asked him to take her on back to the Peabody where her Camry was and he looked at her and asked her did he look like he was running a charity taxi service? So there was nothing to do but get out. And it was snowing again. Little bitty flakes were just drifting around. Probably wouldn't accumulate. Not over a few inches. But you never could tell. It might snow asshole deep to a long-legged Indian in Siberia.

62

The little dog woke up and yawned and stretched and scratched himself some, then went out to the empty kitchen and lapped some water loudly from his bowl. He didn't see anything to eat because there wasn't anything there. Maybe he was hungry and looking for something to eat was why he went upstairs.

He hiked his leg up and peed on a potted plant and wandered on down the hall, in and out of rooms. The door to his goodie room was closed. He whined and scratched at it, but not for long. He'd learned. Dogs do. He went on looking around.

Then he went into another room and stopped dead still. A big white bone was lying on the floor and it was the biggest bone he'd ever seen. There was some noise coming from the top of the bed, only he didn't know it was a bed. He probably didn't have any way of knowing it was Miss Muffett snoring, but maybe in some other way, some secret dog way that people don't know anything about, he did.

He walked around to the end of the big bone and found a hollow place where he could put his teeth into it. It was kind of heavy when he started dragging it, but the little dog went down the hall backward with it, pulling it toward the stairs like a sled dog mushing in reverse.

He got down them one step at a time. Pull a little, rest a little, pull a little, rest a little. In this way he managed to get it down to the kitchen. It must have made him thirsty because he took some more drinks of his water, and then looked around, as if searching for a good place to bury it. Then he saw his own personal door.

63

Arthur was getting worried about her because it was almost ten o'clock and she didn't have any business being out late by herself because she was probably drinking. He was really afraid the cops were going to get her again. She'd sounded pretty mad when she'd thrown the stuff at the door and yelled at him. She'd even used the F word. He guessed she'd lost all her patience now.

He thought about going out to look for her but he would have to call a cab if he did. And, too, if he left, she might come in while he was gone. And then it occurred to him that maybe he should call the pet shop where Eric worked and ask him if he'd seen her. But what was the name of the pet shop? What was it? It was the name of a car. Was it Edsel? No, it wasn't that. Was it the Pontiac Pet Shop? That didn't sound right either. It was some kind of a car they didn't make anymore. DeSoto maybe? Nah. Hudson? Nah. Nash Rambler? Nah.

He sat there with the phone book in his lap. He started going through the Yellow Pages, licking his fingers the way his mother used to, paging rapidly, his gray head bent.

64

Domino slept in a barn.
It was a big barn.
It was a horse barn.
It belonged to a cop.
But he didn't know that.
It had plenty of hay.
It had cat food, too.

He found some Friskies Kitten.

They had those pull rings.

It didn't taste so bad.

And he was powerful hungry.

He actually ate two cans.

One was chicken in gravy.

One was salmon in gravy.

Both were in little chunks.

The gravy was mildly congealed.

It left him feeling unsatisfied.

The barn was pretty dark.

It was good for hiding.

He didn't see any horses.

He pulled hay over him.

Then he slept all day.

Or might near all day.

At dusk he heard something.

Somebody came into the barn.

He pulled out Rico's revolver.

Then another somebody came in.

He was in a corner.

It was dark there, too.

Somebody said something pretty sexy.

Then somebody else said something.

And it was even sexier.

Then he heard some sounds.

There was some hay rustling.

There was some moaning going.

Then he heard some girl say *Oh Randy fuck baby fuck my sweet my fuck my! Randy! Fuck!* and he had to lie there and listen to it for a while but finally went back to sleep to dream of falling endlessly down long dark holes with an ocean roaring far below. Good thing the cop who owned the barn didn't hear him snoring, because he did, mouth wide open, the five or six cats that crept in later from the darkness of their baby-rabbit killing leaning over him where they sat in a circle to smell his tantalizing Friskies Kitten breath.

65

In the pet shop, the phone rang. Eric looked at the clock on the wall and it was ten minutes until ten. Usually nobody called this late. He was afraid it was Miss Helen calling from that bar to see if he was coming. And he didn't know if he was or not. He was afraid that if he went over there, he'd wind up doing something with her. But there was also Mister Arthur to think about. A nice old guy. He'd drunk his booze and smoked cigarettes inside his house. He'd slept inside his house. He'd eaten there. He'd caught his cat.

The phone rang again. He went to it and picked it up. He hoped to God it wasn't Mister Arthur calling for some reason.

"Studebaker's," he said. And then he had to say this other thing. One of Mr. Studebaker's ideas. "'Our puppies are precious.'"

"Eric? This is Arthur."

Oh shit. "Oh. Hey. Uh. How you doin'?"

"Well, I'm not too good, Eric," he said right away. "Helen's gone and I don't know where she is and I'm getting worried about her. I was just wondering if by any chance you'd seen her."

"Seen her?"

"Yes. I was wondering if she'd been by the pet shop."

He had to either lie or not lie. A simple yes or a simple no. How could he lie to him? How could he tell him the truth without hurting him?

"Oh no, sir, I haven't seen her, I mean, not lately." Partly true.

"Well. I'm just worried sick about her. She hasn't seemed herself lately. We've had some . . . problems."

"Oh," Eric said. He didn't know what to say. And he hoped Mister Arthur wouldn't get into the problems and what they were over the phone, either. He was afraid it was something like maybe he couldn't get it up anymore because he was so old. He thought old guys had that problem sometimes. He could remember his granddaddy saying one time with a chaw in his jaw the size of a walnut that the whole head of his had done turned purple. And his grandmother laughing and accidentally farting on her front porch where she was shelling butter beans with a bunch of spotted hound dogs lying around asleep with their long tick-studded ears stretched out on the boards.

"She doesn't usually go off like this," Mister Arthur said over the phone. And then he said: "Well, actually, sometimes she does." Eric could picture him, maybe standing in the kitchen in his house shoes with his hair sticking up. He could see the pans on the stove behind him. The kitten was probably still in the pantry. He almost wished now he'd never gone over there. If he hadn't gone over there, he wouldn't be standing here right now trying to decide whether to go over and meet her for a drink or not. And what was he going to do with Jada Pinkett while it was going on? Tie him to a tree? Put him in the trunk? The whole thing just made him feel uneasy.

"You don't have any idea where she could be, do you?" Mister Arthur said.

Now it was down to the nitty-gritty. A big old lie or not. No way to fudge. A direct question concerning her whereabouts.

"I . . . uh . . . maybe she's in a bar somewhere." *You big old liar.*

"I'm sure that's probably true. She's probably at the Peabody. She goes there quite a bit." There was a long silence. A really long silence. It seemed filled with sadness even though it was so silent.

"Are you okay?" Eric said.

"I'm just worried," Mister Arthur said to him over the phone. "I don't know what she might do. I don't know when she might come in. We kind of had a fight. She didn't leave a note or anything and she hasn't called to let me know where she is. You know there was a murder at the barbershop just across from the coffee shop I go to sometimes."

"Oh yeah. I saw that in *The Commercial*," Eric said.

"You just never know," Mister Arthur said over the phone. "It's a big city. Lots of people. Lots of things go on. Probably some things we don't even want to know about."

"I know that's right," Eric said.

"What are you doing?"

"Me? Aw, nothin'. I'm about ready to close."

"What time do you close?"

"Ten."

"What time is it now?"

"It's about five till."

"What are you going to do when you get off work?"

"Aw. I don't know." Just one damn lie after another.

"Have you got old Jada Pinkett in there with you?"

"Yessir, well, he's out in the car. They won't let me bring him in here. He's asleep last time I looked."

"Is he doing okay?"

"Jada Pinkett? Aw yeah, he's fine. He's old, but he's all right."

"Can he still breed?" Arthur asked.

Eric hated to tell him. He remembered it out by the barn. In the shade under the big mimosa tree. Some of his daddy's buddies standing around drinking beer. Telling dirty jokes. His daddy talking about the whore that had left him and how glad he was she was gone. Eric's mother.

"Well, nosir, he cain't get a puppy no more I don't reckon. He don't seem to be able to get it up. Last time Deddy had to take his hand and kind of guide it up in there and . . . I don't reckon it did no good . . . she never did have no puppies. Not from him."

Puppies. There was no telling how many his daddy had drowned. Maybe hundreds. Sometimes the pit-bull boys dug or tore out of their pens and into another and got ahold of the weenie-dog girls, and made a strange, kind of reddish dog, one that was long and low and brindle striped with a big square head and a deep chest that would dig up armadillos from their dens and kill them, but you couldn't really sell them to anybody unless they specifically wanted armadillo dogs, which, of course, a few folks here and there did. But it took dog food to raise them after six weeks on the teat. And dog food cost money. Eric knew his daddy figured correctly that it was a lot cheaper to put the ones nobody wanted in a tow sack early and throw them in a deep hole in the river. He never had done it himself, and his daddy had always said he was too soft, and sometimes, when he thought about stuff like that, he didn't want to go back home so much. But it was his daddy. What was he supposed to do?

"Oh. I see," Mister Arthur said, and then he brightened. "It was really something the way he caught that kitten. I was really impressed by that. Helen was, too, after she got over her scare. Helen's . . . Helen's really a good woman, Eric."

He had to swallow hard. The shot of the open zipper had burned itself into his brain. But he couldn't say *No she's not.*

"Yessir. She's been real nice to me."

"Me, too," Mister Arthur said. "We've been married for almost twenty years. I'm sure you can tell that she's a good bit younger than me."

"Well. Yessir. I noticed that. I think she's around the age of my mama."

"I know she married me for my money," Mister Arthur said. "But I like to think that she does care about me."

"Yessir. I'm sure she does."

There was some more silence. Eric didn't have any idea what to say and now all he wanted was to just get off the phone. Then he heard Mister Arthur clear his throat.

"Well. I was just wondering if you wanted to come by here and have a drink. I've got plenty of scotch, there's some food here, too, I'm just sitting here by myself, well, not totally by myself, I mean I've got the cat here with me, but of course it's not much company, being in the cage and everything, but I thought maybe you might want to come by here and have a drink and maybe a sandwich. TBS is showing *Red River* at eleven. John Wayne? I thought I'd sit up and watch it and see if she comes on in. I thought maybe you might want to come over and watch it with me. You could bring Jada Pinkett and I could feed him something. I've got some frozen hamburger I could thaw out. It's really a good movie. Have you ever seen it?"

Damn, man. How fucking pathetic was it going to get? And how pathetic was *he*, lying like this to a nice old man who had only befriended him?

"Yessir, I've seen it. It's a good one, sure is. Old Montgomery Clift's in that one."

"Yes he is. And there's probably some other stuff on. The History Channel usually has some good stuff on. Sometimes. Well, they have reruns, but of course some stuff's fun to watch over and over, like those treasure-hunter guys. You ever watch those guys who go out to Arizona with metal detectors and look for buried treasure? I'd like to do that sometime."

Boy, he just kind of rambled sometimes, didn't he? Just jumped around from one thing to another. Maybe Miss Helen thought he was loony. Maybe he *was* loony. Naw, hell, he was probably just lonesome and old. Like his granddaddy after his grandmother died and left him sitting alone in his rocking chair with only the hounds that slept on the porch of the big weathered house to keep him company in his last days.

"Nosir. Well. I'll probably just get on home. I mean, unless I stop for a drink somewhere." *Shit! What the fuck'd you say that for?*

"Well, I just thought I'd see," Mister Arthur said over the phone. "I just thought you might want to." He paused. "But you're a young man. You've got your own things you want to do. I'm sure you've got your own friends your own age you like to do things with."

No. Hell no. That wasn't right. It wasn't like that at all. Eric wanted to tell him that he didn't have any friends up here, that it was hard to meet people, he thought because of his hick accent, and that he'd actually stolen Jada Pinkett from his daddy and run away from Mississippi because his daddy had been going to shoot Jada Pinkett for refusing to fight anymore, and because he couldn't fuck anymore, and that he was lonely except for the old dog, and homeless, and scared sometimes, and that he really wanted to come over and have a drink with him, and a sandwich maybe, too, and tell him some more stories about home, maybe even tell him about how they'd built the rabbit factory, he and his daddy and Mister Nub, putting up the steel posts and six feet of chicken wire around seven acres of grass and brush over two summers, and running boards all along the bottom and tacking the wire to the boards to keep the rabbits in so that they could take the beagles over and run them for practice in the summer, and sit on the benches they'd built, and sip cold beer, and listen to the races. But then, if he did that, he wouldn't be able to go have a drink with Miss Helen, and find out what was going to happen with her, so he just stayed quiet, knowing what he was doing, but not being able to really help himself because he was so badly wanting her, wanting her even worse than he wanted the complete boxed set of *The Civil War* by Shelby Foote, and he wanted it pretty bad.

"Well," Mister Arthur said. "I just thought I'd call and see if you'd seen her. I didn't know but what she came by there to get some catnip for the cat maybe. But you might not even sell catnip. I didn't notice any when I was in there. Of course I wasn't really looking for any. It was a long shot, I guess. I guess she'll eventually come in sometime tonight. I just hope she's not drinking and driving."

"You gonna be okay?" Eric said. He guessed this meant if he went over to the bar and had a drink or two with her at the Peabody and then got her in his car and drove her somewhere he probably wouldn't get to see Mister Arthur anymore. That'd be a shame. Shit. It would be worse than a shame.

"Oh, sure," Mister Arthur said over the phone. "I'll just sit here and watch some TV until she gets in. I've got the cat. I can feed it maybe. I think I may have another can of anchovies in the cabinet somewhere. Maybe I can make friends with it."

"Maybe you can," Eric said.

There was another long pause. It went on for a pretty good while but Eric just waited. He tried, but he couldn't think of anything else to say.

"Well. Come by and see me sometime, Eric."

"Okay. I will." *No you won't. Not if you do that shit.*

"And bring Jada Pinkett, too. Maybe he can play around with the cat some. Maybe it'll be tamed down by then."

"I'll bet he can," Eric said.

"I'll bet he can, too. Well. Take it easy, Eric."

"You too, Mister Arthur."

He hung the phone up, and for a while he just stood there, looking down at the floor. He was thinking about Miss Helen and what she'd said. And how she'd looked. He thought about Mister Arthur at home alone. Then he felt something. He didn't know what it was at first. Then he looked at the animals in the cages around him. They were all watching him, almost like they could tell what he was thinking.

66

Anjalee took the bus downtown and walked the streets for a while. She was kind of putting off going back to her apartment just yet, afraid the cops had been in there and ransacked everything. The snow seemed to be gone, but a lot of people seemed to be keeping themselves inside. The sidewalks were not nearly as congested as they usually were.

She waited at the corners when DON'T WALK was lit on the pole and waited with other people who did not look at her, all except the men. She walked by furniture shops and delicatessens and shoe shops and electronics shops and bars and windows full of lamps and scarves and things carved from wood and ivory in countries far north of there. She didn't see anything she wanted. When she got tired of walking, she flagged a cab the few blocks back to the Peabody. She'd have to go back and see Moe and get her clothes and her coat sometime.

She went to the women's room and made herself up and decided she was okay to be seen. It wasn't very crowded in the lobby since the ducks had already done their thing. At the elegant bar, she took a tall padded chair and waited for a slightly sullen and plainly disinterested woman in pants and white shirt and a bow tie and a short black jacket to come over and take her order for a shot of Herradura and a Bud draft. There was a folded menu and she picked it up and read it. Good thing she was on the pill. But who knew if he had genital herpes? Cops could catch things, too. She'd been tested for HIV four times. She thought she'd have some chicken wings. She looked up at the lady in the black jacket who was pouring the shot.

"Are these wings hot?" she said.

The bartender got a cold glass mug and gave her a shrug and pulled the handle on the tap.

"So-so," she said. "I've got Tabasco."

"Good. Let me have some wings, please," Anjalee said.

The bartender brought the shot and the beer and set them down on some coasters and pushed them in front of Anjalee. She picked up a phone and said the order into it and hung it back up. She went over to the cash register and turned to look back and said: "You want to start a tab?"

"You can just put it on my room."

"What's your room number?"

Anjalee looked at her dumbly and shook her head.

"Why hell, lady, I done forgot. Let me see."

Shit. The key card was in her purse somewhere, in a little paper thing. And the cops had gone through everything in there but had put it all back in. All the money was in there. Good thing she didn't have any grass on her, they'd have busted her ass for that. She pawed through it, pushing aside lipsticks, quarters and pennies, pieces of Juicy Fruit and Big Red.

"It's in here somewhere," she said without raising her head. She wondered if Lenny had ever come in. She could use a house phone and call up to the room after a while. Then she found the key card and pulled it out.

"Four oh seven," she read aloud, and put it back in her purse.

The bartender did something at the register and it spit out a curling white piece of paper that she tore off and brought over with a pen for Anjalee to sign. Anjalee added a good tip and signed it and gave the pen and the paper back to her and picked up the beer and drank some of it. She was almost out of cigarettes, but she'd seen a machine in the entrance to the lobby.

"Can I get a piece of lemon, please?" she said. "And a salt shaker?"

The bartender didn't say anything, just brought them over. Anjalee picked up the shot glass and sipped from it, then put some salt on the lemon wedge and sucked on it. She turned a little on her stool and looked at the fountain. She knew it was almost dark. She'd eat something and have a few drinks and see what happened. She'd get some cigarettes and call up to the room. She wondered again what in the hell had happened to Frankie. What did he mean going out of town and not letting her know? It was starting to look like she might never hear from him again. And would that be a bad thing if it happened? Probably not. As long as she could hang with Lenny until she could get back on her feet. Go back to her apartment. Try to get back to her drawing. Maybe write her mother a letter and try to send her some money. God knows she probably needed it, all those drunks hanging around.

She found her cigarettes and lit one and thought about Ronnie on top of her. Worthless little son of a bitch. It seemed like she was meeting a lot of them. And you could find plenty of them in Mississippi, you didn't need to come all the way to Memphis to find some more. More than anything she was giddy with relief to be away from the police without getting locked up. She didn't want to think about what it would be like if she were doing that now, sitting in a concrete cell with a stainless-steel toilet and some bars on the door, wearing a jumpsuit, instead of being in here, in this nice place, having a leisurely smoke and a cold beer and a shot, waiting for some wings that might need just a little Tabasco.

Two older guys in suits came in and sat four or five stools down from her. Their suits looked expensive and their black shoes were shiny and they had heads of graceful silvering hair. Rings on their fingers and they were tanned. The bartender immediately smiled at them and went over and one of them said something she laughed at. She seemed to have a great personality almost instantly now, kind of a Dr. Jekyll thing. Then he said something to the other guy and they all three laughed. They had to be regular customers, but Anjalee could tell that they also had money. And that caused people to be nice to you. She'd seen plenty of that and not just here.

She turned her face away from them and looked at the mirror behind the bar. She was trying to tell if she looked like she'd just gotten fucked, but she couldn't tell. What were you supposed to look like after you'd just gotten fucked? She guessed if it had been good you would look contented, but she didn't look contented, not even to herself.

That fucking Frankie. She looked around to see if there was a house phone in the bar but she didn't see one. She could ask the waitress. Bartender. Whatever she was. If she ever got through flirting with the two old rich guys.

Anjalee watched her. She was making their drinks now. The two men were talking in low voices, maybe business, she figured. Anjalee looked to see what they were getting just because she liked to know what was going on around her. The bartender filled two crystal glasses with large ice cubes from a scoop and picked up a bottle of Beefeater and made a gin and tonic and added a twist of lime. She poured two shots of Johnny Walker into the other glass and put the drinks on napkins and served them. Then she leaned her arms on the back of the bar and pushed some of the hair away from her face and kept talking to the two old guys.

Anjalee looked around. She sipped at her beer and sipped at the Herradura. She didn't like sitting by herself right now. It would be nice if Lenny would walk in. She could give him a kiss in front of these people and let them see that she had somebody. But would it do to tell him the cops had picked her up? She hadn't been able to have any deep conversation with him just yet, just some really satisfying, energetic sex. No telling where he was now. Resting maybe.

Then she saw the two old guys looking at her. She took a drag off her smoke and thumped her ashes into an ashtray and gave them a look of cool appraisal. Then she glanced away. She could hear murmuring. The murmuring sounded to her kind of like maybe one of the old guys was asking the bartender who she was. The bartender murmured something back, sounded kind of like: "I don't know, she just came in."

The old guy said something else. Anjalee sipped at her beer. She wondered what Christmas was going to be like up here if she stayed. Not worth a shit probably. Now that the cops had turned her loose, she didn't have to leave. And she didn't know if her probation officer would let her leave the state or not. She'd still have to see him sometime, unless she just took off and didn't look back. And would they send somebody to look for her if she did? Did the Memphis Police Department really care if they had one less ho who worked the strip clubs in the city? Back at her place she had a small fake tree that she hadn't decorated yet, hadn't even taken it out of the box. It was only two feet tall. She'd been planning on getting Frankie a few things with the money he'd paid her, and inviting him over to open presents, hoping that maybe he'd have a few little things for her. They didn't have to be anything big. She would have been satisfied with something little. She'd thought about baking a ham and maybe trying her hand at making some potato salad. She could have gotten a can of cranberry sauce. All you had to do was stick that son of a bitch in the refrigerator for a while and then open both ends and push it out on a plate and slice it up. She could have stuffed some eggs and used red-hot sauce the way her daddy used to do, another dim memory now recalled. That would have been almost like a real Christmas dinner. Now the lousy fuck wasn't even around to fuck.

She'd managed to ask Ronnie if she could go back to her apartment after he got through with her and he'd asked her why was she asking him. This was while he was wiping himself off with a moist towelette, which he then wadded up and threw out the window, possibly for some other city employee to have to pick up with a nail on a stick.

She wanted to get to her place. Her probation officer seemed to be a pretty decent guy and she thought she could explain to him how it happened with Miss Barbee and Mr. T.J., but she didn't know if they'd send her back to the old folks' home now or not. She didn't really want to go back there if she could get out of it. If there was some other place where she could go and do her community service, even if it was cleaning a building or something, she thought she'd rather have that. She didn't want to think about the possibility that Miss Barbee had killed Miss Doobis or maybe Mr. Pasternak because what kind of a monster would want to hurt a sweet old person like that who in all likelihood was somebody's daddy or mama? And as soon as she thought that, she remembered the slap and what it had sounded like and knew what kind of a monster it took. Miss Barbee looked like she was about half man.

"Hi there."

She turned her head. She had her legs crossed. One of the old guys was standing next to her, holding his drink. He had one hand in his pocket and his suit was black with thin lines of silver in it.

"Hey," she said.

He extended a tanned hand. Super-clean nails. A deep old scar, perhaps a burn, perhaps shrapnel from a war, which one?

"Harv Pressman," he said, deep voice, just distinguished as hell.

"Hi. I'm Anjalee," she said, and shook his big warm safe-feeling hand. She was trying to figure his age. He was older but well preserved. But what was old? Sixty? Seventy? She didn't know but she figured that to a ninety-eight-year-old facing ninety-nine, sixty-three looked pretty damn good. She didn't think he was seventy yet.

"I don't think you're from here, Anjalee," he said, and he smiled with nice white teeth that looked to be his. "Is that a little north Mississippi hill country I hear in your voice?"

"I reckon so," she said, and stubbed out her smoke.

He set his drink on the bar and lifted one foot and put it on the rail that ran in front of their feet. He clasped one hand in the other like a casual lawyer about to interrogate somebody on the witness stand. She saw a fancy watch. He dressed like he had money.

"I'd guess Tupelo," he said.

"Wrong."

"But not far."

"Not even the same county."

"But not far."

"Far enough."

"New Albany."

"Nope. Pontotoc. Actually Toccopola."

"Did you go to school there?"

She picked up her beer and held it. She could tell that in his youth he'd been one hell of a handsome man. Even now he resembled an aging movie star. She looked at his hand and there was no wedding band on it. The rings he had were really nice. She wondered what he wanted. But that wasn't hard to figure out. Same thing they all wanted.

"Nosir. We ain't got a school there no more. A long time ago we had one, and Elvis played out there one time before anybody ever heard of him. I went to Miss LeAnne's Academy of Curl in Tupelo for a while."

"I think I've heard of it," Harv Pressman said, and picked up his drink for a small sip. As he did so, she looked away for just a moment. His friend was talking to the bartender down there and he was massaging the back of her hand with one of his fingers. The conversation they were having was decidedly private.

"What else do you like to do?" Harv Pressman asked.

"Well." Should she tell him? Why not? "I like drawin'," Anjalee said.

"Oh. You're into art."

"Yeah. I really am."

He seemed to be pretty interested, seemed to be waiting for her to go on, but Ronnie's laughter in the dirty cop room was still a mocking echo in her ears. What did that asshole know about Elvis? What did he know about being sick of being poorer than anybody you knew and trying to get your ass out of it any way you could even if it meant selling it?

"And how does it go these days?"

She set the beer glass down and picked up the shot glass and drank the rest of the Herradura, picked up her lemon chunk, sucked it briefly. She didn't care what it looked like. She'd never claimed to have a lot of class anyway.

"It don't go too good sometimes," she said. "I don't seem to get around to it enough. I want to. But it seems like early in the mornins is the only time I can work. And I don't see enough of those. I'm always up late."

"Do you work?"

"Well . . . not exactly."

He took another sip of his drink and set it back down.

"You mind if I pull up a chair?"

"Please do," she said. He was friendly and nice and easy to talk to. She could tell he'd been around. A mature man who'd seen much of the world maybe. Somebody it might be interesting to talk to. Somebody who might even be sugar-daddy material. Potential sugar-daddy. She took a sip of her beer. Sugar-daddy-in-waiting maybe.

He pulled up a chair and when she fished for another cigarette, he outed with a gold lighter and she bent her face to his flame. She raised her eyes to him and smiled. She was glad now that she'd touched up her lashes.

By the time she'd switched to Dickel and gotten some cigarettes, he'd had another drink and was telling her about fishing for blue marlin off the coast of Cuba, and watching killer whales off the south coast of Africa.

By the time she'd finished her wings and that drink and ordered a second one, they were sitting close together and she was tipsy and wanting to kiss him. He said he knew a great steak house where they could get the best porterhouse in the whole city. Kobe beef from Japan, he said, raised in dark sheds and fed beer mash and massaged daily for the ultimate in tender T-bones.

"Well, let's see," she said, and looked at the clock above the back bar. It was about fifteen till seven and she knew Harv was getting hungry because he'd already mentioned it once. She never had called up to the room or checked the front desk to see if there were any messages waiting for her from Lenny. There hadn't been time. She'd been too busy laughing and talking with Harv because he was just plain fun to be around. One of those kinds of people.

"You need to eat, don't you?" Harv said. He looked at her drink. "Hell, they've got a bar. Come on, let's go." And he started getting up, so she just went with him.

67

Miss Muffett had a dream but it wasn't a wet one, even though there was lovemaking with a guy on a picnic blanket, with a picnic basket. It was springtime. Birds cheeping. Grass green. She had both legs again. It wasn't the first time she'd dreamed it. In that dream she was always swimming in cool lake water either before or after the sex stuff with the guy with the picnic basket and picnic blanket.

When she woke up, she felt surprisingly refreshed.

When she looked out the window, it was getting dark.

When she stretched and yawned, it felt pretty good.

But when she reached for her leg, it was already gone.

68

Domino was actually only two and nine-tenths of a mile from the barn he'd slept in when he stepped out from behind the big silver gas tanks at Rosie Baby's Grocery on 7 South at the intersection of 328, which, if he got on it and stayed on it, would lead him not straight but curvy back to Papa Johnny Road. The red-and-white Ford pickup idling at the pumps after getting ten dollars' worth of unleaded needed a wash job and in the back end had a whitetail's head with two horns. Domino saw it when he slipped out from behind the gas tanks and ran across the twenty yards of open gravel and got in the truck, whose door the owner had conveniently left open for him. He slammed the door and pulled on the headlights and jerked it down in Drive and shot past the two cars parked at the side of the road and turned it back right hard at the exit and went back up the road in front of the store and made a left on 328, just barely making it in front of an oncoming car, its horn blaring WAAAAAAAAaaaaaaa and on down the road past him, fading, his foot hard down on the gas. It would take a few minutes for things to fall into place. It would take the state troopers and the deputy sheriffs who patrolled the county roads a few minutes to get into a position to where they could get behind him or set up a roadblock ahead of him. If he stayed under the speed limit, and didn't attract a cruising cop's attention, he knew he could be back at Papa Johnny Road in probably not much more than ten minutes. If he saw cops near there, he'd drive on by. Or dump this one and get another one. And do it again if he had to. But he needed that weed if he could get it. It was freedom. He had nothing left to lose. Except his life. And it hadn't been so hot so far.

He looked in the rearview mirror. Something was behind him. He had the gun there in his pocket and he pulled it out and laid it on the seat. They weren't going to take him alive if he got a chance to shoot. He'd already made up his mind about all that stuff. Fuck going back to that place. There was a paper sack on the seat and he'd noticed it when he'd first gotten in. The headlights back there weren't getting any closer. He tried not to worry about it. If it was cops, they wouldn't turn their lights on until they could read the tag and determine that it had been stolen. The person at the store was probably just now calling somebody for help. Everything took time. It took time for the truck to get hot. It took time for meat to thaw out. It took time to serve time.

He reached his hand out and felt the side of the sack. It was cold, it was hard. He wasn't going to believe that. But his fingers found the fold of paper and opened it up and he stuck his hand down in it and felt cold round tops with pop-up tabs, meshed in a plastic template. He separated one and pulled it out and held it up. In the dim blue light from the dash, he could see that he was holding a cold Miller tallboy. Like a gift from some ragged angel. It said right there on the label that it was the champagne of bottled beers.

69

Out in Mr. Hamburger's backyard, there was a patch of muddy plowed ground that he'd dug up recently with his red five HP Troy-Bilt tiller in preparation for turnips sometime, and now there was a hole in the middle of it with mud flying out and landing on top of a white plastic leg that was lying there. The mud kept flying and after a while it stopped. Then the leg moved. It slid forward a bit at a time and finally toppled over into the hole, and there was a shoe sticking up on the end of it. It was shiny and black and had a strap around the heel. It looked like a doll's shoe.

Then the leg began to move again.

70

Domino drank fast but he had only one and a half down by the time he got back to the curve he recognized. He didn't see any cars sitting around anywhere. He started slowing down, but not too much. If any cops were parked on the side of the road, he was just some dude going on down the road, man, just out having a little drive, bro, just sipping on a cool one and digging a few tunes, homes. He wished he had time to stop and find that Townes Van Zandt.

It was black as the inside of a tomb down there, which was real good. He just swung on in like he lived there, and wondered if anybody did, because there weren't many tire tracks, just a few, and he couldn't tell if they were fresh or not. If things could go his way, just for a few minutes, he could open the back of the truck, pull the deer out of the way, pull a few boxes out until he saw the one with the red streak, get it, and be on his way. If a cop stopped him, he'd just have to kill him. He was past the point of doing anything else now.

Slow, slow, he pulled around the curve. The truck was sitting right there where he'd left it about twenty-four hours before. Maybe this was just a farming road. Maybe there were some fields on down past the rest of these trees and maybe the only vehicles that ever came in here were tractors and combines and fuel trucks. Maybe nobody who came down this road would think anything about a truck left sitting for a day or so. He'd just have to make it fast.

He stopped right behind the reefer truck and left the stolen pickup running. He got out and went quickly to the back door. When he opened it, he could see the whitetail's horn. He grabbed it and pulled him out, and let him fall to the ground. Then he started pulling out boxes. They had thawed out some and some of them were soft. He pulled out four, then he thought he saw the weed box, but he had to lean in and catch the corner of it with his finger, but he hooked it into a flap and tugged it toward him. He slid it closer and stepped slightly aside so he could read the side of it by the light of the pickup's beams and there it was: PRIME RIB. With a red slash across it. It was money he needed to help him get somewhere else in the country. Oregon was looking pretty good. Rain. Ocean. Cliffs. Hang gliding.

He turned to put it on the seat of the truck or throw it in the back end and Rico stuck a pistol up beside his head and cocked it and said: "For some reason, dumb sumbitches *always* return to the scene of the crime. So, dude, like, where's my little brother?"

Domino looked at him. He had a couple of Band-Aids on his swollen face, and he had one tooth knocked out, but he was grinning through a blood-soaked piece of gauze and he just didn't look real good. He looked like he might be getting a little unstable right here almost at Christmas.

71

Helen was about to get all drunk and messed up. It was already past ten-fifteen and Eric hadn't shown up. He probably wasn't coming. Old Tyrone had bought her a few more drinks, but she hadn't decided what she was going to do with him yet. He'd been telling her all about his job, which involved global-positioning systems for long-haul truckers and a bunch of technical shit about satellites and computers. She'd figured Eric would be here by now, and she wondered if he was having second thoughts. Or maybe somebody had come in late wanting a hamster. Or a gerbil. Or some goldfish.

The bar had filled up with lots of men and women and there was laughter and music filling up all the air. She could smell cigar smoke, which she liked, and folks were starting to crowd in beside them.

Tyrone had switched from scotch to bourbon and he had a couple of them under his belt now. He'd patted Helen on the arm a couple of times during some laughs and had touched her knee lightly once, but it was plain to see that he wasn't one of these guys who was overly aggressive with his advances toward women. He wasn't going to grab her tit or anything. She looked toward the door again, and Tyrone leaned toward her.

"What about your friend?" he said. "He's not standing you up, is he?"

Helen smiled thinly. Was Tyrone being an asshole?

"He had to get off work," she said. "He might have had some late customers."

"What does your friend do? If you don't mind me asking."

Helen picked up her drink and finished it. She didn't know if she wanted to go to bed with Tyrone or not in case Eric didn't show up. And what if he didn't? What was she going to do? Just stay here? If she got any drunker, it would be dangerous to try and drive home.

"He works in a pet shop," she said.

"Oh. You want another drink?" Tyrone said.

"I hate for you to keep buying my drinks. I've got money."

"I know you do. But I'm sticking it all on my expense account."

He called for Ken to give her another round and finished his own drink. Ken gave her another look. The clock on the wall crept closer to ten-thirty and still no Eric came through the door. The drink came and it was getting hard for her now to think of things to say to Tyrone. He was actually pretty boring, kind of like Arthur.

"Are you hungry?" Tyrone said.

"Not really." And it was true. The drinks had removed any appetite she might have had. She knew she'd probably feel like absolute hell tomorrow, always did when she drank heavy and didn't eat, like this morning. Then almost kissing Eric. Then yelling at Arthur. Then going to sleep. Then getting up, feeling like shit with another hangover. Then starting to drink again to get rid of it. And look where she was now. Sitting here with some boring although generous dickhead waiting for somebody to come over who might not even show up. And drunk again. Damn it. How did it happen all the time like this? She didn't ever mean to do this. But this is how it always turned out. And by the time she realized that it had happened again, it was too late to do anything about it but sober up. And she didn't want to do that yet.

"Well, I could use a sandwich," Tyrone said. "I noticed a deli down the street that stays open all night. You want to go down there with me and get some coffee to sober up on?"

"I don't think so," Helen said. "But you go if you want."

"I think that's what I'll do," Tyrone said. "I think I'll get a sandwich to take back to my room. I've got an early flight in the morning."

Helen didn't say anything, didn't ask him where he was going, didn't ask him what time he was leaving because she didn't give a shit and didn't care if she never saw him again. Tyrone Bradbury. Big fucking deal. He wasn't even any kin to Ray. So he bought her a few drinks. So what? He probably had a limp dick, too. Tyrone called for his bill and Ken brought it over and eyeballed Helen with a clench in his jaw and Tyrone pulled out a credit card and paid the bill. After he got the card back, he pushed his stool back and stood up. He was a little drunk, but probably not bad enough for the bicycle cops to get him. He extended his hand.

"Helen," he said. "It was a pleasure to meet you."

She shook hands with him, not too hard.

"It was nice to meet you, too, Tyrone. Tell Ray I said hi if you see him. And thanks for the drinks."

"Anytime," he said, and laughed, and gave her a little wave. Then he turned and made his way through the people and out the door. Helen looked at the clock. It was ten-thirty on the dot. Eric had had plenty of time to get over here from the pet shop. So maybe he wasn't coming after all. And how much longer was she willing to sit here and wait? Till closing time?

She looked at the people around her. Some were laughing and talking and telling stories and others were sitting by themselves just looking down into their drinks. She saw a couple of men looking at her but she broke eye contact with them. She turned on her stool and looked across the back of the bar at the bins of ice and the wineglasses stacked back there and the nozzles that spewed what-ever into the glasses. It was ten thirty-five.

She lit another cigarette and crossed one leg over the other. Arthur was sitting home worrying about her. And what had he done for her to treat him this way? All he'd done was get old. And when she married him she'd always known that was going to happen one day. But it hadn't seemed to matter so much back then, twenty years ago, when he could still do it pretty good or at least regularly, when his hair wasn't solid gray, when he was twenty years younger than he was now. Maybe if she could have had children, it would have been different. Of course it would have been different. She would have been wrapped up in their children's lives and that would have given her a source of happiness. It would have kept her busy and she wouldn't have been able to brood so much. Drink so much. But that wasn't what she had, was it? Nope. What she had was ten-fourty and her glass half empty. She stubbed the cigarette out. The easiest thing to do would be to just finish it, walk out and flag a cab, leave the car here, and go safely home. Not risk a third DUI. Fix herself a sandwich and maybe a cup of coffee. She had a new romance novel she'd bought at Burke's bookstore that she'd been wanting to start reading. How would that be any different from what she'd been doing for a long time already? It wouldn't be. But being so damn tired of that already was the thing. It was old.

She decided she'd wait, have one more drink, give him a little more time. She remembered imagining what his mouth would have tasted like, like tobacco and good scotch whiskey. How strong his hands would have felt on her butt. How hard he would have been against her lower belly.

Okay. If he wasn't here by eleven-thirty, she'd go on home and forget about it. That was all she could do. She didn't see anybody in here she wanted to mess with. Just Ken. And his place smelled bad. And he had roaches. And fucking Barry Manilow all night long.

She'd wait a little longer anyway. Maybe he'd come on in. It still wasn't too late for him to show up. He might have had car trouble with that old thing he drove. But she didn't need to wait too long or get too drunk because she still had to get home someway. If she left the Jag and called a cab, she'd have to call another cab to come back and get it. That would be a pain in the ass tomorrow afternoon sometime. And she wasn't just crazy about leaving it in the parking lot overnight anyway. Arthur had traded in the Seville on it after she'd finished her last alcohol-safety education program and gotten her license back and promised him she wouldn't get in any more trouble with the cops. And she didn't want any more trouble with the cops. It was the last thing she wanted. The classes had been hard for her to take, being thrown in with all those people in the class whose only connection with her was that they all had been caught driving drunk. Some of them looked slimy. Some of them had tried to hit on her while the classes were going on, once a week, for eight weeks straight. But it wasn't just that. It was also the films they made them watch, which were of gruesome car wrecks, and bodies under sheets lying in the middle of highways, and some dead babies on a table who had been killed in drunk-driving wrecks. She couldn't shake those last images from her mind, the cut and torn little bodies, but she couldn't seem to handle her problem either, because here she sat again. Maybe she did need some help.

She kept sitting there and watching the people. There was one couple in one of the booths she couldn't help watching. The young man looked to be about Eric's age, and the girl maybe a bit younger. They were sitting side by side in the booth and he kept holding on to her hand while he talked to her. She had only one hand on the table, so she had to have the other one on him somewhere. And the look on her face was pure love. They were just kids. They didn't know anything. They didn't know shit about the way life could turn around on you and leave you with nothing and no remedy for it except something drastic. Either that or just suffering in silence.

At eleven o'clock she ordered another drink and when Ken brought it, he leaned over the bar toward her and smiled uncertainly.

"You're out late tonight," he said. "What's the occasion?"

She held the straw with her fingers and swirled it around in the glass.

"I don't know," she said. "I just didn't feel like sitting around the house tonight I guess."

"Everything okay at home?"

She looked up at him. He had this terrible-sounding laugh, too, high and in the back of his throat, like a gargling rooster.

"Things could be better," she said. "As usual."

"I can make them better. Always do, don't I?"

"I always have to go home, too, Ken."

"I guess so. Since you're married. Unless you get unmarried."

Ken picked up a cherry from a garnish tray of sliced limes and oranges and lemons and pulled the cherry from the stem and chewed it. She watched his mouth chew it, watched it stop chewing. Then he put the stem in his mouth and his tongue did some things she couldn't see and when he pulled the stem back out of his mouth, he had tied it in a knot.

"How you like that?" he said.

"That's pretty interesting," she said. It wasn't very subtle, but it was pretty interesting. His tongue was the most interesting thing about him.

"It took me a lot of practice to learn how to do that."

"You been getting to practice much lately?"

Somebody yelled for him and he turned away and went to another customer. She picked up her drink and sipped it. She hated herself for doing it, but she kept watching the clock, and the minute hand kept creeping its slow inexorable way around the clock's face. It was about eleven-fifteen. Before long it would be eleven-thirty. Then it'd be time to make a decision. Keep sitting here or go on home. Or . . . ?

"You need another one, Helen?"

She looked up and this time Ken winked at her.

"Yeah," she said. "I think I'll have one more for the road."

But she didn't. She had three, and sat there while people started to go out, by ones and twos, while the level of noise dropped inside the bar, while her mind clouded and hashed and rehashed her problems, while the traffic in the street out front diminished, while the night grew longer, and the hours left before morning ticked off slowly one by one on the clock, and again, one more time, Ken got to gradually looking better and better, at least in her messed-up head.

72

Domino didn't know where in the hell Rico could be taking him. He had to get everything straight in his head. The warden had propped his nicely tooled black cowboy boots on his desk after a big breakfast of whitetail tenderloin and two over easy with wheat toast and told him to go straight and now he was blindfolded and handcuffed and lying in the trunk of a police car with a thawing-out box of meat. He could hear a police radio going faintly sometimes and he could hear the tires rushing on the pavement. His hands were cuffed behind him and he was needing to go to somebody's bathroom pretty bad, pretty soon. He figured they'd get to wherever they were going before long and then they'd get out somewhere and he could use the bathroom there. The only thing was that he'd been thinking that for what felt like close to an hour and they hadn't shown any signs of stopping anywhere yet. He'd felt it slow, had felt it make some turns, maybe go off some ramps, had felt it come to a rolling slowdown a few times, but it hadn't actually stopped. He didn't assume that he was getting transported somewhere to either get charged with his crimes or to get some medical attention since he was blindfolded and handcuffed and lying in the trunk of a police car. He had one hell of a headache and his stomach was going crazy for wanting something in it. That bologna sandwich was the last thing he'd had. Pigskins before that, he remembered. Why did he have to take that road? Weren't there plenty of other roads around just as good? He took that road because he wanted some beer. He took that road because he wanted to ride around and drink some beer and see if he could see a whitetail. Well. He saw one.

He was really tired. His head was on a tire. He needed some sleep. So he tried to ease into a better position on his side and tried to stretch out a little. His feet weren't shackled, and he drew them up and bent his knees. It wasn't the most comfortable way in the world to ride somewhere, but it was as good as he could do for the moment. He didn't want to pee on himself, so he concentrated on holding it.

But that was getting harder and harder to do. There was a bad pain in his bladder that was letting him know that it couldn't keep holding it indefinitely, that something was going to have to give. But they couldn't keep on going forever. They'd have to stop somewhere sometime. He just didn't know where or when that would be. So he lay quietly on his side, and listened to the tires rush against the pavement, and to the crackling of the police radio.

None of this would have happened if he hadn't hit the whitetail. That was what messed him up. Out of the blue. Complete surprise. Something you couldn't account for or figure into any plans. Which was actually bad timing. Which was the worst thing in the world for somebody who was doing something they weren't supposed to be doing. It was something you couldn't see coming and there was no way to predict it. Ten seconds, hell, five seconds, maybe, sooner or later, he probably wouldn't have hit it. It might have jumped before then or it might have gone the other way. Domino knew that life was sometimes measured in small but critical increments. Looking down from approaching traffic for just one second to light a cigarette. Wiping your ass with the winning lottery ticket because it's the only paper thing you have in your billfold besides money. Getting in a hurry zipping up and catching some pretty tender skin in those little brass teeth, standing there so all alone at the urinal, can't go up or down with it, struggling silently, trying not to scream.

So he might have taken another road. That was a possibility. There were all kinds of variables. He wondered what the odds were against he himself hitting that deer on that road before Christmas at that speed at that exact time of night. Probably astronomical. Probably no way to calculate it. Doreen might have been able to. She'd been a whiz in math. She could recite long passages of poetry in Spanish. It never had made any sense. But a lot of stuff in the world didn't make any sense. Just like this stuff right here. This cop had to be crazy if he thought he could get away with doing something like this to him, since this was, after all, America.

He really needed to pee. It was just about to go beyond bad. He didn't want to yell anything, but it was starting to look like he might have to. He didn't think he could take it much longer. He'd thought maybe lying quietly on his side would help it, but it hadn't. If anything, it was worse.

He thought about trying to roll over. But he was also afraid he might pee on himself if he did that. And he sure didn't want to pee on himself in the trunk of a police car. They'd probably beat the shit out of you some more if you did that. He sure didn't need the shit beat out of him any more. His whole head was swollen up already from getting so much shit beat out of him.

He kept lying there, and he kept wondering why he was blind-folded. He'd seen prisoners being transported on television before and none of them had ever been blindfolded. And none of them had been in the trunk of a car. He wasn't being kidnapped by the cops, was he? Hell. That wasn't legal, was it? Didn't the cops have to be legal? He was pretty sure they did since they were the ones who insisted that everybody else in the world be legal.

He sure hoped that was true. He sure hoped they weren't trying to do something illegal with him. He certainly hoped they weren't planning on secretly killing him and then trying to cover it up and hide it or something like that.

Damn, he needed to pee. If he didn't get to, he was probably going to have to yell something before long. Maybe pretty soon. What if they let him out of the trunk and then shot him in the back and said he was trying to escape?

They wouldn't try that shit, would they?

Didn't he have some rights?

Hell. They never had given him his one phone call.

But he guessed that was probably out of the question now.

73

"You want another sandwich, Eric?" Mister Arthur said. "I've got a whole turkey breast in here." He was standing with his head inside the refrigerator and Jada Pinkett was checking out the stuff on the lower shelves, inside the door, sniffing Philadelphia cream cheese, nosing eggs and garlic cloves, sorting the scent of steak sauce from tartar like a visiting wine connoisseur cork-sniffing in a Lebanese vintner's dusty rows of tanks.

"No thanks, I'm stuffed." Eric pulled on his cigarette and thumped his ashes into the cereal bowl in the dim light the television screen threw.

"How about another beer?"

"Yessir, I'll take another beer."

"I'll pour you some scotch whenever you get ready."

"Maybe after this one."

"Just let me know."

Mister Arthur got the beer out and opened it and brought it over.

"Thanks, Mister Arthur."

"You're very welcome."

He went back over to the refrigerator and looked inside it again. Jada Pinkett was still standing there, wagging his nub of a tail.

"I think I'll give him the rest of this spaghetti," he said. "It's been in here a couple of days and I probably won't eat it."

"Okay," Eric said. "But you better get back over here pretty quick. It's just about to the part where they gonna have this badass stampede."

"I'm coming," Mister Arthur said. He took the lid off the Tupperware container and put the bottom part down on the floor and closed the icebox door. Jada Pinkett moved in on the spaghetti. Eric watched them. Damn, he was glad he didn't go over there to that Peabody. He'd decided, after much thought, that this would be the best thing to do, to just come on over here after all and sit around a while with Mister Arthur and keep him company and get something to eat and have a few drinks and see if she came in. But she hadn't. He'd been here for over an hour and she still wasn't in. And Mister Arthur wasn't saying much about it. He'd said a little about it when he'd first gotten there, but now he seemed pretty happy to just pet Jada Pinkett and feed him and watch the television and talk about John Wayne and Ben Johnson and Marlon Brando and John Ford and Alan Ladd. It was pretty amazing how much Mister Arthur knew about westerns, especially the old ones, the ones Eric was most interested in. He knew who Noah Beery was, and Wallace, too.

"You want some pudding, Eric?" Mister Arthur was standing at the kitchen table with one of those plastic four-packs of butter-scotch.

"No thanks," he said, and raised his beer. "I'm cool."

He heard him get a spoon from a drawer and heard the dog eating. Mister Arthur settled on the other end of the couch and pulled the lid off his pudding and put the foil top upside down on the coffee table. He had his house shoes on and he picked his feet up and put them on the coffee table, too. Mister Arthur had one of those really big monster TVs. Cost no telling how much. Digital black-and-white cows were lying on the open prairie, hundreds of them. Mister Arthur dipped his spoon into his pudding. A cowboy on a horse bumped against something on a wagon while stealing some sugar and set the cows off. They all jumped up and took off running. Then it was a stampede. Eric took a cold drink of his beer and watched the rest of the stampede, watched them sadly bury the cowpoke who'd gotten killed in the stampede, watched John Wayne angrily shoot the guy with the sweet tooth for causing the stampede, and then they cut for a commercial.

Out of the corner of his eye, he saw Mister Arthur checking his watch. He hated to think about having to sleep in the car again tonight. It had been so nice to be able to sleep on the couch in here last night. It beat the hell out of his back seat. He couldn't run the motor all night for the heater because cops would stop then, if they saw a car idling for a long time, if they noticed the smoke coming from the tailpipe, because they thought it was maybe somebody getting a quickie from a hooker, because it had happened before, several times. They shined their powerful flashlights in. But they never had done anything to him, just woke him up and told him he'd have to move on. He guessed it wasn't any crime to be homeless in Memphis. But it sure was a pain in the ass. He always woke up cold and cramped in the mornings. He knew he would be a lot colder if he didn't have Jada Pinkett to sleep with him under the blanket. He wasn't that big, but he had some serious body heat. Eric kept his dog food in the trunk with his folded clean clothes and took showers at the Y and ate a lot of meals at McDonald's so that he could use their bathrooms.

"Well," Mister Arthur said. "It's getting close to midnight."

"Is it?" he said. He knew it was. He guessed it was time to leave.

"I figured she'd be in by now," Mister Arthur said.

"Maybe she went to a movie," Eric said, even though he knew where she was. Crap. What he should have done was go on over there and talk her into coming home. But he'd been afraid of that, too. He'd been afraid that if he got close to her again and so much as smelled her perfume or touched her on the arm, or the hand, or the shoulder, he would lose all his resolve and then wouldn't be able to stop himself from going on and doing whatever would have happened.

"I don't think the movies run this late," Mister Arthur said.

Eric didn't say anything. He wondered how he'd feel if he was in Mister Arthur's place. He still didn't know for sure what the problem was between them, but if it was what he thought it was, then there probably wasn't any tactful way to bring it up. Hell, it probably wasn't something he wanted to talk about. Something like that was private as hell. And would probably be pretty scary. But it was pretty obvious that Miss Helen was wanting something she wasn't getting and it wasn't a cat.

A happy guy in a fishing cap came on the TV screen selling cars. It was well-known fisherman Bill Dance again, this time for some car dealership out on Getwell.

"Where'd you and Miss Helen meet at?" Eric said. He was just making conversation, but he wanted to know, too.

"Montana," Mister Arthur said, and spooned some pudding into his mouth. Jada Pinkett was pushing the Tupperware pan around on the kitchen floor with his head, slurping and snuffling and snorting and slobbering.

"I'd say he likes spaghetti," Mister Arthur went on. "Oh yes, we met in Missoula about twenty years ago. I used to have some oil wells and was in partnership with some people in Texas who used to take me with them when they went hunting. They had a camp and a private plane and we'd fly in to the airport out there and then get some pickups and horses and trailers and all that."

"Aw, wow," Eric said. "Montana? What'd you hunt?"

"Well, I didn't really hunt. I just went for the trip. Like a vacation. I usually stayed in camp and played checkers with the cook. He was an old crippled cowboy named Lark Linkhorn. He could cook the best baked beans I ever had, with smoked bacon. And his enchiladas were something else, too. But the people I went with hunted deer mostly. Mulies. What I enjoyed was going to camp and seeing all that beautiful country and eating deer steaks and rabbit stew and playing checkers with Lark and taking naps in my tent."

"I like rabbits myself," Eric said. He started to tell him he had about eleven frozen over at the pet shop that he needed to cook sometime.

Another man came on the TV screen and he was selling paint jobs for cars. Mister Arthur spooned up some more pudding. Then the movie came back on. They watched it without talking and Eric finished his beer just as the next commercial came on. When Mister Arthur saw him set the can down, he went into the kitchen and got a glass from the cabinet and put some ice into it and poured a couple of shots of Chivas over it and brought it back. Eric took it and looked up at him. He guessed it wasn't time to leave after all. That made him feel pretty good. It made him feel wanted. And he hadn't felt that way in a while. Except for those few times with Rae Loni Kaye Nafco and her poodle puppy.

"Thanks, Mister Arthur. A guy could get spoiled hangin' around you for long."

"You're welcome," Mister Arthur said. He had another cup of pudding now and he peeled the lid from it slowly and picked up his spoon. "It's nice to have somebody to watch TV with. Helen usually stays in the bedroom and reads at night. A long time ago she used to play checkers with me, but I think we played so much she finally got burned out on it."

Eric sipped at the scotch and slouched his socked feet out on the floor and rested on his spine. Damn. Was she so hot he just couldn't handle her? Was that what was going on? No wonder he didn't want to talk about it. Hell. How could you talk about a thing like that?

He looked over at Jada Pinkett. He was curled up under the kitchen table, his head on his paws, his eyes looking over at them, and then they closed. He was glad to have him in out of the cold for a while. He was afraid he got cold in the car sometimes when he had to keep him out there during his work hours. On days when the weather was decent, he got him out and walked him. Sometimes he tied him up outside a bookstore but made sure he could see him from the window while he browsed. People didn't try to pet him, though, he'd noticed that. He guessed they were afraid of him because of all the scars he had. And he had a lot. Ears about chewed off. But no wonder. He'd killed six dogs. A dog got a lot of scars killing six dogs.

"She was working in a bar," Mister Arthur said.

"Miss Helen?"

"Yes. We'd go into town sometimes. It was a bar downtown. The Union. They had a long bar and a lot of pool tables and the kids from the university had readings there on Sunday nights. And Helen worked there, but she'd stop working and go in and sit down and listen to the readings until they took a break. Then she'd go back out front and start waiting tables again. She was very popular there. I think just about every man in there knew her name."

Eric sipped his scotch. Boy it was comfortable here. It would be nice to live here, and be able to go to bed anytime you wanted to, in a nice soft bed, some thick covers. He wished he could go back home, but he didn't think he could just yet because he didn't know what his daddy would say, whether he'd let him come back or not. He didn't think his mama would ever come back. There'd been a bunch of yelling and screaming between him and his daddy, and his daddy had been drunk as hell again. He wished his daddy hadn't told him to leave. He figured his daddy probably regretted it now, only thing was, there wasn't any way for his daddy to get ahold of him since he didn't know where he was. He missed everything now, his daddy, taking care of the dogs, riding the four-wheelers through the lanes they'd Bush Hogged in the patches of briars and tall grass within the rabbit factory, fishing, riding around in pickups and drinking beer. Swimming in Yocona River with his friends and diving off the river bridge below Taylor. Sitting underneath a tree at daylight with his shotgun, waiting for squirrels.

"How'd you ever get to talkin' to her?"

"I spilled my drink," Mister Arthur said. "I spilled it on her hand taking it off my tray. But the reason I spilled it was because I was looking at her."

"She's a pretty lady," Eric said. He felt guilty saying even that, knowing that he still wanted to kiss her. What was he doing sitting here? It wasn't right for him to be sitting here thinking the things he was thinking. But it wasn't like he'd made the first move either. He never would have made a move. He would have been too scared to. She looked too good. And she was so much older than him, too. Older was intimidating. Compared to her he was nothing but a kid. But maybe older women knew what they wanted and weren't shy about asking for it.

"That's why I'm so worried," Mister Arthur said. "I know she goes out to bars sometimes. I don't know who she talks to. I guess she thinks I'm kind of boring. It doesn't seem like she talks to me nearly as much as she used to."

Eric swiveled around a little.

"Well, I don't think you're borin'. Why don't you try talkin' to her about Ben Johnson?"

"I have. She's not interested in old movies the way I am. And there's such a big difference in our ages," Mister Arthur said. "I've always secretly worried about that. I've always been afraid it would catch up with us one day." He said this last in a long sigh: "And I guess it has."

The movie came back on then. Jada Pinkett, under the table, began a light snoring. Eric kept sitting there drinking as the ice slowly melted in his glass. Mister Arthur had finished his pudding and sat with his hands in his lap, his head tilted up a little. It wasn't until another light sawing started up that Eric realized Mister Arthur had gone to sleep. He sat up and took a look at him. Yep. Asleep. Eyes closed, glasses down on his nose, mouth partly open.

Well shit. What should he do, wake him up and tell him to go to bed? He thought maybe he ought to just get another drink, so that's what he did. He got up quietly and walked over to the icebox. Jada Pinkett didn't stir. He seemed to be pretty happy here, and why not? Mister Arthur fed him all the time and played with him and scratched his belly and behind his ears and it was warm. Eric thought he liked being around the kitten, too. Earlier in the evening, the old dog had gone into the pantry a time or two to look at the kitten, but it had only bowed up and hissed with its teeth bared. But he knew it would probably tame down if they kept it. Cats were just weird.

He opened the top of the icebox quietly and scooped a few cubes from the bin in there. Jada Pinkett didn't move. He looked over at Mister Arthur, who had rolled his head over onto his shoulder. He closed the top of the icebox and it was dark except for the light from the television screen and a small light that was on over the stove. It held the remains of Mister Arthur's supper: a few small potatoes left in a pan, some green beans in a Corningware dish, half a breaded-and-fried pork chop. He pinched off a piece and chewed it. He turned the light off. The bottle was there on the counter and he poured enough scotch in the glass to cover up the cubes.

He leaned his lower back against the sink and sipped it. He set the glass down and pulled a cigarette from his shirt pocket and lit it. Then he picked up his glass again. Mister Arthur was snoring a little louder now. And Eric didn't care if he watched the rest of the movie or not. He'd seen it so many times. He got to thinking about what Mister Arthur had said about Montana. He wouldn't have guessed in his wildest dreams that Miss Helen was from Montana. But then, on the other hand, what was somebody from Montana supposed to look like? They had elk out there. Bighorns. You could do some serious hunting out there.

He crept past Mister Arthur's feet and reached for the cereal bowl on the coffee table and took it back to the kitchen table and pulled out a chair and sat down. He looked at Mister Arthur. He looked really old in the light from the TV screen. He looked frail and almost helpless. Things must have been a lot different when they got married. Hell, how old was she? If he had to guess, he'd guess about forty. But it was hard for him to tell older women's ages. So, if they'd been married twenty years, she must have been about twenty when she'd married him. Really young. About a year younger than him right now. And Mister Arthur had said something about oil wells. Eric looked around. It was a nice place, yeah, a real nice place, but it wasn't any mansion. It was a hell of a lot nicer than anything he ever expected to live in, but it didn't just shout RICH! from the rafters. But the shiny Jag out front did. He thought that sleek little black baby was about eighty-five thousand. Maybe Mister Arthur was rich and just didn't flaunt it.

He sipped on his drink and smoked his cigarette. If he stayed here, he was going to have to go out and get another pack out of his car. But he didn't want to wake Mister Arthur up opening and closing the door.

And he'd have to go sometime. He didn't want to be here asleep when she came in. If she came in. He hoped to God she would. At least for Mister Arthur's sake. At least before morning anyway. At least if she didn't come in it wouldn't be from anything he'd done to cause it. And what if she was mad at him and acted shitty to him now? He wouldn't be hanging around over here anymore after all. Crap. Maybe he needed to just get up and go.

He watched Mister Arthur sleeping on the couch. The television flickered its colors and bounced them around the dark room. At his feet, Jada Pinkett whistled through his nose. He'd have another drink or two. See what happened. He didn't have to be back at work until tomorrow afternoon. And it was warm in here and it was a home.

Even if it wasn't his.

74

The little dog covered the hole up and when he got through, it all looked alike and he looked like a little dog made out of mud. He was simply coated with it, each hair hanging heavy and dirty and wet on him, his polka-dotted ribbon drooping and bedraggled. He seemed satisfied and trotted back toward the house. Then he stopped and raised his hind leg to pee on a rosebush before he went back through his own personal door to the shiny Mr. Clean kitchen floor.

75

Miss Muffett had a hard time just getting out of the bedroom. She had to hop on one leg and hold on to something, the side of the bed, the bedpost, a dresser, a wall, the door frame.

There was a pair of crutches that she'd stashed in a broom closet downstairs simply because she got tired of wearing the fake leg sometimes and she was trying to make her way down to them. She had a hard time getting up the hall since there wasn't much to hold on to except for a table with some flowers on it and a bench that was too low to do her much good. She could hop about a foot at a time by holding on to the wall. Once she got to the stairs she'd be okay, could hold on to the banister all the way down. Then when she got the crutches she could get them under her arms and look for the leg.

She had to be pretty careful going down. She had to hold on with both hands and kind of turn sideways and hop down one riser at a time. It wasn't a fun way to get around. Nobody understood what it was like to be disabled except somebody who was disabled. She was truly grateful for handicapped-parking spaces because they were always close to the buildings and that meant fewer steps. That mattered to somebody like her.

There was no telling what he'd done with it. He might have dragged it up under the couch. Or hidden it in the utility room. She'd probably have to look in every room in the house.

And when she got to the crutches, she went back upstairs not very easily or quickly and then bent painfully trying to look under beds, checked all closets that had halfway-open doors, and she couldn't find her leg anywhere. Or the little dog, either. She wondered if he was out in the yard.

By then it was totally dark outside and she was ready for a bath and some supper. Maybe even a drink. That whole liquor cabinet downstairs hardly ever got used. And the things Scotty had made for her had sure given her a warm glow before they knocked her on her ass. Maybe she could find some stuff and make something kind of close to it, even though she didn't know what he'd put in it. But the idea of a drink, sitting on the edge of the tub while she soaked in the hot water, started sounding pretty good. Maybe later she could try to call Nub. Maybe something would work out with him. Maybe they could try it again. She did remember vaguely that he was a great kisser. So she went into the guest bedroom's bathroom and leaned one crutch against the wall while she bent carefully forward and put the drain plug in and opened the valves on the faucets. She let the water run awhile and then leaned back over and tested it with her fingers. It wasn't nearly hot enough and she adjusted the left valve. She stood there watching it fill for a while. Then she turned and eased herself down on the edge of the tub and trailed her fingers in the water. It was pretty hot already, but she liked it so hot that her whole ass would be red when she got out of it. So she cut the cold water all the way off and let some pure hot water run in it for a few more minutes, then shut it off. There. By then it was smoking and looked hot enough to scald a hog. Now it would still be hot by the time she got her drink made and got back upstairs with it and got her clothes off and got in.

With practice she was getting better. It didn't take her nearly as long to get back downstairs with the crutches. She went into the great room and behind the little bar and found a glass and got some ice cubes from trays in the small icebox that was there, and then she looked at the bottles. There was vodka, whiskey, rum, scotch, tonic water, gin, Bloody Mary mix, and there were some Cokes and 7-Ups in the little refrigerator, so she mixed herself a stiff bourbon and Coke and left one crutch there, and turned carefully and headed back toward the stairs. Once in a while, she stopped and took a sip. It was pretty good even if she had made it herself.

When she got to the foot of the stairs, she realized she was going to have to drop the other crutch as well since she had only two hands, and needed to hold on to the rail with one of them. She wished she'd thought to leave one of them upstairs. It was going to be hell to get up that way.

What she wound up doing was turning around, dropping the crutch, then sitting down on the second step, setting her drink down, and then scooting her butt up to the next step by pushing with both hands, then reaching down for the drink. Push with both hands, reach for the drink. Push, reach. That was a lot easier, and it wasn't too long before she was halfway up, only thing was, her drink was about half empty by then.

She sat there on the steps, looking down, sipping. Crap. She was only halfway up. So she started scooting back down. That water was getting colder all the time. She got herself up and grabbed the crutch and went back over to the bar and got some more ice cubes and then filled her glass all the way back up with Coke and bourbon, and then she hit the stairs again. It only took her about five minutes to get to the top. And her drink was still almost full.

She hopped her way back along the wall, thinking of how good that hot water was going to feel all over her body. She could lie there and close her eyes and just soak for a while. Then, later, she could go out to the shed in the backyard and get something for supper from one of the coolers. There was probably some fresh hamburger in there since Mr. Hamburger had just been working out there right before he left for Chicago. There was always something to eat out there.

Finally she reached the bathroom and set the drink carefully on the edge of the tub, then put the lid down on the toilet and sat down on it to undress. She unbuttoned her dress and pulled it down off her arms, then raised up a little to slide it from beneath her, and sat there in her slip and panties and bra. She reached for the drink and took a sip. It was good. Maybe she needed to go out more. Maybe somewhere out there was a man who didn't mind an older woman, getting slowly fat, who had a plastic leg. Maybe some widowed man who was lonely like her. She knew love was out there for everybody, if they could just find it. Some found it sooner than others. She hoped to find some herself one sweet day. It wasn't like she hadn't been looking her whole life already.

76

Merlot and Penelope slept as lovers do in the big canopied bed. She was naked next to him and when he woke briefly under the covers he could slide his nose right in the deep brown valley between her breasts and breathe in the scent of her with total contentment. She smelled to him like butter and oatmeal. His hand languidly on her broad hip, the reassuring sturdiness of it. She had a few stretch marks but he didn't mind, loved them, too, since they were a part of her and since his legs were so skinny he couldn't wear shorts and didn't have any room to talk about somebody else's body. He knew he'd inherited those skinny legs from his daddy's side of the family. There wasn't any doubt about it. He'd seen some pictures of his daddy and his uncle on a basketball team at Yocona High in 1949 and their legs were just skinny as hell, like his. A hereditary thing you couldn't do anything about. Some people got handed down buck teeth or big ears.

Hell. Close as they were going to be, they ought to go on down and see Evelyn. It wouldn't be but a few more hours from Natchez. Well shit, it would be, too. You'd have to go down to the coast and cut across to Mobile, and he didn't really want to be gone from Candy for an extra day. Which they'd sure have to stay if they went down there. Ruff would want to drink some beer with him and would wink and ask him if he had any left-handed cigarettes. They'd have to go out and eat oysters. And his mother would raise all kinds of hell with him if she found out that he'd been that close, in Natchez!, and hadn't come to see her. He just wouldn't tell her. He was going down on spring break anyway. That would be the best time to take Penelope. He looked at her.

She didn't snore loudly, but she snored a little. But it was a comforting sound. It let him know gently that she was alive and breathing, next to him. He nuzzled closer to her and drew in a deep breath, held her wonderful essence in his nose for a moment, and then let it out. It was very quiet. It was peaceful. Then a duck quacked.

When he woke again, she was gone from the bed. He raised his head and stretched his arms and yawned hugely. He rolled over and wondered where she was and closed his eyes. He'd just had a dream about going out in some country with snow on the far mountains and on horseback in a golden meadow getting morel mushrooms, some really big fat ones you could ride the horse right up to that grew out of these giant fossilized cow turds from these giant cows that used to roam the earth thousands of years before and that kept a new crop of the mushrooms coming up every year like perennial grass. Then the dream changed as dreams will to him and Penelope in France, drinking Beaujolais wine in a shady garden bower, and then she started having a baby during her birthday party at the new museum and he had to catch it in his hands and it was bloody and slick and already wearing glasses like him and then the baby got sick when it got older and they were in the hospital with it for a while and Penelope had another baby in the waiting room while they were waiting for the first one to get well but everything got okay and then they were all in a car at the Memphis airport and the back seat was full of babies and dogs and Candy was back there playing with them and she was young and beautiful again, and she still had all her hair. And her teeth.

He opened his eyes and threw back the covers. He couldn't hear her in the bathroom, couldn't hear the water running. He got up and went into the bathroom and took a leak for a long time, his head fuzzy from the wine and brandy the night before. They could make it in to Natchez by this afternoon if they went ahead and got some breakfast and packed and got on out of here.

He took a quick shower and washed his hair with the shampoo that was in there, some essence of herbs, maybe, something that smelled like apples. He wondered where she was. He zipped open her bag to see if her gun was in there and it was, small, black, deadly. He didn't like it. Why did she feel like she had to carry it around all the time? Just because she was a cop? He zipped it shut.

He shaved and got dressed and combed his hair and put all his things in his pockets and picked up his jacket in case she was outside.

He went downstairs to find a big kitchen with coffee ready in two pots and some doughnuts and stuff. He fixed himself a cup and saw her through the French doors, on the corner of a deck, sitting at a round table with a hole in it for the umbrella it held in summer. She was drinking coffee and looking out over the yard and the trees. She looked up and smiled when he opened the door.

"Hey, baby," he said. He set his coffee on the table and pulled his jacket on.

"Hey."

He leaned over and kissed her and she kissed him back, but not with much enthusiasm, he thought. Probably still thinking about that Perk guy.

He hoped the guy was all right. He really didn't know how he was supposed to feel about somebody who might be dead who might have been her lover, who might have kissed her the way he did, did to her the things he so loved to do. He pulled out a chair and sat down. She was drinking from a cup of coffee but he couldn't see any steam coming from it.

"How long you been out here?" he said.

She pulled her coat closer around her. She had one of the many mufflers Evelyn had made for him wrapped around her throat.

"Not long. I came down to the kitchen and got some coffee. I thought I'd come out here and look at the goldfish."

"Oh yeah? What are they doing?"

"Nothing. Swimming around."

He hugged his shoulders with his arms. There were a few leaves left hanging in the trees, but not many. Winter had robbed them of their clothes and the trunks of the trees stood in spots of snow. Patches of snow dotted the woods that ran up the hill behind the house.

"You sleep good?" he said.

"I did. I started having the best dreams."

"Oh yeah? What did you dream?"

She picked up her cup and took another sip from it. She looked out over the woods. She had a look on her face he hadn't seen before.

"I dreamed about being with my mamaw," she said. "We were picking blackberries like we used to when I was a kid."

Merlot leaned back in his chair and laced his fingers across his stomach.

"Is your grandmother still alive?"

She set the cup down and rubbed her hands together. It was very cold.

"Yeah. She's ninety-three but she's still going. Goes to church every Sunday. I need to go see her."

"How long's it been?"

"Aw, just a couple of weeks. But I'm always so busy. You know."

"Yeah. I know." Thinking about his mother. But hell, she was all right. Ruff, her second husband, was taking good care of her. She got to walk on the beach every day. He waited a second. "Well, what do you say we pack our stuff and take off? We can make it in plenty of time if we go ahead and get on the road."

"That suits me," she said. But she didn't look happy when she said it.

"Are you okay?"

"Yeah. I'm fine." She paused for a moment. "I was just wondering."

"Yes?"

He knew the coffee had to be cold but she took another sip from it anyway. Stalling?

"Are you going to take me over to your place when we get back?"

He thought of Candy instantly and looked down at the table, then back up at her. Now was as good a time to tell her as any. And she had leveled with him about the cop. She'd been honest, and he knew he hadn't. But she was *old*, damn it, she was *old*, and she'd lived a long time, and yeah, she was in bad shape, but he didn't see some days how he could have her killed. Mainly because he knew she wouldn't do it to him if the shoe was on the other foot. Like always, he waffled from day to day, back and forth on it. Some days it seemed like the sensible thing to do. Some days no way, Renee.

"Yeah."

"I mean, you don't have some woman you haven't told me about or something, do you?"

He laughed then, even though he was uneasy with his secret. But he had lost his courage, too. What if he told her and she didn't understand how things were?

"I do have a woman," he said, and got up and reached for her hand. "But it's not like you think. She's about eighty years old and she's got her own boyfriends. Now don't worry about it. Let's just have a good time. We're on vacation."

She smiled then, and was her old self again. She took his hand and got up. She leaned over and kissed him good on the mouth.

"Okay. I was just wondering."

"Don't worry," he said.

77

When Penelope woke, Merlot had his nose deep between her breasts. She hadn't slept good for dreaming about Gabriel again. She pulled back gently from him and his face slid down onto the pillow. For more than a few moments she lay there beside him, touching the side of his face with the back of her hand. There were a few gray hairs on the sides of his head. Stubble on his chin. On top his hair was thinning a little. He'd told her he was forty-two and tenured. She wanted to know more. She wanted to know everything about him. But there were still so many questions. He was a teacher, she was a cop. He had tenure there, she had twelve years toward a twenty-year retirement. So they had steady salaries, insurance, growing pension funds. There were a lot of things she didn't know about him and there were a lot of things he didn't know about her. Plenty of things he didn't know about her. He didn't know that one of her uncles was in prison doing his tenth year of life for murder or that she had given a baby up for adoption fifteen years ago, when she was eighteen. A fine healthy boy. She didn't know when she'd be able to tell him about that. Not yet. She didn't know him well enough yet. She didn't know his heart yet. But she thought it was good. She wanted more than anything a kind man and a loving man and she thought he was that.

He snored lightly and she got up without waking him. She pulled the covers over him a little better and patted him fondly on the ass.

Naked, she stood at the French doors, admiring the yard. She could see a nice deck down there. Some old Chinese guy raking leaves looked up casually and kind of coughed out his amazement and almost lost his grip on his rake until she jumped behind the curtains with her big titties jiggling and peeked back out. Then he went on, dragging his rake, shaking his head. She thought about stepping out there and flashing him just for the fun of it.

It was very cloudy and the sun was hidden. She thought she'd get dressed and find the kitchen and get some coffee and sit out on that deck for a while.

She peed first, the door almost closed, her elbows on her thighs and her chin in her fingers, thinking. They'd probably be there this afternoon. She hadn't let on to him how scared she'd been the other night, when all that had happened, because she wanted him to think she was strong, that she was fearless, because that was how a police officer was supposed to be, even if the officer was a woman.

She brushed her teeth and flossed and found some long underwear in the bag she'd left on a chair in the bedroom and dressed in the bathroom, the marble floor cold on her bare feet. She put on thick socks. She had half a mind to call the station to see if they'd found out anything, see if they'd found Elwood. They hadn't turned the TV on last night so there hadn't been any news to hear. She guessed she could always buy a paper today at a gas station somewhere if she really wanted to know. If she really did. If he was dead, and she didn't know it yet, wouldn't that be kind of like a blessed ignorance, just for today?

She had some heavy wool pants and pulled them on and put on a sweater and her big coat. Merlot was still sleeping. One of his mufflers was hanging in the closet and she wrapped it around her neck, got her boots, unlocked the hall door, and went down to the kitchen. There was nobody down there, but some coffee was ready and there were some doughnuts and pastries. Some cereal. Bananas. Milk in an iced tub. She pulled out a chair from the table and sat down and laced the boots on. She was afraid she was falling in love with him. He was absolutely nutty and incredibly smart. He was very loving. He was able to make her go dreamy inside her head and make goose pimples jump out all over her. And he wanted children. Lord she did need to go see her mamaw. Tell her she'd found the man she wanted.

Two small stainless-steel urns were sitting on the table beside plastic baskets with the sugar and stuff and Penelope got a big foam cup and drew it full of smoking decaf. She dumped in about five spoonfuls of sugar and stirred it. There were some doughnuts and chocolate eclairs and fruit-filled pastries under glass. She blew on her coffee and sipped it, trying to decide what she wanted. Just a little something to tide her over until Merlot woke up and they could have a real breakfast, maybe ham and eggs if they could find a Shoney's or an IHOP or a Waffle House or a Huddle House nearby. Then hit the road. She set her coffee down and picked up a napkin and lifted the glass top from the eclairs and reached with the napkin for one of them.

She got back out the door by holding the coffee carefully against her breast with her arm and using her free hand for the doorknob. She was glad they'd stopped here. She'd remember this one day when she was old.

On the deck, she sipped her coffee and unwrapped her eclair from the napkin and bit into it. It was filled with sweet white frosting. She got up and went down the steps and walked over and looked at the goldfish pond. The old Chinese guy was out in the front yard, raking out there, and he tipped his hat to her and she smiled back. The goldfish weren't moving much and they looked like they were big enough to eat.

After she'd finished her eclair, she wiped her fingers with the napkin and balled it up and put it in her pocket. She went back to the deck and sat down. The coffee was cooling off some. She kept sipping it. Two nights with him. She wondered what his house looked like, and how big his yard was, and what kind of food he kept in his refrigerator and on his shelves. She wanted to cook for him at his house and make herself at home in his kitchen.

The door opened and he stepped out.

"Hey, baby," he said.

She tried to smile at him because all of a sudden she wasn't sure if this was the right thing to do. Going off for two nights with a man she really didn't even know. Her mamaw probably wouldn't approve of that.

"Hey," she said, and leaned forward a little when he leaned over to kiss her. He pulled out a chair and sat down.

"How long you been out here?" he said.

"Not long," she said. "I came down to the kitchen and got some coffee. I thought I'd come out here and look at the goldfish."

"Oh yeah? What are they doing?"

"Nothing. Swimming around."

He hugged his shoulders with his arms. He seemed so thin now. It was plain to see that he was cold.

"You sleep good?" he said.

And she didn't want to tell him that she hadn't.

"I did. I started having the best dreams."

He seemed interested in that and he smiled at her. He opened doors for her. He left the toilet seat down for her. She hadn't seen him pick his nose.

"Oh yeah?" he said. "What did you dream?"

She didn't want to tell him about the dream she'd had, because she had heard all her life that if you told a dream before breakfast, it would come true. She didn't know if an eclair and coffee counted as breakfast or not.

She'd always had dreams about her baby as he grew up, wherever he was. Even though she had never seen him again since he left her arms at the hospital, age two days, with bright eyes and a curious but happy look and really long black hair, he had aged in her dreams at the same pace she had envisioned him aging in real life. He was now fifteen somewhere, alive and in the same world she walked every day. There was no doubt. She knew he was alive in the same way she would have known if he was dead. And his name was Gabriel, after the angel who would blow his horn. But she didn't want to tell him about all that, wasn't ready to tell him about all that, so she just made up a bunch of bullshit about picking blackberries out in the country with her mamaw, when in reality the itching chigger bites on her private places had always driven her apeshit.

78

Dominic had pissed all over himself long before they got to where they were going. He was sick with shame and knew that a man should not be treated so. It was one of the things Doreen had done to him. Kept him tied in the basement on a bed until he had to pee on himself. When Rico opened the trunk, he just lay there since he could see nothing. But he knew it was still dark. He also knew he was going to die. And probably pretty soon.

Rico got him by the arm and pulled him up out of the trunk. He bumped his head on the lid. The lid went *BONG!* and it hurt.

It was cold on him where he had wet himself, and it had soaked into the bottom of his shorts, and he expected to hear laughter, but there was none.

Finally he stood on the ground. It felt like he was standing on gravel. He couldn't tell if other people were around or not. He could hear wind and not much else. He reached up with his hands to push the blindfold off his eyes and was struck behind his right ear, a blow that caused a bright spark of fire behind his blinded eyes and glanced off his shoulder blade, something heavy, a wrench maybe. And he sank with the pain of it. And could not help it when the tears came. He couldn't hold it back any longer. Why had his parents put him in a garbage can or had him put in a garbage can or allowed him to be placed in a garbage can? Who was that in the bag?

Something else happened to him because he was suddenly lying on his side coming to and gravel was digging into his cheek. There was a roaring in his ears like a coal train coming. He reached to touch his ear to see if there was blood flowing or if the ear was still there and Rico fetched a kick to his kidney that made him piss on himself again. And he began to beg for mercy with the word *"please."* What he heard was a voice above him, crying, hollow with malice, riddled now with bitter laughter.

"Please? You stupid son of a bitch, you better tell me where my little brother is."

"I don't know where your asshole brother is, asshole."

What he didn't expect was to get his pants pulled down. The wind was cold on his already chilled skin and he felt his equipment shriveling. The blindfold was suddenly pulled off. And even in the dark he saw the steel edge of the terrible straight razor down there against the tightly drawn and wrinkled skin of his scrotum. He closed his eyes because he couldn't bear to see it. He knew how the hogs screamed, down on the prison farm, because they'd raised and killed their own.

But Rico bent closer, to slobber softly, sniffling with his runny nose: "Okay, son of a bitch, have it your way. You don't have to say a fuckin' word, 'cause I *know* you killed my brother. You wouldn't have his gun if you hadn't."

Domino lay there. He could feel the blood leaking down the side of his head. He looked around. They were at the edge of a dirt road with woods all around. The son of a bitch was crazy. And the bad thing was that he was right about everything. He should have shot him at the hospital when he had the chance. He wouldn't have been any worse off. He might have been a hell of a lot better off. He might have been headed back to Memphis by now with his whitetail.

Rico was crying with his rage. Domino could see the tears coming down his cheeks. He'd never seen a rage quite like that before and it was a scary thing to see. His words were coming hard. But he seemed about to speak some ultimate truth. As he saw it. As he straightened and stood over him.

"And I ain't willin' . . . to turn you over . . . to some damned. Jury. You're gonna get your punishment from me . . . now . . . and that way . . . when they find my brother dead . . . I'll *know* . . . in *my* heart . . . that by God, I did the right thing by him."

It was a struggle, and every movement hurt him, but Domino pulled himself up off the ground with his hands still cuffed behind his back, and he got up on his knees. It was ridiculous. His nuts were hanging out. The gravel hurt like hell on his kneecaps.

"What if I take you where I saw him?" he said, thinking that if they ran up on some other cops, he wouldn't be able to do this to him, whatever it was he was going to do.

Rico wasn't going for it. He'd made some decision because he was shaking his head.

"Naw. You just tryin' to save your ass. Now you tell me. What's with all that bad meat?"

Why did he want to know that? He already had the weed box in the trunk and it had already thawed out maybe enough to peel the steaks and roasts back and find the package in the center of it but he didn't know if Rico had done that or not. He didn't know if he should tell him what was in the package or not.

"It's for the lions."

Rico just looked at him for a second.

"The lions?"

"Yeah."

Rico was frozen, hanging in front of him, still bent over, still gripping the razor. He was trying to understand, too.

"Lions. Do you mean . . . the ones that guy keeps on Yocona River Road down close to Water Valley? That's got three legs, some of 'em?"

Domino's legs were trembling. He felt weak and sick to his stomach. And he could taste blood in his mouth. A place on his head was throbbing.

"Yeah. He's got a contract for meat with my boss, in Memphis."

The look on Rico's face changed again, and it turned into something that was almost like a smile, only it wasn't a nice one.

"Well why in the hell didn't you say so?"

"You just now asked me."

Rico stood there looking down on him, and then he folded the straight razor and slipped it back in his pocket. He motioned toward the trunk.

"I got a key to that place," Rico said. "The sheriff insisted we have keys after that one got loose and killed that dog. Now you just get back in."

79

Miss Muffett in her gown and robe almost broke down and cried when she saw the kitchen floor and the great-room carpet. There was mud in slick trails, and little muddy dog footprints were scattered around. She knew she didn't have the energy to try and clean it all up tonight. She would have to get down on her hands and knee to clean it, and she just wasn't up for it. So she went into the great room and mixed herself another drink.

She sat on the couch and wondered if maybe it was time for her to move on. She was tired of being alone with the dog but not actually *with* the dog. It might have been different if he would be just a little friendly and be some company for her. And she didn't have any idea where her leg could be. She sat there and got sadder and sadder and sipped her drink. It didn't seem fair for a dog to be able to do something like this to a person. He didn't even know what he was doing. He didn't have any idea what he was doing. He had it made and he didn't even know it. He had a warm place to sleep and plenty of food to eat, and he didn't appreciate any of it. All he knew how to do was shit on the floor and make a mess. Show somebody his teeth. Make more work for her.

That was when she heard what sounded like splashing in the tub upstairs. She raised her head and looked at the ceiling. It sounded like a five-pound bass flopping around up there. Then she remembered. She'd forgotten to pull the drain plug when she got out of it. Just one more thing she'd have to clean now. Didn't he care? Couldn't he see that she had only one leg?

80

Helen was in a dark room on a water bed covered with some dirty cotton sheets and she was naked below the waist. She saw shapes, shelves, things on the walls. Her shoes were off and her head was on a pillow. He was gripping the tops of her thighs with his warm hands. Her sweater was open and one of her breasts was exposed, the bra on that side pushed down under her breast. It was too hot in the room, and he was burrowing with his mouth like a mole at the junction of her thighs. But it felt too good to do anything but just lie there and take it.

She reached out a hand and touched his hair. It was too dark to see much. She licked with her tongue around her dry lips. She thought she'd been asleep. She cleared her throat.

"That's good," she said. "That's . . . yeah." And she trailed off in a sigh.

There was some faint music playing somewhere, so low that she couldn't even tell what it was. More Barry Manilow probably. Some of her hair was in her face and she pushed it away. She reached to the catch in front of her bra and undid it, and pulled the two sides away, and let them lie beneath the edges of her sweater, let her breasts lie at ease. She hated to have to wear a bra. She was beginning to remember now as she looked at the ceiling.

Oh fuck. What damn time was it?

"Ken?" she said.

He didn't answer. He just made some pleasurable sound in his throat and kept doing what he was doing. She knew she was very drunk. She knew that much. She thought she must have gone to sleep for a while.

All those drinks. They fucked you up over the long run. It was fun at first, when everything was happy and warm and there was music and people to talk to, and then, if you kept sitting there drinking long enough, you started to feel a little sad, and a little sorry for yourself, and you started to feel lonely. And if you were talking to somebody, then you might start telling things that you might not have told if you hadn't been drinking. You began to confide, is what you began to do. You began to tell about your unhappiness if you had some. And she remembered that happening with Ken. Again. Even after she'd told herself she wasn't going to with him again. He had listened to her, agreeing, taking her side, touching her hand. And then he had kissed her on the mouth in a room somewhere in the hotel, behind the bar, after it was already very late. He had unzipped her sweater and pulled her breasts free of the bra and had sucked on her nipples very hard, so hard she'd been afraid he was going to cause her to have some hickies, and he might have. And then he had driven her here. Back to his place. She'd have to look later. She'd have to lock the door to the bathroom, where Arthur couldn't see, when she got home and check herself for hickies. She couldn't let Arthur see. He'd get mad. But wasn't she going to divorce him anyway?

She twisted her fingers through his hair and sighed deep in her chest. She held his head and moved her legs languidly, searching for the best position. It was too late now to worry anymore about Eric. Too late to worry about what time it was. Too late to think about how embarrassing it was to be taken to jail in handcuffs. Too late to think about those dead babies they'd made her look at.

"Ken," she said. "Make me come again 'cause I've got to go."

81

Anjalee was sitting on a sleek leather couch in Harv's den and he had his stereo going at a nice listening level, not too loud. He had a really nice place and he hadn't been wrong about the steaks. She'd never known that a T-bone could be that tender. She was full, comfortable, and a little bit sleepy. But she wasn't quite ready to go to sleep. Not yet.

He wanted to go over to her place sometime and see her drawings and she was nervous about it. Frankie had been to her place only a time or two and never had said anything about any of them, had only turned on the television and plopped down on the couch and called for a drink. She thought of Christmas with another tinge of regret. But there wasn't anything she could do about that. Not unless she wanted to go all the way home and have Christmas there. But she already knew what that would be like. Her mother would have some man over at her trailer. He'd be divorced or maybe even still married. Maybe he'd have a stubble of beard or bad breath or a pot gut or a human bite mark on his nose, and she again wouldn't be able to understand why her mother had spent almost her whole life fucking a bunch of losers. She wished she could have known her daddy better, longer. He was such a dim memory. She knew he'd been a real good man. Her mother had said it enough times: Honey, your daddy was a real good man.

She was still worried about not getting in touch with Lenny before she left the hotel. She hoped he wasn't mad, because she didn't want to blow a possible good thing with him. What was she doing with Harv anyway? Lately could she not stick with one man for more than a few days at a time?

She heard him coming out of the bathroom. He walked into the den and took his coat off and dropped it onto a chair. Who was it he looked like? Was it Cesar Romero? Errol Flynn?

"I love your place," she said. "Who's that you got on the stereo?"

"Patty Griffin," he said. "It's her new record. Isn't she great?"

"She's mighty good. I can't believe I've never heard of her," she said. "But I guess you can't keep up with everything."

"I guess not. I can make some coffee if you want some after a while. There's some brandy here. Or I could make you a drink."

He ducked his head for a second to start loosening his tie and she could see that he had no bald spot. His hair looked as strong as a twenty-year-old's, only flowing silver. She wondered what kind of shape the rest of him was in.

"I might have a drink," she said.

"It's right here," he said, going over to a little cart where there were some bottles and a small tub of ice he'd brought from the kitchen earlier. He took the knot out of his tie and pulled on one end of it and slid it from his collar. "I know you like bourbon. I've got Maker's, Crown, Wild Turkey. What would you like?"

"Maker's on the rocks is fine."

He folded the tie and put it on top of the stereo and started fixing her drink. It wasn't that late, only a little after ten. She watched him pour the bourbon over the ice and then he walked over with it.

"I'm sorry I don't have any cocktail napkins," he said.

"Thank you," she said. "This is fine."

Suddenly she didn't know what to say. He was just so fucking *distinguished*. He looked like he could be president of a university or something like that. Maybe a bank.

"You want to get stoned?" he said. "I've got some good grass."

She took a sip and smiled at him.

"I'd love to. Mine's back at my place."

"Okay. I'll be right back."

He went past her and touched her briefly on the shoulder and walked into the kitchen. She heard him opening a drawer.

She hadn't told him anything about her recent troubles. For some reason she'd felt it wouldn't be the right thing to do. He still seemed a little mysterious and when she'd asked him about what he did for a living, he had said only that he dabbled in this and that. Which could mean almost anything. There were some nice paintings on his walls and pictures of him holding big fish that had come from some ocean.

He came back in and sat down beside her and handed her a tiny green glass pipe and some brown weed that smelled pretty good when she opened the top of the bag. She set her drink down on the coffee table and loaded it and got her lighter from beside her cigarettes and fired the bowl up and took a hit. She handed him the lighter and the pipe and held the smoke in for a few seconds, then blew it out. He fired the bowl up and took a hit that made the little pile of marijuana glow red. He blew a plume of smoke toward the ceiling. He handed the pipe and the lighter back but she smiled at him to let him know she was fine and set them back on the coffee table. He patted her on the hand. He let it rest there and she was glad to feel it. Then for a few minutes they just listened to the singing in the darkened living room. Anjalee leaned back. She didn't want to be alone tonight. She could tell Lenny just about anything she wanted to once she saw him again. If she did. Who knew if she would, even though he'd given her money and said in the note that he'd hook back up? Who'd have thought that Frankie would just up and disappear?

But maybe he'd decided to dump her and this was just his way, to stop coming around, to stop calling, to stop coming by Gigi's Angels.

Harv was listening to the music. And then her cell phone rang. Just once because she reached into her purse and cut it off. She didn't know who could be calling unless it was Moe, and she didn't want to talk to him right now.

"I'm not gonna answer that," she said. He just nodded.

It was driving her nuts who he looked like, but she couldn't think who it was. Hopalong Cassidy? One of our cowboy heroes. She couldn't help herself. She leaned to him and kissed him full on the mouth. His hand went naturally to her breast and cupped it, and her hair swung down beside her face and she put her other hand on his chest. She kissed him some more without taking her mouth away from his and reached lower and found something about the size of a Jimmy Dean smoked sausage in his pants.

"Hot damn," she said. "Where's the bedroom?"

82

It was cloudy and overcast outside and looking like more snow but warm inside the Four-Runner, which they were both almost ready to buy since it was so nice. Merlot had already mentioned maybe trying to trade in the minivan on it once they got all the bullet holes fixed. They'd loaded up on pancakes and sausage and eggs at a Waffle House just outside Mathiston and had gotten back on the Trace there. He said they'd have to get off the Trace for a short while near Jackson since it disappeared for a stretch there, but that he'd catch it again at Ridgeland, and then it would be a straight shot on down to Natchez. They'd already passed through Kosciusko and he thought it was about an hour to Jackson from there, and then probably about two more hours or a little more to Natchez. Which would put them in there early. They'd have plenty of time to stop for a good lunch somewhere, and could take their time eating. They listened to music as they drove.

The land beside the road was sometimes filled with woods, sometimes fields where hay had been cut and baled in large round bales and covered with rolls of either black or white plastic, and set in straight rows. Or she saw farms with red barns and neat brick houses where the fields were filled with the dead stalks of the fall's crop. Corn. Cows. Once in a while some horses. There was not much traffic. Sometimes they saw creeks and there were deer feeding openly beside the road in places and she even saw a small one that had spots. She was still a little apprehensive, and didn't really know why, only that she was. She was already getting a bit hungry but hadn't said anything about it because she didn't want him to think she ate too much. She wasn't starving or anything. She just wanted maybe a Coke and a candy bar to tide her over until lunch. Or some Nabs. She decided she'd wait a while longer before she said anything. He didn't eat as much as she did. Or as often. She couldn't help it, she liked food. But he didn't seem to mind her size. It was just the reverse. He'd told her she was his dream come true, big hipped and big breasted. He'd said that the women in all those old paintings you saw in museums were built like her, that the old masters knew what a good woman was supposed to look like naked.

Merlot pointed.

"Look at those turkeys."

She looked but didn't see them. They rode in silence for a while.

The highway was clean now with only scraps of white that lay in the shady places along the sides of the road. She remembered snow from when she was growing up and having snowball fights with her grandmother, who would go out every evening in the summer into the little garden she kept and pick some peppers for her supper, tiny curled and wrinkled green things that would bring tears to Penelope's eyes, but which her grandmother would munch calmly along with her corn bread and buttermilk and fatback.

If she hadn't given her baby away, she wouldn't have wound up here today, with this man, going to spend the night in the oldest house in Mississippi. If DeWayne had been willing to marry her, it might have turned out different. She might not even be a police officer.

She was going to have to call sometime and see what they'd found out about Perk. She was going to have to know. If he was dead, it was going to be hard to deal with. She couldn't believe that guy had gotten away from Rico. Everybody knew Rico was a bad son of a bitch. The only soft spot he had in him was for Perk.

"What else you got to listen to?" Merlot said.

"I've got some more back here," she said, and reached back between the seats and into her bag for her CD case without unfastening her seat belt. It was a little black zippered box that held ten discs. She put it in her lap and opened it up.

"What about Al Green? You got any Al?" Merlot said.

"I did have but he got to skipping. Let me see what else I've got." She looked.

"I've got Lightnin' Hopkins," she said.

"Stop right there," Merlot said.

They'd been listening to mixed Motown and she pushed the button to eject it. She got Lightnin' out and pushed him into the player. Guitar strokes like bolts of velvet lightning started throbbing up in the Four-Runner.

They rode with the music for a while and she watched the land go by. She watched the curves go by and sometimes she saw roadside stands where pumpkins or vegetables had been sold, but now they were empty and deserted, lightless and abandoned until next year. There were small windmills for sale in yards, draft horses in pens beside the highway. Once she saw a DEER CROSSING sign, a black deer in silhouette outlined against bright yellow. But in a way she didn't really see any of it. Things passed that she didn't notice.

She wanted to see Gabriel again, that was what she wanted, to hold him, or if that wasn't possible, to maybe just stand somewhere at a distance and be able to watch him for a while. Like at his high school graduation, wherever he was. He could be anywhere. He could be in Louisiana. Or Texas. Or Wisconsin. Or Florida. Anywhere. Maybe even overseas. She'd checked already, lots of times, but hadn't been able to find out anything. The records had been sealed, they'd told her. She'd signed a bunch of papers, but she didn't remember now what-all they said. There were so many of them, and she'd been crying so much she had wet all the pages. Smeared the ink with her signature. Maybe she wouldn't ever see him again. How was she going to know? What if he was sick? What if whoever had him was mean to him? How would she ever find that out? What did she ever give him up for? Other girls raised their babies by themselves. Or with the help of their mothers. If they had mothers who were around. Or sisters. Or aunts. Or grandmothers. And her mamaw had begged her not to do it, had come to the hospital and told her she'd take it and raise it until Penelope was out of school and had a job and was able to take care of it herself. But she'd been so confused. And so embarrassed. And so scared. And so young. You could make a mistake when you were young and then it would follow you around for the rest of your life. She wanted to tell Merlot. She was going to tell Merlot. But she wanted to wait until the time was right. If he really loved her, maybe he'd help her find out what had happened to her baby. He was smart. He'd been to college. Hell, he taught at a college. Maybe together they could find him. Was that too much to hope for?

"How much longer you think it'll take?" she said.

Merlot reached up and turned Lightnin' down some.

"We'll be there in a couple more hours. We'll stop and eat some lunch somewhere. You getting hungry?"

"I could use a snack."

"We'll get you one next place we see."

She reached out and put her hand on his arm.

"I like going places with you."

Merlot smiled and she watched his eyes.

"I can stop at the next town and find a gas station and get you a snack to tide you over if you want," he said. "A hot dog or something till we can get to a place for lunch."

"That'd be great," she said.

That made her happy and she settled back in her seat. The nameless worries she'd had earlier had about gone away now. She was looking forward to seeing where he lived when they got back, what he had in his house, what his yard looked like. He'd tried to describe it. He'd said it was lovely in the summer when the leaves were on the trees.

After a while she got sleepy and closed her eyes, reached for the knob on the side of the seat, and leaned it back. She kept listening to the music and Merlot kept driving. It was absolutely wonderful being off with him. Once in a while the sun broke through and she could feel it through her eyelids.

83

Eric didn't even hear the Jag pull up to the curb outside but it wasn't because he was asleep. It was partly probably because the Jag had such a good muffler, but it was also partly because he was concentrating on a movie. He was on his second glass of scotch and he'd opened another pack of cigarettes from his car and Jada Pinkett was asleep under the coffee table. Mister Arthur had slipped in his sleep down deeper into the couch earlier and Eric had gone over quietly and lifted his legs up onto the couch and had taken his house shoes off and then wandered into another room and found a folded comforter that he brought back and spread over him. Carefully he'd removed his glasses and put them on the coffee table. Mister Arthur had turned in his sleep and put his face to the back of the couch. Now he was snoring and the only light was from the enormous television screen, and Eric was watching *Shane*, with wonderful sound quality and digital enhancement that you had to actually see to believe. It was one of his favorites. It had been made before Eric was born and it had everything. It had good guys, it had bad guys, it had a kid, the kid had a dog, it had a hardworking man and his hardworking wife, it had the new little guys trying to carve out pieces of land they could homestead being pitted against the big old guys who were trying to hold on to all of it for themselves. It had gunfights, and drinking, and fistfights, and thunder, and everybody was still pissed off about the Civil War, and a small man in buckskin who'd seen enough of gunslinging and only wanted peace showed up one day, but wound up having to unlimber his fists and duke it out with Ben Johnson because Ben Johnson got to calling him Sody Pop in the saloon, and he eventually had to strap on his gun one more time because hot lead was the only thing some people understood. And the kid, the young Brandon de Wilde, running after him down the dusty road, almost at the end, yelling for him to come back. And it was almost to that part now. Alan Ladd had already outpulled two-gun Walter Jack Palance in Grafton's saloon, had blown him into a bunch of wooden beer barrels, and he'd gone down shooting through a cloud of smoke. Alan Ladd had twirled his gun, and spun it back into the nicely tooled holster, and the kid had seen everything from the bottom of the bat-wing doors. But upstairs a board had creaked, and the kid had yelled for Shane to look *out!*, and he had spun, and fired, killing the guy with the gun at the rail upstairs, who shot and crashed down to the floor, but he might have hit Shane. It kind of looked like he *did* hit Shane, because Shane flinched and staggered. And now the kid was going to follow him out to the dusty road, and run along after him once he'd mounted his horse and ridden away, yelling for him to come back, and you knew he was hurt, because one arm looked real limp, and he was kind of leaned over sideways in the saddle in the last few frames, and you knew with a sick feeling in your soul that he was probably going to ride over the mountain and die somewhere up there in the black woods all by himself after he'd been such a good dude, and had helped all the new little guys in the valley, but the movie didn't show that. That was the cool thing about it. The ending was left up to you. And just as Shane was going outside to untie his horse from the hitching rail and tousle little Joey's hair, and say a few things to him about growing up strong and straight, Eric heard the door opening and turned his head to see Miss Helen standing there. *Fuck.* Talk about bad timing. Now not only was he going to miss the end of *Shane* after investing almost two hours in it, he was going to have to talk to her, and she looked like she was drunk.

She also had what looked like a half gallon of Edy's Rocky Road ice cream in her hands. For a moment she didn't say anything. For a moment she just stared at him. Then she came on in and stumbled a little and shut the door and locked it. Turned the dead bolt, too. He wondered why she did that.

He should have already gone, he knew that, but he hadn't wanted to just go off and leave Mister Arthur there asleep on the couch all fucked up and alone. And plus he'd wanted to watch *Shane* in a warm place with a full belly and have a few drinks. What was wrong with that?

But was it just that? Or was he sitting here this long also because he wanted to see her again, even if he hadn't gone over to the Peabody to have drinks with her? Could it be that he was still wondering what might have happened? Mister Arthur was asleep. Mister

Arthur wasn't doing her any good evidently. He hated to think that, but it looked like that's the way it was.

"Hey," she said quietly, her hair swinging gently as she turned.

He took a drink of his scotch. Then he looked up.

"Hey." Just as quietly.

She stood there for a moment looking at Arthur on the couch.

"How long's he been asleep?"

"Hour or two I guess. I was just watching some TV. I probably better go, I guess."

Arthur moved on the couch and seemed to settle deeper into it.

"You ain't going nowhere," she said.

She walked into the kitchen and he saw her open the top section of the refrigerator and put the ice cream in there and then shut it. She turned the light on over the stove. That gave just a little light to the kitchen, but it was still mostly dark. She got something down from a cabinet. A bottle.

"Why don't you come in here?" she said. "We can talk and he probably won't wake up. And no big deal if he does."

Eric stood up, with his drink. He looked down at it for a few seconds, then back up at her. He didn't know if he needed to be driving or not. He probably didn't. These Memphis cops were hell on drunk drivers. They'd take your ass to the Shelby County Jail and he knew he didn't want to go there. But his car was out front. He could get Jada Pinkett up off of the floor and get their quilt out of the trunk and get him on the back seat with him, and curl up, and cover them both up, and sleep until he was okay to drive somewhere for breakfast. Maybe if it would warm up a little tomorrow he could take Jada Pinkett over to Overton Park for a while and let him walk. He was tired of all this. Being in a big city and not having a place to stay. Not having much money. Being cold at night. He wanted to go home. See if his daddy would let him come back. Maybe he would by now. It had been almost three months. But what if he wouldn't let Jada Pinkett come back? Or what if he still wanted to shoot him?

"I better go," he said. "It's done got pretty late."

"Come on in and sit down," she said. "I'm fixing myself a drink."

He didn't know what to say. He didn't know if sitting around here drinking with her was the thing to do right now. He didn't want to stick around because he was afraid something might happen. And Mister Arthur was right there.

"Let me fix you another one," she said.

Eric looked back at Mister Arthur, and glanced at Brandon de Wilde trotting down the road behind Shane, and moved on into the kitchen. Miss Helen was standing there pouring whiskey over ice in a glass. Her lipstick looked smeared and he wondered if she had been kissing somebody. He figured she probably had. Maybe even something else. Maybe it had been somebody she'd met in the Peabody. Or maybe she had some regular guy there she saw. Met there maybe.

He moved up behind her and stopped.

"You all right?" he said quietly.

She turned around to him. She looked tired and she looked pissed off.

"Why didn't you come?" she said, just as quietly.

He felt helpless to give her an answer. It was too complicated to try and explain it here in the kitchen while he was listening to Mister Arthur snore on the couch. But if he was snoring, he wouldn't hear.

"Different reasons," he finally said. "I'm scared of you, I guess."

She shook her head and walked over to the refrigerator and got a Coke out and opened it, then poured some in on top of the whiskey. Then she picked it up and sipped it and turned back around to him.

"Why are you scared of me, Eric?"

"I don't know." He picked up his glass and headed for the refrigerator, and opened the top and reached in for some more ice cubes. He shut the door and picked up the scotch bottle and poured some more in. He lifted the glass and took a drink. She was standing there watching him. He walked back over to her. He stood there in front of her and took another sip.

"You're about the same age as my mama, for one thing," he said. And after that he didn't know what else to say. So he sat back down and just sat there, drinking with her in silence. The silence went on for a while. She put that drink down her throat quickly and then mixed another one. He could tell she had something on her mind. She just stood there drinking and thinking. He really wanted to go now.

"Fuck," she said, and she started crying. And it seemed just a natural thing when he got up for her to come into his arms. He was still holding his drink but he set it on the table when he saw what was happening, just in time to get both his arms around her. He turned his head and looked back at Mister Arthur. What if he woke up and saw this? But there wasn't anything he could do. He could feel her face up against his and he could feel the wetness she was smearing on him. She wasn't crying loudly. It was mostly shaking. He could feel her breasts shaking against him and he didn't mean to do it but he started getting hard. And before he knew what was happening she had her mouth on his and she was kissing him. She pushed him backward. He felt her at his zipper even while she was pushing him back and in just a few seconds she had pushed him into the den and around the corner where she stopped and reached into his shorts. She leaned her mouth against his throat and he could feel her hot breath against his skin. She pushed him against the wall and started going to her knees and the kid was hollering *Shane! Shane! Come back!*, and when she opened her mouth and put it on him, Eric almost fainted and also because he heard Mister Arthur stirring on the couch and pulled back and fastened his pants together before he could get up and come in there.

"You go first," she said, and he was terrified. When he stepped around the corner, Mister Arthur was turning over on the couch but he wasn't getting up. He was just moving around. Now he was still again.

Eric stood there with his heart in his throat and his breathing was only now starting to slow down. What if he'd walked into the den and turned on the light? It felt like the world was sucking a hole in him.

He went back over to the table and made sure his clothes were in order. He looked back at her. She was standing inside the door frame, resting her hand on it. He didn't know what to do. He needed to get out of here was what he needed to do. Before she had another chance to get him in trouble. Hell, Mister Arthur might have a heart attack if he saw her doing that shit.

"Eric," she said. He looked up. She was motioning him toward her with her hand, wanting him to come back in there. He knew he didn't need to stay here. He knew he didn't need to be in the middle of their problems, which he saw now were pretty bad if she was trying to suck him off with her husband on the couch about twenty feet away.

He walked back over to her and whispered: "I'm scared to."

Her answer was to put her arm around the back of his neck and pull him close again. She turned him so that she could be facing Mister Arthur on the couch and watch him while she was kissing Eric and he saw what she was doing. And he pulled back again.

"I cain't do it," he whispered. "It ain't right."

She leaned to his ear and whispered: "Don't you want me to? Doesn't that feel good?"

"It feels great," he whispered. "But it ain't right."

And by then Jada Pinkett had already woken up. Eric felt him nuzzling at his hand and he looked down and rubbed his head. Miss Helen saw him, too.

"Shit," she said, and didn't bother to whisper. "Hell, fuck it, forget it," she muttered, and walked past him and back into the kitchen. He just stood there looking at her.

"I'm sorry," he said. He didn't know what else to say.

"What are you sorry for, Eric?" she said, raising her voice, and she picked up her drink. "Life's too short to go around being sorry. You'd better get what you want while you're young. 'Cause you're only young once."

She looked up at him and he could see more tears coming down her face. Now he was really sorry he'd stayed. But only because of her. He started to pull out a chair from the table and sit back down, because he was afraid Jada Pinkett was getting on her nerves by walking all around in the kitchen, and he was going to hold on to him or try to get him to lie back down, but she just finished her drink and turned and walked past the couch, and Mister Arthur turned over and sat up.

"Helen?" he said. His hair was twisted up on the side of his head and he reached for his glasses, on the coffee table. She didn't stop, just kept going, out of sight. She turned on a light that lit up the hall and Eric knew there was a bathroom down that hall because he'd used it last night. Mister Arthur sat up and looked at the television, and then he looked at Eric. He looked kind of bewildered.

"Hey, Mister Arthur," Eric said. He waved, too.

"Hey, uh . . . Eric," Mister Arthur said, and he found his house shoes and slipped them on his feet at the same time the bathroom door slammed very hard. "Is that Helen?" he said.

"Yessir. She just come in."

"What time is it?"

Eric looked up at the clock on the kitchen wall.

"It's about three-thirty. I guess I better go."

But Mister Arthur got up and didn't answer him. He went after Miss Helen, and he disappeared down the hall. Eric heard him knocking on the bathroom door.

"Helen?" he yelled. He was knocking really hard.

Eric heard the muffled answer from behind the door.

"Go away. Leave me alone."

"Open this door, Helen. I want to talk to you."

"No," she said dimly. And then she started yelling a bunch of stuff and Eric couldn't make out what all she was saying. Then they were both yelling at the same time and he couldn't make heads or tails out of what they were saying except that Mister Arthur was threatening to break the door down and she was yelling for him to go ahead and do it. Damn. Why in the hell didn't he go on when he had the chance? He started looking around to see if he could find Jada Pinkett's leash, and his jacket, because he was thinking about trying to sneak out while they were making all that noise and maybe then they wouldn't notice him. But he didn't know where the leash was, and he didn't want to get up and start looking for it in case she came busting out of the bathroom and they brought their fight in here. He'd heard his mother and daddy fight like that before she'd left for good. Their fighting had gone on for years before she left. He guessed she just got tired of it. And he never had understood what it had all been about, except money sometimes, and his daddy's drinking. And his daddy's carousing. And the people he hung around with that she called worthless white trash. But he knew Mister Nub wasn't like that. And the thing that killed Eric's heart the worst was that she never had written him even after all this time. He knew where she was. She was in Seattle. She lived in some kind of a hippie commune, his daddy said. His daddy said she smoked dope and fucked hippies, and his constant comparing of Eric to his mother was another thing that had driven him away from home, that and the knowledge that his daddy was going to take Jada Pinkett out behind the barn and blow a hole in his brain just like all the other dogs he'd seen him do it to all his life. For different reasons. For being too old. For being too weak or too skinny or even for being just one of too many to feed that week. He wished now he could have told Mister Arthur all that. But there hadn't been time. And now maybe there never would be. He was still screaming at her and she was still screaming at him and the next thing that happened was something he could hardly believe.

Mister Arthur broke the door down.

There was a moment of silence.

And then a long bloodcurdling scream like you'd hear somebody make in a horror movie and something that sounded like a roar from Mister Arthur.

"Come on, Jada Pinkett," he said, but Jada Pinkett only stretched out under the coffee table again and put his head down on his paws.

"What have you been doing!?" Arthur screamed. "Whore!"

And he heard Miss Helen start crying. And then, amazingly, she ran out of the hall, holding her arms over her lovely naked breasts, which were bobbing delightfully, and she ran up the stairs. And up there the door slammed.

Gosh damn. He sipped at his drink. The credits were rolling on *Shane*. Then a commercial came on, Miss Cleo selling fortunes. Mister Arthur came walking around the corner like a zombie, shuffling his feet in his house shoes, not picking them up even an inch, and he walked slowly to the couch and sat down with his hands between his knees. He didn't even seem to notice Eric. But he must not have forgotten that he was sitting there either. He turned his face and looked at him. It took him a long time to say anything. There were slamming noises coming from above. Eric could hear faint cussing, too.

"She's got suck marks on her," Mister Arthur said. "Hickies."

Eric was struck too dumb to say anything at all. Mister Arthur turned his face back toward the TV screen, where somebody was selling Monster Hits from the Swinging Eighties. He watched the ad for a while.

"And I didn't put them there," Mister Arthur said to the television.

"I guess I better go," Eric said. "Looks like y'all need some privacy."

"Suck marks," Mister Arthur said again. "About five or six maybe."

"I was just lookin' for his leash," Eric said, getting up, wondering where in the hell he'd left it lying, wishing there was some more light in here, but not wanting to turn one on, because he could hear the old man crying now, and he didn't want to look at him, and he truly hated himself for ever putting his arms around her and letting her do that to him.

About that time a loaded suitcase came flying down the stairs and tumbled over a few times and came to a halt. Mister Arthur turned his head and sniffled and looked at it.

"That's her luggage," he said, like a question.

"Yeah. I was just huntin' his leash. Have you, uh . . ."

"I guess she's leaving," he said. "Is she leaving?"

"I don't know," Eric said, and stopped. "I was just—"

Then a small bag flew down.

Then a medium-size one.

And then she herself came down, hair brushed, clothes changed, wearing a long black coat with a scarf around her throat, looking in her purse. She appeared to be enraged.

Mister Arthur stood up. "Where you going?" he said. "You're drunk."

She stopped right in front of him. "You damn right I'm drunk! I'm getting the fuck out of here! I'm taking the Jag and I'm getting some money out of the ATM! You can do what you want to with this house! I'm going back to Montana! Where you found me!"

"Where you fucked everybody in Missoula!" Mister Arthur shouted. And she started picking up her bags. They must have been pretty heavy because she looked like she was having a hard time with them. Eric didn't know whether to try and help her with them or what because Mister Arthur was just standing there. He looked like he was getting mad.

"Okay, Helen," he said, and his voice had begun to shake with anger. "If that's what you want to do. Just leave me. Then get the hell on out."

"I *will*," she said, and pulled the strap for the small bag over her shoulder. "Eric, will you please help me get the fuck out of here before I scream?"

He looked at Mister Arthur. Mister Arthur looked extremely pissed. But he turned his head slowly and nodded slightly at him.

"Go ahead and help her if you want to, Eric. If she wants to go, she can go right now."

And he sat down on the couch but turned his face back toward Helen for a moment. He looked really pissed. "You can just forget about getting anything for Christmas this year," he said.

84

Texado was even better than *Southern Living* had said it was. They got there long before dinner and had time to admire the whole house with the middle-aged lady who showed them the rooms and the furnishings and recounted the history of the house for them.

The lady put them in an elegant upstairs room whose back doors opened onto a fine wood gallery that overlooked a brick courtyard like those you'd find in New Orleans. The furniture looked so old that Merlot was almost scared to sit on it. It was still plenty early enough to go out, not even close to dark yet, so they locked their room with the key the lady had given them and took off down the sidewalk and it was only about thirty minutes before they were in the casino, which was basically a big floating boat that was moored in the Mississippi River by two very thick ropes that were hooked to the bank. It had a wide gangway, a huge parking lot, and buses gladly ferried suckers back and forth twenty-four/seven, even on Christmas, even on Christmas Eve, Thanksgiving, Fourth of July, Rosh Hashanah.

Inside it was lit brightly and there was music playing and people talking and bells were going off and all manner of folks were walking around, old ladies with bad legs on walkers and slick young pomaded dudes with girls on their arms, people in muddy overalls who looked like they'd just stepped from a cotton field, and probably had, security people in good suits, semiprofessional gamblers out of Vegas with flashy diamond/gold rings and gold chains around their necks, retirees up from Florida in print shirts and berets, a wide mixture of humanity, all come to be happy in risking their money in the hope that they might not lose what they already had but instead hit the big jackpot and get some more.

Merlot couldn't get over how loud it was. There were no windows or clocks. Penelope bought twenty dollars' worth of quarters right away and got a free beer and started playing the progressive slot machines with an intensity Merlot found a little bit scary. She got to where she would hardly even talk to him. Once in a while she'd hit for twenty or thirty dollars and the quarters would come rolling out and she'd put them in a large plastic cup that she pulled from the stacks of them that sat on each side of each machine. And there were a lot of machines. Bells were ringing everywhere, lights flashing, skimpily dressed girls with short dresses and net stockings and push-up bras carrying around trays of free drinks.

Pretty soon she had a couple of cups half full of quarters and when she started betting fifty cents at a time, he told her he was going to walk around for a while and see what was happening. She just nodded and kept playing.

He stopped a cashier and gave her a twenty and got some dollar tokens and went over to the bar where a country & western band was doing covers of Merle and Waylon. He hated like hell that Waylon died. He got the bartender to give him a beer and tipped him one of the tokens and started playing the poker machines in a row in front of him. He kept looking around. He hadn't said a word to her yet about Candy. And they'd probably be back at his house before tomorrow night. She was getting really insistent about seeing where he lived and he knew there was no good reason why he shouldn't be able to take her over there. No reason that she'd be able to understand anyway.

There was some older lady a few machines down and she was playing the same kind of machine he was on. She wasn't winning anything and he wasn't either. Not for a while. Then he got to playing five-card stud and won a little. He punched the Pay button and when the quarters rolled out, the old lady turned to him and leaned over. She had glasses thicker than his and she had several black and decayed teeth. A nearly toothless hag.

"You like it. Don't ye?" she said, and he nodded.

"Oh yeah."

He went back by and checked on Penelope one time and she was still playing, but she was losing now and pissed off and was feeding the machine very slowly and had gone back to betting a quarter at a time.

"How much were you up?" he said.

"Shit, baby. Almost two hundred one time." She stopped one of the cashier carts and gave the lady another twenty-dollar bill for a roll of quarters.

"I think I need to move to another machine."

Merlot stood there and watched her for a while. He clinked together some of the dollar tokens he had left in his hand. Idly, without half looking, he shoved a token into one of the dollar slot machines just across from her and pulled the handle.

"You still want to go back to the place for dinner?" he said.

She said something but he couldn't hear it because it was lost in the sudden scream of sirens. He looked at his machine. All the lights were going off on it and three cherries were lined up in the glass and the machine started going *BONGBONGBONGBONGBONGBONG-BONGBONGBONG!* and spewing dollar tokens into the tray with a steady clicking noise and while he stood there stunned they filled up the tray and started spilling over onto the floor. All around him people were looking at him and pointing and shouting and smiling. Some casino officials were coming toward them. They were smiling, too.

The machine finally ran out of its coins and stopped spewing them out but by then they were scattered all over the flowery carpet and the machine kept binging and somebody came over with a street broom and started pushing them into a pile for him.

Later: Lying in the darkened bedroom in the oldest house in Mississippi, built by slaves and a Spanish governor long dead, with a full belly, in a high four-poster bed under a canopy, with a small cheery fire burning in the grate, he held her in his arms just before she went to sleep.

"I still can't believe you won twenty-seven hundred," she said.

It *was* pretty hard to believe. But the cashier's check from the casino was lying right over there on the dresser next to his car keys and wallet and change. They'd already taken out the state and federal income taxes. She yawned.

"What you gonna do with all that money?" she said.

"I was thinking about getting me a dog," he said, just kidding.

"Oh," she said, drowsy, almost asleep. "My mamaw had one when I was little. The meanest thing. I was scared to death of that dog the whole time I was growing up. I used to have nightmares about it."

That worried Merlot, to hear that she'd had nightmares about a dog, of all things. He'd never had a nightmare about a dog.

"Oh yeah?"

The flames flickered in the grate. Little shadows were moving around on the walls. A car passed, down the street. He held on to her, listening to their breathing. Nearly silent. So drowsy in the soft pillowy bed with its thick white sheets and mattress. So good. So warm. So sleepy.

"Aw yeah. It got old and got to where it couldn't walk and just drug itself around and my mamaw wouldn't have nobody shoot it." She snuggled closer to him and he touched the side of her face with his cheek.

That worried him even more, to hear her talk so casually about somebody *shooting* a *dog*. He wondered again if that gun of hers was loaded and why she thought she needed to bring it along with them. He hated to say anything about it. She was a cop, yeah, but why did she need it with him?

"So what do you think about dogs now?" he said, listening carefully in the dark.

But she never did give him an answer because she was already asleep and beginning to snore very lightly, a gentle hmm . . . hmm . . . hmm . . .

85

The marines canceled Wayne's fight because Johnson had just been given orders to join a guard company somewhere in the Third Fleet and there wasn't time after all to schedule a match with him at Camp LeJeune before Christmas. They told him they'd give him some Christmas leave instead, which was a big relief. Now he could go on back to Memphis and try to find Anjalee when his leave orders were ready. They gave him and Henderson a place to stay in an old almost deserted marine barracks close to the base library as well as the movie theater. They said they'd figure out what they were going to do with him later, would reassign him somewhere since his ship was coming back in, gave him a number to call when he got through with his leave. They paid them and they ate well at the marine mess hall. Everywhere he walked he could feel the marines looking at him.

There was a small color TV with a remote in the old barracks and he turned it on the first afternoon and sat on his rack and flipped it over to CNN. Henderson had gone over to the PX for a while. They were still talking about all the whale shit, speculating about this, speculating about that. A few groups were outraged and somewhere were carrying signs. One said "U.S. Navy: Baby Whale Killers." He just wanted to get back to Memphis. He knew what he ought to do was go back to Bowling Green and see his mother and father and their two dogs, Georgie B. and Big Mama, for Christmas. Spend some time on the farm with them. Go hunting with his dad maybe. See all his friends. Hit all his old hangouts. But he couldn't stop thinking about her. He was almost sick with love for her. There was a yearning in him he'd never had. He didn't know how much longer he could go without seeing her again. She was all he was thinking about.

Then somebody from the XO's office brought over a message from his captain, who had sent him a fax on his personal stationery. He sat there on his rack and read it.

Dear Petty Officer 2ND Class Stubbock:

I heard you won't get to fight Johnson after all and I'm sorry to hear it. Too bad me and the admiral won't get to win some money on you. It looks like they're going to relieve me of command, although they have allowed me to navigate the ship back to port in Norfolk. Hell, Stubbock, I'm an old fart anyway, and I'm only getting out a few months early, and it's nice and warm down in Tampa. Don't let what happened to me affect your decision on whether or not to stay in the United States Navy. I joined when I was eighteen and now I'm forty-two, and I've been lucky enough to see the world many times, and I've never regretted once being in uniform, not even today. Okay, well, maybe a couple of times on my birthday.

So take care of yourself, kid, and if you're ever down in Tampa, my wife and I are in the phone book. We'll fix you a margarita, boil you a shrimp or two. Keep your chin down and your gloves up.

And good luck with the girl in Memphis. Stay at the Peabody.

Sincerely,

Louis B. Goode, Captain, USN, Commanding

On the second day at LeJeune, they were just waiting on their leave to start the next morning. After lunch they walked around for a while and got bawled out for not saluting some second-lieutenant marine officer because they just thought he was some kid. They watched some marines standing in formation while two officers went through their ranks inspecting them. They went to the movie theater and saw, with popcorn, *Pearl Harbor*. They went over to the base post office so Henderson could mail a few letters he'd written. When they got back outside and stood on the marble steps, it had turned windy and some sand was blowing. There was sand all over this place. It was full of pine trees and deer.

"So what you up for this evenin', Wayne?" his buddy said.

"I don't know. Maybe go get a beer. What about you?"

Henderson stuck his hands in his pea-coat pockets and looked up and down the street.

"I'm talkin' about supper, bro. I mean what we gonna eat?"

Wayne shrugged.

"Go to the mess hall, I guess. What we always do."

Henderson stood there and rocked back and forth from his heels to his toes. It would be dark in about another hour.

"I'd like to get me a real civilian meal tonight."

"Where you gonna find a real civilian meal around here?" Wayne said. "Anyway, I like all that stuff in their mess hall. The marines eat good."

Henderson wasn't having any of that. He burrowed his neck down in his pea coat.

"Aw come on, Wayne, shit. We get the same stuff seven days a week. All comes out of the same government bunghole, baby. Look here. Why don't we catch us a cab into town and find us a steak house? You know they got to have a Sirloin Stockade or somethin' in that town, as many marines as they got here. Sink our choppers in a prime porterhouse. You up for that?"

Wayne stood there nodding. It was probably exactly what he needed to do. They could go into town, find a bar somewhere, have a few drinks, then find a restaurant, and over the course of the evening he could tell Henderson about Anjalee. He had to tell somebody. And it didn't matter what Henderson thought. He could think he was crazy if he wanted to. He just wanted him to listen to him. Just listen to him.

"Cool," he said.

"You know where the cabstand's at?"

"We'll find it."

And they stepped off, walking side by side.

"We'll ask one of these jarheads," Henderson said.

They went on down the street and jeeps and Humvees sometimes came by them. They saluted one once in a while just to be safe.

They crossed the street just ahead of a platoon of young marines in green T-shirts and camo pants who were sweating heavily and running in step. Henderson turned his head when they went by with their boots slamming.

"Check out that shit, man. Them boys is hard-core."

"Aw hell, they ain't got nothing on the Seals."

"I wouldn't want to be one of them neither. Man, you know them dudes can kill you with their bare hands?"

"Yeah," Wayne said, but he wasn't listening very closely because he'd just seen something that interested him. There was a small brown building set off the road and it had a plywood plaque over the front, painted red, the letters etched in yellow: USMC BOXING.

He stopped and nodded toward it.

"Hey. Look at that."

Henderson stopped with him and rubbed at his nose.

"Aw yeah. I guess that's where their guys practice."

Wayne stood there and thought about it. Vehicles kept going up and down the street and the wind was getting colder.

"Yeah. It's probably where Johnson practices."

"Yeah. Probly so. You want to go in there and ask 'em where the cabstand is?"

"We might as well."

There was a path through worn grass and it had pea gravel scattered over it. The door was open and when they got closer, Wayne could hear the *rat-a-tat-tat* of four-ounce gloves on a speed bag, and when they stepped through the door and stopped, the smell of all of it hit him again: sweat and leather and the taste of something like brass in your mouth when a hard fist wrapped in a padded glove slammed into your face, and pain and jumping rope and slamming a heavy bag until your arms were worse than dead and every inch of your body was dripping with sweat, and running in the cold mornings in the fog with the dogs barking and the lights coming on in the houses, and the ring lights and the people in the rows out there yelling and the smoke hanging up in the roof of an aircraft hangar.

He missed it. He hadn't realized how much he'd missed it the whole time he'd been on the ship. He'd been thinking so much about a life with her.

He knew right away Johnson was the guy on the speed bag. He

was too good to be anybody else at that weight in this place. He had on some long silver shorts and he was wearing red-and-white boxing shoes with tassels on the laces and a couple of USMC athletic shirts he had sweated through and he hammered and danced with the bag in a movement that Wayne knew well. His arms were thick with muscle and his black hair was cropped in a way that resembled a crew-cut Mohawk. Had to be Johnson.

Wayne had heard a little about him from one of the Seals on the ship in the armory one night when the Seal had been carefully cleaning the bolt of his M-60 with a toothbrush. Johnson had enrolled in OCS at Quantico to be a marine officer but had washed out like a lot of other people always washed out and had been sent to Parris Island with the enlisted slobs to goob around for a couple of months of recruit training in the sand fleas and graduate as a private and he was still pissed off about it, the Seal said. He'd also said he'd seen him fight and that he was bad news plus dirty but that Wayne could probably take him if he watched his balls.

Nobody was up in the ring, but a couple of guys with their shirts off were doing sit-ups and an older black guy in a sweatshirt and long pants who looked like he might be a trainer was doing something on a bench with some towels, and Wayne nodded toward him. They walked over. The speed bag kept rattling steadily in the back.

The guy in the sweatshirt looked up when they got close.

"Hey. How you men doin'?"

"Pretty good," Wayne said. "We were wondering if you could tell us how to get to the cabstand."

The rattling bag in the back stopped. Wayne looked over there and the guy was standing next to the bag, swinging his gloves back and forth across his belly in a sort of mindless way, twisting his hips, looking at him.

"Aw yeah. It's right down here a couple of blocks." He pointed over his shoulder. "Go right on past this buildin' and turn left at the parade ground there? That big place looks like a parkin' lot but they ain't no stripes? And go on down here till you get to the—"

"You Stubbock?"

Wayne turned his head and the fighter was standing right next to him. Henderson was watching the dude with something that was near a scowl. Wayne could see tiny beads of sweat on the guy's face. His nose had been broken and either hadn't healed properly or never had been set correctly in the first place. He shook his head to sling some of the sweat off his face and Wayne felt a few drops land on his cheek. Asshole.

"Yeah," Wayne said. "That's me."

The guy who'd been giving them directions stood up then.

"Aw hell," he said. "You the guy we's supposed to fight."

"Yeah," Wayne said. "This is my buddy Henderson."

They shook hands with the trainer and Wayne could feel the guy watching him, so he turned his head and looked at him.

"How'd you know who I was?" he said.

The guy spit on the floor.

"We been watchin' a few of your matches," the trainer said. "On videotape. Look here, I'm Joe Montesi."

"You got lucky, Stubbock," the guy with the gloves said.

Wayne turned his head to look at him.

"So you're Johnson," he said. He looked him up and down. "Well, I don't know about lucky. Maybe just bad timing."

The guy had cold eyes and a smile you couldn't like.

"I meant lucky you didn't get your ass whipped in front of all your navy buddies."

"All right, now, that's enough of that," the trainer said, and made moves to get in between them, but it was already too late. The one thing Wayne had never been able to do was take any shit off anybody.

"Oh, were you gonna kick my ass?" Wayne said.

Henderson shoved his small and now belligerent face forward and said: "Whup his ass, Wayne. Smart son of a bitch."

Maybe Johnson knew exactly what to do to push his buttons. Maybe Wayne was so sick of wondering if she'd still be there when

he got back that when Johnson reached out and pushed his little
buddy, it was only natural for Wayne to tap him on the shoulder
and get his attention and then when he did get it pop his head back
with a short right and maybe it was almost a sucker punch but the
one he caught on his left ear was lightning quick in retaliation and
even though the trainer was still trying to get between them it might
have gone on right there on the floor if somebody hadn't yelled:
"Ten *hut!*"

And when Wayne saw Johnson stand still and lock his eyes he
knew that an officer had entered the building. He went to attention
as did Henderson, but not the old trainer, who was obviously a
civilian.

"Evenin', Colonel," he said.

Wayne turned his head slightly and there was a full bird marine
colonel in his winter greens, about fifty-five, shoes spit-shined to a
gleam, tall and gray haired and looking hard as nails. Then he realized that he shouldn't have turned his head since he was supposed
to be at attention. Johnson had it locked up and was staring straight
ahead when Wayne looked back at him. He heard quiet steps on the
concrete floor. And then the colonel stepped in front of him.

"Hey, Joe," he said, and reached out and shook hands with the
trainer. Then he looked at Wayne. "I don't know what attention
means in the navy but in the marine corps it means attention."

"Sorry, sir," Wayne said.

"You men on assignment here?"

"Uh. Just temporary, sir," Wayne said.

"This the guy we's sposed to fight, sir," the trainer said.

The colonel turned his head slightly. He looked like he had a
poker up his ass. Maybe a broom handle.

"Is that right?"

"Yes, sir," the trainer said. "This here is Stubbock, sir, he's the one
we's supposed to fight."

The colonel looked him up and down then.

"The hell it is," he said. He looked down at the floor and took a few steps away. Wayne followed him with his eyes but not his face. He looked like he was thinking something over and that maybe the answer was written on the floor. He turned. He stopped. "At ease," he said.

The guys who'd been doing the sit-ups got their gear and went into the showers. All Wayne wanted to do now was just leave. Fuck Johnson. He'd already popped him anyway. Fuck all these damn marines.

The colonel walked back closer to him. Henderson rolled his eyes and Johnson started slipping off the gloves.

"Yes, sir," the trainer said. "We were sure lookin' forward to that match. Colonel was, too. Colonel's a big fight fan."

"You know Admiral Hoozey?" the colonel said.

"Well no, sir, I don't know him personally," Wayne said.

"Hmm," the colonel said. "All right, then. What's going on here?"

Wayne looked at Johnson to see if he was going to say anything but he could tell at a glance that he wasn't going to say shit.

"Nothing much, sir. We came in here to get directions to the cab-stand."

"Where you going?" the colonel said.

"Out to supper, sir. Somewhere in Jacksonville, I guess."

"Don't like that good old marine corps chow, huh?"

Damn. This fucker. But he'd seen pricks in the navy, too.

"Ah, sir, well, we just . . . we were hunting a steak house."

The colonel stepped up right in front of him.

"And so you thought you'd just take a swing at another enlisted man while you were here."

Uh-oh. He could almost quote the next thing that was coming. And he was right.

"Because that's punishable by a court-martial, hitting another enlisted man. At least it is in the marine corps. I'll bet you ten bucks the navy has the same rules."

"It was just a misunderstandin', sir," Henderson said.

The colonel turned his bored face away for just a few seconds.

"If I need anything out of you? Petty Officer Third Class? I will pull your chain for it. Is that okay with you?"

"Yes, sir," Henderson said, and clammed up.

And then those hard green eyes were on him again. One side of his immaculate uniform, on the breast, was covered with bright multicolored campaign ribbons, lots of reds, blues, yellows, stripes, little bronze stars, oak-leaf clusters. The two silver eagles sat on his shoulders with their wings spread. Another was on his cap. No telling how many people he'd killed or had killed and where. One hard-ass old son of a bitch chomping at the bit to be a general. And Wayne even knew what was going to happen. So when it came it wasn't a real big surprise. The colonel's voice took on a philosophical, almost fatherly tone.

"I suppose I could overlook it if I wasn't so damn disappointed in us not getting the match. What would you say to sparring a bit with Corporal Johnson? He's leaving soon. When are you out of here?"

"Tomorrow morning, sir. But I don't have any gear."

He didn't want to do this. And he knew there was no way the colonel could make him do it. But if he didn't do it, all the colonel had to do was go to the wall and pick up the phone that was hanging right there and call a couple of MPs over here and then he and Henderson wouldn't be going out to Jacksonville for a juicy porterhouse. And maybe not even out of here in the morning to go back to Memphis. Oh shit.

"We can loan you some gear. And I can assure you it's quite all right to stage a little sparring match right here in our boxing barracks with qualified personnel. We do it all the time, don't we, Joe?"

The trainer was old, and he had a job and a paycheck he probably needed, and he just nodded his head. Probably didn't make a shit to him anyway.

"Yes, sir. Sure do. Do it all the time."

So Wayne just said okay. He wasn't even mad anymore. He just wanted to get it over with.

86

Eric slipped his coat on before he went out with the big bag and the middle-size bag. From the corner of his eye, he saw Mister Arthur gather Jada Pinkett to him on the couch like you would a favorite beloved child.

"I'm gonna shut this door," he said, since it was standing wide open.

Mister Arthur nodded but didn't answer or look up. So he went out and pulled it closed behind him and his breath frosted out white in front of him. He could see the red taillights of the black Jag out there at the curb and smoke was curling in a froth from the twin exhausts. He saw her get out, saw the interior light come on, saw it go off, saw her walk to the back of the car, where the trunk lid had raised slightly. He didn't think she needed to be driving but he went down the step and past the trees that flanked the little walk and she raised the trunk lid. The trunk was brightly lit.

He wondered if she was really going to Montana. She damn sure sounded like she was. And suck marks. God. What'd he do, rip her bra off? And how'd he knock the door down, old as he was? He guessed maybe it was one of those things like when somebody turned a tractor over on him and his grandmother picked it up off him.

Miss Helen was standing by the trunk waiting for him when he got to the sidewalk. She was angry and very beautiful in the cold. Eric turned his head to see if he could see Mister Arthur watching through the front window, and he could. Mister Arthur had his hands up beside his face and he was pressing his face right against the glass. Jada Pinkett was beside him, looking out.

The car was idling at a rough stutter and the smoke curled and scattered into the air. He set the middle-size bag down and stepped off the curb with the big bag.

"You can put it right in there, Eric," she said. He looked at her for a few seconds and then swung it in there.

He turned his face toward the house. Mister Arthur was still watching. He turned back to her.

"You really goin' to Montana?" he said.

She nodded before she answered, looking down at the asphalt for a moment, where Eric could see a flattened sardine can. She had her hands in her pockets and the cuffs of her jeans came down low over her black cowboy boots. She was weaving just a little. Eric put his own hands in his pockets. It was very cold. It looked like a bad night to head out anywhere. He didn't even know where Montana was. It was way up there somewhere. Up in the north and over to the west. It was up near Canada. He remembered looking at some of it in *Lonesome Dove*. And *Stand by Me*. And *A River Runs Through It*. And she was from there. Ranches. Mountains. Bears. He would sure like to see that country for himself.

"Yeah," she said, and looked up. "You want to go with me?"

"Huh?"

"I can take care of you," she said, and stepped closer. "We'll be there in three or four days at the most. It's a beautiful place. It's got mountains and the biggest sky you ever saw."

Damn. Just take off with her?

He looked back at the window. Mister Arthur wasn't looking out it any longer. And he knew that the old man's world had to be coming apart. And he even felt like in some way he'd caused it. He looked back at Miss Helen. There was more than one reason he couldn't go with her. There were plenty of reasons he couldn't go with her. But he just named the first one that came to mind.

"What would I do about him?" he said.

She smiled and lifted her hand and brushed some hair from her face.

"You mean Arthur?"

"Naw," he said. "I mean Jada Pinkett."

87

After the crowd had started to gather and old Joe Montesi rang the bell, Johnson moved out of his corner in a bobbing weave, and fired a few swift jabs that Wayne blocked and counterpunched against. He got two hard jabs in and saw them blister Johnson's face inside the headgear. Wayne wasn't in shape and he knew it. He hadn't been able to run. He had no wind. This fucker had probably been running all over Camp LeJeune ever since he'd been here. And it wasn't long before Wayne knew he was in for a bad one. This was no sparring match. This was the colonel's boy. And the colonel wanted to see some more blood before his boy shipped out.

Johnson had surprising speed and he popped Wayne hard twice on his left cheek and then missed with a left that Wayne ducked under.

"Come on, Wayne!" Henderson yelled from down below the ring apron.

Then Johnson hit him hard on the side of his head with a punch he almost didn't see coming. He went backward and another one slammed into his ribs down low on his left side, and he felt a hard pain, and then he was against the rope, and Johnson was trying to take his head off, was all over him, and Wayne tried to go sideways and was able to land a couple of shots that caused Johnson to back off long enough for him to get a little breather. His wind was going already. He was starting to realize that this was a pretty stupid thing to do. He could get hurt here for nothing, real easy.

Johnson stopped in the middle of the ring and Wayne was vaguely aware that more and more people were coming inside the building because they were getting louder. They'd started drifting in when he'd walked out in borrowed shorts and boxing shoes and headgear. More had gathered while Joe Montesi put the gloves on him and taped them up, wrapping them tightly on his wrists. But he wasn't going to stop and see how many spectators there were. They were starting to yell, though:

"Come on, Johnson! Smoke his ass!"

"Show him what the marines are made out of, man!"

Wayne tapped out with his jab, searching, and stuck it hard in Johnson's face a couple of times, and then Johnson hit him in the balls.

It made him instantly sick to his stomach, and it felt like it flipped over, and he even heard a few boos from the crowd, which spoke well for some of the marines, he guessed, but then since he expected the bell to ring, or for somebody to call time, he forgot for just a crucial second to protect himself, and Johnson's glove came right into his face, and he saw fire for a second, and all he could do was grab hold of the man in front of him through a red mist, and pin his arms, and stagger around with him. He thought he was going to throw up. He was trying not to. But he sure wanted to.

"Pussy," Johnson said into his ear.

"Dirty son of a bitch!" he heard Henderson yell.

Johnson's headgear was rubbing up against his cheek and then Wayne felt the laces scrub across his face. This guy was as dirty a fighter as he'd been up against. Johnson was hitting him on the back of the head, rabbit-punching the shit out of him. Lousy bastard. But two could play.

"Time!" he heard Joe Montesi yell. "Time, Johnson!"

Then there was a lot of yelling and talking down on the floor and the old man was between them with his arms spreading them apart, saying: "Don't hit, don't hit, time, time!"

Johnson turned loose of him and walked away.

The old man's worried face was in front of him, and Wayne could see the tiny old wounds that told of his own years in the ring. The scar tissue was thick around his eyes, and Johnson was leaning in the corner with his glove on the top rope. The marines were yelling and Wayne blew his breath out a few times and walked around in a little circle. His balls were killing him. He looked out past the ring apron and the whole place was full of marines, some in uniform, but most not. He could tell from the haircuts, their youth and their hard young faces, and some of them had beers in their hands and were smoking cigarettes. Smoke was starting to gather in the air above the ring. He couldn't see Henderson, then he did, waving, yelling to him, but covered by human bodies in jeans and pea coats and sweaters and tank tops and he was drinking a beer, too. And they were betting. There was money held in hands and they were yelling louder and louder and more people were coming in through the front door. It was turning into a party. They'd emptied out of all those barracks he and Henderson had walked past this afternoon. Bored to death. Nothing to do. Writing letters home. Wanting to be home. Drinking beer at the PX. No women.

Joe Montesi was following him around, touching him on the elbow, asking him: "You all right, sailor? I'll give you as long a break as you need. This ain't nothin' but a sparrin' match. He done hit you low but I don't think he meant to."

"Whatever," Wayne said through his mouthpiece. He shifted it around some with his tongue. His whole mouth was filled up with it. But the pain was starting to ease a bit. He wasn't going to throw up. But he was going to be sore for the rest of the fight. And there wasn't a thing anybody could do about it.

"How about just give me a few minutes," Wayne said.

"Take what you need," the old man said.

So he did, and walked around in the ring, swinging his gloves lightly, eyeing Johnson in the corner, who was leaned over the rope talking to some of his buddies, who were yelling and shouting happily at him.

He saw the colonel, too. He had taken his piss cutter off to expose his large gray head and he was standing against a wall with a space cleared of bodies in front of him, except for a couple of older enlisted men in dress greens with long stacks of red chevrons on their sleeves who stood beside him, guys who'd been in as long as the colonel. Master sergeants or gunnies or sergeants major maybe. They were all looking at him and they weren't yelling like the younger marines. They were just standing there next to the old colonel and looking at Wayne. Sizing him up. He couldn't tell if they approved of the low blow or not.

"Hey, Wayne, hey, Wayne! You all right?"

Henderson had crowded up to the ring apron and he stuck his face underneath the bottom rope. He was almost hopping up and down. Wayne walked over there and looked down at him.

"I will be," he said. "They betting, huh?"

"Hell yes they bettin'! I got fifty dollars on you myself, man! With this dude right over . . ." He turned to look for somebody in the crowd. He pointed rapidly. "This dude right over here. My man Julian from Boston. He knows where the steak house is!"

Wayne looked where he was pointing. Some blond young guy with a California tan and a beer in his hand and a flowered shirt and khaki pants grinned and waved his beer at him.

"Johnson done told all his buddies he gonna knock you out. "They bettin' if he can or can't. I'm bettin' he can't. How's your balls?"

"Like they went up in my throat," Wayne said. "You got me some water for between rounds?"

"I got it, man. Joe give it to me."

"Okay."

He turned away from Henderson and the noise level steadily rose. When he walked back to Joe Montesi, it went up to a scream.

Johnson was going up and down on his toes in his corner. Wayne turned to Joe Montesi.

"Okay. I'm ready."

"Time!" Montesi yelled, and Johnson moved out toward him. As soon as he got close enough to him, Wayne punched him square in the balls, and Johnson curled up hugging his jewels with his gloves and hit the canvas with his eyes closed. More boos went up, even louder than before. Wayne walked away and looked over at the colonel. It was easy to see that he was infuriated. But one of the old sergeants grinned at Wayne and said something to one of his buddies and the buddy grinned, too.

It only got louder while Johnson slowly got back on his feet and took his own walk around the ring. But Wayne thought the message had been passed since Johnson gave him a grudging pissed-off nod.

By then you couldn't have gotten any more marines in there with a shoehorn. They were wall to wall and they'd even crowded in close to the colonel and his cohorts. They were packed all around the ring apron, and Wayne could see a couple of well-pressed MPs with pistols on their belts and white stripes on their helmets standing guard at the door.

When Montesi called time again, Johnson rushed at him, swinging at his head, and Wayne closed with him in the center of the ring. He could feel Johnson's gloves slamming hard against him, all over him, too many punches to count, but he doubled over just a little and kept his gloves close to his face and fired from there, short hooks and jabs that slapped the leather on Johnson's face. The marines were going crazy and the sound rattled against the roof. Wayne drifted to another place he went to when he fought, where he could focus and block out everything else. He slammed Johnson's face with one hard right after another and stood easy on his feet and leaned against him and worked on his ribs, and heard the breath grunt out of him each time he hit him. Montesi rang time and had to get between them again. Johnson's face was red and he was saying something to Wayne that he couldn't understand as he turned away.

"Fuck you, son of a bitch," Wayne said.

There weren't any stools in the corners. No place to rest between rounds. Rounds? Hell, it wasn't a match. There weren't supposed to be stools. But when he looked out at those faces around the ring, he knew exactly what it was. It was the marines against the navy.

So he rested his forearms on the top rope and drank a little of the water that Henderson gave him, and talked to him, and decided he could go about one more round and that would be it. Whatever they said. This was bullshit and he was tired of it.

He leaned down to Henderson and gave him the water back and said: "One more round and let's get our asses out of here. I'm about ready for that steak."

"It's your call, Wayne."

When Montesi called time again, Wayne could barely hear it for the yelling. Johnson moved close to him and peppered him with jabs, and Wayne backed up and let him come on. The jabs were landing on his shoulders and his face and he knew his face was getting red. His breath was coming harder and his arms were getting heavy. His forearms were tight and his hands felt cramped. And then some sweat got in his eye and he got caught with a hard right hook on the jaw. It jarred his whole head. As hard a punch as he'd ever felt. He started to turn and jab back but a fluid feeling almost like heat passed across the back of his head. His vision blurred for just a second and he didn't see the next one coming and didn't know he was down until the canvas slammed him in the back of the head. Then there was a roaring in his ears and the next thing he saw was the lights overhead tilting and sliding and going out of focus.

The steak house was dark and had the stuffed heads of longhorns on the walls and on all the tables there were little ruby glasses with candles burning. They were in a back booth and Henderson was sighing with pleasure as he mopped the last cool puddles of porterhouse juice from his plate with the last pieces of his Texas toast. He leaned back against the booth and chewed. The remnants of his wrecked baked potato lay on his plate. And it had been a big one. His salad bowl was full of empty cellophane cracker packs.

"I don't know where in the hell you put it," Wayne said.

"Hoo," Henderson said. "Have mercy."

Wayne caught the waitress's eye and held up his beer mug. He was still working on his T-bone, and there was a small nagging pain at the back of his head, but he hadn't said anything about it. And Henderson hadn't said anything about him getting knocked out. He was glad for that.

He picked up his knife again and sawed a few more pieces away from the bone. He reached for the A.1. sauce and dribbled some of it over the steak.

"What time's your flight?" he said.

Henderson had it memorized.

"Ten-twenty. Flight two thirteen, Northwest. What time you got to catch the bus?"

"Shit. Eight o'clock. I thought maybe we could ride back to town together but I don't want you to have to leave early 'cause of me."

"I can come on in to town early. We can get some breakfast."

Wayne picked up a piece of steak and put it in his mouth. The waitress brought his beer and she was a cutie but not as cute as Anjalee.

"How you guys doing?" she said. "Can I take that stuff for you?" she said to Henderson.

"Yes, ma'am. Can I get a piece of that chocolate fudge cake with some vanilla ice cream on it?"

"He's a bottomless pie hole," Wayne told her.

She laughed and picked up Henderson's plate and his salad bowl and went away to get his dessert. It was getting on in the evening and people were starting to clear out of the place some. Waitresses were setting up other tables. At the bar the bartender was wiping glasses and telling customers good night as they went out.

Wayne ate two more bites and then pushed his plate back away from him.

"I'm about to die," he said. He picked up his beer and took a sip from it, then set it down and toyed with the handle.

"Hey, man, I got somethin' for you," Henderson said, and reached into his pea coat, which was folded on the seat beside him. He took out an envelope and opened the flap and pulled out a small stack of pictures.

The waitress brought his cake and ice cream and he looked up and said Thank you ma'am and she went away. He was going through the pictures, looking at all of them, taking his time. Finally he picked one out and handed it across.

"Look here, man. This is my baby. I ain't gonna give you a picture of me. I'm gonna give you a picture of her. And you stick it in your wallet or whatever. I don't know when I may see you again."

Wayne took it and turned it around so he could look at it. She was sitting up on what looked like a piece of carpet and she had white barrettes in her hair and she was smiling a big smile for the camera. She looked like she was about two years old. Then the vision of her blurred. Just for a moment. But there was no pain. And then his vision was clear again. It hit him that the smart thing was to go to the hospital. Now. Tonight.

"Okay, man. Thanks. If you're ever in Bowling Green, Ohio, say, twenty years from now, come by and look me up."

They dawdled, talked. Henderson started in on his cake and ice cream. He never did tell him anything about Anjalee. It just didn't seem to be the right time. Maybe it never would be. And he could always go home. There were some people who would be more than glad to take care of him for a while up there in Ohio. Yeah, but . . .

88

Penelope loved Merlot's house at first sight. It was down on North Fourteenth, a quiet, narrow street where it looked like there wouldn't be very much traffic. Probably a good place to raise a kid. They could ride bicycles. There were big trees all up and down it, but of course they didn't have any leaves on them now. Merlot had said that his backyard was very shady in the summer and a cool place to hang out on a hammock and read and listen to the radio and cook out on weekends and the long summer evenings after school was over each May.

The house itself sat back from the street with a small yard and a railed porch and a high peak on the left, old timey looking, blue with red trim, with that gingerbread-looking stuff on the front. It had a tall brick chimney with sharp stones set in the top of it, like teeth. Seemed like he'd said it had been built in 1948 but was solid, no termites in the foundation.

He pulled into the black drive next to a silver car and shut off the Toyota. He opened the door and the light came on.

"Well, this is it," he said. He looked a little worried, and she'd noticed that the closer they'd gotten to town, the less he'd said. He had something on his mind and she wondered if it was because she was over here.

"It's beautiful," she said. "Whose car's that?"

"That's Marla's. The lady I told you about."

"She house-sits for you when you're gone, right?"

"Yeah," he said, and pulled the key out of the ignition because it was making that particularly irritating *Bing! Bing! Bing! Bing! Bing! Bing!* noise.

"Thanks for doing that," she said, and unstrapped her seat belt. "Should I bring my stuff on in?"

"Whatever you want to do," he said.

She waited a moment.

"Well. I guess what I was wondering was if I was going to spend the night."

"Spend the night?" he said.

What was up with him? He was acting like half the people she stopped. Nervous.

"Well. Unless you don't want me to. But I guess you'll have to take me home if I don't. I'm not going to sleep on the porch, baby, it's cold out here. Are you okay with this?"

Merlot nodded rapidly and fiddled with the keys.

"Sure I'm okay. You can spend the night if you want to, I mean it's fine with me."

Only thing, it didn't seem fine with him. It seemed like he was just saying that. She wondered what the reason was. She poked his arm playfully.

"What? Are you afraid your house sitter won't approve?"

"Are you kidding?" he said, and unstrapped his own seat belt. "She's a semiretired nympho."

She got out and reached for her little bag she'd packed in Natchez that had just a few things in it, her gun and a toothbrush and some underwear, and a gown in case she stayed. And she couldn't think of any reason she wouldn't. He was hers now. Wasn't he? But there seemed to be something else on his mind. He looked like he was wanting to say something.

"What is it?" she said.

"I hate to say anything."

"Go ahead, baby."

He rubbed his chin.

"Well. It's just that gun. I didn't have guns in my house when I grew up and they kind of make me nervous. Is it loaded?"

"Yeah. You want me to unload it?"

"Do you mind?"

"Not at all."

"Okay. Thanks."

"You're mighty welcome. I'll do it when we get inside if it makes you nervous. I just carry it out of habit."

"I know."

Merlot opened the door on his side and reached in for his stuff, got the straps over his shoulders, and closed the door. When Penelope walked back around in front of the hood, she could see some curtains hanging in one of the side windows, and past that there was a glimpse of a tall floor lamp and shelves of books. He was waiting for her in the dead grass of the yard but she saw that there was a little brick path. She looked up. There was a wispy trail of smoke coming from the narrow chimney.

"You got a fireplace, huh?"

"Oh yeah. It's nice on cold winter nights like tonight."

She walked up next to him and kissed him and put her hand around his shoulder. When she pulled back, she was still very close to his face.

"Is everything all right?" she said, and looked into his eyes.

But he wouldn't make very much eye contact with her.

"Sure. Come on in and meet Marla."

"Okay."

She followed him up the walk and turned a tiny curve and went up the two steps to the porch. There was a swing with stuffed pillows.

"Oh and you got a swing!" she said. "My mamaw's still got one. I grew up swinging on a swing."

There was a screen door and he opened it and tried the knob on the door and it opened.

"Hey, Marla! It's me," he said, going in, turning back to her for a moment to say: "Oh yeah. I sit on that swing and grade papers whenever it's warm outside."

She held the screen door away from his back so that he could get in with his bags and she was looking around as she went in. There was a room to the left and she could see a nice black television and a stereo system against a wall that held lots of CDs on shelves. A couch and a long coffee table. The hall was wide and well lit and there was a coat tree with several coats on it, one of them a long flowery number with spotted white fur on the cuffs.

"Come on in," he said, and walked into the room on the right where his office was. There was a walnut desk with a computer and papers and books on it and the walls were filled with books on shelves but there was also a stuffed black fabric love seat and matching chair along with a glass coffee table where a tall vase of flowers was sitting. A crystal ashtray. An Ole Miss flag on one wall. Pictures in frames of some people she didn't know. Even a picture of a dog. A boxer. And his house smelled good, like recent air freshener.

"This is *so* nice," she said.

"Thanks."

He dropped his stuff on the love seat and somebody at the back of the house spoke his name.

"It's me, Marla," he called, and he started taking off his coat.

She set her little bag on the coffee table and unzipped her coat. Just as she was coming out of it, footsteps came up the hall and a tall older woman walked into the room. Who once had probably been gorgeous. She had black hair that you could tell was dyed just because of her age, which had to be around seventy or somewhere. She was wearing a lot of makeup and a green gown with a high collar. And she had long black fingernails. But she had a nice smile and Penelope liked her right away. She came forward just as Penelope was putting her coat down next to his on the love seat.

"You must be Penelope," she said. "I'm Marla and I've been just dying to meet you."

"Hi," Penelope said, and held her hand out, but was surprised when the woman threw her arms around both her shoulders and laid her cheek against her. The old lady was very skinny but very strong. Penelope wasn't weak herself, and could manhandle a lot of men, and had had to do it more than once, but the old lady's grip was like a bear hug, tight, powerful, sincere.

Then she pulled back and looked at Penelope with that steady, strong smile. She had faint red eyebrows.

"Welcome," she said. "Merlot's told me so much about you." She turned her head to him for just a moment. "How are you, Merlot?"

"I'm doing pretty good, I guess," he said, and he still looked kind of worried or uncertain or scared or something Penelope couldn't quite decide on. "How's everything been around here?"

"Kind of shitty if you know what I mean," the old lady said, then stepped back. "Well. I must be off. It's very nice to meet you, Penelope, and I hope you enjoy your stay. There's cold beer in the fridge and a bottle of wine that's been opened is on the kitchen counter. I set out some glasses. You're almost out of laundry detergent, Merlot. 'Bye."

And she turned and walked over to the coat tree and pulled off the long one with the spotted cuffs and put it on and buttoned it rapidly while smiling steadily and happily and wrapped a scarf over her head and gave a quick wave and was out the door. Penelope looked at Merlot. He was acting really nervous now. Didn't want to look her in the eye. *Kind of shitty?* He was shifting around like he didn't know what to do with his hands and he took a couple of steps one way and then he stopped and looked toward the back and came over to Penelope. Outside, the car started and left.

"Come on in the living room," he said. "Well. Come on in the kitchen. Maybe we should go back there first."

"A glass of wine would be great," Penelope said. "I want to see your whole house."

He gave her that look again. Then he nodded.

"Oh. Yeah. Sure. Right this way."

Down the hall there were several Monet prints that had been framed and matted at no small cost. A wide pot about four feet tall whose neck narrowed near the top like a beehive held painted cattails and reeds, odd thin sticks of driftwood, a peacock feather. There was a closed door on the left and an open door on the right that showed a neat bathroom, towels hung on racks, a glass shower door in a clean chrome frame. But she noticed that the hall floor itself was very badly scratched. And there was a bit of a bad odor in the air right here.

"I just love your house," she said, lingering in the hall, wondering what was behind the closed door, wondering where his bedroom was, wondering what that nasty smell was. "Where's your bedroom?"

"It's back here," he said. "I'm glad you like it. Come on."

She turned and pointed back to the closed door.

"What's that room there?"

Merlot stood there for a second and looked at the closed door.

"That's the other bedroom," he said. "I don't sleep in there. Come on and I'll get you that wine."

And he turned and walked on down the hall. She followed him. Maybe it was full of junk. Everybody had junk. He was standing back, facing her now in the hall.

"Here's my bedroom," he said. He reached inside the door and flipped the switch and the lights came on. He stood aside so she could look in.

"Wow. Very nice," she said.

There was a king-size bed with thick posts and a high headboard and a white knitted spread that filled up most of the room, and there was another television on a shelf with books and pictures of more people she didn't know. A tall bedside table with a phone and a lamp. One reading chair with a lamp over it. On the dresser a small colorful globe of the world.

"I like it," he said. "You can watch television in bed. Or grade papers. Kitchen's back here."

She liked it, too. She looked at it from beside the back door. It wasn't big but it was very functional. It had gray marble counters a knife wouldn't scratch and there were plenty of cabinets and an old gas Chambers stove. You could do plenty of cooking on that baby. And once you walked in past the off-white refrigerator it was kind of small, but the white cabinets with their brass pulls wrapped around the dark green tiles on the floor so that there was a cozy enclosed space where you could sit on one of the three high stools and talk to somebody and have a glass of wine while they were making the roux and quartering lemons and getting the water ready to boil for the shrimp. She rubbed her hand on the marble top. There was a wide window with lace-trimmed curtains over the sink.

"This is great," she said. "I wish my place was this nice."

"I'm a bachelor," he said. "I've got nothing to spend my money on but this house. How about that glass of wine?"

She guessed that was true. But she wondered why he didn't get the scratches in the hall floor fixed. That wouldn't cost that much. Would it?

"Cool. Look here, baby. You got any of those joints left?"

He picked up the wine bottle and pulled the cork from the mouth.

"Sure. I think there's three in the side pocket of that Lakers bag. They're in with the Q-Tips. Why don't you go get us one?"

"I think I will, since we're home."

She went back up the hall and when she went past the closed door, a small noise came from behind it. It sounded kind of like a low whine.

She looked at it and didn't know whether to say anything about it or not, the way he was acting. All the way back from Natchez he'd talked about teaching and his students and the carjacking asshole who was running loose somewhere probably terrorizing some more innocent people and how he hoped they'd catch him pretty soon. She should have called into the office already to see about Perk, but she just hadn't. They hadn't watched any TV, they hadn't bought any newspapers, so she really didn't know what was going on, if they'd found him or not. She remembered what it had looked like when she'd walked up on his cruiser where it was parked down on Papa Johnny Road, slightly bobbing up and down, and she'd known he was in there screwing somebody, but when she'd shone her flashlight in the window to find out who, she'd been very surprised to see Earleen Lundt's fat face looking over his shoulder, and him with his pants down and his big white hairy ass bobbing over her, until he'd grabbed for his pants and put one hand up in front of his eyes. Asshole. And to think that she'd been pretty close to thinking about getting almost ready to consider maybe fucking him. By God, times had been hard.

She unzipped the side compartment on the Lakers bag and was standing there looking through the stuff in it when she heard the door down the hall open. She stopped. There were some noises. It sounded like that whining again. Then there was some kind of hissing noise. Then the door closed again. What the hell was going on?

Damn he had a lot of stuff in his bag. Aspirin. Excedrin. Aleve. A tiny box of Kleenex. Baby lotion. What was that for? Bottles and bottles of pills. Toothpaste, and there it was. She pulled out the little blue box and slid the cover open. She got one of the joints out and put the box back in. Then she went back to the kitchen. She didn't hear anything when she went by the door but she could smell again something that smelled kind of bad, just a whiff of it, and something that smelled like air freshener. When she got back to the kitchen, Merlot was sitting on one of the stools, smiling, and her glass of wine was already poured and sitting there, but he picked it up and got off the stool.

"Why don't we go up front?" he said.

"I thought we were coming back here."

"Let's go up there where the fire is."

He seemed to be kind of in a hurry. It was like he was trying to rush around but wasn't moving very fast. What he acted like was that he was trying to get her out of the kitchen. So she turned in front of him and went back up the hall and into the living room, where the fire was burning.

And that was very nice. There were some overstuffed pillows on the couch. He set her wine down and walked behind the coffee table and sat down on the couch. She put the joint on the table and went over to the fire and sat down on the floor.

She started unlacing her boots and looking around. There were lots of tiny cars and some antique toys scattered around on shelves and small tables. A big calendar with two kittens in a sock, for December. Over the fireplace there was a low mantel that held some seashells and starfish and the horn of a goat, and there was that quiet sound of crackling embers and that good smell of wood smoke that reminded her of sitting and doing her school lessons at night on her mamaw's hearth out in the country when she was little.

"You don't mind, do you?" she said. "I've got to get these boots off my feet. And then I'd love to stretch my toes out toward that fire. I will if you'll toss me one of those pillows."

"Sure." He reached over for one and it landed next to her. She smiled at him. Why was he spraying air freshener around? Maybe Marla smoked. Maybe he had something he didn't want her to see yet. But if he did, that was okay. This was his home and maybe he hadn't been quite ready for her to pay a visit and spend the night. Maybe he really was a sloppy bachelor and the old lady didn't get everything completely cleaned up while he was gone. But she was pretty old, too, so that was understandable.

"You know," Merlot said. "I think I'll go wash some clothes."

She took the first boot off her foot and looked up at him.

"Wash some clothes? You mean the ones you brought back? You didn't even wear all of 'em, baby. What you want to wash now for?"

"Just to get it out of the way," he said.

She just nodded.

"Well, whatever you want to do. I thought we's gonna smoke this joint."

"Oh, you go ahead. I just need to stick a few things in the washing machine. It won't take me but a few minutes. Just stay in here and relax and I'll be right back."

And he set his wine on the coffee table and went down the hall. The room was made so that you couldn't see all the way down the hall from where she was sitting. She heard his feet go all the way back. She started unlacing the other boot, listening. A few things banged back there. One sounded like the lid of a washing machine.

She stopped with the boot and leaned way over and got her wineglass and took a sip. She listened some more. She couldn't tell what he was doing. Washing clothes, she guessed.

She set the wine back down and got the other boot off and stood both of them neatly beside the hearth. And it sounded like the back door slammed. She kept listening. It slammed again. He was doing something. And she had decided that he wanted her to stay in here while he went on and did whatever it was he was doing. So she did.

Well, there the joint was. She reached and got it and stuck it in her mouth, and leaned back and ran her hand down in her pocket, but her lighter wasn't in there. Merlot had it. She took the joint out of her mouth to call to him.

The hall door opened. There were some noises. The hall door shut. She listened for about five seconds. The back door slammed. Then the back door slammed again. Then Merlot's feet came back up the hall.

He poked his head in the door at an angle.

"You doing all right in here?"

She smiled and nodded.

"Yeah, baby. Have you got my lighter?"

He grabbed all his shirt and pants pockets rapidly with a blank look on his face and then pulled it out with a look of relief.

"Here go," he said, and handed it to her.

"Don't you want some?"

"I'll get some later," he said. "I've got to finish with these clothes."

"What are you doing, taking your garbage out?"

"I'm just cleaning up," he said, and ducked back out before she could say anything else. His feet went down the hall and she struck the lighter and put the joint back in her mouth. The paper fired at the end and she pulled on it and let the lighter go out. Then the door opened again. There were some more noises in there. But nothing like what she'd heard before. Not that whining sound.

She held the smoke in her lungs and crossed her legs on the floor. It was so nice and toasty warm by the fire. Maybe later Merlot would let her bring in some blankets and make them a lovemaking bed right in front of the fire and make some more sweet love with him. And then she could start to tell him about Gabriel. She blew the smoke out. Oh, how she could tell him all about Gabriel. She could tell him that he probably looked like a young black god by now. DeWayne had been a good-looking young man. And how long had he been dead now? Lord God, was it twelve years already? She guessed it was. He got shot one night at the Turning Point after she'd been a deputy for only three months. Hanging around all those people. Getting drunk. Running drunk. Running his mouth. Bunch of drunk fools with guns in their pockets thinking they were gangsters. That same bunch was still out there. All of them too sorry to work. Didn't want to do nothing but smoke a crack pipe. Get somebody pregnant. Then just ignore the child. She knew all about it.

Merlot's feet went back out and the door closed. Then his feet went some more. She heard the lid go down on the washing machine, and the very faint sound of water running into it. She guessed he *was* washing clothes.

She took another hit on the joint and thumped the ashes through the wire grate in front of the flames. She watched the fire. Red neon coals in the split oak were glowing and going out and coming back and changing shape, like worms crawling around under logs in the woods.

The back door slammed. Maybe that old lady made a lot of garbage while he was gone. Merlot had told her she liked to party. She hoped she could still do it when she got to be that age. She took another hit on the joint and then stubbed it out on the bricks, just below the grate. She put the roach on the coffee table and got another drink of her wine.

God, where was she going to start about Gabriel? At the beginning, when she was seventeen, she guessed. Kissing a boy and getting worked up. Wanting all of it, not just some of it. Just because it felt so damn good. But there wasn't any need in telling him all that stuff because he already knew how making love was. She had something right here that was real good, real positive. He was such a smart man. He knew all that stuff from all those books. If anybody was smart enough to help her find Gabriel, it was probably him. And if they did find him, and he was happy, that was fine, and she didn't have to meet him or interfere in his life in any way. If she wasn't going to get him back, and she knew she wasn't, it would probably be better not to meet him. Because that might hurt him. He'd want to know why she'd given him up maybe. And what would she say? She didn't have to say anything. She didn't have to meet him. She just wanted to look at him. She just wanted to see what he looked like. At a graduation or whatever it was.

The back door slammed again. There was a bump, a thud, a muffled bang, and Penelope heard Merlot clearly say: "Fuck!"

In just a few moments, his feet came back up the hall. Then there was some more hissing. Then his feet went back to the kitchen. Then it sounded like a cabinet door slammed. Then his feet came back up the hall. He walked in and sat back down on the couch and smiled at her.

"How you doing?"

She reached for the pillow and put it where she wanted it, up under her elbow, and pulled her wineglass closer. She smiled at him. She loved him so much already it was scary and crazy, but what was crazy about love when it came? What was crazy about having a man who drove you almost out of your mind with his need for you and satisfied your own with it? Who was always funny and not a deadbeat like so many men she knew? The washing machine started doing a chugging number somewhere back there. Faintly.

"I'm doing great. Your place is so comfy. You want to come over here and lay down beside me?"

"Well," he said. "I got a few more things I've got to do."

"What are you doing?"

He shook his head steadily for about three or four or five seconds.

"Oh, you know. Just the regular old shit you take care of when you get in from a trip. Just cleaning shit up. You know how it is."

"Well, it looks pretty clean to me. You thought anything about supper?"

There was a horrific noise and bang at the back door, something that sounded like a cross between a yelp and a scream and a woof and a bark and Penelope said : "What is *that?*"

Merlot acted like he didn't hear it. Then he did.

"Oh, *that?* Aw hell, it's probably a coon."

Penelope leaned toward him.

"Coon?"

"Yeah. We've got a coon or two that lives in the neighborhood and they come around and bang on the door once in a while. Hey, you want to listen to some music?"

Penelope was getting pretty stoned now and she knew she was smoking way too much these last few days. She'd have to slack off before she went back on duty and let it start getting out of her system because they had random pee tests sometimes. But it sure felt good right now. And some music would be really nice. But now, stoned, she suddenly wanted to see the coon.

"Cool, baby, put something on. You got any Alejandro over here?"

"Shit no," he said. "Somebody borrowed my *Thirteen Years*."

The terrible noise at the back had subsided.

"I want to see the coon," she said, and picked up her wineglass and took another sip. "Can I see the coon?"

"See the coon?" Merlot said.

"Yeah. See the coon. Can I see the coon?"

Merlot sat there with his hands between his knees.

"Well, I don't know," he said. "They usually run off if you try to look at them."

"Can't you just turn on the light and look through the back door?"

"I think my bulb's burned out," he said.

"Oh. Okay. Well, what about supper? What we gonna eat?"

And she turned her wineglass up and had another sip.

Merlot got up.

"I don't know," he said, and moved toward the stereo. "How about if we go out somewhere?"

She leaned back on her pillow. It felt so good here. It was so warm and cozy in here. The washing machine was still chugging. Faintly.

"Go out? Oh, baby. We just got back from a long drive. I don't have any clothes ready. I think I want to just stay right here in front of this fire. I can eat a frozen pizza or anything. Or we could just order something and get somebody to bring it. All these places around town deliver."

He was fiddling with the stereo, doing something. There was another noise at the back door. It sounded like something scratching at it.

"I wish your lightbulb wasn't burned out. Have you got another bulb you can put in it? Or give me the bulb and I'll put it in. I want to see that old coon."

And she did, too. One of her mamaw's neighbors, Harold Washington, had kept one in a rabbit cage he had out beside his barn, up under the shade of a huge catalpa tree. Fish-bait tree. In her memory it was the biggest one she'd ever seen, and in her memory she thought it was probably bigger than the one they had out at Ole Miss, beside the student union. And that one was enormous.

"I don't know if I've got any bulbs or not," Merlot said. "What you want to listen to?"

"I don't know. Just put on something good."

And that old coon would wash everything Mr. Washington fed him. Even if you fed him a biscuit, he'd wash it in a pan of water he had in his cage. She could remember petting that coon. It had long whiskers.

"There's a new place in town I was thinking about trying," Merlot said. "They're supposed to have really good food. You sure you don't want to go out? I've got all that casino money I won. We ought to go out and celebrate. I could buy you a big steak."

She reached for her wineglass.

"You know what I want to do?" she said.

"What's that?" he said, without looking up. He had his head turned over sideways, reading the titles on his CDs.

"I want to stay here and make us a love nest right in front of this fire. How's that sound, baby?"

He turned to look at her with his head still on the side. She rolled over on her side and unbuttoned one of the buttons on her blouse. She saw his eyes go to her breasts and she grinned at him. She took another sip of her wine and then lowered her eyes and looked up at him from under the lids. That always got him excited when she did that. But for some reason it didn't this time.

"Well, the bed would probably be a lot more comfortable," he said, and then turned back to the CDs. He pulled one out of the shelf and stood looking at it.

Well shit. Here she was, first night with him in his house, and he wasn't wanting to be romantic. What could be more romantic than lying naked on a cold winter night next to a good warm fire with plenty of quilts and pillows to lie on with your man? He wasn't getting tired, was he? She sure hoped not because she was just getting started. It had been a long time since she'd had a man but that didn't mean she hadn't wanted one in all that time. Now that she had one, she was going to get all she could. Like tonight. Right here. She was too comfortable to move. And she sure didn't want to go out nowhere just to eat.

"How about Leonard Cohen? I've got *The Future* and *I'm Your Man* both."

"Great."

He bent over and turned on the stereo and it lit up with blue digital numbers. He pushed a button and the tray slid out and he started taking the CDs out of their cases. Of course he had a few already in there and he had to stop and find the boxes for them. She heard scratching at the back door again.

"You must have a trained coon," she said, and laughed.

Merlot looked at her.

"Why's that?"

She took another drink of her wine. It was really good and she was starting to float a little bit on it and the weed together.

" 'Cause. He's scratching like he wants in."

Merlot just gave out this little nervous noise and went back to what he was doing. And she was going to have to get up and go pee. She'd meant to do that before she came in here.

"You don't mind if I use your bathroom?"

"Oh no, go right ahead," Merlot said. He was putting the Leonard CDs onto the tray. He pushed the button and the tray slid closed. He pushed another button and the upbeat tempo of "Closing Time" started up. She set her wine on the coffee table. It sounded good. She got up and heard her knees creak a little.

"I'll be right back," she said.

"I'm going back to the kitchen for a minute," he said.

"Why don't you see what you got to eat while you're back there?"

"Well . . ."

"Or we can order something. I've got some money."

"Well . . ."

She went down the hall ahead of him and looked at the door when she went by. It was closed, but the bathroom door was still open. She went in and he went past her and she shut the door and went over to the commode and put the seat down. She thought she heard the back door open just as she started peeing and she thought she heard it close but it was hard to tell because of the music and because she was peeing so hard into the water. She stopped peeing to listen for a moment. Then she heard it, just barely. It sounded like he was *talking* to somebody. He wasn't talking to the coon, was he? Man. She hadn't been this stoned in a long time. She guessed she'd better slow down. And oh. She needed to go ahead and unload her gun. He seemed kind of nervous about that.

She finished and got up and pulled her panties and pants up and flushed the commode and glanced at herself in the mirror. She patted at her hair. Maybe she'd get something new done with it before long. She was about tired of the way it was now. And she wanted it to look nice for him.

She opened the door while the commode was still filling and went out into the hall and back into his office for her bag. Leonard was really booming and it was almost too loud, so she bent over and found the volume knob and turned it down to an easier-listening level when she got back in the living room.

She thought she'd better sit on the couch to unload the gun so that she wouldn't risk dropping the bullets on the floor, so she did. She unzipped the side pocket of her bag and took it out and pulled it from the holster and started to push the release button on the side of the frame to free the cylinder, but suddenly Merlot was standing in the door of the room, and he looked kind of scared. She dropped the gun to her side and could see him take a big gulp.

"Penelope," he said, and his voice was a little shaky. "I've got somebody you've got to meet."

She looked at him curiously.

"Now?"

"Yes."

Well, who in the world was it? She guessed maybe one of the neighbors had come over. Through the back door. Unless they came in the front door while she was in the bathroom. But she didn't think she'd heard the door open.

"Oh," she said. "Well. Maybe I should turn the music down," she said, and she started to get up to do so, but he stopped her.

"No, it's okay," he said. "She likes Leonard."

She?

And then she heard something coming up the hall, and it was that whining again, and it sounded like something scratching on the floor. No it didn't. It sounded like something heavy *pulling* itself along the floor. And the whining was getting louder, faster, rising with excitement.

"Penelope," he said. "I want you to meet Candy."

Penelope looked at him. Then she looked at the floor, where he was looking. And then a nearly hairless boxer with scabs and open sores scattered over its hide pulled its skinny self around the corner and stopped. Under its two bright black eyes she could see two raw red open gaps like underlips. Its back legs were twisted sideways, flat and lifeless like her mamaw's awful dog, and it was drooling and it had no teeth, only black gums, and it was grinning at her with them, and it started pulling itself toward her faster on its front legs with its toenails making more scratches on the floor and it was whining excitedly and it smelled like dog shit and when it opened its mouth and puked on her feet she freaked out and shot it four times *BOOM! BOOM! BOOM! BOOM!* as fast as she could pull the trigger.

89

Wayne woke up again, just at dark, just as they passed the exit for Dollywood in the mountains near Knoxville. He pulled his cap from over his eyes and looked through the window of the bus. There was a billboard in tall grass lit by spotlights on the side of I-40 and there was a Dolly on it about fifteen feet high and her blond coif stuck up above the sign a good two or three feet.

He was getting hungry. The driver had let them off the bus for twenty-five minutes at a Waffle House near Asheville and he'd eaten some ham and eggs there and now he was wondering how much longer it would be before they stopped for food again.

He knew the plane was faster, but the bus was cheaper. Much cheaper. They didn't serve drinks on it, but it had a bathroom, and you could sleep, or read, or watch the countryside go by. The time passed eventually. All you had to do was sit there and the different parts of America would roll past. You didn't have to worry about anything. You could think about all the money you saved by taking the bus instead of a plane. And that was important if you were thinking about saving your money for the future. Because the future was an unpredictable thing. Oh yeah.

He'd had to ride all the way to Raleigh to catch the bus to Memphis. Three hours up there, then waiting around in the bus station, looking at the people, some guy with glasses on a microphone, calling out arrivals and departures.

His head had been hurting a little. He'd picked up a fishing magazine from where somebody had left it in the seat pocket in front of him, and had flipped through it, looking at the pictures, reading a few of the ads, but when he'd tried to concentrate on an article about hand-grabbling for monster Mississippi River catfish, his vision had blurred on him again and it had scared him so badly he'd put the magazine away and just contented himself with looking out the window at the rapidly fading daylight and thinking about her. And then he'd gone to sleep.

There wasn't a lot to see now that it had gotten dark, mostly just a black highway with the same stuff passing by over and over. Red Roof Inn. Huddle House. Texaco. BP. Holiday Inn. Buick. Toyota. Days Inn. Kentucky Fried Chicken. Hardee's. Harley-Davidson. There were always cars passing, and trucks, and even other buses, and Wayne liked sitting high in the bus seats, able to look down on the cars, and right across the windows into the cabs of the trucks. Sometimes the drivers waved, but it was dark on the bus except for a few reading lights people had turned on here and there, and Wayne knew the drivers wouldn't be able to see him if he waved back. So he didn't.

He knew now that there was something wrong with his head. But he didn't want to know what it was yet. That was too scary a thing to think about. So he watched things pass through the night in Tennessee, and thought about a country girl who was growing ever closer to him.

90

Penelope was gone, and Merlot knew she wouldn't be coming back. He was sitting in the living room and he had mopped up all the blood. The bucket and the mop were still sitting there. There were four bullet holes in the floor in a tight group. And he had turned off Leonard now.

Candy's tortured breathing, the ragged sound of her breath through her nostrils, was missing from the silence of the night. She was lying close to the back door now, wrapped in an old quilt that his grandmother had made, and slipped inside a plastic garbage bag to keep the blood off the linoleum. He would bury her under one of the trees in the backyard tomorrow, and maybe one day he could go down to the Yocona River and find a small suitable stone to mark her grave. Something smooth and round maybe. A river stone.

He saw now that he'd done wrong by her. What man who truly loved his dog wouldn't put it to sleep when it became too hard for it to live? Even Marla had agreed, Marla who was old and wise, Marla who knew she'd be out of a job dog-sitting if the dog was no longer around. Her purpose around here would completely disappear. But even she had said a long time ago that it was time.

Giving Candy a bath had been the worst. It was such a job to get her out of the tub, because she was dripping water everywhere, and it was running off her legs, and you were getting your clothes wet, and she still weighed almost forty pounds, and she couldn't do anything to help you with her. But she knew you were trying to help her, that was the thing. She'd look at you with eyes of love after you got her dried off and back in her bed. Sometimes, when she felt good after a bath, she'd even try to bark, but of course nothing came out except the same half-yelping noises she'd made at the back door when Penelope was sitting right over there.

He couldn't blame Penelope. He couldn't blame Candy. He should have been straight with Penelope about it from the start. But that wasn't what he'd done, was it?

No. He'd chosen to try and evade the whole thing, had tried to hide what he couldn't, not with her in the house. He had tried to hide his best friend. And why? Because he was ashamed of what he had let her become.

She'd gotten to where she couldn't eat much anymore in the last few months. What little Purina she did eat he'd had to soften with warm water and mash up with a spoon. She'd let him know with whining when she needed to be carried out and laid down in the backyard, away from the walk. If he wasn't asleep. Sometimes in the middle of the night he was, and didn't hear her, and had to clean up a mess the next morning before he met his first class. But that was over now.

Her eyes had been open before he'd wrapped her in the quilt and they had glassed over in a way Merlot had seen on a deer that had been in the back of somebody's pickup in the parking lot of James's

Food Center one fall afternoon before they'd torn it down. They'd always had the best tomatoes.

He didn't cry. He turned the light off and went into his bedroom and turned that light on and got a favorite sweatshirt from the closet, and pulled it over his head and chest, and looked down at it. It was a black one from Wofford College, with yellow letters, and the team name was on the sweatshirt: "Wofford Terriers." He took off his boots and found his house shoes, and slipped them on, and went back to the kitchen and reached into the cabinet for a short clean glass. He put some ice cubes in the glass and bent over and pulled out a canned Coke from a twelve-pack that was open on the floor and then he reached into another cabinet and pulled out a fifth of Crown in its little blue cloth bag. He mixed a good strong drink and then sat down on one of the stools and sipped it.

It was quiet in the kitchen. The overhead light buzzed just a bit, but it was one of those things you get used to that keeps everything sounding safe and the same. After a while he turned it off and turned on the one over the stove. That made it a little dark, but not too dark to see. After he'd finished that drink, he mixed another one, and went back up the hall to his room.

The weathered case was upright inside the closet, and he set it on the bed to unfasten the snaps. When he lifted the lid, he looked at the sleek black finish and the shiny bronze strings and the single mother-of-pearl word inlaid above the ivory tuning pegs: *Gibson.* He pulled it out of the case and got a pick and his pitch pipe and a capo from the worn velvet box inside the case and went back to the kitchen with all of it.

He tuned it sitting on the stool, knowing she was lying back there by the door, dead, knowing she was getting cold, knowing nobody else would understand because she was just a dog. He had to go back to the top string a couple of times and blow on the pitch pipe and hit the string with the pick while turning the peg until he was sure he had that string in tune, and then he worked his way down, going from one to the other, going back and checking to see how it sounded, turning the pegs slightly, listening, comparing how one string sounded as opposed to the one pressed to the fret above it. He was very patient with it, but it had taken him years to learn it as well as the patience. And he didn't play as much as he used to. Work. School. Taking care of Candy, too. So he took his time now and sipped his whiskey and made sure all his strings sounded in tune before he tried to make a chord.

When he thought he had them all good, he made a G chord and hit a downward stroke with the pick. It rang like a bell, the opening sound of something that wanted something else to follow it. He set the pick down for a second and took a sip from his drink. And then he got the pick back in his fingers and started playing and singing a song Elvis had done once, "Old Shep," there in the kitchen with a full bottle of Crown, and a dead old dog on the floor, by the door, and the rest of Oxford mostly asleep around him.

At two he was still sitting there and playing. His fingers hadn't completely lost their calluses but they were starting to get a little sore. So he stopped for a few minutes and put the guitar carefully on its back on top of the counter and mixed another drink.

What did you do in the middle of the night? Who was there to talk to since even the bars were closed? And who would listen to such a story? Would anybody want some stranger's dog troubles poured on him?

He picked up his guitar again and looked at it. It was very old, the reason it sounded so good. The one good thing his daddy had left him, made in 1945. The more it was played, the better it sounded, to the point where it would fairly resonate on its own after a couple of hours of playing. Merlot was trying to get it to that place. He was trying to get it warm with its own music from within itself. And it was going to take more whiskey.

And the crazy asshole cigar-smoking butcher running around, escaped from the hospital, no telling who he was or where he came from. And if it hadn't been for him, he wouldn't have even met Penelope. He might have seen her in a patrol car one day somewhere, and maybe would have glanced at her for just a second, and then he would have turned his face back to the red light in front of him, and waited for it to change.

He sipped at his drink and picked up the guitar again and got his pick. He sat there, just strumming, and picking out notes on the strings, doing little runs he'd known for years, things he didn't even have to think about much to play. It sounded good in the kitchen, and the gentle sound of it rang into the corners where maybe the mice listened.

He put the capo up on the third fret and made a D chord and teased the strings with the pick, making little ringing notes that warbled and floated.

Then he put the guitar down and went out on the front porch and looked down the street. It was too cold for crickets, or those vivid green tree frogs that sang their little songs so sweetly in the thick heat of summer nights. But he'd heard them many times from here.

He'd stood on the sidewalk and watched her go out of sight down the dark street, with her head down, and her small bag under her arm, and her hands in the pockets of her coat, passing from pool to pool of street lamp light like something that had stuck with him from an old black-and-white TV program he'd watched once with his daddy when he was just a little bitty thing, Jimmy Durante closing his show. Taking his hat off to show the few hairs combed over on his head. It had been a long long time ago, but Merlot remembered what he'd said: *Good night, Mrs. Calabash. Wherever you are.*

He went back inside and closed the door. It was cold out there.

91

Just like Miss Muffett had figured, the tub was full of cold dirty water and the bathroom was a sight to make a housekeeper want to puke. It looked like the little son of a bitch had pulled a couple of clean white towels down from the hangers with his teeth and rolled in them to dry off, but now they were more brown than white, and soggy and wet on the tiles. And not only that, but he'd evidently slung the water from himself as dogs do, after he got out, she guessed, or maybe even while he was still in it, and the dirty water had splattered all over the walls, and run down them, had splattered all over the toilet and the vanity, all over the floor and the tub curtains and the neat little blue rugs that stayed in there. It made her want to actually kill him. And hell. The gun was right down there in her purse. Fucking thing was loaded, too.

But some people will shoot a dog and some won't.

And where was he now? Where was her leg? Why would anybody want to keep such a crappy job? What if she just walked out the door?

But she didn't. She couldn't. She was trapped and she knew she was trapped. So instead, she made herself a big hamburger patty out of some of that fresh meat Mr. Hamburger had been working on for the last few nights, had gone out to the shed on her crutches and looked in the cooler and there was some meat that looked like fresh hamburger, but since it didn't say "Hamburger Dog" on it like the dog meat always did, she figured it was for her instead of the little dog. She'd taken it back inside and opened it and made that nice thick patty, had the black iron skillet hot already, laid that baby in there and salted and peppered it good, grabbed an onion out of the crisper and peeled it and cried some stinging tears and then sliced it on a wooden board with a sharp knife and dropped those white round beauties in there as the meat started sizzling.

There were Roma tomatoes and a fresh head of lettuce in the

crisper, and after she got everything out, she sat down at the table and sipped her drink and sliced up half a cucumber and made a nice little tossed salad and then got back up and flipped over the burger, which was talking to her. Already the onions were going soft and brown and translucent. She microwaved a Larry's stuffed potato, turned down the heat under the skillet, and found the ranch dressing in the fridge. There was still some tea in there from a couple of days ago, heck, it was still good probably. She turned on the oven and stuck in some rolls. She finished her drink and put the glass in the sink.

And when she had it all ready, she put on some Perry Como and poured herself a glass of iced tea with a wedge of lemon in it and sat down and started eating, thinking to herself, with the first juicy, dripping bite, one that held a strange and delicate new flavor: *Yum*, and knowing again, like she had all her life, even after she lost her leg to her daddy's boat motor, that things could always be worse. She might have lost both legs. And hey. It was almost Christmas.

92

When Anjalee woke in the dark of his bed, late, and turned over and touched him, Harv was on his side and cold as a fish, naked beneath the sheets. He'd made gentle and very satisfying love to her and after that they'd gone to sleep, but somehow he'd caught the big nap, eternal night or eternal light.

She rubbed her fingers over the side of his throat and there was no pulse there. His skin was cool, like he'd just come from a shower, but it was dry. And his eyes were closed. She wished hers still were.

She'd been having a Technicolor dream like a drive-in movie about her daddy and in the dream he had not been killed in a truck wreck in Alabama but had come back home to wreak everlasting happiness with them in Toccopola instead. They cooked out in the yard on summer evenings and drank beer with the radio on. They fished down on the riverbanks among the willows with cane poles and caught catfish and bream. They went to the fair in Tupelo and saw the rodeo and ate cotton candy. And in the dream her mother didn't have those other men hanging around and they didn't have cars that kept having flat tires and her mother didn't live in a trailer that was run down and ragged and cold in the winter and they weren't surrounded by garbage and they lived in a nice house. But she had wakened from the dream, to hold what was alive and real beside her, and now he who might have turned into the fabled sugar daddy was worse than out of town with his hair not even messed up.

She cried for a long time, up close to his back, wetting his arm and the sheet with her tears. She kept rubbing his cold shoulder. Harv had been so nice. Such a gentleman. And nobody had ever kissed her quite the way he had. So it was very hard to see him dead, see death so close so suddenly. But it had been like that with her daddy, here one day, gone the next, so in a tiny way she was almost kind of used to it.

She dried her cheeks with her fingers and turned her back away from him and lay on her side. She'd have to call the fucking cops.

But she didn't want to just yet. She could wait awhile. She had to hide his weed so they wouldn't think it was hers. She had to make sure she didn't get in any more trouble. She was about tired of trouble. It seemed like it had been following her around for too long. But she knew it had all started when her daddy died.

She didn't want to get up. She didn't want to have to mess with the police again. They would be in here, taking pictures, asking questions, looking around. She might even have to go with them. She hadn't thought about that, but it might be necessary. They might insist. There might be a law. Probably was. Or they might have to have an investigation. What if they revoked her probation over this shit and put her in jail anyway?

She kept lying there, staring at the dark window, the closed blinds where light from the street seeped in around the corners. She wondered what would happen to her if she just left. What if she just got dressed, and ready to leave, and called a cab, and waited for it to get here, watched out the window until she saw it pull up on the street outside, and then called the police the last thing, going out the door, and told them his address, and that there was somebody dead in here that they needed to come get?

That seemed the only sensible thing to do, so she got up and put her clothes on and went into the kitchen and looked around until she found some mail that had his name and address on it, and then she found the phone book and looked up a cab company and left the book open to that page.

She hated to go off and leave him dead and alone like this after he'd been so nice to her, but she couldn't stick around and wait for the cops to get here. The cops would want to know what had happened. They might think she had something to do with him dying. And maybe she had. Maybe she had gotten him too excited. Maybe he'd had a bad heart and hadn't mentioned it.

She heard a siren somewhere far off. The firemen stayed up late. She wondered if it was some of the ones she knew on that truck going somewhere in the dead of night. She still remembered those nights in Fifi's Cabaret, and Fifi herself, with her cool black clothes and her glass of red wine and her dark and lovely Mediterranean features. Back when a girl could make a little money and have some fun at the same time. Before it got to be not fun. Not like now, when there were so many cops around looking at everything that it was hard to get away with anything. It had just gotten too risky. That's why she'd been so glad when Frankie had come along. He'd kind of saved her from all that for a while, from doing it with strangers almost every night, back behind the closed frosted-glass doors on the darkened couches while the thump of heavy metal came through the walls, worrying about the undercover police. And now where in the hell was he? Out of town. And what was she going to do about Lenny?

She got her cigarettes and walked into the den. The lamp was still on and she sat down in the chair that was in front of the TV. She lit a cigarette and crossed her ankles on the footstool.

What if it had happened when he'd been on top of her? When he'd been inside her? What if he'd been coming and then died? Oh God. That would have been awful. And she didn't know anything about him or who he really was or what he'd been doing all his life or if he had children or even grandchildren maybe. If he had children, they were probably older than her. Who was going to go to the morgue and get him? She wouldn't even know.

She sat there and smoked her cigarette, wondering if this was the right thing to do. She couldn't think of anything else. And she needed a drink. So she got up and went into the kitchen and found a bottle of mezcal in the refrigerator and a lime in the crisper. She found some sea salt in a little round box up in the cabinet and she got it down.

This shit was just like all the other shit. She got a knife from the drawer and sliced the lime into quarters and then eighths. Drawing. What good was it? What could you do with it that would make any money to live off of and not have to do what she'd been doing for the last three years? The cops knew her now. She needed to get out of this fucking town. Maybe even find something else to do for a living. Find, hell. She had a perfectly good license from the state of Mississippi to fix hair. She'd gone down to Jackson and taken her state board exams, had passed, still had the certificate framed somewhere. She thought it was in her mother's trailer. But fixing hair was a lot of work, too. Fixing hair you had to stand on your feet all day listening to women bitch. But getting humped by strangers all the time wasn't exactly the world's best scenario either, no matter what she'd told Ronnie the cop about liking the way it felt. It looked like there would be a happy medium somewhere in there. Why couldn't she find a nice guy? Somebody like that sailor boy?

There was a clean shot glass in the drain board and she opened the mezcal and poured it full. She did the shot and bit the lime and shook some sea salt onto her hand and licked it off. Wiped her mouth. And Ronnie Boy got a freebie. Big deal. And in another way it was the same thing as raping her. She wished she could kill the little son of a bitch. He didn't need to be a cop. Cops were supposed to be good.

"Brrrrrrrrrr," she said, when the rush from the mezcal hit her, and kind of shivered her shoulders. Maybe the thing to do was just get fucked up before she called the cab and the cops.

And maybe she needed to go on home like she'd been thinking about. It had been a while. Her mother never called her because she didn't want to run up her phone bill because her beer bill was already so high. It had been about a twelve-pack a day for a while. And when you had a bunch of deadbeats hanging around eating your food and all your microwave popcorn and helping you drink the beer, you needed even more than that for one day and night. Mostly night. Watch movies and jewelry channel shows all night long. Wait for some guy or guys to come over at two A.M. Let dirty clothes pile up. Leave dirty skillets and plates with bad food all over the place and garbage overflowing in the trash can until a person didn't even want to sit in there. Anjalee had cleaned up that trailer more times than she could remember, and her mother would always let it slide back into something pretty bad for people to try and live in. That was another reason she'd left.

There was some cold beer in Harv's fridge. Five tallboys of Stroh's. She got one out and popped the top, and picked up her cigarette from the ashtray, and took a drink, and pulled on the cigarette, and then decided that she could probably use a toke or two off his stash and his pipe. Or just take it with her, hell, Harv wasn't going to need it. It would be a shame to let good dope go to waste. And a good pipe, too. All the cops would do if they found it was just confiscate it. Some asshole like Ronnie would probably keep it for himself. Harv'd probably want her to have it instead of them. He'd seemed to be a pretty unselfish man. The bill for the two steak dinners and salads and appetizers and drinks had been $127.60 and she knew that because she'd picked up the bill and looked at it while he was gone to the bathroom in the restaurant, just because she'd wondered how much it was.

She went back in and looked at Harv again just to make sure he was still dead. He was. He wasn't moving at all. But it was the damnedest thing. Except for his chest not rising and falling with his breathing he just looked like he was asleep.

"Old fart," she said, in a sad but loving way, and she was kind of mad at him for just up and dying on her. She stood there and looked at him for a bit, then she went back to the kitchen and did another shot.

"Son of a *bitch*," she said, standing in the kitchen, doing that little shiver again. All those firefighters got her to doing that stuff, that mezcal. Claimed if you ate the worm, you'd have a vision. And she had eaten the worm one night. It tasted pretty bad, was tough and chewy, and she didn't think she had a vision, just got drunk as hell.

She put her cigarette out and loaded up the pipe, then wrapped the rest of the weed tightly in its little bag and stuck it in her purse.

She couldn't believe this shit. But it wouldn't do any good to cry. Crying never had gotten a damn thing done. That was the other thing her mother did, cry. All the time. From unhappiness. From missing her father. From being drunk. From being depressed from being almost constantly drunk. From living the way she did. But she wouldn't try to change any of it. That was the thing. She just wanted to lay around on her ass all the time and feel sorry for herself and draw a check off the government. And drink. She was going to drink herself to death if she didn't slow down.

She fired the pipe up and took a long hit and held it, then blew the stream of smoke out. Would she have ended up like this if her daddy had lived? She liked to think that she wouldn't have, but she didn't have any way of knowing for sure. She guessed she'd always been a little man crazy, but she sure enough got it from her mother. After watching her long enough, she knew she had.

She did another shot of mezcal and already a warm dizziness was spreading through her. She could feel it wrapping around her as surely as a cloak or a coat. It wasn't the worst thing in the world. It wasn't the end of the world. Here is how it was. She had fucked up Miss Barbee and violated her probation. Frankie was gone. Harv was dead. She had some money. It was close to Christmas. She still had time to go home, pack a few things and get them in the car, and gas it up and head out. Just go back home. Just see what things were like. Maybe they were better. There was always a chance. And her mama would be surprised.

She hoped she'd be glad to see her. Maybe she could give her some of the money Lenny had given her. She needed to get his number somehow before she left. And was she coming back? The rent was going to come due in about three more weeks. If she stayed here, she'd have to pay it. And it looked like Frankie's money was out of the picture. And how was she going to get ahold of Lenny again, without going back to Gigi's Angels to wait on him, or sitting around the Peabody bar, hoping he'd walk in?

There was too much going on at once. She stood in the kitchen and sipped her beer and then lit another cigarette. She was going to have to call the cab and the cops before long. She couldn't just put it off all night.

She was stoned now on top of the booze. And maybe she needed another toke off her pipe, too. Maybe she hadn't smoked enough yet because she wasn't to the place where she wanted to be yet. She didn't want to feel anything or have any worries. And she wanted to be somewhere with some people she knew before this night was over. And she wanted her good black leather coat. Something to remember Frankie by.

So she smoked some more weed and stuck the pipe in her purse and went back to the kitchen for a fresh beer. She braced herself. She got her cell phone out of her purse and walked over to the phone book she'd left open and called the cab company. Some sleepy-headed-sounding woman answered and Anjalee gave her the address and the woman told her the cab would be there in ten minutes. Then she pulled up the blinds in the den so that she could see the front of the building, sat down with her fresh beer, and settled down to wait. But then she got up, went into the room where Harv lay, and bending over, kissed him good-bye on top of his graceful silver head.

93

The fight was over, now, but the lions were still growling. It hadn't been much of a fight anyway, with his hands cuffed behind his back, but he'd fought all he could, once he saw what was going to happen, had tried to butt with his head, had tried to kick, had even tried to bite, but it hadn't worked, since Rico had simply knocked him out cold again. And that was getting old. Domino's brain felt fuzzy and damaged. He thought maybe electrons were ebbing, going weak like old bad batteries. Some blood was probably loose in there, too, and maybe some of his brain cells were getting drunk on it. And Domino felt more than a little light-headed, but considering the blood he was losing that wasn't any big surprise. Rico had cut his balls off and was holding them in his hand. Then he threw them over the top of the cage and one of the lions started eating them.

And that made Domino throw up. He panted hard afterward and threw up again. Really just gagged, nothing came up, just that choking gasping dry retching, eyes streaming, going into shock.

The lions in the cages behind him were snarling and lashing their half tails. There was one with a missing back leg that stumped back and forth, coughing with its hunger or just its rage at being in the cage. He could hear Rico going through the keys looking for the right one.

He was too weak now to resist anything much. He heard the

enclosure door open and felt the blood leaking into the crack of his ass. He thought maybe he would have had a chance if they hadn't put him in a fucking garbage can. Maybe if he'd been given a chance, instead of being given to some inbred person full of fear and hate. Then some pimply prison employee punk shoots a shotgun in your ear. But the warden likes whitetail, too, and says go straight. Another guy says give him a cigarette or else. Then you're fighting somebody. Which way to turn? And who do you call on if there's nobody you know?

His arms and hands were really hurting. There was some blood in his eyes. Why didn't he just go straight? Why didn't he just listen to the warden? The warden had made it plain as day.

The lions would probably be quick. He knew from watching the nature shows that they could pierce the brain with their long teeth and he probably wouldn't feel a thing. He knew they'd eat him, but he also knew that was their nature, and besides that, he'd eaten a lot of animals himself in his life. Cut them up for a living. Untold tons of them. What was so crazy about one of them eating him? He wouldn't need his body after he was gone. He was sorry for killing the cop and wished he hadn't done it. And all those people in those wrecks. He wished he'd gone straight. As it turned out, like the flip of a coin, he hadn't, but easily might've.

So maybe everything in the universe balanced out. Maybe there was some sort of scale everything got stacked on, and it evened out over eternity. He didn't know. He never had been religious, but he'd never had anybody close to teach it to him either. Who knew? He might have liked it. He liked the stars and all that astrology stuff. Like which house your planet was in and all that. In prison they'd made them go to church on Sunday, and he'd always liked the gospel singing, which he'd cupped a hand to hear. But now he couldn't remember any of the songs, just watching the big titties under the rich blue robes of the pretty black girls in the choir. Like that deputy sheriff that got him. She was a brick house. And hell. Who knew? Maybe under different circumstances . . .

He felt Rico take him by the collar and start dragging him. So much blood was leaking out of him that it was starting to soak all through his pants. He was about to get very light-headed. His head fell over and he couldn't help it.

This guy wasn't going to get away with this. Who did he think he was? Was the guy who owned the lions not home? Was he on vacation?

And all that time down on the prison farm, waiting to get out. Waiting for all the stuff he was going to do. Find a woman. Find out something about what a normal woman was like, since he didn't really know. And now he never would. Not in this life.

But there had to be more to it than what he and Doreen had done. That was just sex. There wasn't any lovemaking in it because there hadn't been any love. That was just fucking. He'd had plenty of fucking. That was all animals had. Just making little animals. Oh but then some of them had *dens*. Maybe if he'd had a good *den*.

He slid on his back across the rough ground, and on his hands. The collar of his shirt was choking him, the way Rico was holding it. But in just a little bit, from blood loss, he didn't know so well what was going on, only that it was very cold out here and that he was getting numb and that something was going to happen and then everything would be over and he wouldn't be feeling this way anymore.

There were noises close to him but he didn't know what they were. His butt was cold. His butt was wet. He remembered from long ago a bright parking lot with cars and trucks and somebody holding him up, horns honking, the smell of what he knew now had been gas and oil. He remembered Doreen sucking him off but hurting him on purpose with her teeth. Not being able to make her stop with his hands tied behind his back. Screaming on her bed, the world not hearing, the world never hearing, for years, and years, and years.

He was choking. Something had him by the throat. It was getting cold. He wished he could sleep.

Like in the warm barn.

Next to the happy fucking he'd heard.

Then somebody was speaking to him. Somebody was saying something to him, and for a time he couldn't figure out what it was, and then he could. It was somebody asking him did he want to say anything before he shut the enclosure door and opened the cage door. And he couldn't think of anything, so he just said: "Thanks, I think I can make it fine from here."

And the cage door slammed, and another one opened, and then something big and hairy was on him, and it had teeth, and very bad breath, and then it felt like teeth closed on his head.

94

Wayne went down to the bar at the Peabody in the evening with his uniform on and grabbed a tall chair near the fountain. The bartender had a tag that said *"Ken"* and he got Wayne a cold Budweiser in a bottle and a shot of Quervo Gold with a piece of lime on a napkin. Wayne told Ken to start him a tab and Ken nodded and then left him alone. He was glad because he needed to think about everything before he did it.

His head felt okay now. He just needed to get it checked. Maybe it was nothing. Or maybe it was something they could fix. They could fix about anything these days. People had artificial hearts. People had synthetic knees. They had very good doctors in the navy. And they might let him out if there was something wrong with his head, but he wouldn't tell Anjalee about that. Not right now. Not tonight. Other stuff was more important. And a medical discharge was not really anything to be ashamed of. It just meant that you got hurt during service to your country. It happened to people in the service even when there wasn't a war going on.

He took a long cold drink of his beer and set it back down. There were more people starting to come into the lobby and the bar now and everybody seemed to be happy. There were Christmas decorations set up and there was a tree with lights in a corner and a bunch of probably fake wrapped gifts under it. He took another drink of his beer.

The thing was, he didn't want to let himself get over there too early and get drunk. He wanted to go back around the same time he'd seen her before, since that was one of the few things he knew about her, the time she'd been there, which he thought had been between nine and ten.

So he was just going to sit here, be cool, sip some beer, sip a few shots of tequila, and just hang out, and watch the people, and then later on, when he got hungry enough, he'd go eat somewhere, and then he'd come back and give the bellhop a few bucks to call him a cab, and he'd tell the driver to take him to the place on Winchester. Gigi's Angels. And maybe she'd be there when he walked in. There was a hope for that like a great happy birthday balloon in his heart. He could see her face in his mind. He hadn't seen her naked, so he just imagined all that. And he'd already done that a lot of times.

He'd been rehearsing what he wanted to say to her. The first thing he'd ask her was did she remember him. He hoped she would. He was sure she would. The second thing he'd ask her was did she want a drink. And then they'd go from there. And if she wanted money to talk, he had plenty in his pocket. He was going to have to talk to her, a lot, to get her to understand what he was talking about. What he was talking about was life.

And maybe it wouldn't happen all at once. Maybe he didn't need to rush things too much. Maybe he'd only be able to get her address, so that he could write her, and he had to tell her about his situation, that he didn't know if he was going to stay in the navy or not, but that he had twenty-one more months to think about it, and that he'd get some more leave in there somewhere, and that he wanted to come back to Memphis to see her, if that was all right. And that if he had to pay her again to go to bed with her, that it was all right, and he'd pay it gladly, but he wanted her in a bed this time, and not in that dirty place upstairs, but maybe here at the Peabody, up in his room, where it was private. Up in that nice bed within those nice walls, on clean sheets, in a place where he could talk to her, and tell her that he'd been thinking of almost nothing but her, and touch her face, and her skin, and her hair, and all the other wonderful things she had. That was his plan. But the plan changed, as the best-laid ones sometimes do.

95

Helen didn't make it over four blocks before she ran a red light trying to get through under the yellow. Blue lights surged out from a parking lot and pulsed behind the Jag, cold cold light that washed into her heart.

And just like that, the commonwealth of Tennessee had her ass again.

96

Eleven o'clock found Wayne in loud music, almost drunk, and sitting on a bar stool away from the stage in Gigi's Angels, and Anjalee wasn't there. He'd been looking for her, and he'd asked almost everybody in there if they'd seen her, the bartender several times, and he'd already said he didn't know where she was tonight.

He didn't mean for this shit to happen. How in the hell had it? Did she work here or did she not work here? He never had seen her on the stage. Maybe she wasn't a dancer. Maybe she was an off-duty dancer. Maybe he didn't know what the fuck she was. He knew he needed another beer, though. He flagged down the bartender again. The music was really loud.

"You think she might come in later?" he said, when the bartender brought the fresh bottle. Some of his money was in a crumpled pile in front of him and he picked some bills from it and pushed them across.

The bartender picked up some of the money with a bored look and put one bill back in the pile. He spoke just as he was turning away.

"Like I told you, buddy. I don't know where she is tonight."

He motioned toward the stage when he stopped at the register. A slim redheaded girl was slinking up and down and around a pole with blue lights winking over her pale skin.

"There's plenty other women in here. I can introduce you to one if you want to hook up."

Wayne looked around. There were some girls sitting in men's laps here and there. They were mostly naked. They didn't seem to be dancing. He waved a hand.

"I think I'll just sit here and see if she comes in," he said.

"Suit yourself," the bartender said, like he'd missed some great opportunity, and moved away to wait on some other people down at the end of the bar.

He should have eaten. It always messed you up if you didn't eat. He should have gone right on down the marble steps to the street and found a place to eat, but he'd daydreamed different scenes with Anjalee that always ended in lovemaking, and he'd gotten comfortable where he was, and everybody was really friendly to him, and some even told him they appreciated what he was doing for the country, and the whole evening had seemed to turn into a big pre-Christmas party, and he'd just stayed on his bar stool, drinking beer, drinking shots, buying shots, telling the whale story to new friends.

But all those new friends were gone now. And he was drunk again. And she wasn't here.

Sometimes when Wayne got to drinking, he got to feeling that people were looking at him. And he was feeling kind of like that now. There were five or six guys sitting at a table twenty feet away and they were husky young men, about like him. One had on a Memphis Fire Department T-shirt, so he figured they were all fire-fighters. He'd noticed a couple of them look at him. But that wasn't really unusual. People always looked at a man or a woman in uni-form because you didn't see them that often out in the civilian world, just mostly in airports unless you lived in some place like Washington, D.C., where the whole city was full of uniforms.

He watched the dancer on the stage for a while. She was okay but she wasn't anything special. Maybe when she came off the stage he needed to ask her if she knew Anjalee.

He guessed Henderson had been home for a while already. They should have swapped phone numbers. Then maybe they could have kept up with each other that way. He could have called Henderson's house or Henderson could have called his house. His mother could have told Henderson where he was and how to reach him. He didn't know why he hadn't thought of that. But Henderson evidently hadn't thought of it either.

He kept sitting there sipping his beer. He'd probably had seven or eight, counting the ones at the Peabody. And if he didn't see her tonight, what was he going to do? Come back over here tomorrow? Yeah. He had ten days to do something. But he couldn't afford to stay ten days in the Peabody. It was a nice hotel, yeah, but it was too high for an enlisted man's pay. A Howard Johnson's would be a lot cheaper. Or even a Motel 6. But it wouldn't be any big deal to move, with just one duffel bag. Maybe he could find a motel near here. Cut down on cab fare. And then the other thoughts came back, the ones that were always nagging at him.

That this was crazy. To even be here. It didn't make any sense. She was a prostitute. A whore. She fucked people for a living. But what had made her that way? What had gone wrong in her life that caused her to sell herself to men all the time? The questions he wanted to ask her were driving him nuts. And she might tell him to mind his own business. And she wasn't even anywhere around to ask anyway. He hated to keep bugging the bartender about it. And at the same time he wondered if the guy might have a phone number for her. If she worked here, the bartender might need to call her to tell her to come in to work, might need to tell her *not* to come in to work, might need to tell her any number of things over the phone about her job. And did they punch a clock? Did they have insurance? Did the club get a percentage off a blow job? He guessed they did since she was using their building.

People kept coming in and there was more and more cigarette smoke floating around. The girl got off the stage and some people whistled and clapped but she didn't come by where he was sitting, instead went over to the other side of the room and sat down in a man's lap. He guessed he could get up and go over there and ask her if she knew Anjalee. Somebody in here had to know how to get in touch with her. That old girl might be the one.

He kind of kept his eye on her and drank his beer. He looked back behind the bar to see if there was any tequila back there and there was.

He looked at the bartender a couple of times but he was talking to some woman and not paying attention to his customers. Wayne tried to be patient. But he was getting a little aggravated. The bartender knew her. But he didn't want to tell him anything about her. What did he care? What was it to him? Was he the boss? Did he own this place? Maybe he did. Or maybe he just worked here. He could ask him if he ever got his attention. He waited and waited and got tired of waiting.

"Hey, man," he said, and raised his hand about halfway, but the bartender didn't hear him. The woman the bartender was talking to saw him, though, because she looked at him, but then she cut her eyes back to the bartender and kept listening to whatever bullshit he was blowing.

Wayne took a deep breath and a big drink of his beer. He was about halfway done with that one. He might as well order another one when he ordered the shot. Keep from having to call him back again. If he ever got the shot ordered. He waited and waited some more, long time, long time.

"Hey, bartender!" he said, kind of loud, and the bartender turned mid-bullshit, and Wayne saw a flash of anger go across his interrupted face, then he said something harsh to the woman and came on over. He put his hands on the bar. He looked like a man trying to be an asshole. His reasons unclear. His scarred and warred-on face.

"You don't have to yell at me, sailor. What you want?"

"Sorry. I want to get a shot of that tequila. And let me have another beer. I couldn't catch your eye."

The bartender muttered something and went to the row of bottles and pulled out the tequila and reached for a shot glass. He half-turned to Wayne.

"Lot of people in here, you know? I can't watch everybody the whole time. All these dipshits."

"I got you," Wayne said. "It's loud, too."

"Fucking aye. And it's just me."

Wayne nodded in silent agreement while the bartender poured his shot. He set it down hard in front of Wayne and some of it spilled. He didn't put a napkin under it either. Wayne sat there. The bartender got him another beer and opened it on the cooler-box lid and set it beside the shot glass.

"That's nine-fifty," he said, and stood waiting. Wayne gave him a ten and a couple of ones for a tip. The bartender was the one who'd fixed him up with Anjalee. Same guy. No doubt about it. He thought his name was Moe. Was it Moe?

"Have you got her number, Moe?" Wayne said.

The bartender had been turning away with the money but he stopped. He was still pissed. But he guessed his name was Moe.

"Whose phone number you wanting again?"

"That girl I was asking you about. Anjalee's her name."

"Oh yeah," the bartender said, and nodded as he turned away, and muttered something about how he didn't give out the girls' phone numbers. Wayne wanted to talk to him some more, but a few more people came in and walked to the bar and the bartender had to start waiting on them. And a girl showed up with a tray and an order for drinks. Then another one came from the other side of the room with the same thing. And looking all around he didn't see anybody in there who even vaguely looked like Anjalee.

So he turned back to his shot. The bartender hadn't given him any lemon or lime, either one. And he didn't want to do it without that. Only now he was tied up making all those drinks. Some more people were coming to the bar. Another girl was climbing up on the stage and a rock tune was starting up, some distorted and fuzzy moaning of *wah wah waaah* . . .

There were some lemons and limes both, in a tray on the back edge of the bar. Wayne could see them. They were sliced into wedges and he really needed one for his tequila. The bartender should have given him one.

Couldn't he just reach back there and get one? He wanted to try and talk the bartender out of Anjalee's number, because that would be a big help, but he didn't want to do anything to piss him off now that he knew he had her number.

So he sat there and took a sip of his tequila, but it was pretty bad without a piece of lemon or lime to bite into, so he waited awhile and thought about it and then got up and walked a few steps down the bar and reached across the bar into the tray for a piece of lemon and the bartender saw him.

"Hey. Hey!" he said, loud enough for everybody at the bar to look around. "Keep your fucking dirty hands out of my garnish tray, sailor."

"You were busy," Wayne said. He had the lemon wedge in his hand. He could feel and see everybody looking at him and he felt like he'd been caught stealing. He could feel his ears getting red.

"How do I know where your hands been?" the bartender said, loud again, and it was easy to see that he was mad. For no reason. People. Shit.

"Hey, mister, take it easy, okay? I just wanted a piece of lemon with my shot 'cause you didn't give me one."

"You didn't ask for one."

"Yeah, well most bartenders serve them with one."

The bartender had his arms at his side and he took a step closer. Like an invalid relearning to walk. Then he pointed toward the door.

"You don't like the way I serve drinks, you can get your fucking ass out of here, navy. Right now."

Everybody within earshot was listening now because the bartender had gotten so loud. This was all going badly wrong. And Wayne wanted to stop that if he could. He started backing away.

"Take it easy, mister. I'm just going back to my drink. I don't want any trouble."

"I'll give you some fucking trouble," the bartender said.

Wayne sat back down in front of his beer and his shot glass. Damn. The bartender glared at him for a few more seconds and then he turned away, went back to what he was doing. But he was cussing under his breath. One unhappy man. Wayne looked at the beefy bouncer at the door who was watching him with his arms crossed.

And one of the firefighters laughed. Wayne caught eyes with him. About two-ten, about five-ten. Hair razored down to the skin of his tanning-bed tanned head but a short black beard with no mustache. Going for the semi-Ahab look. Had a diamond stud in one ear. Probably didn't wear it on smoke calls. He didn't look away. But Wayne did. He had to keep sitting here. He had to try and make peace with the bartender and he'd seen the bartender joking and laughing with the firefighters before, calling them by name, so it was plain that they were regulars or at least knew each other. He was the outsider here. He knew how it was. He knew how dogs were about their yards. He didn't want any trouble. Some trouble would mess up everything. He should have just waited for the lemon. He wished now that he had.

There was a salt shaker within reach and he got it, licked the web of his hand, and sprinkled some salt on it. He was hunched over the bar with the toes of his black oxfords hooked on the rungs of the stool and he lifted the shot glass to his mouth and drank about half the tequila, then set it down and bit into the lemon, and licked the salt from his hand. He sipped his beer.

He hadn't called his mother and daddy yet. He knew he should have done that this afternoon, and told them what had happened with the whales, but he'd known it would turn into a long conversation with his mother, and she would have insisted that he talk to his daddy, too, who might have been out in the barn or up in the loft or out in one of the fields on the tractor cutting down cornstalks or just anywhere on the farm. Then he would have had to wait while she called him to the house on the walkie-talkie. Wayne had given the little durable Motorolas to them for Christmas last year and they used them all the time between the farm and the house, said they didn't know how they'd ever gotten by without them before. They sat in their chargers each night with their tiny red lights burning in the dark of the kitchen. His. Hers. Home.

And he could always go there for Christmas. He knew they were hoping for that, and he knew that the right thing to do was to go see them. Go right back to the bus station, he could be home in fourteen hours of riding. Put on his old clothes. Eat some of his mother's cooking. Go mess around in the fields with his daddy. They could probably find some pheasants to shoot. Deer season would be open. They could hunt. They could watch TV. They could drink beer. See all his buddies and aunts and uncles and cousins, maybe even Stella. His mother said she was working at the telephone office in town now. Hell. If he went home, maybe they could go have a beer. He still liked her okay. He sure didn't have anything against her now.

But shit. What good would that do? That was over and done

with. She didn't want to make love anymore if they weren't married and that was all there was to it. Said it had gotten to where it made her feel like a whore. As much as they'd done it, for eight months, and then for her to come out with that shit. Just because she wanted to get married. He wanted to be married, yeah, he wanted to have kids, but not before he was ready, and not just because somebody said it was time for him to. Not just because Stella said it was time for him to. Nope. He hadn't seen the world yet. But after that he joined up to do just that. And his daddy was really proud of him. He needed to go see them. They were getting old. Slowing down.

He took another drink of his beer and the firefighter laughed again. It pissed him off but he tried to ignore it. He didn't want any shit to get started in here. He had to stay in here. He had to apologize to the bartender again and tell him he was sorry and tip him good even though actually he'd been tipping him pretty good already and see if he couldn't find out how he could get ahold of her. But he'd had four or five beers and some shots. And he was upset that she wasn't here. And he hated for some wise son of a bitch to be able to sit back there and think he could laugh at him. He didn't have anything against firefighters. Hell no. The ones on the ship had a hell of a job. All that jet fuel, all those rockets and bombs, and missiles, all those tons of explosives, if any of that shit went off, it was the firefighters who had to get the hoses and go in there and put their asses on the line to put it out. No, he had respect for firefighters. But this one was acting like an asshole. He knew he was going to have to look at him again.

So he did.

The guy was watching him with his head kind of laid back on his thick neck. He was smiling at Wayne, and sipping on a drink, and just kind of chuckling to himself. A private joke maybe. Wayne smiled at him, too, and picked up his shot glass again.

"Fuck you," he said to the guy, through the music.

The guy stopped smiling then. He was out of his chair in just a second and almost up in Wayne's face within the next few.

"You got a problem, sailor boy?" he said. He wasn't sober either.

Wayne wasn't excited but he stood up just in case the guy took a swing. People were watching, he knew.

"I got a problem with you laughing at me," Wayne said.

Some of the guy's friends were yelling at him to shut up and sit his ass back down but he didn't pay any attention. Wayne was afraid of getting sucker-punched and knew that if he didn't step carefully here, there would probably be some police involved within a few minutes. Maybe a quick trip to the friendly local jail. And he didn't need that. He knew he didn't need that.

He risked a glance at the bartender. Everything had stopped but the music. He was going to explain things to the firefighter. He was going to calm everything down and make friends with the bartender and get Anjalee's number and call her when he got back to his room in the Peabody and everything was going to work out tonight. He was going to go to the doctor when he got back and get his head seen about. Stop boxing for sure since that obviously was causing his problems, getting hit with too many straight rights. He was good but not great. And that was a vast difference in boxing. He was lucky. He could always farm.

And, shit, in a bar like this? It was just stupid. It was small-time punk stuff. Which didn't change the fact that you could get hurt in it. You could get hurt in it even worse than in the ring. Where there were rules.

"I'll laugh whenever I get damn ready," the firefighter said. He was young and stocky, and his eyes were rimmed slightly with red. And Wayne didn't want to fight a drunk. He sure didn't need to get hit in the head.

"Look, man," Wayne said, and held up a hand. "Let's just sit back down and call it over. Call it even. Call it whatever the fuck you want to call it. I don't need no trouble. If you think I'm scared of your ass, that's fine."

The firefighter stared at him with drunken intensity, and Wayne took a step back, and felt himself weave just a bit. Hell. He didn't have any business fighting. And just like that it all changed.

"Just get your fucking troublemaking ass out!" the bartender said. And he waved to the guy on the door. "Tommy! Get this asshole outa here!"

"*Wait* a minute, man, I ain't done nothing," Wayne said, and the bouncer was coming over, and the firefighter was still standing there, and he knew somebody was about to put their hands on him, and he didn't want that either, but the bouncer, big, dark clothes, in loud music, made a grab for his arm, and Wayne snatched it away, and ducked a punch he barely saw coming, and then his instincts took over, and he coldcocked the bouncer with one hard shot to his jaw, so that his knees bent, and he fell over and knocked over a table with some drinks. And everything seemed to stop except for the blaring music. He was watching the faces. He was watching the other firefighters getting up from their table, and he was watching the girls watching from the stage while the loud music kept pouring out of the speakers, and he didn't see the bartender at all, who had reached somehow for the same fifth of tequila, and raised it high, and leaned out over the bar, and was just about to bring it down on Wayne's head in a splinter of glass and tequila and blood, like an explosion, when the front door opened and Anjalee walked in.

"Don't!" she screamed.

So he didn't.

97

The cops at the Shelby County Jail were not overly nice to Helen since it was her third trip in there. There were cops everywhere and there were people screaming and shouting and begging in the bedlam that was going on, cell doors slamming, but the police didn't seem to pay any attention to any of it. They fingerprinted her and photographed her while she sobered up and she only wished that she could go back and do the last few hours over again. All Arthur's money couldn't do her any good in here. Or in that courtroom where she would have to face that judge again. She was too scared to even cry.

But the worst was when they put her in the cell. It was so crowded there near the holidays that they had to stick her in with another woman, a large and mean-looking black woman with big feet and titties and some bandages on her melon head and who looked like she was about half man. Helen tried not to look at her when the cell door slammed. But she did. And the woman stood up, towering over her, and said: "The hell you lookin' at, *bitch?*"

98

In Wayne's heart the love beat deep for the country girl sleeping beside him in his nice room at the Peabody. He knew the big river was out there flowing, and he heard the sad horn of a tug going down to maybe New Orleans blow a long flat note out across the water he couldn't see. A little moonlight shafted in through the window, and he knew that same moon was hanging over his daddy's farm in Ohio. He could picture the house in shadow, the old white barn dark except for the single light his father left on over the front so that you could read the big numbers, hand-painted, *"1928,"* the trucks and tractors and corn pickers that were parked out there beyond the gate with frost all over them. The two rat terriers, Georgie B. and Big Mama, would be sleeping in the barn. And his parents would be sleeping now, too, upstairs in their bed. He had already imagined taking Anjalee there one fine spring day, to their house, to the back door inside the screened porch with all the flowers and plants, opening it to the kitchen, stepping in, holding her by the hand, and his mother in her apron would turn from the stove, and she would rush to hug him, and laugh, and kiss him, and then she would look, smiling, past his shoulder at the girl he would be turning to, and he would say, with pride in his voice: "Mother, I've got somebody I want you to meet."

99

Rico was not crying but was mercifully sleeping for a little while when the knocks on the door woke him. His dog, Fred, was in the bed with him, as it usually was, now that Lorena was gone for good, and it got up and howled with its nose pointed up. It only weighed about four pounds, and shook sometimes, and it had bugged-out eyes, and he told it to hush and got up and put on his robe and then picked the dog up and put it under his arm like you might carry a loaf of bread or a football.

He could see the blue flashes of light through the curtains of his living room, and he knew then that they had found his brother.

He stopped, and stood there just short of the door, very afraid, and remembered a Christmas long ago when he'd been hoping to get a guitar, only to see a red one with plastic strings show up on Elwood's side of the tree. And he remembered that he had gotten a model train, and had cut his finger putting the track together, and he could remember pushing Elwood into a mud hole when he was about three or four, and making him cry. Now he hated so bad he'd done that. He would have given anything if he could go back and do some things over. With his brother. With his wife. With his life.

He knew that his brother was dead, had known it all along, but he didn't know why. He didn't know how. He didn't know where they'd found him, only that they had. He pushed the curtains aside, and looked out. The whole road in front of his house was filled with cruisers, and people were walking around in his yard, and all the blue lights were winking, making flashes of color on his curtains, and on the face of Fred, who howled bravely, fiercely, loudly at what was out there in the night, safe in the warm crook of his large buddy's arm.

100

It was only a few nights before Christmas, and Arthur had put up a small tree and strung multicolored blinking lights that made the living room look warm and happy. The tree held some last-minute presents under its narrow lower branches, and dishes of pecans and English walnuts were sitting on the coffee table with a new nutcracker set. Also displayed were some nice fake holly leaves and red wax berries in a pleasing configuration.

The cool thing going on with WTBS tonight was another twenty-four hours of Clint, back to back, around the clock. *Hang 'Em High.* *Coogan's Bluff.* *For a Few Dollars More.* All his favorites. He had his occasional gin and tonic going and was feeling comparatively good, relatively speaking. It had been four days now since he'd heard from her lawyer, and sent the lawyer the money for her bond, so he guessed she was still staying in the Peabody. He guessed maybe she wasn't coming back in time for the holidays. He'd already accepted that. But it was her decision. She was the one who chose to drive drunk this close to Christmas. But he guessed he'd wind up being the one who paid the fine again for her anyway. He hoped the judge wouldn't really send her to the penitentiary like he'd threatened, but would maybe let her do her time at the jail here so that he could visit her a little easier. He'd always known what she was in Montana.

Town pump they called it out there. They even had some gas stations named that. But that hadn't mattered to him and it still didn't. She'd get through this somehow or other. Then maybe she could come back home, if he wanted her to, if she wanted to, and maybe they could work things out from there. If they couldn't, it wouldn't be the end of the world.

He sipped at his gin and tonic. It was just the way he liked it, with a bit of lemon peel in it alongside the lime chunk. Eric had told him that he'd learned how to make drinks from his daddy. And he'd told him about the rabbit factory. And they were going to see it soon. And there wasn't anything much better than having a few drinks in the warmth of your own home and sitting down to a real good western movie with your supper. Like the one they were getting ready to watch in about thirty more minutes, *Once Upon a Time in the West*. Directed by Sergio Leone. With Henry Fonda. Charles Bronson. Jason Robards. And Claudia Cardinale. Now there was one fine woman. That was the main reason he'd been attracted to Helen in Montana that night, because he'd had a few gin and tonics and she'd gotten to looking like Claudia Cardinale. But even after he'd sobered up the next day and had taken a good look at her lying naked in the bed next to him, sleeping, with her wild hair around her face, it hadn't mattered that she was the town pump. He'd always feared he wouldn't be able to hold on to her. He'd always secretly known she'd married him for his money. He'd known this day might come. He'd known she liked men. So now that it had happened, it wasn't like some big surprise. And it wasn't like he couldn't find another woman if he did split up with Helen, now that he had his equipment in good working order again. If he wanted one. He didn't know right now. But if he did, all he'd probably have to do was put on a good suit and go down to the Peabody one evening, order a gin and tonic, and hang out a little. Find a young one looking for a sugar-daddy. The world was full of them. Like Helen twenty years ago.

He looked around but he didn't see it. Hiding probably.

Jada Pinkett had been playing with it but maybe it was taking a nap under the couch now. He thought it was going to tame down, now that they'd let it out of the cage and let it walk around where it could see that they weren't going to hurt it. That had been Eric's suggestion, and Eric had been right.

He seemed to be real good with animals. He'd evidently had hundreds of dogs in his lifetime. And the kitten was already house-trained. It was using the kitty-litter box Eric had brought home from the pet shop.

And the frozen rabbit he'd brought over from the pet shop smelled heavenly now. He sipped his drink and turned his head to look at Eric. He was quietly cooking in the kitchen, turning the rabbit in the skillet, making mashed potatoes, and they were trying to time it so that they'd have their plates loaded and on their laps with their napkins and their drinks on the coffee table when the shot of the train station opened, and the creaking of the windmill started up, and Jack Elam was sitting in a rocking chair, with a fly buzzing loudly around his head.

"How's your drink?" Eric said from the kitchen. He'd already taken over just about all the cooking, and everything he did was good. He could make biscuits from scratch. And the best gravy you ever tasted. He could *fry* some chicken. Said he'd learned how cooking for his daddy when he was little.

"I'm good," Arthur said. "You sure you don't need any help in there?"

"Everything's cool," Eric said, and slid the lid back over the skillet where the rabbit pieces were browning nicely. He picked up his beer and came on in the living room and sat down on the couch. He had a towel stuck in his belt to wipe his hands on while he was cooking.

"It sure smells great," Arthur said. He was glad Eric had all his stuff in the house now, his books and clothes, his dog food.

"It's gonna be more than me and you can eat probly," Eric said, and took a drink of his beer. "It's a lot of meat on a grown rabbit."

"What day you want to go see your daddy?" Arthur said. He had the Jag back now. Some nice police officer had driven it over from the jail. Helen couldn't use it anyway since they'd taken her license again.

"I don't care. I can call him first. See how he is."

Both of them looked at the big TV screen for a while. Some woman who used to be a wrestler was selling something. Then they cut back to the last scenes of *Dirty Harry*, and watched Harry shoot the punk, and toss his badge in the water, and then Eric got back up to go check on the rabbit.

He knew one thing he was going to do. Arrange a good hunting trip for Eric next year out in Montana. Just the two of them. He could hire all the help over the phone, find a guide, get somebody to wrangle the horses, carry the tents, set up a camp, find a cook. But he'd probably never be able to find anybody who could cook enchiladas as good as Lark Linkhorn.

"Well, it'll be ready in a little bit," Eric said from the kitchen. "I'll start makin' the gravy in a minute."

"I'm ready," Arthur said. "You're really going to love this movie."

"I can't believe I never have seen it," Eric said.

Jada Pinkett came walking up and put his chin on the cushion next to Arthur's legs. Arthur put his hand out and petted him. The old dog whined and looked around. Arthur looked up at Eric.

"I think he misses Helen," he said.

Eric didn't say anything. But he had a look on his face that Arthur hadn't seen before. And then it went away from his face as he went back to his cooking, just as the kitten came walking down the hall, hugging the wall, its crooked tail arched up, and it was mewing softly, and it sounded like a question, like somebody looking for friends.

About the Author

Larry Brown was born in Oxford, Mississippi, and lives happily on a cattle farm near Yocona with his beloved family. He is the author of nine books of fiction and nonfiction, and his work has been translated into other languages around the world.